AUTHOR'S NOTE ON LANGUAGE

Please note, as the author and the main character of this book are both from Ireland, it is written in the version of English that is standard there. So recognise is spelled recognise and not recognize etc. The author recognises some North American readers may find this upsetting and while he is of course scared of them, he is considerably more scared of his Mammy, who taught him how to spell. Nevertheless, as an apology, here are a bunch of Zs for you to mentally stick in as and when you choose.

ZZZZZ

Look, they look like a mummy duck and little ducks. Adorable!

CHAPTER ONE

"What's healthy?"

Marcy Wainwright was hacking furiously at the rock-solid stalactites of chewing gum under the counter and had been for nearly twenty minutes. She'd left them for a week, expecting Beatrice or Valentina from the day shift to crack and actually do some cleaning. She'd done it the last two times and they knew damn well that it was their job – part of the deal for getting the sweet day shift. They were either blind or straight-up couldn't give a rat's ass. All those two did was turn up and milk those sweet tips. Damn, she wanted that day shift so bad.

"'Scuse me?" said Marcy.

"What've you got that's healthy?" repeated the woman. She didn't look like the typical customer that Murphy's Diner got at seven o'clock on a Sunday morning or, indeed, at any other time. She was pure soccer mom, in her mid thirties, with Pilates thighs and a lemon-sucking expression. Behind her stood a little bald man with round glasses on a tiny round head.

"I got a healthy disrespect for authority darlin', but that ain't on the menu."

The woman gave one of those smiles that wasn't a smile. "Are there any additional vegetarian options?"

Marcy dropped her scraper into the bucket and wiped the sweat from her brow. "Honey, cook's name is Freddie. He's on two strikes, he's trying to quit the cigarettes and his wife ran off with an honest-to-God postman. I mean, who in this day and age even knows their postman's name? I ask you..."

Marcy had never met this woman before but the confused look on her face was all too familiar. "Sorry, I got a tendency to wander off the point – terrible affliction of mine. Lost me two husbands and at least one cellmate."

The woman reflexively clutched at her purse.

"Oh, don't worry none, honey, I just embezzled a little money from my old employers at Quincy Shipping. I was in a bad place is all. Second husband had left me; I was drinking a smidge. That's how it goes, though. A person steals off a company, person goes to jail. Company steals off a person – hey, that's just business. I do have a tendency to talk too much though; people hate that in a cellmate. Sorry now – what was your question?"

"Additional vegetarian options?"

"Oh yeah – point is, Freddie is the cook and he does exactly what it says on the menu. He's kinda hardcore on this particular point. You want something different, you best head on down the road. If you're heading north though, be warned, there ain't much for quite a stretch at this time of the morning. We ain't got fine dining but what we do have is location, location, location."

Murphy's Diner was busier than normal for that time of the morning. In other words, it actually had customers. It was a glorified truck stop on I-95, truth be told. It was the last stop on the city bus routes and a pick-up for some of the Greyhounds and private hires. Nobody came here to eat. They ended up here and were hungry.

A Canadian trucker who was a semi-regular was sitting in the corner booth, grinding his way slavishly through a double pile of pancakes. He must've been 350 pounds and Marcy felt bad for giving them to him, but it wasn't her job to live the man's life. Besides, he brought his own maple syrup and he was a crappy tipper. Then there was the Mexican lady with her ten-year-old son. Looked like they were waiting for one of the buses that started up at 8am. They didn't have much luggage. Marcy guessed they were visiting relatives – or running from one in particular. The mom had ordered food for the kid but nothing for herself. Marcy had times two-ed it and then told her she'd made a mistake and the second one was on the house. Momma had protested but then eaten it like it was manna from heaven. It's easier to be proud on a full stomach.

There was a sweet old grandpa type in the back booth who was steadily working his way through the eggs Benedict while trying to keep his eyes open, and then there was the squirrely thin dude who had that twitchiness that anybody who'd been near the streets would recognise. He'd shown her cash on his way in, guessing right she'd have asked to see it before taking his order. He was moving the huevos rancheros around his plate like he was trying to divine the future. If he went to the bathroom she'd have to time him and get Freddie to go in there with the bat to give him the rush if he was up to something. Freddie was in a bad mood; Marcy hoped this guy wasn't going to find out how bad. There was also Miss Lonely Hearts, who had barely touched her salad as she sat there, staring out the window. When she'd first stepped through the door, Marcy would've taken her for a teenage runaway – she was five-foot-two tops, with a slight frame and a thin face. She wasn't wearing any make-up either, which added to the little-girl-lost look of her. On closer inspection, she was revealed to be probably mid twenties, but she could still get ID'd going to the movies. She looked like Little Red Riding Hood who got lost on the way to Grandma's house. Marcy was guessing nasty break-up, not that it was any of her business. The sweet little thing had spoken so quietly when she ordered that Marcy had needed to lean in to hear her. She wasn't showing much enthusiasm for her salad either; she'd been picking at it for twenty minutes now. Marcy just hoped Freddie didn't see. He got awful touchy about people not being keen on his work. He had the soul of a tortured artist in the body of a longshoreman from Queens.

The soccer mom gave the menu another look, regarding it like she'd just scraped it off her shoe. "Alright then. I guess I'll have two scrambled eggs on rye toast, no butter, with a side order of onions."

Marcy nodded and then hollered at the top of her lungs, "Hey, Freddie – Adam and Eve on a raft, then wreck 'em on whiskey, 86 the cow to cover and breath in the alley."

A grunt from the area of the fry station indicated Freddie was still alive. Marcy turned her attention to the little fella standing behind his wife. "And for the mister?"

The soccer mom pushed the menu back at Marcy. "He'll have the oatmeal with skimmed milk."

"And a no-fun special, please, Freddie." She gave the soccer mom a wide smile. "It'll be right with ye, honey."

As Marcy watched the soccer mom eye the various booths, as if deciding which one to marry, she noticed the 217 bus pulling up on the far side of the road. "Freddie, 217 special!"

Grunt.

Isabella drove the 217 bus and this was its final stop on her shift. Every morning, five days a week, she stopped in for her bowl of muesli and a doughnut. She'd chew the fat and then do a little of her college homework, waiting for the morning shift driver to pick up the bus and bring her back into New York. She'd drop her two kids at school and then catch her four hours. Marcy didn't know how she did it all on such little sleep. Marcy herself barely saw daylight in the winter. She'd love to get herself another job but there ain't nothing worse on a résumé than embezzling. Employers will forgive murder sooner than that. Only reason she got this job was that Mr Choi reasoned there wasn't much for her to steal around the place at night. Besides, wasn't nobody here could tell her to shut up and Marcy liked that.

Marcy went back behind the counter as soccer mom plus one took up one of the booths by the window.

Freddie was wordlessly handing Marcy the bowl of muesli for Isabella as the bell above the door tinkled.

"Here's my girl."

"Hey, Marcy, how you doing?"

"Oh, you know, laughing on the outside, crying on the inside, keeping out a good eye..."

Isabella joined in for the last bit: "For a sighting of the upside."

She was sitting at the end of the counter as per usual, two big textbooks propped under her arm, looking more cheerful than she'd any right to be. Marcy placed down the bowl in front of her.

"How's the population transportation business, honey?"

"Oh y'know, the usual. Had some tweaker losing his shit, screaming he was on fire."

"Damn."

"Yeah. Had to pull over and call the cops. Guy is rolling around, screaming the place down, while this lady starts banging on my booth telling me to get moving."

"You're kidding."

She shook her head. "No. She was all like, 'Dude ain't on fire, I'm gonna be late for work. Boss'll have my ass.' She ended up arguing with the cops when they eventually showed. It was some fun times."

Marcy shook her head. "Ain't right, young woman like you all on your own with all that crazy."

Isabella shrugged. "Hey, I just stay locked in the booth." She patted the textbooks. "Fourteen more months and it's bye-bye, 217 – hello, data management on easy street."

"That's my girl. You got yourself a plan."

Isabella nodded and picked up the spoon for her muesli. "Alls I gotta do is stay awake long enough to see that finish line."

Marcy laughed and turned around. "Jesus!"

"Guess again."

The man spoke with a strong Irish accent – not that it was the most noticeable thing about him. He was a big man in all senses, with a thick beard and air of disrepair. He looked like one of those poor dancing bears they're always trying to raise money for. He wore a sheepskin coat and looked like he might've slept in it, only he didn't look like he'd slept. His eyes were bloodshot and the left one was lazy. She assumed that wasn't part of the hangover, but who knew – Marcy once knew a man who'd drunk himself to actual blindness. This dude was still able to see but he was clearly on the downswing of the mother of all benders. He ran his hand across a brow glistening with cold sweat.

"Damn, honey. If you don't mind me saying, you look like death warmed up."

The man winced and scratched at his beard. "You have no idea. Is Jackie around?"

"Jackie who?"

"Jackie Murphy. He's the owner."

Marcy shook her head. "Sorry, honey, that guy ain't been the owner here for a while. It's a Mr Choi now."

"But it says Murphy's Diner outside?"

"It sure does. I guess Mr Choi thought it sounded more inviting than Choi's Diner. People love the Irish thing."

The man puffed out his cheeks and sighed. "Not as much as you'd think."

He winced as Marcy slapped the counter. "I just got it – it was Saint Pattie's day yesterday, wasn't it?"

He shook his head. "No. It's Saint Patrick or Paddy – Pat at a push."

"Excuse me, I'm sure. You had a big ol' celebration for yourself then, I'm guessing?"

"In a manner of speaking."

"Was Mr Murphy a friend of yours?"

The man shrugged. "Not as such, but I did save his life."

"Oh, well, I'm afraid it didn't take. Him dying is how Choi owns this place now." Marcy leaned across the counter and lowered her voice. "Matter of fact, one of the girls who worked here back in them days told me all about it. Murphy died back there in the disabled bathroom. Caught himself a heart attack while in the middle of being in flagrante with one of the waitresses."

The man sighed. Marcy leaned back slightly; he wasn't the most delightful olfactory treat.

"Yeah, that's him alright. It was being caught doing something similar with the wrong man's wife that nearly had him dead the first time. The gobshite clearly never learned his lesson."

"So, you two weren't close then?"

"Nah, but he was the only man this side of the Atlantic that owed me a favour and I happen to suddenly find myself in need of one."

Marcy ran a cloth along the counter as she talked. "Sorry to be the bearer of bad news. Hope the rest of your visit to this green and pleasant land is going better?"

"Not so much."

"So, were you looking to eat or was this just a social call?"

"Oh God, yeah. I could eat the arse off a donkey."

Marcy wrinkled her nose in disgust. "I'm afraid we don't have that. Here's what we do got." She picked up a menu and handed it to him.

He looked it up and down. "Right so, can I get two fried eggs, some baked beans, mushrooms and three sausages, please."

"Sure, honey," said Marcy, taking the menu back. The man winced again as she raised her voice. "Hey, Freddie – flop two, whistle beans in the alley, funky fungus with a triple Zeppelin chaser."

She turned back to see the man rubbing his hands over his eyes. "What you people have done to the language."

"I could say the same, honey."

"Oh, and a cup of tea, please, too."

"Iced tea?"

"No, like tea tea."

Marcy raised her voice again. "Freddie, did those teabags ever come in?"

Her extensive experience in speaking Freddie meant that Marcy was one of the few people on Earth who could identify the grunt that followed as a firm negative.

"Sorry, hon' – we're out of tea."

The man looked like she'd just offered to chop his foot off and cook it for him. "You've got no tea?"

"Afraid not."

"That's... that's... like none at all?"

"Unless you want iced."

"But... you've... are you allowed open without having tea? Surely there's like a rule or something?"

"We got coffee."

"Well, of course you've got coffee. This is... I can't begin to... you've got no tea?"

Marcy put her hands on her hips. "Honey, it's been a long night. Sorry about the tea thing. Now can I get you some coffee or do you just want one of them hari-kari swords?"

The man opened and closed his mouth, like a very confused goldfish whose castle had just disappeared. "Jesus, how do you run a country without tea?"

"By drinking coffee. We're up all night while the rest of the planet is sleeping."

He sighed again, looking like a dog who'd had the fight beat out of him. "I'll have a coffee then."

Marcy slapped her hands together. "That's the spirit. When in Rome. One steaming hot cup of java coming right up. Fair warning, I keep it hotter than hell."

The next few minutes got surprisingly busy for the time of morning. In a massive non-surprise, Soccer Mom decided she didn't like her order when it landed and asked for it to be changed. Her hubby just sat there eating his oatmeal like a man looking forward to death, either his own or hers. The old guy in the corner booth dozed away with his head back, his mouth wide, catching flies. The young twitchy guy went to the bathroom. Marcy had timed him and was about to introduce him to Freddie's sunny disposition when he came slinking back out. The mother watched the son colouring in a notepad, all kinds of worry running through her eyes. Miss Lonely Hearts split her time between looking out the window, staring at her watch and glancing at her phone. She'd not set up a date for Murphy's, had she? I mean, young folks did all kinds of weird stuff these days with all them apps on their phones and what not, but Murphy's had never been seen as a romantic rendezvous point before. Well, at least not by anyone bar old Jackie Murphy in the disabled restroom – and look how well that had turned out.

Freddie dinged and the Irish dude's plate spun up. She delivered it to him at the counter and picked up the hot pot of coffee, topping him up without asking, for fear of another tea-based meltdown.

He nodded his thanks. "Much appreciated. And sorry about earlier. I didn't mean to be rude."

"That's alright, sugar. I been where you are. In fact" – she leaned in conspiratorially – "I ain't gonna give you the twelve steps speech, but how's about a couple of aspirin?"

"You're a wonderful woman."

"You ain't so bad yourself, although, no disrespect, you might want to ease up on the sauce a little."

"Madam, I assure you, I am never going to drink again – and this time I mean it."

Marcy gave him a wink and moved down the counter to go find her purse with those aspirin.

The Irishman lifted his knife and fork, a look of determination on his face.

The bell over the door dinged and Marcy looked up.

Two men.

The first thing she noticed were the ski masks.

The second thing she noticed were the guns.

CHAPTER TWO

"Everybody, be cool – this is a robbery."

The two men wore ski masks: one dark blue, one red. The blue ski mask covered the head of a taller guy, maybe six-foot-three, his black hoodie failing to conceal his muscular gym body. The red mask guy was considerably shorter and slighter of frame. They were standing in the doorway, each waving a handgun around.

Red stepped into the centre of the room. "Any of you fucking pricks move and I'll execute every motherfucking last one of you." Then he gave an excited giggle.

Marcy stepped back from the counter and put her hands in the air. This wasn't her first rodeo, although normally the cowboys didn't quote Tarantino movies.

Isabella flinched as the blue mask moved behind her so he could see Freddie in the kitchen.

"You. Hands where I can see 'em. Hands where I can see 'em! Don't do anything stupid."

Freddie moved slowly out from the kitchen and stood with his hands above his head near the register. "Alright, man – take it easy."

"Who else is back there?"

"Nobody."

"Bullshit."

"Look around; we ain't exactly rushed off our feet."

Freddie was a big guy, six-six and muscles with it. He didn't work out, he just worked. Marcy knew he did a warehouse job four days a week too, and some other stuff she didn't ask about. Not that Freddie spoke much. Mister Choi said that he put him and Marcy working together as, between them, they averaged out to two reasonably talkative people. Freddie wore an apron over his wife beater and cargo shorts, it being too hot in the kitchen for much else. Fat burns speckled his bare upper arms, the black skin turning purple in places. You could also see the scars of the shoulder operation that'd cost him a football scholarship and his shot at having other people make him breakfast.

The guy in the red ski mask was scanning the room again. "Hands in the motherfucking air, yo. Don't make me ask again."

Marcy looked around. Soccer Mom and her husband had their hands obediently held up in the air. The Mexican mother had grabbed her son and was using her body to shield him from the men, while still holding one trembling hand up in an effort at compliance. Isabella, the trucker and Miss Lonely Hearts held their hands up too, as did the squirrely guy, who was almost cowering under his table as he did so. The old timer in the back booth was, against all probability, fast asleep. Either that or he was dead. Everybody else had their hands in the air. Well, everyone except...

"Didn't you hear me?"

The short guy pointed his gun at the Irishman, who sat at the counter, calmly shovelling baked beans into his mouth.

The man swallowed. "I did, yeah."

"So, put your motherfucking hands in the motherfucking air, motherfucker."

"Jesus fella, you'd really want to work on your vocabulary."

The man spiked a couple of mushrooms with his fork and calmly put them in his mouth.

"Are you for real?"

The Irishman belched and then patted himself on the chest. "No offence, lads, but I'm not that intimidated by arseholes in balaclavas. I come from the country that invented the concept."

The taller one shouted down the counter. "You see the guns pointed at you, dipshit?" Marcy noticed the guy spoke with a Boston twang and then tried to stop noticing. In this situation, noticing stuff could get you killed.

The Irishman calmly sliced off a piece of fried egg. "Ara, big deal. You're in America, champ – land of the free, home of the armed. Everybody's got a gun. D'ye really think you're the only ones in this room packing hardware?"

Marcy watched as the two men in masks glanced at each other before looking around the room again.

The Irishman continued talking, never turning from his food, speaking around mouthfuls. "There's that jumpy little sod over there; he's either got a piece or he sold it for whatever is making him so jittery."

The squirrely guy spoke in a squeal. "I ain't got nothing, nothing, nothing – straight up."

"Well," continued the Irishman, "if you can't trust a junkie, who can you trust? You got a woman travelling with a kid; she might've brought along a little protection."

The Latina lady said nothing, her eyes wide with terror, but she shook her head furiously.

"Father Time in the back there – Vietnam vet, maybe? Bet he's packing, all set to shoot the next unlucky gobshite that cuts him up in traffic."

On cue, the old man grunted softly in his sleep. So not dead then.

"Now there's a man who could sleep through artillery. The young girl travelling on her own. Be daft if she wasn't packing something."

Miss Lonely Hearts shifted in her seat. If Marcy was giving out prizes, she'd been winning least terrified looking. Well, apart from the snoozing old guy and, of course, the man who wouldn't shut up.

"Then," continued the man who wouldn't shut up, "you got the big fella – trucker, I'm guessing?"

The big guy's face was an alarming shade of red and he was

rubbing his hand on his chest in a way that worried Marcy. She felt bad enough about the heart attack he had coming without having to be present for it. "You better believe he's packing, and it's either on him or he's regretting leaving it in the cab right about now. And as for the staff" – he winked at Marcy – "they don't even serve tea. Back home, if you tried that, you'd have to be armed. As for the Jetsons over there…" The Irishman glanced over his shoulder for the first time. "Well, who knows what their deal is."

"Would you shut up," hissed the soccer mom. "Just let them get on with robbing the place."

"I'm only making conversation." The Irishman slurped a sup of coffee and grimaced.

The man in the red balaclava stepped towards the Irishman. "Put your goddamned hands up now. This is a robbery, bitch."

"Ah, but it isn't though, is it?"

The red balaclava glanced back at his compatriot. "What?"

"A robbery. It isn't one. Look at your shoes." He said it in a tone of voice that implied no other explanation was required. Marcy would've sworn blind that the Irishman was yet to turn around enough in his seat to have even seen the guy's shoes. He dipped a slice of toast into his egg yolk and crunched it into his mouth. Marcy took a step further away from him. It'd be her damn luck that someone would go to shoot this lunatic and catch her instead.

Blue raised his voice. "Alright, asshole, enough. I'm giving you to the count of five and then I'm shooting you in the head. One…"

The Irishman calmly cut up one of his sausages and addressed himself to Marcy instead of either of the men. "No offence, but this place makes what, a few hundred bucks a night, at best?"

Marcy found herself nodding. "We bank on the early breakfast crowd." She clamped her hands over her mouth. Her mamma had always said her inability to keep quiet would be the death of her.

"Two."

"Exactly, so there'll be feck all in that register right now. Which raises the question…"

"Three."

"Why is a guy in designer leather loafers, which look to be worth a few grand, robbing it?"

Despite themselves, the whole room looked at Red's footwear.

"He's got a point," said the soccer mom's other half.

"Shut up, George," snapped his wife.

Marcy jumped as George unexpectedly slammed his fist down onto the table. "No, I won't, Janice. Doctor Steinberg said I should be allowed to express myself."

"Fair play to you, fella," said the Irishman. "Whatever this is, it's not a robbery. So, if it's all the same to you, I'll finish my breakfast."

"Four!"

"I'm sick of this loud-ass Scottish motherfucker." Red stomped across the room towards the Irishman. "You are going to be..." Red raised his gun-holding hand aloft, as if he were about to pistol-whip the Irishman on the back of the head.

What happened next, happened fast. So fast that Marcy spent the next few days trying to piece it together over and over again in her mind.

The pot of steaming hot coffee that'd been on the counter suddenly wasn't. It was in the Irishman's hand, its contents being hurled into Red's lap.

Red yowled in pain as the boiling hot liquid made contact. He dropped his gun, sending it skittering across the floor. Marcy watched it thump against the base of an empty table and stop.

When she looked back, the Irishman was up and standing behind the screaming Red, the coffee pot having been thrown into the air. He grabbed the back of Red's mask with his right hand as the other hand appeared at his neck, pressing the fork into it.

The coffee pot smashed onto the floor.

Instinctively, those in the room that were able had dived for whatever cover they could find. Marcy cowered back against the serving area; she could feel the heat of the metal against her lower back.

"Jesus, Jesus, Jesus, Jesus!" screamed Red. Despite the fork to his throat, his entire attention was focused on his own groin area, trying to tug the soaking material of his chinos away from it.

At the far end of the counter, Blue now had his gun pointing at the Irishman and shouted to be heard over his compatriot. "Let him go!"

"The feck I will. This fork is jammed right up to your pal's carotid artery, the one that pumps blood to the brain. A jab of my wrist and he bleeds out on this floor in under sixty seconds. What in the hell? Would ye stop wriggling!"

The last bit wasn't directed at Blue, it was directed at Red, who, ignoring the fork pressing against his neck, had undone the belt of his chinos and dropped them to the floor – quickly followed by the boxers underneath. "My balls are burning!" His voice was now a tearful whimper.

The Irishman leaned forward and looked over Red's shoulder. "OK," he said, "well, that just happened."

"Let him go or I'll shoot you in the head!"

The Irishman bobbed around behind Red while still keeping the fork firmly jammed to his throat.

"Jesus, you'd have to be some shot from there."

Blue took a step forward. "Ex-Special Forces, asshole."

The Irishman's voice carried a lilt of joyous mockery to it. "Sure you are, and this fella is Captain America, that's how he's standing here with his boiled bollocks hanging out."

"Fuck you," said Red, with the kind of venom only roasted genitalia could bring. Marcy had been told before not to keep the coffee so hot, but it kept it smelling fresh.

The Irishman leaned into Red's ear and spoke in a stage whisper. "By the way, I'm Irish, not Scottish. You've no ear for accents."

Isabella was crouched down in front of the counter, out of Marcy's line of sight. She yelped as Blue reached down and grabbed her by the hair, dragging her to a standing position.

"Let him go or I shoot this bitch in the head."

Freddie moved towards Blue, but he was stopped dead by the gun being turned in his direction.

"Back away – now!"

Freddie stepped backwards, his hands once again up in the air.

"So," said the Irishman, "your play is to shoot someone I don't know and get your friend killed in the process?"

"Let him go, nobody dies."

The Irishman laughed a humourless laugh. "Oh, I seriously don't think that's true. Even if you don't kill me, Burning Balls here strikes me as the type to hold a grudge. How did you find me anyway?"

"What?"

There was a long moment's silence.

"Oh for... you're not here for me, are you? So, who are you after?"

"I don't know who the fuck you are but let him go now."

The Irishman shook his head. "If this isn't a robbery, and it isn't, and you're not here for me... You're here for something or somebody, that's for sure." He looked around the room. "Well now, ain't this like an Agatha Christie book, only the twist is we're all gathered around trying to guess who the victim is supposed to be."

Blue snapped. "Let him go or I shoot her..." Isabella yelped as Blue tugged more tightly at her hair. "And then I shoot him." He pointed the gun at Freddie.

"Really?" said the Irishman. "A room with, what, a dozen people in it, and you're going to shoot the only two black folks?"

Freddie turned towards the Irishman. "Hey, man, welcome to America."

Blue fired a shot into the ceiling. Isabella screamed and tried to run, only to be dragged back by the hair.

"Everybody shut the fuck up, right now," said Blue. "I'm done with this."

"Alright," said the Irishman, "take it easy. It's your lucky day. I'm not keen on the cops turning up either. You just walk out the door, then I'll let the Boy Wonder here go and this never happened. Deal?"

It was hard to tell behind the mask, but Marcy reckoned that Blue was at least thinking about it. They never did get to hear his response though, as the window behind him exploded.

CHAPTER THREE

Marcy ducked behind the counter as the bullets started to fly.

She was shocked as the Irishman dived over the top to join her, him being lighter on his feet than she would've expected.

Marcy clamped her hands over her ears as, on the other side of the counter, shots rang out. A steady boom on one side met by a rat-a-tat rapid burst from the other. Glass smashed, plaster exploded, people screamed, the air stank of gunpowder. Then, suddenly, as quickly as it had started, the gunfight at Murphy's Diner stopped.

Beside her, the Irishman crouched on his haunches. He popped his head above the counter quickly, then down, then up again, then he stood properly. He offered Marcy his hand.

"The coast is clear now, love."

Marcy stood and surveyed the scene of devastation. The glass was shattered in several of the windows, the gumball machine had taken a hit, covering the floor in its contents, and several of the pictures on the wall now had bullet holes through them.

The old timer was still pulling the trigger on his *Dirty Harry*-looking hand cannon, despite the fact it was out of bullets. It click-clacked through empty chambers. "Did I get him?"

"That depends," said the Irishman. "Were you aiming for the jukebox?"

The old man lowered his gun. "I can't shoot a damn without my glasses."

They looked out the shattered windows as Red, with his ski mask still on and his pants still down around his ankles, hopped towards a sports car. In a screech of tyres, it zoomed away before hitting the brakes and reversing to pick him up.

"Fecking amateurs," said the Irishman. "Is everybody alright?"

Mumbled assents issued from under tables and behind counters.

"Ah, man, I'm hit, I'm hit!" It was the squirrely guy, red splattered across his battered windbreaker. Freddie ran over to him.

"OK, take it easy. Where are you hit?"

"I'm gonna die, man. Ah, fuck!"

Freddie lifted up the guy's T-shirt and then moved him around to look at his back, running his hand over him. Then he looked down on the floor and shook his head. "Damn junkie idiot." He picked up a plastic bottle from the floor and held it aloft. There was a bullet hole right through it. "Ketchup, you dumb son of a bitch. Ketchup!"

Freddie threw the bottle back down on the ground again.

The trucker stood up on shaky legs. "Shouldn't someone call the cops?"

Marcy noticed the Mexican lady with her young son still strapped to her side, shaking her head furiously again.

"Erm," said the old timer, "I don't have a permit to carry in this state."

"Yeah," said Freddie, "no kidding. You can't hit a damn thing. It's a miracle nobody's dead thanks to you."

"How dare you! I was defending myself!"

Marcy watched as Freddie, fists clenched, took a step towards the old man.

"Freddie!" said Marcy, stepping out from behind the counter. "You don't want to do anything silly now, honey, do you?"

Freddie took a deep breath and stomped back towards the kitchen, muttering darkly to himself as he went.

At this point the soccer mom had re-emerged from under her table and had her phone clamped to her ear. "Yes, hello. Police please, immediately."

The Irishman hopped back over the counter, his feet crunching on broken glass. "That's my cue to leave. Best of luck folks – it's been emotional." He bent down and picked up Red's discarded gun from where it lay on the floor. He turned and placed it on the counter in front of Marcy. "Don't forget to tip your waitress."

Soccer Mom glowered at him. "You're not going anywhere."

"Guess again."

"George, restrain that man!"

She looked at her husband, who was sitting in the booth, staring out the window. He didn't even turn his head as he spoke. "Shut up, Janice. I want a divorce."

CHAPTER FOUR

Bunny McGarry ducked behind a tree and watched the police cruiser zoom by, sirens blaring and lights flashing. With a sigh, he stepped out and started walking back up the verge of the road. His leg ached, his head throbbed and his stomach rumbled. He'd not slept properly for a couple of days now and he'd managed barely half a breakfast, just enough for his body to decide it did indeed want food. His whole body had been building itself up for a doozy of a hangover, but the wild burst of adrenaline from the gunfight had rather thrown a spanner in the biological works. Bunny had no doubt that, when it sorted itself out, retribution would be had. In the meantime, he needed to get off the road. He'd not actually broken any laws – well, bar leaving the scene of a crime – but still, the cops would start asking questions that Bunny wouldn't have answers to.

He had no idea what direction he was walking in, other than away. He realised the sun was in front of him, not yet high enough to warm the biting chill in the air. So that meant he was walking east. If he kept going for about three thousand miles, he knew a good pub in Galway where a man could get a pint at any hour if he knew who to ask. They'd do you a decent cup of tea too.

He'd gone to Murphy's hoping for a solution to his problem and he'd come away with yet another one. It had not been a good couple of days. In fact, it'd not been a good week, but it had been a disastrous twenty-four hours.

Nineteen years ago, Simone Delamere had walked into his life and accidentally stolen his heart. It hadn't been love at first sight but that was because he'd been mesmerised by her voice before he had ever laid eyes on her. Against all odds, she'd loved him too. In the darkest moments since, he'd doubted that but he didn't now. Those couple of months they'd had together had been the happiest of his life. Then, her past, the thing she had run to Dublin to escape, had caught up with them and brought the dream to an abrupt end.

Together they had managed to deal with the problem, but that had left two bodies buried in the Wicklow Mountains and left Simone with no choice but to run again. Bunny hadn't known it at the time, but she had done so to protect him, just as he had been trying to protect her. He had only found this out a few months ago when the two long-buried bodies had been discovered and all hell broke loose. Simone was now the prize in a battle between two opposing forces within the US government. Her, and the video tape they believed she had, could bring down a powerful man. Bunny didn't care about any of that. He'd almost died twice to protect her and when the opportunity had arisen, he'd made third time the charm. Alive, he was a point of weakness they could attack to get to Simone, dead, he could disappear and then try and find her before anyone else did. That was his mission, his purpose – the reason he had to still be alive.

He had only one advantage over the chasing pack. He knew that she had been originally sneaked out of New York by an order of rogue nuns known as The Sisters of the Saint. He was also guessing that they had spirited her out of Dublin too. At the very least, they could give him a starting point, somewhere to go looking. The problem was that the Sisters had left Ireland long ago and Bunny's entire plan was pinned on the hope that they would still be active in New York. He was realising that searching a city of eight and a half million people for a bunch of nuns – who, if they were still here, would not want to be found – was even harder than he had expected.

Plus, he was a fish out of water, having spent the last thirty years policing the streets of Dublin. It'd been a long time since he'd turned a corner and not known what to expect. Over here, it felt like he couldn't even find the damn corner.

He had briefly considered taking the gun. If he had it and could find whoever it was who had robbed his stuff, he could be guaranteed their undivided attention. Not that Bunny would actually use the gun. No. He had every intention of killing whoever did it with his bare hands.

The road he was walking along was what he'd have called a dual carriageway, although he had no clue what it was called over here. Everything in America had a different name and he was getting sick of it. That and the inexplicable lack of a decent cup of tea. These people were savages. There wasn't a footpath as such, and he guessed nobody walked along this road, although judging by the state of the verge, they slowed down to chuck out rubbish quite a lot. Amidst the fast food wrappers and beer cans, there were cardboard boxes of God knows what, mud-encrusted plastic tubing and what appeared to be a stuffed moose head with its lower jaw missing. Who the hell threw out half a moose?

Bunny's options were limited. He needed to get back to New York and find whoever was responsible for him waking up in Times Square minus some incredibly important possessions. He'd not been wild about having to call in the debt Jackie Murphy had owed him, but he'd had little choice. Nobody was supposed to know Bunny was alive, but given that almost everyone thought Jackie was dead too, it had been an acceptable risk to take. Seeing as the randy bastard had gone off and actually died, that was much of a muchness now anyway.

Bunny had nothing to his name but the clothes he was wearing, the random crap in his pockets and a very bad mood. The fact that most of his current predicament was his own damn fault made the whole thing feel worse still. He worked best when he had someone to take it out on, although remembering the sight of that gobshite with the balaclava on his head and his pants around his ankles brought him a half-smile. If nothing else, he may've at least taken away one gobshite's chances of adding to the gene pool.

A dark green car pulled up beside him. Bunny didn't make eye contact. "I'm fine, thank you, just out for a walk."

He heard the passenger-side window lower with a whir.

"Get in."

Bunny stooped down to look into the car. It was the girl, the one who'd been on her own in the diner. She had shoulder-length straight brown hair and was the dictionary definition of petite.

"No thanks," said Bunny. "I'm fine walking."

He started walking on. The car rolled forward to keep pace with him.

"Stop being an ass and get in the damn car."

"Fine language for a young lady. Are you even old enough to drive?"

The car pulled in front of him at an angle, blocking what path there was.

She sounded exasperated. "Look, I don't know who the hell you are, but get in the damn car before someone else spots you and starts asking questions. I get the definite impression you don't want to answer any."

"I'll be grand."

He started to move around the car, but she moved it further forward, forcing him to jump a step back.

"For God's sake, love, what's your problem?"

She rubbed her knuckles into her eyes for a couple of seconds and then looked up, a decision made. "It was me."

"What are you talking about?"

"They were after me!"

CHAPTER FIVE

"Wake up."

The Irishman turned in the seat slightly and farted.

Amy wrinkled her nose in disgust and shook the guy's shoulder firmly. "Wake up," she repeated more loudly, to no noticeable effect.

She turned the radio back on and treated her passenger to three seconds of Imagine Dragons at ear-splitting volume. The Irishman reared up with a start.

"What in da feckin—!"

"Oh good, you're up."

He looked around, dazed and confused. "Where am I?"

"You're in my car. I picked you up about fifteen minutes ago. We didn't get much chance to make conversation – you complained about the song on the radio then fell unconscious."

"Oh." The Irishman nodded. "That makes sense, alright. And where are we now?"

"I pulled over at a McDonald's drive-through." She held out a brown paper bag and a lidded cup. "I got you an Egg McMuffin meal with a coffee."

He looked at the cup. "I don't suppose they had tea?"

She pulled both the bag and the cup away. "Seriously? I just saved you from the cops and bought you food."

He held his hands up in contrition. "Sorry, sorry, sorry – it's just – never mind."

She handed him the bag and cup and he plunged his hand in to start shovelling hash browns towards his face. She had gotten herself yet another coffee. She was too nervous to eat.

She pressed the button to bring down the window. "And by the way, you could stand to take a shower. It smells like a wino's ass in here."

He tried to talk but was unable to do so around a mouthful of food. He held his finger up for a second's grace, chewed expansively and swallowed. "I could do with a lot of things; a shower would barely scrape the top five. So, why'd you pick me up?"

Amy looked out the window at the empty parking lot. A chill breeze cut through the car. It was just shy of 8am. There was a reasonably steady stream of customers pulling up to the drive-through window, but nobody was pulling over. Anyone who had McDonald's for breakfast this early on a Sunday was eating it with one hand on the wheel, driving to wherever they needed to be.

She turned back to him. "What do you think was happening back there?"

"In Murphy's Diner?"

She nodded.

"I'll tell you what wasn't happening – tea! Fecking disgraceful."

She gave him a look.

"Those two guys weren't robbing the place. That was pure nonsense."

"How so?"

He had pulled out the wrapper holding the Egg McMuffin and he was now inspecting it like a dog did with something it found on the floor, as if trying to decide if it was food or not. "Well," he said, "I'm only guessing, mind, but if you have someone or something you need to get hold of in a hurry and it's in a public place, like a restaurant, you pretend you're robbing the place and then you take everything, to hide what you were actually after. Only those two idiots hadn't got a clue what they were doing."

"What makes you say that?"

She waited as he took a large bite of the Egg McMuffin and chewed through it industriously before swallowing. He nodded approvingly. "Not too shabby. What was your question?"

"What made you think those guys were amateurs?"

He shrugged. "Because pros wouldn't pull such a gobshite move, and if they did, they'd have controlled the room. If that bloke was Special Forces, then I'm Ronald Mc-Fecking-Donald. They let me talk. A pro would've identified the threat and shut it down."

"And in that room, you were the threat?"

He nodded. "Well, outside of the geriatric gunslinger, but yeah. If they knew what they were doing they also wouldn't have let me annoy them into getting close enough that I could flash-fry one of their bollocks, pardon my French."

"I speak French," she said absentmindedly, looking out the window, "and that isn't French."

"Excusez-moi." He said it in a sing-song voice around another mouthful of McMuffin. "So," he continued, "what's your story?"

"What?"

"Who were you meeting?"

"Who said I was meeting anyone?"

He said nothing, but raised his eyebrows at her.

She turned away. "It doesn't matter."

"I'd lay good money it does."

"Alright, then it's none of your damn business." She turned her head away from him again and looked out the window. A woman in a minivan appeared to be arguing her order at the drive-through window.

"Fair enough."

They sat in silence for a minute, just the three of them – Amy, the constantly chewing Irishman and his overpowering aroma.

Eventually, Amy turned back. "So, what's your deal then?"

"Excuse me?"

"Why were you at Murphy's Diner? And who comes to a roadside diner without a car?"

He licked a spot of egg from the corner of his mouth. "I got the bus. I was hoping to meet the eponymous Mr Murphy. He owes me a favour and I happen to be in need of one. I find myself suddenly with an absence of funds."

"Was he not there?"

He shook his head. "He is not receiving any visitors, owing to him being dead as the proverbial dodo."

"I see. And how did you... who are you that... how did you know how to handle that situation?"

He shrugged.

"I mean seriously," she continued, "you figured out what was happening just from the guy's shoes. You weren't just talking; you were distracting them and drawing them into a mistake. Then you managed to disarm the guy. How'd you know how to do all of that?"

He shrugged. "Ah, I've always been good in a scrap."

She turned towards him. "Yeah, but seeing the guy's shoes, knowing straight off what they were doing there..."

"Do you know how some people are just good at maths? Or are natural singers? Or they can just, I dunno, they just understand computers and stuff?"

"Yeah."

"Well, I was never much for the sums, I can't sing to save my life and I can barely check my email – but that... that I can do."

"Have you been in the States long?"

"Seven days."

"Why did you run from the cops then? I mean, until you left the scene, you'd not broken any laws. Hell, you were a hero. You'd foiled a robbery and God knows what else."

The man took a sip of his coffee with a grimace. "Let's just say I don't particularly want to draw attention to myself."

Amy turned further in her seat. "No, that's not it though, is it? You thought they were there for you."

"Maybe I did."

27

"You did. You asked how they found you. Are you on the run?"

"No. It's complicated. Those lads definitely weren't after me though."

"Why? Do you not warrant two men with guns?"

"No. I don't warrant two amateurs with guns. So anyway..." He shoved the now empty wrapper into the bag and scrunched it up. "Any chance of a lift back into New York?"

"That depends."

"On what?"

She stared out the front window as she spoke, running her hands up and down the wheel nervously. "I need your help. Clearly, these guys are after me and you've got... Well, you beat them with a fork and a pot of coffee. I think I could do with your help. I'll pay you. No questions asked."

"I'm afraid there'll have to be questions. For a start, why are they after you?"

"I won't tell you that."

"Why don't you just go to the police?"

"I can't."

"OK then, the answer is no."

She turned her head to look at him. "Excuse me?"

"Look, my arse is hanging in the wind here, but I'll figure it out. I need less trouble, not more. I've got a lot of shite of my own to deal with and not a penny to my name. I could do with a lift and the money, I won't deny that, but I'm not helping you unless I know the whys and wherefores. If this is drugs or anything dodgy, I'm not interested."

"You're awful picky for a man who's running from the cops!"

"Avoiding. And that makes me shy; it doesn't make me a criminal. Look, I've my own way of looking at this, and I don't expect you to understand. So, thanks for the lift and the food and all that, but I'll make my own way from here."

He opened the car door.

"Wait."

He did. They sat there, him with one leg out of the car, her trying to weigh up her options. Although "options" implied plural, and right then, she could only see one. "Alright."

He pulled his leg back in and shut the door.

"I work as a dom in Manhattan."

"A what?"

Amy was annoyed to feel herself blush. "A dominatrix."

The man scrunched up his face. "Like with the whips and the chains and all the spanky spanky, 'who's your daddy?' stuff?"

"Well, that's a rather juvenile interpretation of it, but yes, essentially."

The man raised his eyebrows. "And that's a job now, is it?"

"Yes," said Amy. "And as it happens, a rather well paid one."

"Well spank my bot-bot and call me Susan." He scratched his beard. "And you're trying to get out of it and those guys are your pimps or something?"

Amy didn't try to keep the anger from her voice. "No. See this crap is why I don't tell people. I'm not being forced or coerced into doing it. I like my job. I'm good at my job. I appreciate it's a bit different, but fundamentally I believe that what happens between two freely consenting adults is entirely their business."

"The law might take a different view."

"And the law is wrong."

"Well, that aside, you're like five-foot-nothing and you'd blow away in a strong wind."

"And? I'm a dominatrix, not a professional wrestler. I don't need to physically overpower someone. In fact, that's the last thing I should be doing. Look, it's just a job like any other."

"Really?" he said. "So, if I asked the lady at the drive-through window there if she'd like to whip me and shove a dozen chicken McNuggets up my—"

Amy cut across him. "Forget it. If you're going to be an asshole about it, just get out and walk."

He thought for a second and raised his hands. "Alright, sorry. Honestly, 'tis not my sort of thing, but I don't care what gets anybody their ya-yas as long as all involved are enjoying themselves. It's a short life with a lot of queues; get your happy wherever ye can find it, that's what I say. So, did someone take offence to how you booted them in the knackers or something?"

"No. Look, are you going to shut up so I can just explain this to you or not?"

He shrugged. "Alright, fine, fire away."

"OK." Amy took a deep breath and then continued. "Last week I was having a session with a regular client of mine. He's been coming to see me for a couple of years. We were just doing the normal stuff."

"Normal?"

Amy shot him a look. In response, he mimed locking his mouth and throwing a key away.

"So, yes – anyway. The client, out of nowhere, breaks down, starts confessing stuff to me. About his work. Discretion is a big thing in the job, but I knew he was a Wall Street guy. I've got a few of them. It's a weird thing but, well, a lot of these guys like someone else being in complete control for a while and, y'know, surrendering..." She kept her eyes on the steering wheel in front of her as she talked. Having to explain herself irritated her. She wasn't ashamed of it and yet she still got embarrassed when forced to justify it. "Thing is, afterwards, it's like the other self kicks in and they try and reassert their dominance of life. Start telling you how big and powerful they are back out there in the real world. It's a common enough occurrence that you learn to leave a bit of time at the end of a session for it. Friend of mine calls it the 'rebuild' – like they're rebuilding their all-important self-image before your eyes. Anyway – I'm rambling. So, I knew this guy was a big deal on Wall Street. He'd been... Another thing that happens – guys think they're in love with you." Amy could feel her cheeks flush with embarrassment. "It happened with him last year. You do all this stuff that they've always wanted to experience but have mostly never had in their personal life, so they build up this dream that you're amazing and imagine how incredible life would be with you. You've got to sit 'em down and explain it isn't real life and it's a professional relationship. You wash your undies, sing off key, get irritated by the way someone breathes through their nose, just like any real person. Some guys you just stop seeing, but this guy, Matt, he seemed cool with it. Still, we're having this session and he just breaks down. Starts telling me all this..." Amy paused, searching for the words. "I dunno, confidential business stuff, about shady dealing and screwing some guy over. To be honest, I wasn't really listening. There's rules to this stuff and when someone, y'know, steps out of the game, then it's over. I just calmed him down and focused on getting him out of there. He was... weird after. Like, I could see he was already regretting it. Texted me the day after, saying to forget all he said. I assured him that whatever happened in the room stayed in the room, like it always does. Not a problem. Then I didn't think anything about it until last night..."

Amy absent-mindedly rubbed her hand over the logo on the steering wheel and ran her tongue over her dry lips. "I came home and some guy I don't know was standing on the landing outside my place. He said he was a friend of Matt's and wanted to talk to me about something important. I said I don't let people I don't know into my apartment and he could call and make an appointment like anybody else. Then he got aggressive. Put his hands on me, so I Maced him and ran."

He spoke softly. "Fair play."

"Then I called Matt and asked, y'know, what the hell. I told him I was going to the cops. Said this shit was completely unacceptable." She chopped at the wheel with her hand. "I was really, really clear."

"And what did he say?"

"He said it was a massive misunderstanding and that the guy was completely out of line. He promised he could fix it and he'd explain everything in person. So, I said I'd meet him somewhere public..."

"And he picked the diner?"

"No," said Amy. "I did. I'd stopped there before when I was driving back home. I wanted somewhere public but somewhere way out of town, so if he caused another scene..."

"Right," he said. A long moment stretched out between them. Amy glanced back over and noticed that the drive-through altercation had now expanded to involve three members of staff and another driver.

"Can I ask the question anyone would ask in this situation?"

Amy puffed out her cheeks. "Let me guess – why am I helping you get away from the cops rather than running to them?"

She looked back to see him nodding.

"Because – surprise – I'm currently in my final year at NYU Law. Being a dom is legally... murky. Opinions vary on whether it is actually illegal. I'd make an excellent test case if it came to trial. It'd also be the only time I'd see the inside of a courtroom, because the New York State Bar Association has what it calls 'fitness tests'. Once the truth was known, I'd have a hell of a time trying to get a licence to practice law here or anywhere else, and even if I did, no law firm worth a damn would touch me."

"I see what you mean. Was it not a big risk becoming one then?"

"Well, yeah, but do you have any idea how much law school costs? Spoiler alert, it's a lot. I didn't get a scholarship and my dad hasn't got that kind of cash, so I funded myself by working and..." She nodded back towards the McDonald's. "Believe me, you don't make NYU Law money flipping burgers. And, again, I'm not ashamed of what I do. I like my job. Consenting adults should have a right to express themselves how they see fit in private. I believe that to be enshrined in the Constitution and, if I ever get a licence to practice law, I'd argue that case."

The man rubbed his hand around the back of his neck. "Yeah, no, fair enough. You'll get no argument from me. One question though, this whatchamacallit, 'client' of yours—"

"Matt."

"Yeah. Do you think he could've been one of them lads in the balaclavas this morning?"

She shook her head. "No. I've been thinking about it. Neither of them seemed like him, although the taller guy, the one you didn't, y'know – I think he could've been the guy outside of my apartment."

He nodded. "Right. Did this Matt fella give you anything?"

"No."

"You didn't record him or...?"

"No! That'd be a massive no-no."

"Yeah. That's what I was afraid of. You see, if those lads weren't trying to get something off you, then there's limited options for what they were doing."

"But if they wanted me dead, couldn't they just have..." Amy had a sinking feeling in her stomach. She had suspected this but hearing it didn't make it any easier.

"Think about it from their perspective. Some poor girl gets shot by a masked gunman, the police are going to want to know why. Law student, good girl, all that. They're going to go looking. They'll find out your part-time job pretty fast. Then they'll go looking for clients. Maybe you've said something to somebody..."

Amy lowered her head onto the steering wheel. "But if she gets shot in a robbery gone wrong then the police aren't looking at her, they're looking for who would have robbed a diner."

"Afraid so. A whole other motive. Look on the bright side."

Amy looked up. "There's a bright side?"

"Yeah, you're lucky those two gobshites couldn't pull it off. May your enemies always be fucknuggets – Sun Tzu's *The Art of War*."

"That does totally sound like him."

Amy thought for a second, then reached down into the pocket of her car door and came out with a wad of bills held together by an elastic band. "Alright, ten grand. It's yours if you help me sort this out."

He pushed her hand away. "Jesus, what are ye like? Don't go offering men you've just met wads of cash in a car. Ye don't know me from Adam!"

"Well, you seem sort of trustworthy."

"Did this Matt fella seem trustworthy too?"

She narrowed her eyes. "That is a low blow."

"I'm just saying like, be sensible. How do you even have that kind of money knocking about?"

She rolled her eyes. "I work in a cash business."

"I suppose, yeah. I can't imagine you take credit cards."

"Oh, I do, just not everybody uses that. It shows up as being from a tailor's in Soho."

He pursed his lips. "Fair enough. Still though, what do you want?"

"I want you to help make this go away."

"I'm not muscle for hire."

"You haven't got a cent to your name and you're stuck out here in the middle of nowhere. Are you sure you can afford to be that proud?"

He turned away and she could see him thinking about it, his fingers drumming on his knees. "I'm not going to like, kill anyone or nothing like that."

"Good. Matt and these asshole buddies of his clearly think I'm going to rat them out. All I need them to realise is that I've no interest in whatever insider dealing bullshit they're doing. I just want to be left alone. I want my life to go back to what it was twenty-four hours ago."

"Don't we all."

"Speaking of which, what's your deal?"

"My deal?"

"You've been here for a week and you're penniless and, frankly, stinking of booze. Are you a sailor just off a ship or something?"

"We don't need to discuss that."

Amy shoved the money back into the side pocket. "Yeah, we do. I just got told I'm too trusting. How do I know I'm not tossing myself from a relatively warm frying pan into a blazing inferno? You could be some Irish serial killer for all I know."

"Well, I'm not, although if another person tries to fob me off with iced tea…"

"Noted." She gave him a long, searching look. "Still, I need to know why you're on the run from the cops. What did you do?"

"Ah for…" He drummed his fingers on the door irritably. "I'm not… I'm not legally in the country."

"I see. So, what? Are you here looking for work or something?"

"Not exactly. I'm here looking for a woman."

"Oh God."

"A particular woman. She's in trouble. I'm trying to help her, but to do that, I need to find her first."

"OK."

"You don't need to know the details. Let's just say that if I get picked up, it'll be very, very bad and cause all sorts of hassle. I've no ID or anything and..." He paused and looked out at the empty car park like it was suddenly fascinating.

"What?" she asked, wondering what he didn't want to say. It was hard to tell behind the big beard and with the lazy eye, but Amy could've sworn he was embarrassed.

He shifted around in his seat. "I got... I got robbed yesterday."

"You? The guy who took down two armed men with a cup of coffee and a fork? Who the hell robbed you?"

He scratched at his beard irritably. "Well, if you must know, I was... I'm here alone. It's been... a while since I've been home. It being Paddy's Day, I got a little – well, I suppose... homesick, you could say."

"OK?"

"And I went out drinking."

"As I believe is traditional for your people."

He shot her a dirty look. "That's a bit of a stereotype."

"An accurate one, apparently."

"Well, anyway, I suppose, one thing led to another. I'd a few drinks and then... somebody robbed me."

"What, like they pulled a gun on you or something?"

He mumbled something she couldn't hear.

"What?"

"No," he said, considerably more loudly. "If you must know, they must've spiked my drink."

"Right. Are you sure you weren't just drunk?"

He reacted like he'd just been slapped in the face. "No, I was not. I'm not a lightweight. I'm telling you, I was spiked!"

Amy raised her hands. "OK, OK. I'm only asking. I thought I was hiring some fork-wielding badass. Turns out he's a bit of a pussy."

He folded his arms and glowered over at her. "I can see why you got a job booting people where it hurts, you've a real eye for it."

She smiled as she turned the key and the engine ignited. "OK then, let's go see if we can sort this all out, shall we?"

He gave a curt nod.

A thought struck Amy and she stopped the car and extended out her hand. "Oh, by the way – Amy. Pleased to meet you."

He looked at her hand and then shook it. "Bunny."

"What?"

"Bunny," he repeated.

"As in Easter Bunny?"

"Well, it's not my proper name, obviously, but it's what I'm called."

"Bunny what?"

"Just Bunny."

"Seriously?"

He nodded. "I like to keep a low profile."

"Really? Because I've known you less than an hour and you've already been in a shootout and left a lasting impression on at least one of your opponents."

He looked out the window. "I said I *like* to keep a low profile, I didn't say I was actually managing it."

CHAPTER SIX

Chicken. Chicken. Chicken.

Matt stood on the balcony watching a fresh Sunday morning spread itself around Manhattan, fourteen floors below. The wind tugged at his T-shirt, causing goosebumps to rise on his skin. He liked it. The coke and tequila buzz had gone stale in his blood. He'd hit Brad's room and taken a couple of pills he'd found. He didn't know what they were – the high had felt a little like ecstasy, but now there was a weird taste at the back of his throat. With Brad, it could be anything. That Philippe guy he bought from specialised in what he called "boutique tailored" experiences. What it meant was that he'd found a way to get Wall Street assholes like Brad to pay through the nose in the belief that, somehow, their highs would be higher than what you got from the dude outside the men's room with the switchblade and the tattoo of Tupac on his arm. Matt corrected himself: Wall Street assholes like Brad and him. He was one too; in fact, he might just be the worst.

They'd met in college – Matt, Brad and their other roommate, Charlie. Six-foot-three, blond, built like a brick outhouse, as Uncle Chip would've said, Charlie was all athlete, attending on a lacrosse scholarship. In contrast, Brad was a full foot shorter and a walking, talking cliché about short guys and Napoleon complexes. Charlie seemed posher than he was, his sporting ability meaning he'd gone through a Boston prep school beyond his parents' means. Brad meanwhile, came from serious "house in the Hamptons" money, and yet underneath the party boy act, he seemed inexplicably full to bursting with a burning resentment, like he'd never been given a fair chance at life.

Matt came from chicken. His family had owned a chicken farm. They'd been getting by, hanging on in a tough economy, and then his mom had got sick. Real sick. They hadn't been able to afford the bills. The debts had built and built until the day Matt had found his mom collapsed on the porch when he'd come home from school. Uncle Chip had quietly gathered some of the neighbours and collectively they'd paid for the funeral. By this point, the Clarkes didn't have two cents to rub together. The bank sympathised and then foreclosed. Everyone up the chain had apologised but said there was nothing they could do, a corporation proving to be a protective bubble that ultimately insulated you from the consequences of your decisions.

Matt's dad had sent him and his sister, Jennie, to stay with Uncle Chip and Aunt Jane for a couple of days while he'd gone off to visit some old war buddies. He'd said he knew a couple of guys who might be able to help them out. "Never leave a man behind" and all that. He'd waved them off and then gone into the chicken barn and blown his brains out. He had left a note. Matt had never read it – he had already known what it would say. Uncle Chip had called on the same people and they'd got some more money together for the funeral. Matt had noticed that his dad's coffin had been of a much cheaper-looking wood than his mom's. The big conglomerates were squeezing the margins tight on chicken farmers. At the time, he had commented that if he went the same way soon, he'd be buried in a refuse sack. Jennie had gotten really upset about that and Matt had watched his mouth from then on.

Uncle Chip and Aunt Jane had been great, but it had been a strain. Quietly, Matt had explained it to Jennie. The little bit of money their folks had left, he'd use to go to college. He'd work his damn ass off and when five years later it came to her turn, he'd make sure the money was there. She'd agreed. Of course she had. Matt could remember, in happier times, his mother explaining to him that, yes, his little sister following him around all day probably was annoying, but that was how it was. He still remembered her words: "She thinks her big brother raises the sun and moon." At twelve, it'd been annoying. It felt different now. On the day of his father's funeral, Matt had felt the weight of his father's coffin on one shoulder and his responsibility to Jennie on the other. He was all she had left, and try as he might, Matt couldn't figure out how to make it better. Some things don't get better.

So, he'd gone to college and worked his ass off. He'd delivered a thousand pizzas and worked warehouse jobs when he could. When it came to finals, in a cosmic dump from a universe seemingly not running short on spite, he'd gotten the flu. He'd tried to power through with a temperature of one hundred and three. His final grades were poor if you didn't know the circumstances, but impressive if you did. Still, the interest from the big firms, who typically don't stray far from the Ivy League or the big schools anyway, had dissipated.

Charlie, for his part, thought he was going to be one of the many college athletes who went on to flourish in Wall Street's alpha male environs. It turned out that if you can't cope with numbers flying by fast, you crash and burn pretty damn hard as a trading desk assistant. He'd made it two months. He'd also punched a trader on the way out the door.

So when Brad had come calling, the timing couldn't have been better. His uncle Rudy ran a hedge fund, which sounded exciting, at least in principle. If Wall Street was Broadway, Lanark Lane Investments was off-off-off Broadway. It managed the investments for old ladies and a couple of orphaned pension funds of small companies that'd disappeared. They were technically on the buy side of Wall Street, but they were such small fry that they could hardly get the big houses to take their calls. Uncle Rudy was virtually retired for health reasons, only coming into the city two days a week, and he spent one of them seeking the consolation of his mistress. After six months, Brad, Matt and Charlie found themselves captains of the ship, for what it was worth. Matt was the analyst, wading through the data single-handedly, trying to find that holy grail. Charlie worked the phones, that down-home charm working to get some new clients onto Lanark's previously moribund client list. Brad was ostensibly in charge. And so they'd gone, batting above average, but not enough to get them noticed and a call-up to the big leagues. Their first year, the Christmas bonus had been $800 and a really nice letter opener complete with its own sharpening stone.

Then, chicken. Chicken, chicken, chicken.

Jennie had taken a year off before going to college. That's what they'd called it. The reality was that the money hadn't been there to pay her tuition. Matt would have somehow preferred it if she'd got angry, bitched at him and moaned about how unfair it was. Instead, she'd been infuriatingly understanding. She had taken a job at the local day care and stayed home, helping out Chip and Jane on the farm on her days off. She'd started seeing Jimmy Nightingale, who worked as a manager at the distribution centre for the chicken wholesaler. He'd been in the year above Matt in high school and Matt considered him too old and nowhere near good enough for his sister. Still, Jimmy had invited Matt out for a beer and, at Jennie's insistence, he'd gone.

Despite Matt's reservations, Jimmy was an OK guy. Still, they'd had precious little in common, so they'd made up for the gaps in conversation by drinking. Eventually, after striking out on attempts to find common ground on sports, music, TV, Jimmy had resorted to bitching about work. The company had swapped haulage companies in a highly competitive bidding process and it turned out the lowest bidder had been so damn cheap because they'd entirely misunderstood what the job required. The software didn't work to tell the trucks where to go, and even when the trucks did find out where to go, it took way too long. The hauler blamed the software company, the software company blamed the existing software at the wholesalers – the whole thing was a disaster. They were going to be the laughing stock of the whole industry. Worst thing was, they couldn't go back to the old system if they wanted to, as losing the bid had sent their old hauler to the wall. In three days, half the chicken franchises in most of the South were going to run out of chicken. Chicken shops with no damn chicken!

Matt had listened intently as Jimmy had talked and talked, delighted to have finally found something of interest to Mr Wall Street, as Jennie affectionately referred to her big brother.

Matt had flown back to New York the next morning and, despite it being a Sunday, he'd headed straight to the office and run the numbers. Then he'd run them again. Then he had called Brad and Charlie. Things might have been very different if Rudy hadn't been off on a cruise – the latest apology to his wife. For a man who screwed around so much, he seemed spectacularly bad at hiding it. Brad had been given access to the trading accounts in his absence.

They'd cleared their whole investment portfolio by midday on the Monday. Some of it had been a fire sale to clear non-liquid assets. Brad had called it going all in. By Tuesday, they were one hundred per cent committed to the plan – every last cent that Lanark Lane had under management. Then, they'd sat there silently watching screens as they had taken the mother of all beatings. Wednesday came and went with more of the same. Brad had been dodging calls from his uncle for over a day at this point. Somebody from one of their brokerage firms had rung Rudy to find out what was going on. They had shorted the wholesaler, the haulage company, the fast-food chains. They'd invested heavily in their rivals. By the time it had started to break their way on Thursday night, Matt was alone in the office. Brad was somewhere getting wasted and Charlie had rung an ex-girlfriend, in the hope that getting laid could distract him from his career imploding before his eyes – again.

It had been a fun news story on local TV, the shop with the sign up saying no chicken. They'd found the most redneck SOB imaginable to interview and his incoherent rage had been pure clickbait. The video had been auto-tuned and remixed by Friday morning and the chicken shortage had made the morning talk shows. By close of business Friday, Lanark Lane's portfolio had doubled in value over the space of a week. Rudy had gotten off a plane, looked at the numbers and promptly fired his three employees. They'd won it all and somehow still lost.

Brad, of course, had his job back by the end of the weekend. His uncle Rudy was terrified of the SEC coming to audit their funds but, if anything, he was even more afraid of Brad's mother.

Four weeks later, Matt found himself sitting at the bus station, hungover, with all of his earthly possessions in a rucksack at his feet, when it happened.

A stocky black guy with a shaven head and tightly trimmed beard had sat on the bench opposite and given him an appraising look. Matt had sat upright and pushed his rucksack further under the seat. The man looked out of place; nobody else in this zip code was wearing a tie, for starters. There was something about the way he was looking at Matt that he found unnerving. Given that they were in a bus station where an old lady was arguing loudly with Jesus and a dude in a tracksuit had been rummaging vigorously in his pocket for eight minutes, looking for change he didn't have, that was really saying something. The black guy's eyes stayed locked on Matt's.

"Can I help you." Matt didn't say it as a question. He said it as a back off.

"Come with me."

"Excuse me?"

The man had stood up and spoken to Matt while scowling at the gangly kid in the tracksuit who was still trying to find that quarter.

"Come with me," he repeated.

"Yeah – no, thanks. I ain't interested in... whatever."

The man sighed. "Your name is Matt Clarke, you're twenty-four years old and you're about to get on a bus back to your shitty life in Falstaff, Ohio. Or you can come with me for a few minutes. Woman wants to talk to you."

"About what."

"If she wanted me to talk to you then she wouldn't be waiting to talk to you."

"Who says I want to talk to her?"

"The forty-seven bucks in your checking account means you can't afford not to."

A chill went down Matt's spine. He'd checked his account on the way to the station. Aunt Jane liked snow globes; he'd kept promising to get her a New York one and he hadn't managed it yet. He'd figured now might be his last chance. Then he'd realised that he didn't have enough to be blowing his last few dollars on cheap junk.

"I'm walking over there. Come, don't come – up to you, kid."

Then the man had walked off.

Matt had followed and was surprised when, instead of exiting the bus station, he'd led him through the door that said "Staff Only". In the middle of what looked like a break room sat a woman of about sixty, with a black bob streaked with grey. She wore a tailored pantsuit and a tight smile under green eyes. Everything about her said she was in charge. "Mr Clarke, take a seat."

"What is this?"

"It's a job interview. I believe you're in the market."

"For who?"

"Lanark Lane Investments."

"I've already been fired from there."

"Excellent, so you have relevant experience. Sit."

"Is this some kind of joke? Did Brad put you up to this?"

"No, Mr Clarke, Brad Bradley did not put me 'up to this'." She said the last words like they were beneath her. "Sit."

Matt looked behind him and did a double take. The first look was because a tall brunette woman he hadn't even realised was in the room was standing right behind him with a chair. The second look was because the woman was frankly gorgeous – a dazzling smile, perfect olive skin and blue eyes that sparkled. The sound of the older woman clearing her throat made Matt realise he may've been staring too long. He could feel his face flush as he placed himself down on the chair. The brunette moved silently to stand behind the other woman. As she did so, she gave him a wink that, despite the circumstances, was distracting.

"So, Mr Clarke. The Grandino Poultry Distributions deal that you made."

"I don't know what you're talking about."

"Of course. Still, I do. Lots of people get information, but what you did with it was the impressive part. You have an eye for weakness. I respect that."

"Are you with the SEC?"

"Does anything about this meeting strike you as being the kind the Securities and Exchange Commission typically engage in?"

"No, but then maybe that's the point."

She nodded amiably. "Good. That's a good instinct, Mr Clarke. Trust no one. You do not need to confirm or deny anything. Let's just say that you are a man who has shown an ability to appreciate the value of information. I" – she smiled – "am someone who, on occasion, comes across information. I am looking for someone who can understand and act upon that information."

"The last time I did that, it got me fired."

"It won't the next time. You will also not need to worry about the SEC, or any other combination of letters you care to mention. Not if you do your job correctly. Or maybe you'd prefer to go back to little old Falstaff?"

Matt bristled. "How in the hell do you know so much about me?"

"We are the US government; it's our job to know about you."

"Exactly which part of the government?"

"If memory serves, the Interstate Commerce Commission regulates bus travel. If you need a name, use that."

"OK. Well, in that case, there's a dude outside who has been choking the chicken for the last ten minutes. Who do I complain to about that?"

In the corner of his eye, Matt noticed the brunette grinning at that last statement and his heart skipped a beat. Her boss looked at her watch.

"This is a limited-time offer, Mr Clarke."

"You haven't actually made me an offer yet."

"A job. To be exact, your old job back."

"Rudy won't go for it."

She carried on as if he hadn't spoken. "I am in charge of managing a retirement fund for the, ahem, Interstate Commerce Commission. I would like you, under the guise of Lanark Lane Investments, to manage it for me."

"How do I know I'm not being set up?"

"Because you're currently not important enough to set up." She stood up and looked at her watch again. "It's fourteen minutes before your bus leaves. Your phone will ring before then. If you're who I think you are, you have enough information. Take the offer, don't take the offer, the decision is yours. But if you do take it, know that you work for me. I'm offering you everything you ever wanted, Mr Clarke, I don't need to negotiate."

She walked briskly to the door.

"But – wait – I—?"

A surprisingly firm hand on his shoulder from the brunette made it clear that the meeting was over and following them was not an option.

Seven minutes later, Brad rang, sounding thrilled. Rudy had just been in touch, saying he'd reconsidered and was offering Matt his old job back.

"Tell him no, not unless he doubles my salary."

"But dude, I—"

Then Matt had hung up the phone.

The next morning, he'd returned to work at Lanark Lane Investments at twice his previous salary. As had a grateful if extremely confused Charlie. Rudy didn't even speak to them. He carried on as if afraid to make eye contact.

The next week, the new high-value clients had started rolling in. When the third one showed up out of nowhere, Charlie had begun asking questions. Matt had taken him and Brad into the meeting room and briefed them on most of the details. Brad was thrilled, but

Charlie – despite now understanding how he'd managed to get his old job back, was less sure.

"Who are these people?" he asked.

"I don't know, but they're clearly government and they clearly know what they're doing."

"Yeah," agreed Brad. "The CIA are always running drugs to get money to fight terrorists and shit. Hell, this might be patriotic work."

"I'll tell you something else," Matt had said, slightly embarrassed. "This woman, the client, she reminded me of Mrs Miller."

Charlie pulled a face. "From that dumbass sitcom you like?"

"Dude! *New in Town* was an underappreciated classic."

"It didn't even make it to midseason before it got canned."

After three months, their assets under management had doubled in size and on the rare occasions any of the three of them referred to their client, the name Mrs Miller was used. And on they had gone.

On a Friday night two months later, Matt had been in a bar waiting for his date to show up. She was a trader at Morgan; Charlie played pick-up basketball with her brother and he'd set them up. There had been an ongoing discussion in the apartment, which he, Charlie and Brad shared, that Matt really needed to get laid. Sitting there, nursing his drink, Matt had been deciding how long a grace period he'd leave before assuming he was being stood up and bolting when the brunette from the train station calmly sat down opposite him. She'd smiled and wordlessly handed him a phone. The voice had been who he had expected. "In a few weeks, a Solaranda oil tanker is going to have an accident in the Persian Gulf. It will be quite messy."

"OK. Should I... "

The line went dead. Matt handed the phone back to the brunette. "Your boss isn't much for conversation, is she?"

The brunette stood, leaned across and placed a wet kiss on his lips. Then, with a giggle, she turned and left. Matt looked up to see his date standing looking down at him, truly appalled. As she stormed out, Matt couldn't help but laugh.

This time he was considerably cleverer about it. He produced a detailed position paper on why Solaranda Oil was a bad bet. The thing is, with any company, you dig around enough and you can always find a reason why it could all go wrong.

When the SEC came asking – and they did – Matt had been able to produce the paper, which he'd taken the unusual step of sending to a few select clients in order to explain investments he was going to make on their behalf. One of the clients had forwarded it to his broker at Merrill and been assured it was crap. Then, three weeks later, admittedly not from overexposure to volatile Saudi Arabian politics but due to a fire starting in a ship's galley and some seriously faulty design, Solaranda had spread oil all over a large part of the Gulf and their names over every newspaper on the planet that used three-syllable words. They'd gone bankrupt and Lanark Lane Investments had made a killing on behalf of their clients. Their reputation had continued to grow. If you get it right, nobody cares that you got it right for the wrong reasons.

After that, their client list had really started to swell. Matt couldn't be sure who was a front for Mrs Miller and her associates and who was just an ordinary client trying to jump on the bandwagon. They'd hired a trading desk and three other analysts, all of whom were, of course, in the dark about Mrs Miller and the fund they were managing on her behalf. Matt instructed Brad to engage in a significant increase in daily trades – dipping in and out of funds in the medical, energy, retail and property sectors. It was a fairly bullish market, so he was coming out even or slightly down most of the time, which was absolutely fine. What Matt wanted was volume, white noise, so that when the time to make another move came, there would be cover.

Initially, Matt hadn't paid much attention when Rudy had come in for a few days and started looking through the accounts. He'd said he just wanted to check in on some of his old clients, make sure they were doing OK. Matt didn't get it – they were making money, why wouldn't they be happy? But whatever, as long as Rudy stayed out of the way, he didn't care. At this point, all he did was sign paperwork when instructed to do so.

Then, one evening, Matt had been down in the parking garage, admiring his new Lexus, when Rudy suddenly appeared from the shadows.

"Jesus, Rudy!"

"Do you have any idea what you're doing?"

"What the fuck are you talking about?"

Rudy grabbed Matt's arm, his grip tight. "I built this company from the ground up."

Matt shrugged him off angrily. "Big deal. It wasn't that far off the ground until recently."

"You goddamn pissant."

Rudy threw a punch. It didn't land with much force; it was more the shock of the thing. Matt leaned back against his car. He could taste a trickle of blood on his bottom lip as Rudy stood there, his fists by his side, the knuckles clenched rollercoaster-white, his face taut with strain.

"Calm down, old man, you'll give yourself a heart attack."

Matt got into his car and drove away, angry and embarrassed.

Two days later, Rudy had another heart attack – his last.

The funeral had been a surreal affair. The widow had been merry to an undignified degree, possibly prompted by her first and only visit to the offices of Lanark Lane Investments, which she had made that morning and discovered exactly how much of a nest egg she was sitting on. But at the back of Matt's mind, there had been a nagging doubt. Then two days later, the man from the bus station had been waiting for Matt at the end of his jog around Central Park.

"Your old boss asked too many questions. You need to make sure you and your two boys keep the ship running tight."

Matt had stood there, panting – leaning up against a tree, watching the man walk away, carrying whatever his old life had been with him. A line had been crossed and it wouldn't be the last one.

The road had led down and down and down, until he'd found himself here, two years later, on the balcony of a penthouse on West 88th Street, where, try as he might, he couldn't convince himself to jump.

Chicken, chicken, chicken.

He turned at the sound of the apartment door thumping open behind him. A vase of three-hundred-dollar flowers was sent crashing to the ground as someone stumbled in.

"Fuck!!! My balls, my balls, MY FUCKING BALLS!!!"

CHAPTER SEVEN

Disaster Incorporated – that was the name Brad had come up with for them. Matt had loved it. It sounded like one of the tag teams he'd grown up watching on Saturday mornings after he'd helped his dad with the chickens.

Matt sat on the massive oversized corner couch in the sunken living room, while Charlie paced up and down in front of the fireplace, which was illuminated by fake fire. In the background, Matt could hear Brad in the bathroom, alternating between whimpering and screaming. Matt had suddenly reached a moment of zen-like tranquillity amidst it all. It was like when a plane was about to crash and the people who were terrified of flying were always the calmest people onboard – or so he'd heard. To everybody else, the world was ending and the sky was falling, while to them, what was happening was just what they had expected. A part of Matt had been waiting for this moment for a while now; there was a sense of relief to no longer having to wait. Or maybe those pills he'd dropped had finally kicked in.

Charlie leaned up against the mantelpiece. "We are so screwed, dude. Totally screwed."

Matt sipped at his drink. "You've still not explained exactly what happened."

Charlie looked back at him, his face contorting into that constipated look he got when life wasn't going his way. "Are you high?"

Matt giggled. "Of course not, Mom. Honest Injun."

It was a peculiarity of Charlie's that he did not indulge in narcotics, instead tutting none too quietly as Matt and Brad did. Brad had always been enthusiastic in this area but, recently, Matt had been catching up fast, self-medicating himself into being the chilled eye of the storm.

Charlie stood there, clenching and unclenching his fists, glaring down at Matt. "You asshole, this is all your fault."

"What'd I do? I've been here all night."

"Yeah, while I've been out, trying to fix your damn problem."

They both looked over towards the bathroom as Brad howled. "Oh Jesus, oh Jesus, oh Jesus."

"Seriously, what happened to him?"

"He got a lap full of hot coffee."

"Damn. I take it she didn't take the money then?"

Charlie turned away and looked into the fake fire.

"Charlie? You said you were just going to buy her silence."

He turned back, anger in his eyes. "Do you really think Mrs fucking Miller would be happy with someone out there knowing what she knows?"

Matt felt a horrible sinking feeling in the pit of his stomach. "What did you do?"

"We did what we had to. I tried talking to her before, remember? Bitch Maced me."

"Because you threatened her." Matt leaned back on the sofa and looked up at the ceiling. "Like I told you the first time, if you'd just let me—"

"Shut up. Seriously, shut up, or I'm going put you through a fucking wall."

Charlie clenched his hair between his fingers and scrunched his eyes shut. "You came to me, remember? 'Help me, Charlie, I've run my damn mouth off to my whore.'"

"She's not a whore!"

"The fuck she isn't. I'm not interested in whatever gets you off, but she does that shit for money. Bitch is a whore."

Matt rose unsteadily from the couch and pointed angrily. "I said, don't call her that."

"Oh man, this – this right here, this shit is going to get us killed. You came to me, told me you'd screwed up. All the talks you'd given both of us, talking about how we couldn't say anything to anyone, all of that, then you – yes, you – blew it. So, I went to talk to her, to try and fix it."

"Look how well that turned out."

"Fuck you, man. You said try and scare her."

"Scare her, not attack her."

"I didn't."

"So how come she was calling me and threatening to go to the cops unless we met?"

Charlie picked up a cushion and hurled it across the room. It was a ridiculously expensive piece of soft furnishing designed by someone French. The interior designer they'd hired when they'd moved in six months ago had assured them that it tied the room together beautifully. It hit the Dalí print on the wall and sent it to the floor with a thunk.

"We did what we had to do," said Charlie.

"Is that why Brad's in the john screaming about his balls? To return to my earlier question – what the fuck did you do?"

Charlie stood still for a few seconds, breathing in and out, clearly trying to calm himself. "We – Brad – had an idea. Said we could deal with her and make it look like an accident."

"Deal with her? As in kill her? I never said kill her! You fucking…"

Matt lunged at Charlie, tripping over the step from the sunken living room as he did so. Charlie neatly stepped to the side, letting Matt fall gracelessly to the ground. Then he was on top of him, his knees pinning Matt's shoulders effortlessly.

"I'm going to kick the shit out of you, you ungrateful asshole—"

Charlie's train of thought was derailed by Brad's balls appearing beside his head. His voice was a high-pitched whine. "Jesus, Charlie, look at it. I got burns all over my—"

"Fuck dude, get it out of my face, man." Charlie pushed Brad away.

"Don't touch me!" cried Brad. "Everything hurts when I move. I gotta go to the doctor."

"For the last time – no. The cops will be looking for a guy with burns down there."

Matt interrupted. "The cops? What stupid shit did you pull?"

"What did you say?" asked Brad, a demented look in his eyes.

Charlie managed to jump to his feet in time to stop Brad stomping on Matt's head. He had switched from being the guy about to whale on Matt to the one protecting him.

Brad flailed around like a wild animal, so much so that, despite the height and weight advantage, Charlie had a hard time holding him against the wall.

"I'm gonna kill him, I'm gonna fucking kill him."

"Shut up, man," said Charlie. "Think! We ain't got time for this."

Matt got to his feet and gingerly moved towards the drinks cabinet. "I need a drink."

"The fuck you do," said Charlie. "We gotta call them."

"Them who?"

"What the hell – *them*. Mrs Miller."

Matt shook his head. "Do you really want to risk telling them how badly we screwed this up?"

"We've got no choice. We can't contain this. We don't understand this shit."

"Yeah," said Matt, "remind me again, what exactly are you two experts in?"

"That's it," hollered Brad, "give me my gun. I'm gonna pop a cap in this bitch's ass."

Charlie shoved him back against the wall again and then clamped his hand over Brad's mouth. "Keep your fucking voice down." Charlie turned his head back towards Matt. "Do it. Call them."

Matt laughed. "I can't."

"What?"

"You think they've given me a number to call? They just show up."

Charlie looked at him for a long moment and then shook his head. "Man, we are screwed."

"Hey, look on the upside," said Matt, "at least Brad won't be breeding any time soon."

What Charlie was about to say next never made it out, as their argument was interrupted by the doorbell.

With a drunken smile, Matt wafted his drink towards the hallway. "That'll be them now."

CHAPTER EIGHT

"I see."

Charlie had done most of the talking for the last twenty minutes. Matt had been too freaked out to say much; he was coming down fast, and he now had paranoia crawling all over his skin. He had said what he needed to: the truth, unvarnished and as brief as possible. Mrs Miller, ever since their first meeting at the bus station, had made clear her appreciation for brevity.

They were in what looked like some kind of disused homeless shelter. Benches sat beside long tables that stretched down the room. On the wall was a worn-looking mural, the features of a group of happy, smiling people fading away amidst chipped paint and water damage from a leak in the roof. The word at the top was missing its first letter, but Matt guessed it had once been "hope". Beside it, the Latina with the dazzling smile was leaning against the wall and casually spinning a yo-yo, of all things, up and down in a hypnotic fashion. In her Converse sneakers and figure-hugging jeans, she could pass for a teenager. She caught Matt's eye and beamed at him. He looked away, embarrassed. He had still never heard her speak.

"I see," repeated Mrs Miller.

She sat very still, listening intently as Charlie spoke. He'd gotten to the part where he and Brad had their brainwave of "eliminating the problem" of Amy once and for all. Assholes. Matt would never have agreed to that and they knew it. Charlie had promised to buy her silence; God knows they had the money. Luckily, all their hare-brained scheme had resulted in was an embarrassing screw-up and, well...

"He burned my goddamn balls!"

Matt could happily go the rest of his life without hearing Brad say that again. He was sitting on the long bench beside him – although sitting wasn't quite the right word. Brad was squirming, same as he'd been in the car on the way over. Most of the burns, from the limited view Matt had seen, were actually on the skin on his thighs, but Brad had chosen not to focus on that.

The knock on the door had been the black guy from the bus station who Matt had come to know as Mr Cole. He'd instructed all three of them to follow him and he'd led them downstairs to a car. He'd then driven them out towards the docks. Brad aside, there had been very limited conversation on the ride over. All around them, the hustle and bustle of a city waking up to an ordinary day had carried on regardless. Sunday wasn't a day of rest in New York. Matt had wondered if he would ever see another sunrise.

"This man," Mrs Miller continued, "did he work at the diner?"

"No," answered Charlie. "He was just some random Scottish dude."

"Was he with the girl?"

"He didn't appear to be. I looked in the window before we, y'know, and she was on her own. This guy was just a customer, far as I could see."

"Yeah," chimed in Brad, "he stunk of booze and looked like some homeless loser."

For the first time, anger flashed on Mrs Miller's face. "A homeless man that managed to disarm and very nearly neuter you."

"Fuck you, lady."

Mr Cole was in Matt's field of vision, so he saw the swift movement as he delivered the backhand slap to Brad. It didn't look like he'd put much behind it, yet it was still enough to send Brad spinning to the floor.

"Thank you, Mr Cole. I assume Mr Bradley has learned a valuable lesson."

Charlie leaned forward and picked him up. "Sorry, he... sorry. He's in a lot of discomfort with the... he's not thinking straight."

"From what I can gather, none of the three of you have been thinking straight for some time. This is quite a mess you have made. And you're sure nobody saw your faces?"

Charlie nodded emphatically. "We wore masks the whole time. We're golden."

Mrs Miller favoured Charlie with the kind of look normally reserved for dogs that had taken a dump on new carpet. "Indeed."

She said nothing for a full minute, instead looking at her nails intently, seemingly lost in thought. Matt noticed she wore no jewellery on her fingers – so Mrs Miller was a Miss. She didn't look up as she spoke next.

"Mr Bradley and Mr Fenton, please wait out beside the car and try not to get into any trouble for a couple of minutes. I will speak to Mr Clarke alone."

Brad moved his lips as if to speak, but a look from Charlie stopped him dead. Instead, he allowed himself to be pushed out the door.

Mrs Miller watched them leave. "This is not good, Mr Clarke, not good at all."

Matt nodded. "I know."

"I don't think you do. The timing of your... let's call it an outburst, could not have been worse."

"Look, I know that. I'll make it up to you. It's not too late to stop this."

"Stop this?" Mrs Miller leaned forward in her chair, her tone incredulous. "Stop this? There is no way on Earth we can stop this. Wheels are in motion. We have taken loans of money from people you do not take money from lightly. People who are not as understanding as we are. I blame myself. I have allowed you to be utterly oblivious to the seriousness of our situation. You picked an interesting time to grow a conscience. Regardless, we proceed as planned."

"But?"

"Exactly. As. Planned. Do I make myself clear, Mr Clarke?"

Matt ran his tongue around his dry lips and nodded. "Yes. I understand."

"You are useful, Mr Clarke. Do not make the mistake of confusing useful for irreplaceable. Please join your friends."

Matt nodded and stood. He hesitated, then thought better of what he was about to say and took a step towards the door. Then he stopped again.

"Yes?"

He turned to face Mrs Miller. "The girl – Amy. I don't want anything to happen to her. OK? This is my fault, not hers."

Mrs Miller gave Matt a look he couldn't read and then nodded.

He headed outside to stand in silence beside the other two thirds of Disaster Inc.

Cole watched as his boss stood and dusted off the seat of her skirt.

"Lola," she said, and the brunette immediately stopped yo-yoing and stood to attention. "You will take Mr Fenton back to this woman's apartment and, assuming she is smart enough to not be there, you will do what is necessary."

Lola gave one of those big smiles that sent a chill through Cole's heart.

"Are you sure that's a wise idea, ma'am?"

The boss turned towards him. "Really, Mr Cole? Given your immense and catastrophic failure in the task assigned to you, I would have thought you would not be of a mind to question my orders."

"It's just—"

"You had one job. One. That was to sit on those three buffoons and make sure that our affairs were being taken care of while they stayed nicely contained and deniable."

"I—"

"I have read every one of your reports. I know Mr Bradley's family history, his proclivity and preferences in the field of pharmaceutical entertainment and even the fact that he is sensitive about the alliteration of his first and second names. I know Mr Fenton's vice of choice is the pleasures of the flesh, something he has indulged in to such an extent that a trip to a clinic last month confirmed he had chlamydia. And yet, through all of this, you somehow managed to miss that not only was Mr Clarke availing himself of the services of a dominatrix but, as we have just seen, has developed feelings for her. How did this manage to slip by you?"

Cole shifted nervously. "Clarke had another phone I didn't know about."

"Really? You were bamboozled by the same trick every cheating spouse has used for twenty years?"

Cole said nothing, judging rightly that nothing he could say would improve this situation.

"So," she continued, "Lola will get us some breathing room, while you have the delight of taking Mr Bradley and his scalded scrotum to visit that veterinarian friend of ours."

Cole closed his eyes and nodded. Today was not going to get any better. "Yes, ma'am."

"I, meanwhile, will have to engage some additional resources and put in place measures that should not have been necessary in order to ensure docile compliance and the completion of the plan. That is all."

CHAPTER NINE

Amy hit redial and held the phone up to her ear.

"Hi, this is Matt—"

She stabbed at the disconnect button with her finger and for a half a second toyed with the idea of hurling the phone across the room. It would feel good to do something that finally had an effect, even if it was a bad one.

They'd been back at Jonathan's for over three hours now and, so far, a whole lot of nothing had happened. She'd tried to call Matt's phone every fifteen minutes and got the damn voicemail every time. Her new "associate", meanwhile, had come in, gone to the bathroom for what he referred to as "a cleansing upchuck" and then collapsed onto the sofa.

She had asked him if he had any ideas on what the plan of action should be. He'd answered that he needed a few moments to ponder the best way forward and then promptly fallen into a deep slumber, accompanied by a cacophony of snoring, farting and belching. Twice already Amy had needed to intervene to stop Evil the cat from launching some kind of attack on her new unwanted houseguest.

Evil was why Amy was there. She belonged to Jonathan, aka the fabulous Jonathan. He was away for two months miming to show tunes on a Caribbean cruise liner and Amy had agreed to cat-sit by dropping in every couple of days.

She had to admit, there were worse places to hide. The Victory hadn't actually been a hotel since the 70s. It had tried to be a high-end establishment, but at the wrong end of the Village, back when the Village still had a wrong end. The original owners had bet on the area rocketing upwards and they'd been right – just a few decades too early. Still, the Victory had a colourful history, even by the standards of New York, where any hotel worthy of the name collects incidents of infamy just by existing in the city that doesn't sleep – or if it does, it sleeps with someone else's partner. A visiting senator had passed away in the loving arms of a hustler with a rap sheet longer than the Bible. A prog rock band had named the album that caused them to break up *Five Nights at the Victory*. Despite claims to the contrary, no famous beatnik authors had penned works there, but quite a few had blown advances. It had been scheduled to get torn down until a dotty old lady stepped in and offered to take it off the city's hands. She'd then converted it into apartments and made a fortune, so not so dotty after all, thank you very much.

The apartments had high ceilings, wooden floors and gloriously big windows, even if they only offered views of the buildings and billboards on the far side of the street. Its former life as a hotel was still visible in the decor in places with odd little touches here and there. Until recently, it had still had a doorman. Legend had it, he'd come with the building as part of the deal, a favourite of the building's original owner who'd been guaranteed a job for life as a condition of sale. He'd been eighty and had still turned up to work every day, even if it was only to fall asleep behind his desk.

Speaking of things that came with the building, then there was Evil. The cat was named that as a compromise. Jonathan had initially wanted to call her Hitler due to an unfortunate small patch of black under the nose on her otherwise white fur. She had been born and raised in the Victory and Jonathan liked to tell people that she was possessed by the place's evil spirits. He'd heard crying one night and, being unable to find the source, had initially believed it to be something supernatural. Jonathan was an intelligent man, but in Amy's opinion, he went to the woo-woo way too fast as an explanation for damn near anything. He'd heard it three nights running, the same desperate mewing. Eventually, much to the delight of the neighbours, he'd taken a sledgehammer to a wall at 4am and discovered one of the Victory's many hidden secrets. A dumbwaiter had been covered up and a cat had found her way inside when searching for a quiet place to have her babies. Evil, it seemed, was the runt of the litter, who'd lacked the strength to get herself out of there and so had been left to die. Amy wondered if that trauma was responsible for how the cat had turned out, or if this was a case of "give a dog a bad name", as she had certainly grown to fit her moniker. Evil was your best friend one second and then drawing blood the next. Amy had learned the hard way not to wear a dress around the little monster. She clearly viewed the Victory as hers and only Jonathan was to be tolerated.

Jonathan actually owned the apartment through chicanery he had never fully explained other than to hint at a bad romance. From what Amy knew, he had been given it in the late 80s by what he termed "an admirer". At the time, he'd been in a chorus line on Broadway, with a lucrative sideline working as a drag queen. He'd never quite made it in musical theatre, even before the throat cancer had taken away his singing voice, but while he bitched about it often and at great length, he was still in demand as the diva of divas. Amy had seen him perform and it was quite the sight to behold. The fabulous Jonathan could destroy a front row, saying the most horrible things about people, worse than they'd probably heard in their whole lives, and they'd love him for it. They'd applaud through tears of laughter then stomp along enthusiastically as Jonathan mouthed "I Will Survive" in outfits that Liberace would have considered a bit OTT. While much of the fabulous one's wardrobe was on the high seas, there were still three racks' worth over beside the kitchen. He had merely taken "the essentials" with him.

Amy had found something to do to fill her time, when not fending off the cat and liberally spraying air freshener around her houseguest. She'd taken to Google and tried to find out as much as she could about Matt Clarke. While it was a relatively common name, when searched alongside financial services, it brought her to the hedge fund of Lanark Lane Investments. There was a picture of him, with two men, one she recognised, one she didn't – although her best guess was that she had met both. The one she definitely knew was the tall blond guy she'd met on the landing outside her apartment last night. God, was it really only last night? It felt like a lifetime ago now. The other guy was shorter. She couldn't be sure, but if she had to guess, she reckoned he'd be feeling pretty sensitive about now, after having had his nuts napalmed with hot coffee.

Matt didn't have any social media accounts that she could see, but the short guy, Brad Bradley, did. His Facebook account was thankfully set to public and it had pictures of him and his two "bros for life" moving into their new place with a view of Central Park, and the epic party they'd thrown to celebrate. Admittedly, the view of the park was a restricted one – it was essentially a hint of foliage between two buildings, but Amy knew enough about Manhattan real estate to know that anything in that zip code would be worth some serious coin. So, while she didn't know where they lived exactly, she knew enough to maybe figure it out. It wasn't much, but in a situation where she was feeling all but helpless, it was comforting to know she had managed to do something. Of course, what good it would be, if any, depended on what their next move was. And currently her tactical advisor was still resting his eyes.

As always, at times like this, there was that part of her that wanted to call her father. But, of course, she couldn't. She'd grown up a daddy's girl by default, her mother having died when she was three months old due to complications after childbirth that had got progressively more complicated. A little part of Amy felt she remembered her, but she knew that couldn't be the case. Her mother lived on in her because of how often her father spoke of her. That light in his eyes when he did so, even to a little girl, was a special thing. It was a peculiar thing to be a little jealous of your own dead mother, but there it was. Growing up, there had only been the two of them. Her childhood looked a whole lot different when seen through Amy's adult eyes. Her father had tried to enter her in beauty pageants, ballet classes, doll clubs, which, even now, Amy was surprised were a thing. She had hated it then, but she got it now. An irrigation engineer – an expert in sewage – he'd been terrified that he didn't know how to raise a daughter right. He'd tried to suppress her tomboy tendencies out of nothing more than well-meaning panic that he was doing something wrong. Her father was a handsome man. He would invite ladies over to the house, and at the time, Amy had thought he was dating. But it turned out she was the one he'd brought them there to see, hence why so many tried to have chats about make-up etc.

Eventually, they'd hit on a happy compromise with horseback riding. Her father had been called out to the Regency Riding School to help them with a sewerage problem they were having. When he'd seen all the young girls out riding, he'd expressed an interest and promptly been paid off with thirty free lessons for his daughter in lieu of cash. From the first, Amy had loved it. Always a small child, she was suddenly massive on the back of a horse. She loved animals, too, and had a great natural feel for it. By the end of her stint of lessons, she was riding better than any student they'd ever had – so Carol, who owned the place, said. Horseback riding was expensive though, so her father did odd jobs around the place to help out Carol and her partner, in exchange for lessons. That's how it was that a working-class kid from Pittsburgh ended up with a room full of horseback riding trophies. It was also how, a few years later, when Carol fell ill, her father became the owner of a riding school that'd never in its entire existence managed to make money. Pittsburgh was not an area that was traditionally big with the horsey set.

Since moving to New York, Amy had managed to keep up with the riding almost by accident. While out jogging, she'd met a woman bringing tourists around Central Park on horseback. One of the horses had come up lame and Amy had assisted her with calming it down, so they could get it on a trailer. They'd got to talking, and now Amy went down every Saturday and Tuesday morning and helped out at the stables in exchange for early morning rides. Her horse of choice was Mabel. A former showjumper for a rich kid, she'd been cast aside when a bad leg and an inability to breed had made her not worth anyone else's while. They went out at the crack of dawn and Mabel got to pin her ears back and run – really run. It was the best part of Amy's week.

Speaking of big dumb animals... As if on cue, Bunny farted loudly and extensively. It had been a while since Amy had played much music, but it sounded like he'd hit most of the notes on the major scale. She was still very doubtful about getting him involved, but it wasn't like she had a lot of options. Besides, he had gone up against "the enemy" once already and managed to destroy them with a tasty beverage and the second-most dangerous of the three most common kitchen utensils. He had been able to cause them problems; she just couldn't be sure he wasn't going to do the same for her. Despite all of that, and for no logical reason she could give, Amy found herself trusting him. As much as she could put her finger on why, it was the notion that untrustworthy people, in her experience, put considerably more effort into presentation.

Bunny snorted, belched and aggressively scratched at his nether regions. The man was like a biological orchestra.

Amy was done with waiting. She picked up one of Evil's extensive collection of cat toys that were strewn about the place and tossed it at Bunny's head. It bounced off his nose, and he snorted and pulled himself into an upright position before it had landed on the ground. "What in da fuck?"

"Oh good," said Amy. "You're up!"

Bunny looked around, scanning his location as if he was seeing it for the first time. "It smells of cat piss in here." He turned around and noticed Evil the cat sitting on the arm of the couch, giving him an appraising look. "Right, well that explains that, I suppose."

Amy spoke under her breath: "I'm surprised you can smell anything over..."

"What?"

"Nothing. Come here and look at this."

Amy turned the laptop towards Bunny and he stood and walked over.

"See this picture: that guy is Matt and that guy" – she indicated the tall blond – "is the one who was outside my apartment. His name is Charlie Fenton. They work together."

"Right, yeah. And I'm pretty sure short-arse there is the bloke whose bollocks I boiled."

"I agree. I also think I've figured out where they live. I think. Rough area anyway."

Bunny nodded. "Fair play to you. I was thinking the best way to deal with this is to go pay them a visit."

"I don't know the exact address, but I think it's a penthouse off either the east or west side of Central Park." She turned the laptop and opened up the Facebook page with the picture of their view. "Look, there's a Starbucks, which probably doesn't narrow it down much, but there's a dry cleaner, which probably does."

Bunny looked at it and nodded. "Excellent news." He stood and drummed his hands on his belly. "So, will we grab a bit of grub and then get cracking?"

"Yeah." Amy pointed behind Bunny. "First things first though."

"What?"

"You need a shower."

CHAPTER TEN

Charlie stood nervously on the pavement outside the brownstone in Astoria and looked at his watch.

He'd been here yesterday, and it had not gone well. All he had wanted to do was talk to that Amy girl and make sure she understood that, regarding what Matt had blurted out, silence really was golden. She'd not been willing to listen and, well, things had gotten a little out of hand. Still, there'd been no need for the bitch to Mace him – that stuff really burned. His eyes started to water slightly at the sense memory.

Speaking of crazy, then there was the woman he was currently waiting for. He'd been nervous as hell going to the meeting with Mrs Miller. It had been excruciating, enumerating the ways that they'd screwed up in the last few days. Matt had started it but, between Charlie's own failed attempt at intimidation and the disaster that was Brad's plan for elimination, they now all looked like clueless idiots. Still, for all that, it'd gone better than Charlie had expected – they weren't wearing concrete slippers at the bottom of the East River, or whatever else was currently in vogue for body disposal.

Instead, he'd been put in a car with an insanely hot chick. She was a ten, straight up, on anyone's scale: Latina, perfect skin, full, pouty lips and a smile that could make some things melt and other things go exactly the other way. She'd sat opposite him and not said a word. He'd tried to make conversation, and each time, she'd just smiled. It was weird. She said nothing but there was no indication that she couldn't. Were people still mutes? Was that still a thing? His cousin Winston was deaf, but he could speak OK. There was no sign of hearing aids or anything. The girl did respond to what he said, albeit non-verbally. Maybe she just read lips? Still, for all that, with the smiles and the fluttering eyelashes, there did seem to be something there. Chemistry. Charlie knew he should be focused, but that was just it: every time they'd had a big game coming up in college, he'd been horny as hell. He figured it was an excess of adrenaline that needed somewhere to go. His body was a machine and it ran hot.

The black dude, Mr Cole, who'd picked them up had told Charlie that he and the girl, Lola, were going to go back to Amy's place. Charlie had asked if they expected her to be there, and when he'd said no, he'd asked what the point was. Cole hadn't answered – he'd just given Charlie a look he couldn't read.

They'd been six blocks away when this Lola chick had tapped the driver on the shoulder and he'd pulled over. Then she'd opened the door of the car and nodded her head for Charlie to get out.

"But this isn't the place?"

She nodded that she understood.

"Are we walking from here then?"

Lola shook her head and then pointed at him.

"Am I walking from here?"

She gave him a big smile and nodded.

"Oh, OK."

He'd gotten out and stood on the sidewalk. "So, I'll see you there?"

She mimed running, blew him a kiss and closed the door with a giggle. Could mute people giggle? Charlie needed to figure that shit out. That giggle was driving him crazy and he wanted to hear more of it.

He had taken off at a fast walk, always a man who loved a challenge.

He'd been standing outside the building for a good fifteen minutes now and there was no sign of Lola. The car had driven off in this direction. They'd hardly got lost, had they? Maybe this was some kind of game to mess with his head? Part of him was tempted to leave but the other, much bigger part of him, more than anything, wanted to do nothing to piss off Mrs Miller any further. He got the definite impression that there would be no more free passes on that score.

It was a dry day. It was therefore odd when Charlie felt water hit the back of his head. He put his hand there and looked up at the cloudless March sky. More water hit his hand. He turned and got some right in the face.

"Hey."

He looked up to see Lola, four stories above, leaning out the window with a water pistol in her hand. He could see her giggling away.

The door opened and an elderly lady with a shopping bag on wheels started to slowly make her way through the front door. Lola crocked her finger and motioned for Charlie to come upstairs.

He stepped forward and held the door open for the old lady. "There you go, ma'am. You have a great day."

Her initial look of suspicion gave way to a smile of gratitude. If you couldn't trust a well-groomed, athletic, blond white boy, who could you? He smiled back and then slipped through the door.

Charlie ran up the stone steps two at a time. When he reached the top landing, the point where his previous disastrous chat with Amy had taken place, he was breathing a little hard. He'd been hitting the weights more than cardio recently. The door to Amy's apartment was ajar so he gingerly pushed it open and stepped inside.

A song was playing on the stereo; not something he recognised. He wasn't big into music. It was something old – he could see a record revolving on a turntable in the corner. Some woman was singing about putting a spell on a dude. The spring sunshine coming through the big bay windows illuminated the main room. Off to the left, the door was slightly open, and he could see a dim light playing against a sliver of wall.

Charlie opened the door. Candles threw flickering light against the walls. A large wrought-iron bed lay in the centre of the room. The decor was a mix of blacks and dark reds. Lola stood on the far side of the room, standing in front of a large oak wardrobe. She beckoned for him to come inside. Charlie did so, closing the door behind him.

"So..." said Charlie, suddenly nervous. "Erm, what's up?"

She smiled and leaned back against the wardrobe. Now he noticed she had a riding crop in her right hand, which she tapped against the side of her leg. As he reached her, she giggled and grabbed his T-shirt, pulling his lips down to hers. They kissed briefly and then she pushed him back firmly, until the backs of his legs hit the side of the bed. Then she turned and opened both doors of the wardrobe with a flourish. Inside lay a cornucopia of objects and implements. Some leather, some rubber. Some things he recognised; a lot he didn't.

"Yeah," he said, "that's some freaky stuff. Not really my bag."

Suddenly the smile dropped from Lola's lips and Charlie felt like the world had tilted slightly in the wrong way. She looked crestfallen.

"I mean, y'know, I'm open to new ideas."

Her face brightened and her eyes twinkled once again. She gave him a big smile. With her left hand, she twirled a finger, motioning for him to turn around.

"OK." Charlie laughed nervously.

He heard something heavy being slid against wood. "I mean, nothing too – y'know. Maybe we could take turns or..."

His train of thought was derailed by something heavy slamming into the back of his head. His legs buckled from under him and he crumpled to the hardwood floor.

Everything swam before his eyes. "What the fuck—"

As he tried to pull himself upright using the side of the bed, someone punched him in the kidneys, causing all the air to expel from his body.

A hand roughly grabbed his hair and pulled his head back. Then he felt wet lips brush against his ear.

"The reason I don't like to talk is that I know men don't like to listen."

Then she giggled again.

It didn't sound so cute now.

CHAPTER ELEVEN

"I'll tell you what would go well with this."

Amy diverted her gaze from the street and looked down at the plate in front of Bunny. "What?"

"A nice bit of bacon."

"It's a bagel."

"Sure, don't I know that! I ordered the fecking thing. I'm just saying, nice bit of bacon would go fantastic with it."

"You're in a deli."

"And?"

"A Jewish deli."

Bunny shrugged. "What? So the Jews don't eat bacon, does that mean I can't?"

"You don't come here to eat bacon. There's like a thousand places within walking distance where you can eat bacon. If you want bacon, you've got to go somewhere else or, y'know, bring your own."

"Do you think they'd let you do that?"

"Well, I doubt they have a rule forbidding it, mainly because nobody has thought to do it."

"I don't suppose—"

"No, I do not have any bacon on me."

On the street outside, exhausted and elated people walked by, wrapped in silver recovery blankets. On the way over they'd seen signs warning that there was a half-marathon happening today. It seemed odd to Amy. At ten o'clock last night, some guy had tried to rough her up. At seven o'clock this morning, somebody had tried to kill her. With her world so utterly screwed up, it was surreal to realise that lots of people were just having the Sunday they had been planning for months.

Bunny interrupted her train of thought.

"Are you a member of the Lost Tribes yourself?"

"No."

"So, what's your problem with bacon?"

"I'm a vegan."

Bunny rolled his eyes, which was particularly unnerving, given the lazy one. "Oh, for feck's sake." He lifted the bagel and shoved half of it in his mouth. Amy wrinkled her nose in disgust.

"You're a pig."

Bunny gave three energetic chews and swallowed. "Thanks very much. I'm assuming you meant that as a compliment."

Amy thought better of what she was about to say, instead clamping her lips shut and turning back to look out the window. They had been at this for over an hour now, not counting the almost two hours it had taken to find the place. She was sure this was the street. Almost definitely sure. West 88th Street. The picture on Brad Bradley's Facebook page had been taken from a height, but Amy was pretty sure the tree-lined street in the background was this one. It was harder to tell than she'd expected. It turned out most of the streets around Central Park were lined with the same kind of trees. They were also similar in width. The deli in which they were currently sitting was opposite a currently closed-for-renovations dry cleaners, which she was ninety per cent sure was the one in the picture. She really wished they'd left the signs up though.

The understandable anxiety she already felt was, if anything, exacerbated by the tedious time spent watching as nothing much happened on the street outside. She was still trying Matt's number every fifteen minutes, hearing the opening two words of the same voicemail message again and again.

"When you think about it," said Bunny, "I feel sorry for chickens."

Despite herself, she turned back and looked at him. "What?"

"Think about it. The Jews and the Muslims, Lord knows they don't agree on much, but neither of them will eat pig – or prawns, come to that."

"So?"

"So," continued Bunny, "the Hindus won't eat cow – sacred animal and all that."

"So?"

"So," Bunny repeated, "everybody eats chicken. Poor delicious little fuckers are the entire planet's go-to dish."

"Well, I don't eat chicken – or any other meat."

"Do ye mind if I ask why?"

"I don't believe in animal cruelty."

"That's ironic, given your job and all."

Amy turned back to looking out the window. "No, it is not."

"So, hypothetically, if a chicken asked you to spank it on the bot-bot and call it a naughty boy, you'd be fine with it?"

Amy ripped at the cardboard of her coffee cup with her fingers. "No, because chickens do not possess free will and they're also not boys. Now can we stop talking about nonsense and start doing what we came here to do?"

"Relax, would ye? You're awful tense."

She turned back to him, the anger that'd been building finally bubbling to the surface. "Well maybe if you even attempted to do the damn job you've been hired to do I'd be a little more chilled. As it is, we've spent an hour here and all you've done is spend my money stuffing your face while paying no attention to the street where the guys who are after me hopefully live."

Amy took a deep breath. By the end of that little speech it had gotten away from her and she'd ended up putting more venom in it than she'd intended.

Bunny calmly picked up the second half of his bagel and spoke without taking his eyes off it. "The woman who walked by fifteen minutes ago was walking the same poodle that the fat guy with the beard was walking an hour ago. I'd lay good money that they're a couple having an argument who can't stand to be in the same apartment together, so that poor little sod is going to get walked to death. The same white van has passed by here three times in just over an hour – maybe the guy is just doing deliveries, maybe he's lost or maybe it's something else. Speaking of deliveries, the guy with the neck tattoos who delivered pizza just up the road there has been inside for fifteen minutes, which makes me think he's not just delivering pizza. Best guess, someone is right now having a joint with their dealer. The dude smoking on the corner is doing so because his wife won't let him in the apartment and he's none too happy about it. And of the forty-six cars currently parked on this street, thirty-four of them have stayed put the whole time we've been here, but the guy on the third floor above the dry cleaners keeps looking out his window, possibly because he's the new owner of that gaudy penis extension of a Porsche sitting over there and the sad gobshite just likes looking at it. And the couple at the table behind me... The woman is having an affair, guessing by the way she looks at her phone when he goes to the counter or the bogs. I could be wrong – maybe she's planning a surprise party. Any questions?"

"How did you...?"

"Because the trick to seeing is not watching. You should always be doing something else. Now, you've had nothing but coffee all day and it's making you cranky. Relax and have a fecking bagel, would ye?"

"Fine."

"I'll have one of them twirly jobs. Thanks."

"A pretzel?"

"Yeah. I've always wanted to have one of them. Could you ask about the tea again?"

"The guy said they were out an hour ago. They're not going to have had a delivery on a Sunday."

Bunny shook his head. "How in the feck did you people ever become a superpower?"

"I've not studied a lot of history, but I'd guess a combination of can-do spirit and big weapons."

Bunny licked a blob of mayonnaise from the corner of his mouth. "Well, bit of bad news for you then – the Chinese have both of them now, and a shitload of tea. Famous for it."

"Oh well, I guess we…"

Amy stopped talking as she noticed a change in Bunny's facial expression. She turned to see an SUV with tinted windows driving past. It stopped at a canopied entrance just up the street. The rear passenger door opened and Brad Bradley got slowly out, walking in a cautious manner that indicated they had correctly identified him earlier.

"That's him," hissed Amy. "That's him! The asshole…"

"Relax," said Bunny. "Keep your head down. Don't stare."

"Let's go over there and you…" Amy raised her finger to point and Bunny's hand shot out and snatched it down. A black man in a suit with a tightly trimmed beard and a shaven head got out of the other side of the car.

"What are you doing?" asked Amy indignantly. "Don't put your hands on me."

The couple at the next table, who wouldn't be a couple in two months, looked at them in concern.

Amy watched as the black guy casually followed Bradley into the building's foyer.

"We've been made."

"What are you talking about?"

Bunny threw twenty bucks of the two hundred Amy had fronted him down onto the table top and headed straight out the door. Amy followed.

"Seriously, what's your problem?"

"The black fella made you."

"He didn't. He never even looked our way."

Bunny glanced left and right. "Run down towards the park now, head straight across and through and don't stop until you reach the far side."

"But..."

"Then grab a cab or keep moving fast until you can find one."

"But my car?"

"Anyone tries to stop you, scream rape."

"But..."

Bunny pushed her in the back towards the park.

"I'll meet you at the apartment in two hours – or else get out."

"But where are you—"

"Go!"

It was the way he said it, the certainty in his voice. Something primal in her responded to it – like even though her brain wanted to rationalise what the rustling noise in the bushes could be, her body was not in the mood to find out. So, she ran. When she had nearly reached the corner, she slowed and looked back up the sidewalk behind her – and what she saw made her run for all she was worth.

There, about sixty yards behind her, with a mobile phone clamped to his ear, was a black guy with a shaven head and a tightly trimmed beard, running after her at full pelt.

CHAPTER TWELVE

As soon as Cole stepped into the lobby, he moved to the side and pulled his cell phone out of his inside jacket pocket. Brad Bradley stopped huffily and looked at him.

"What are you—"

"Shut up and get upstairs now."

"But—"

Cole ignored him and dialled a number. "I'm at their building. She's here now. Possibly someone with her. Send backup."

Bradley took a step back towards the door. "Fuck, she's here?"

Cole grabbed him by the scruff of the neck and hurled him roughly towards the elevators. "Upstairs now, asshole."

The building's concierge, a Puerto Rican man in his sixties called Raul, watched this exchange in confusion. On the one hand, a man had technically just assaulted one of the building's tenants. On the other hand, he more than anyone knew that the tenant in question was indeed an asshole.

As Bradley started and then reconsidered a couple of retorts, Cole speed-dialled another number. "She's here. The deli across the street. Bring the car back around the block and..."

Cole took a couple of casual steps towards Raul, although Raul noticed that he wasn't actually looking in his direction. "Shit!"

He ran out the door and looked left and right. "She's in the wind."

He ran across the street and saw the figure of Amy Daniels running down the sidewalk. He took off in pursuit, still holding the phone to his ear. "She's running towards Central Park – blue sweatpants, red hoodie. There was a man with her…"

Cole stopped talking as two things struck him in quick succession. The first was the thought that the man in question had disappeared. The second was the man in question.

Bunny McGarry's philosophy on fighting had been developed over many hard lessons. He had then gone on to teach it to other deserving souls, through the dishing out of even harder lessons. It was built around five fundamental beliefs.

Firstly, the easiest way to win a fight is if the other fella only realises he was in one when he wakes up in hospital. In his youth, Bunny had been a good, but not great, boxer, mainly because he knew how to take a punch. He was an excellent street fighter though – mainly because he knew how to throw a punch before the other fella had heard the bell. Or, in this case, how to leap out from behind a car and rugby tackle him before he knew you were there.

The two men collided, and Bunny sent his opponent crashing messily into a half-dozen stone steps leading up to the stoop of an apartment building.

Although he'd long since lost track of exact numbers, in his life Bunny McGarry had won more fights than he'd lost. His winning percentage rose considerably in those scraps where his opponent made the mistake of letting him get the first shot in. It was therefore an unpleasant surprise when he reared back to deliver a roundhouse right into his current opponent's face only to have his head sent snapping backwards as an elbow, delivered with velocity and precision, connected with the bottom of his chin. A gush of blood filled his mouth as he bit his own tongue. This was closely followed by a kick to the chest.

Kicks, as far as Bunny was concerned, with the dishonourable exception of the boot to the kneecap, were largely useless in a hand-to-hand combat scenario. They looked fancy, but Bruce Lee would've still had his arse handed to him in a disagreement over a car parking space in Ballyfermot. Yes, there was the all-time classic boot to the bollocks, but while in the McGarry fighting philosophy that region was often targeted, it was rarely through a kick. He'd more often use the punch, elbow, knee or headbutt to the nether regions. Once, memorably, the bite. And, come to think of it, including that morning, the hot drink, twice. His current opponent, however, was forcing Bunny to re-evaluate his prejudices vis-à-vis the kick, because he seemed to really know what he was doing with it. This one caught Bunny right in the solar plexus and sent him flying backwards to slam against a car, briefly knocking the wind out of him.

The second tenet of the McGarry fighting philosophy was that hesitation meant defeat. Never giving your opponent a second to gather themselves was an essential concept. This was why he instinctively bounced straight back, aiming the aforementioned boot to the kneecap at his opponent's standing leg.

Unfortunately, his opponent must have also been familiar with this move, as his kicking foot came down with unerring accuracy to slam into Bunny's instep, causing him to howl with pain. It would have hurt anyone, and most other people hadn't previously been shot in the foot by a psychopath.

The third principle of the McGarry fighting philosophy was to go for the weak spots. In no particular order, his favourites were the eyes, throat, knees and knackers. Ideally, within the first three seconds, your opponent should be unable to either see, speak, walk or conceive.

Bunny was nothing if not eager to learn, which was why the open-handed smash, delivered to his left ear that made his head ring and his balance desert him, was certainly educational. He'd never considered the ear slap as a go-to move, and it turned out he'd been missing out. Bunny's re-education continued as he found himself in the middle of one of those full-body judo throws, which he had previously scoffed at as being only good for people who believed in bowing first and fighting in your pyjamas.

As he flew through the air, the thought struck Bunny that he was very definitely losing this fight. Nothing about his bone-crunching landing on the stone steps dissuaded him from that conclusion.

He heard a shocked gasp and looked up to see an elderly white-haired lady standing in the doorway, looking down at him through jam-jar-thick spectacles. She looked horrified by what she was seeing. To be fair, Bunny wasn't wild about it either.

The fourth principle of Bunny's fighting philosophy was to use anything to gain an advantage. Therefore, on an intellectual level he could not fault his opponent for using this gap in proceedings to pull a gun on him, but on a personal level, he found it a disappointing development.

Bunny looked around and quickly raised his hands in surrender. He was dimly aware of the old lady shuffling back towards the door.

"Who the fuck are you?" asked the black guy. He sounded dishearteningly in control as he did so, not to mention not even being out of breath. He held his gun like a man who'd held one quite a lot, and nothing about him said he might not use it.

"I'm just... I'm just a guy trying to buy a little time."

The black guy shrugged. "She got away, but I got you."

Bunny nodded. "Fair play to you, fella, you did – you got me bang to rights and there's not many who can say that. Although you misunderstand me."

"Do I?"

"To put it another way" – Bunny raised his voice to a frankly girlish trembling falsetto – "please don't shoot me! I'll give you my wallet."

The thing with the "use anything you can" nature of the fourth principle was that it worked both ways. Bunny watched as several emotions flitted across the face of the man who'd just kicked his arse seven ways to Sunday:

Surprise at Bunny's sudden appeal.

Realisation of what it meant.

Anger at what the realisation meant.

Then the quick flicking of his eyes right and left to confirm.

"NYPD. Put the gun down!"

They both turned to see a nervous-looking patrolman with his service weapon drawn and trained on the big guy with the gun.

"It's not…"

"Drop it, motherfucker. Last warning."

The lad looked barely old enough to drink. Bunny would have laid good odds that this was the first time in his life he'd ever pulled a loaded weapon and aimed it at another human being in anger. The situation could go one of two ways: either he'd lose his nerve and be unable to pull the trigger, or his nerves would cause him to pull it immediately. A lot of people had ended up dead over the years after calling that coin flip wrong.

"I'm—"

"Now!"

With a wince, the black guy dropped his gun and raised his hands in the air.

"Back away, back away!"

The patrolman, his hands jittery with excitement, stepped forward as Cole retreated as instructed.

"Now get on the ground…"

"But…"

"GROUND! NOW!"

As he slowly lowered himself to the ground, Cole registered the sound of the door of the building opening and his opponent slipping through it.

He swore quietly to himself.

The fifth and final principle of the McGarry fighting philosophy was that when all else fails, run like hell.

Fifteen minutes later, down by Central Park, runners from the half-marathon stood with silver recovery blankets wrapped around them, rehydrating while comparing personal bests. To the left of the main group, one man stood alone. While he was wrapped in a recovery blanket, it was over a black sheepskin overcoat and street clothes, because he hadn't been in the race. He took a gulp from the complimentary water bottle he hadn't actually earned, swirled it around his mouth and spat some bloodied fluids into a nearby trash can. You'd have to have been watching closely, but if you were, you'd have noticed that while he didn't appear to be doing much, he was regularly looking up West 88th Street, where three NYPD patrol cars were currently blocking traffic. Some of the runners were looking in that direction too, curious as to what was happening. They soon turned their attention elsewhere though. Whatever it was, it appeared the excitement was over. A nearby resident stood on the street, not interested in the incident so much as he was keen to confirm that it wasn't going to in any way damage his new Porsche, which he had bought in the mistaken belief he could afford it. Now even he, with one last lingering look at the object he loved more than life itself, was about to head inside. The patrol cars were starting to pull away. On the sidewalk, a discussion was taking place between a sergeant, one of his fresh-faced new patrolmen and a well-built black man in a suit. The sergeant handed the man back his wallet and gun and then looked at the patrolman, who dutifully offered an apology while his body language screamed that he wished the ground would open up and swallow him. The black man put his gun back in its shoulder holster, shook his head in disbelief, turned and walked back up the street.

Half a block away, the man wrapped in the recovery blanket unnerved some of the nearby runners by saying "bollocks" slightly too loudly and then turning to limp off.

CHAPTER THIRTEEN

Amy sat on the sofa stroking Evil the cat, who sat in her lap. She'd been back for an hour and she'd heard nothing from Bunny. It dawned on her – too late – that she didn't actually have a number for his cell. When she'd left him, she'd run like her life depended on it, shooting across four lanes of traffic on Central Park West and dodging runners who'd just finished their half-marathon. Also, as per Bunny's instructions, she hadn't gone back for her car, which was parked over at the Time Warner Center on Columbus Circle. Normally, Amy wasn't wild about following anyone else's instructions, but she felt she should this time, seeing as her arguing had allowed whoever that big black guy was to almost catch up to her. On the rare occasions she'd chanced a look back over her shoulder, there had been no sign of him – she assumed that was something to do with Bunny. When she reached Fifth Avenue, she'd managed to grab a taxi someone was getting out of and then she'd come straight back to Jonathan's place, watching out the back window all the while for any sign that she was being followed. She was now terrified, more than anything, that her dithering and obstinance might have got Bunny killed. She'd only met him twelve hours ago and knew almost nothing about him, but she was still racked with guilt that she might've got him into trouble – or worse.

Just then, there was a knock on the door.

"Who is it?"

"Bacon delivery," said an irritating voice she was delighted to hear.

"Hang on a sec— Ohhh, fuck you, you little douchebag!"

"Thanks very much. Great to hear yer voice too."

"No," said Amy. "I mean, sorry. The damned cat just dug her claws right into me."

"Well, it's been a rough day for all of us."

Amy flung the door open.

Bunny McGarry limped in, holding a bloodied paper napkin up to his mouth. "What in the hell are ye doing just opening the door?"

"I knew it was you."

"Yeah, well, I could've had a gun to my head. You'd want to be more careful."

Bunny reached the big armchair to find that Evil was now sitting on it. "Believe me when I say this, cat, this will not go well for you."

Evil gave him an appraising look and then casually hopped down, like she'd been about to do so anyway and Bunny's presence had no effect on proceedings.

Bunny sat down with a wince and a groan.

"Are you OK?" asked Amy.

"I've been better, to be honest. I've got a lump on the back of my head that feels like a golf ball. Any chance of a bag of frozen peas or something?"

"Right. Yeah. Sure," said Amy, hurrying over to the refrigerator. "So, what the hell happened to you?"

"Well, the good news is – I found out quite a lot about that black fella who it seems is now working with the three amigos."

"OK." Amy looked at him across the counter. "Did you, like…"

"What?"

She lowered her voice. "Beat it out of him?"

Bunny gave a humourless laugh. "No, quite the opposite. I figured some of it out while he was kicking the bejesus out of me."

"Oh."

"The only good news is the fact there's news; everything else is bad, I'm afraid. For a start, I've taken quite a few kickings in my time, but none delivered with that much panache. Whoever the lad is, he knows what he's doing. I mean, he's had some serious training. I'd guess military or something. Either that or he's a very keen amateur."

Amy found a bag of ice in the bottom drawer and brought it over to Bunny. "He can't be that good. I mean, you got away from him."

"Not exactly."

Bunny put his hand out to take the ice but Amy shook her head. "Lean forward."

With a wince, he did so, and she moved around to stand behind him. "So, where is this – holy shit!" She'd assumed he'd been exaggerating, but there really was an alarmingly large lump on the back of his head. "What did he hit you with?"

"The ground, mostly."

"Have you got a headache?"

"Yes."

"Woozy? Nausea?"

"Yeah."

"We need to get you to a hospital," said Amy, carefully placing the ice against the large lump clearly visible below Bunny's hair.

"No, we're definitely not doing that. Besides, a lot of them symptoms might just be a hangover. You're lucky, being in your twenties. Your hangovers are like an alarm clock – first thing in the morning, a short, sharp shock, then you're up and on with your day. At my age, it's like a series of painful packages being delivered in the post. You can never be sure when the next one's coming, and half the damage is done waiting for the bloody thing. Don't suppose you happen to have a bit of hair of the dog about the place?"

"What?"

"Booze. Whiskey. Beer. I'll even make an exception and go wine."

"No. I don't drink and neither does Jonathan."

"Did the two of you meet in rehab or something?"

She could sense Bunny tense slightly after he said it, as if the flippant remark had come out of his mouth first and then his brain realised it might be something uncomfortably close to the truth.

"No. If you must know, I've never drunk."

"Jesus. Do you've any bad habits at all? I mean other than the spanky-spank who's your mammy stuff?"

She ignored the last part. "If you must know, I met Jonathan at a vegan cooking class."

"If ever there was something you'd need to be pissed for."

"Shut up. Even if I had it, I wouldn't give alcohol to somebody with a probable concussion. What I am doing is calling you an ambulance."

Amy left the ice balanced on Bunny's neck and moved around to go and get her phone. He grabbed her wrist as gently as he could. "You can't do that."

She pulled her hand forward slightly and he released it. She didn't look at him. "If you haven't got insurance, I'll pay."

"No, it's not that. Sit down for a second, will ye?" He said it in a quiet, measured voice – one she hadn't heard before. It was probably meant to be calming, but if anything, it had the opposite effect. She sat on the couch, pulled her legs up and hugged her knees to her chest. He held the bag of ice with one hand and leaned back in the chair. "I only got away from the guy because he pulled a gun on me and a cop intervened. I got lucky."

"Well, that's good right? He's been arrested."

"No, it isn't. I got away and then I circled around just in time to see him getting handed his gun back with a grovelling apology."

"But..."

Bunny put his free hand out, asking to be allowed to finish.

"Sorry," she said. "I'm... sorry."

"'Tis OK. What I'm trying to tell you is, the guy was clearly some kind of law enforcement."

"But…"

Bunny shook his head. "I know it doesn't make sense, but that's what we've got to figure out. It also changes the rules. Now, does anyone know you'd be here?"

"No. Jonathan is away for another month and he thinks I'm just popping in to feed Evil."

"OK. Friends? Family? Boyfriend?"

"I don't have a… and no, nobody. Jonathan and I are friends, but we have no friends in common, if you know what I mean. Nobody else would know about this place."

"Good. Did you leave the car where it was?"

Amy nodded.

"Right, you're going to have to forget about it for the time being. You also need to turn off your phone."

"I can't. I…"

"Amy." There was a firmness to his tone now. "Look, love, you need to listen to me now, alright? I can help you, but you need to listen. Turn off your phone."

Amy nodded and then reached across to pick it up off the arm of the sofa and turn it off.

"OK. Good. Now, the next thing is—"

Amy put her hand to her mouth. "Jesus. This is… what the fuck is happening? None of this makes any sense."

Bunny nodded. "I know. I don't…"

"I mean, these assholes try and scare me, then almost kill me and now the law is on their side? Seriously?"

"I know; it's shite."

"I mean…" Amy stopped and thought for a second before nodding to herself. "Look, this isn't what you signed up for. You've already taken a beating from this guy. I'm not having your… y'know. I don't want to get you into trouble."

He shook his head. "No can do. I've taken your money and I offer a strict no-refunds policy."

"You can—"

"No. End of discussion. You're not getting rid of me. I'm not the type to run away from a fight."

"You just did!"

She felt bad as his face scrunched up, like she'd inadvertently added to the pain he was already in. "I retreated in order to regroup. Plenty of fellas have got the best of me, but nobody has got the best of me twice."

He gave her a lopsided smile, which she tried to return.

"Now," he said, "given the change in circumstances, we need to discuss what we've been avoiding. Namely, what this Matt fella told you that you really aren't supposed to know."

Amy gave an exasperated sigh. "I've been thinking about that, and honestly, I have no clue. None of what I remember makes any sense."

"Take me through it."

"Well, we were..." Amy started to mime something with her hand, then looked at Bunny and thought better of it. "It doesn't matter exactly what we were doing."

"Leave it to my imagination."

She nodded. "Then he suddenly breaks down and starts crying. He said, 'It's gone too far, I can't stop it. I'm sorry.' And then... 'Admiral Ackbar is screwed. We're taking out the *Millennium Falcon.*'"

Bunny gave her a long look. "Isn't that..."

"*Star Wars.* Yes. I mean, I'm not a big fan or anything, but I think so. I looked it up just now. It doesn't mean anything. Not in the real world, at least. Admiral Ackbar doesn't even fly the *Millennium Falcon* or whatever. It's gobbledygook."

"That's all he said?"

"He said lots of stuff, but it was hard to decipher. He had a..." Amy flushed slightly. "He had something in his mouth for most of it. There was also a lot of him saying he was an asshole, piece of shit, blah blah blah."

"He was right on that front at least."

"But, you see what I mean – it doesn't make any sense. It's gibberish."

Bunny nodded and leaned back in the chair, moving the bag of ice around as he looked up at the redbrick ceiling.

"So, what's our next move?" asked Amy.

"Honestly," said Bunny, "I'm not sure. But that's not what worries me."

"No?"

"No. What worries me is what their next move is going to be."

CHAPTER FOURTEEN

In a Manhattan bar, a man sat alone at the counter. He had stopped in for one drink about six drinks ago. Any other night, this bar would be rammed, but Wall Street doesn't work Sundays. The reason he had been passing was that he had just worked Sunday, for fourteen hours straight – trying hard to fix his own mistake. Halfway through, he'd realised that he couldn't fix it. Tomorrow he was going to have to go in and confess all. He fully expected to be fired. He wished he'd stolen some stationery, maybe a printer, on his way out this evening. Tomorrow he was going to be escorted off the premises by a security guard and would need to print résumés fast. He'd have to get them circulating quickly, in an effort to outrun the rumour mill that would carry news of his incompetency far and wide. Maybe he wouldn't bother; it seemed like a futile gesture. As he sat there, he could swear that he could feel himself morphing into a cautionary tale.

He looked over at the booth in the corner. A statuesque lady with black hair streaked with grey sat alone, nursing a drink. She was a little older than he was, but then, he wasn't exactly in the best shape of his life – so a little slack worked both ways. He didn't want to go home. He wanted a distraction to take his mind off tomorrow.

He slipped off his bar stool and made his way over to the dimly lit booth. Sure, he was a little drunk, but he was feeling OK.

"Hi there."

"Hello."

She really was a good-looking woman. Maybe a little severe, but hey, she could be warmed up.

"I'm Mike. Would you like a drink?"

"No, thank you, Mike. I'm waiting for someone."

Mike plonked himself down opposite her. "Me too!"

"I didn't say you could sit down."

"Hey," Mike said, with what he was sure was an endearing grin, "I took a chance."

"Not a good one. Good night, Mike."

"Hey, c'mon. Relax! I'll just keep you company until your date gets here. I'm a good guy."

When he thought back on these moments later on, one of the most unnerving things would be his memory of her facial expression. Namely, the fact that it remained exactly the same throughout. Glacial.

The woman took a sip of her drink. "Here's the thing – Mike, was it?"

He nodded.

"Mike," she repeated. "You've misjudged body language, verbal cues and now you've ignored a straight no. You've also crucially misjudged your own limited charm. So now I'd like you to leave."

"Hey," said Mike, all hurt feelings and soured bravado, "you don't even know me."

"I do, Mike. I know you. I've known a thousand yous. You are nothing special."

"Fuck you."

"That's just your fragile little ego talking, Mike. Utterly, tediously predictable. You remind me of a Venezuelan man I once knew."

"Did you screw him?" said Mike, with a bounce of his eyebrows, incorrectly deciding this might turn into a really good hate fuck.

"In a manner of speaking, Mike. He lied to me about something important."

Mike shook his head expansively and tutted. "I knew it. You've been hurt before."

"Not as much as he was. I took a Stanley knife and ran it straight across his gut."

The smile on Mike's face froze as his brain struggled to keep up with the left turn the conversation had taken.

The woman steepled her fingers together and rested her chin on them as she spoke. "Have you ever seen someone bleed out from a belly wound, Mike? It isn't pretty. Most people defecate themselves. This guy, let's call him the other Mike, certainly did. He died trying really hard to get one word out. Just one word. But it's hard to speak when your lungs are filling up with blood and you're effectively drowning in your own life."

Mike went to speak but stopped as the woman raised a finger.

"So, one of two things is going to happen now, Mike. One, I'm going to take my thumb and, before you manage to get one more word out, smash it into your trachea in such a way that you would be unable to speak for the rest of your life, which would admittedly only last about a minute, as you endure death by oxygen starvation. I'm reliably informed that those sixty or so seconds are excruciatingly painful but, well, who can say for sure? By the time the waitress notices you sitting here slumped over the table and gets the burly barman to come over to throw the drunk out, you'll be long dead, and I'll be long gone – in another bar, enjoying a quiet drink. Or, option two, and I do urge you to consider this option carefully, Mike, you stand up and without saying another word – not one single word – you leave this bar and don't come back. And the next time you find yourself tempted to impose your sweaty charm on a woman who is having a quiet drink alone, you'll remember the time that other woman almost took your sad little life, and you'll think better of it. So, what's it to be, Mike? Are you talking or are you leaving?"

Mike stood up and, on unsteady legs, headed straight for the door.

"Good choice. Bye, Mike."

When Mike got outside, he threw up over the faux-flame lighting beside the bar's door, which earned him a disgusted look from a man walking in. Mike half ran for six blocks in the wrong direction and then stopped and took a very hard look at his life.

Meanwhile, the other man walked into the bar and looked around. He saw her waiting for him and, without a word, slid into the seat opposite her in the booth.

"Hello, Jeremy."

"What the hell, Victoria? We have guests over at the house tonight. My wife is pissed."

"My apologies." She took a piece of paper out of her clutch and slid it across the table. "Name and social security number. To start with, I would like taps on this woman's phones and those of all family members. Email as well. We'll be in contact with any others we need."

He pushed the piece of paper back across the table. "The hell I will. I told you the last time was the last time. The NSA is not your personal Gestapo."

She gave a slight roll of her eyes. "There's no need to be melodramatic, Jeremy. And this is not personal; this is related to the fund."

"Well, that's – I mean I'd like to help, obviously, but I can't."

She nodded. "So, I should go back to those people whose retirements are at stake and explain this?"

"Well, I mean... I... I... I..."

Victoria let him stammer for a while as she got the attention of the passing waitress. She raised her glass. "I'll have another one of these." She looked across at Jeremy – his face pale, his eyes wide. A man lost in his own personal hell. "So will he."

The waitress nodded and departed.

Victoria turned her attention back to her companion. "'The last time was the last time'? You're not really naive enough to believe that, are you? We own you. You know it, we know it, so let's not drag this out."

Defeat spread across his face, but he kept fighting for the show of the thing. "We can't... innocent civilians."

"Well," said Victoria, calmly raising her glass to her lips to drain the remains of her drink, "if it's any consolation, the woman in question will be of interest to an awful lot of people by morning."

CHAPTER FIFTEEN

Three quarters of a million people pass through Grand Central Station in a day. Some are at the start or end of a long, globe-spanning journey, but most are just commuting in from the suburbs. As one of the busiest such terminals in the world, studies have been made of the ever-shifting flow of humanity that rushes daily through its doors, although such studies are tricky, because a true New Yorker is never going to stop for someone with a clipboard.

In the midst of the Monday morning rush, a seemingly ordinary woman, dressed in a smart business suit, stopped right in the middle of the station concourse and screamed. It was not some girlish squeal of delight or some slasher movie fakery. No – this was something dredged from the depths of her soul and unleashed into the world. This was a scream because not screaming was not an option. Amy Daniels, as it happened, had been looking in that direction, so she'd seen the well put together middle-aged woman stop for a second, close her eyes and let rip.

This stone being dropped into the rushing flow had caused a splash and some ripples. Nearby people stopped to look for the source and the cause; others walked by oblivious. More than a few pulled out headphones for a moment, unsure what they'd just heard.

A couple of transit cops rushed towards the noise only to find nothing when they reached it. The woman, having screamed for a couple of seconds, opened her eyes and resumed walking, disappearing back into the flow. Before she did, an older man with a kindly face tried to talk to her, but she brushed by without making eye contact, as if he were the weird one. Talking to strangers is not something that New Yorkers are particularly known for, the line between stranger and just plain strange often being whether or not they want to chat.

Whatever was behind it, the woman clearly didn't appear keen to explain her outburst. Maybe perversely, the Grand Central Station rush was the only place in this woman's day of home, train, office, train, home where she was "alone". Where she could unleash her frustration at a life that was not going as planned without having to admit it to anyone else.

Amy could sympathise. On Saturday evening, she'd come home after being the last to leave the NYU library only to have a man threaten her because she'd heard something she not only didn't want to hear but also didn't understand. Then, the next morning, the same man and his friend had tried to kill her, and probably would have done but for the intervention of fate and a drunken Irish lunatic. Then, she'd had to run once again from a man she'd subsequently found out was with law enforcement. Her life had been turned upside down. She had been so careful to keep her unconventional job and her ultra-conventional life separate. She had few close friends and nobody who knew the truth of her whole life. Well, nobody except the aforementioned drunken lunatic. He was now shaping up to be her only hope of getting out of this mess with any form of life left. She'd worked her ass off to make it on her own and the sheer frustration of finding herself reliant on some man she hardly knew for her salvation was galling. She too felt like screaming.

Amy jumped as a hand was placed on her arm. Bunny pulled back slightly. "Sorry. You alright?"

"Yeah."

"Right. I've double-checked – no cameras directly on them, so we're good."

Amy nodded and then took the little black book from the inside pocket of her leather jacket. She had two address books. One was full of old friends, college buddies, a couple of ex-boyfriends. This was the other one.

She flipped to the page with Matt Clarke's number on it. On Bunny's insistence, she'd gotten rid of both of her phones the night before, once they'd realised that the man who had chased her towards Central Park was some kind of law enforcement agent. That had changed the game – not that it'd felt like much of a game to begin with.

"Do you want to go through it again?"

"No. For Christ's sake Bunny, I'm going to be a damn lawyer. I don't need you to hold my hand through a negotiation."

Bunny held his hands up in apology. She knew he meant well, but he could be a little overbearing. Amy needed to feel like she had some form of control, that she wasn't just a passenger in her own life. She walked over to the bank of payphones, four quarters sitting sweaty in her hand. Bunny trailed casually behind her.

They had carefully planned it all out the night before. The reason they were in Grand Central Station was that even if they traced the call, she was one person amidst a mass of humanity and she could be on a train or subway to countless destinations a minute after she had hung up the phone. It told you so much that it really told you nothing.

She would calmly lay out their options, all with the desired goal of Amy's life returning to what it had been forty-eight hours ago, before all this madness had started. This was the moment she would finally retake control of her life.

Amy dialled the number and held the receiver to her ear, trying to not think about how often it might be cleaned. She looked up at the high ceiling with its mural of zodiac signs then across at Bunny, who was giving her a wonky-eyed smile of encouragement that was quite off-putting. He had a face for belligerence; hope didn't suit it. She steeled herself, expecting the disappointment of hearing Matt Clarke's voicemail again, the script for the prepared message she would leave ready to go if required.

The call was answered on the second ring.

"Hello."

Amy was taken aback. The voice was female. Older.

"Hi... Umm, sorry – I may have misdialled. I was looking for Matt Clarke."

"Ah yes. Hello, Amy. Do you mind if I call you Amy? I know Daniels is your real second name, though Matt knows you as Ms DeSilva."

Amy felt a cold icicle of dread in her stomach. "Who are you?"

"The who is not important. The what, however..." The voice sounded calm. "You may consider me, for want of a better word, your opponent. If it is any consolation, I share your annoyance at Mr Clarke for dragging you into this. However, I must deal with what is and not what should be. I'm afraid he has made you into a problem for us."

"A problem? You have no idea, lady. You all need to leave me the hell alone or I'll tear this whole thing down."

"No, Amy, I'm afraid you won't."

A part of the prepared script popped into Amy's head. "I've left details of what I know with several people who you—"

"No, you haven't."

"Excuse me?"

"I was relieved to see that you had kept your normal life and your 'hobby' so separate. Sensible, I suppose, on your end. It does, however, make things so much easier for us. You see, the people I represent cannot afford to have a wildcard running around, shooting off her mouth about what she thinks she knows. We have elected to seize the initiative. You have considerably bigger problems than us now."

"What the hell is that supposed to mean?"

"I'm afraid you went too far, didn't you? I guess it is understandable, in the heat of the moment. Only, when the authorities find your online private diary, well, it'll be very hard to make the case that it was an accident. Such dark thoughts you have."

"What diary? I don't have a diary."

By way of an answer, the woman just laughed. "The story will hit the news outlets soon. I'd imagine first reports will be out within the hour. You know how ravenous the press are for titillating angles, and this is undeniably juicy."

Amy tried hard not to scream. The words came out with a slow calmness she did not feel. "What have you done?"

"Oh, me? Nothing. You, on the other hand – dear oh dear. What will your father say?"

Amy felt like she had been punched in the gut.

"You should get going, Ms Daniels. Very soon, the whole world will be looking for you and nobody will be interested in whatever nonsense the monster has to say. You need to run. Run and hide. The very best of luck to you."

Then the line went dead.

CHAPTER SIXTEEN

Cole lifted his eyes to the rear-view mirror when he heard the sharp intake of breath from the back seat.

They were in an SUV with the rear windows heavily tinted, hence why they were able to drive through downtown Manhattan with two men with black bags over their heads without attracting any undue attention. They had their hands bound too. Neither of those steps was strictly necessary, but it was good practice. Yesterday, Matt Clarke and Brad Bradley had expected the hammer to fall on them and had instead been greeted with a consoling arm around the shoulder. Today was the day that the reality of their situation was to be brought home to them. Standard operating procedure. Disconcert the subject and then assert control once dependence has been established.

When they'd first got into the SUV, the two men had been concerned about their friend Charlie, who hadn't come home last night. From his research on them, Cole knew that Charlie was a sport fucker of some renown, verging on the pathological, so him having spent the night with one of his several fuckbuddies wasn't exactly unusual. But still, given the circumstances, his friends were surprised that he wasn't answering his phone. Once Cole had pulled the gun on them and Lola had taped their mouths, tied their hands and placed the bags over their heads, he imagined they weren't so worried about Charlie anymore. They'd both be coming to terms with their own mortality in a very private hell inside those bags. Or at least, they would have been, if Lola hadn't kept interfering. The reality was, they were both required for the next step of the plan and if they were thinking clearly, they'd figure that out. But the whole purpose of the theatrics was to make sure they weren't thinking clearly. Not right now. Now, the message needed to be reinforced and full and meek compliance ensured. There could be no mixed signals.

"Lola!"

Cole felt ridiculous, like he was the stern parent trying to settle the kids down in the back seat. Lola, being Lola, was seemingly unable to resist toying with Brad.

Cole had been given the tedious job yesterday of bringing Brad to the vet to have his burned "area" dealt with. For a man who didn't have any pets, Cole had spent too much time in veterinarians' offices. When you needed someone with access to medical equipment and pharmaceuticals and with a willingness to not report a gunshot wound to the authorities, the veterinarians of America were the unofficial emergency service. What they lacked in an understanding of the finer points of human anatomy they made up for in discretion. Many a veterinarian had paid for a holiday home or a messy divorce by making sure a certain kind of person didn't die or end up in prison. Having said that, some of them also had their own incinerators, which could prove very handy should their best life-saving efforts be in vain. They were full service.

Brad Bradley, being the whiny little shit he was, had bitched and moaned about where he had been taken. If Cole had been so inclined, he could have explained how lucky he was. Doctor Novachov wasn't a drinker and his surgery was immaculately clean. Under Cole's instruction, the vet had put Bradley under general anaesthetic to deal with the burns he'd received from the application of hot coffee to his genital region. He'd not actually needed to be knocked out, but it had served a purpose, and besides, he was such an irritating little whelp that the break from his incessant chatter had been most welcome. He'd been bandaged, given a cream to apply and sent on his merry way. Lola was now using this opportunity to run her hand up his inner thigh, like a cat toying with a helpless mouse. Crazy bitch.

Bradley gave another pitiful whine.

"Lola," Cole repeated.

She withdrew her hand and gave Cole an OTT pout in the rear-view mirror. He shifted nervously in his seat and looked out the window. He didn't like to admit it, but she freaked him out. Cole was, by almost anyone's reckoning, a dangerous man. His CV was impressive. He'd been in the SEALS, then seconded elsewhere – disappeared from the system, an asset for a part of the CIA they don't much discuss at dinner parties. Their team was "self-funding", so what Congress doesn't know... Only, of course, they knew. Not the details – nobody wants those – but anyone with a brain knew that such teams existed. What they wanted was to not *definitely* know. Deniability was currency in Washington. They wanted to just let them get on with it, doing what needed to be done and, if the shit ever hit the fan, the politicians could cry foul and express outrage at the dark deeds that had been carried out in the name of national security. Meanwhile, those same people would quietly expect that, even while they were busy ripping down what was there, someone somewhere would be equally busy rebuilding it, because the need for the medicine did not go away just because the public didn't like the taste.

Technically Cole wasn't on the government's payroll and hadn't been for a while – but that depended on where you thought the government stopped and the private contractors took over. The lines were blurry. Still, Cole was a undeniably dangerous man, but he was a professional. Lola, on the other hand, was a stone-cold psycho bitch.

He would never say those words to her face, of course – not if he ever wanted to enjoy a good night's sleep again. They'd worked together a few times. She was the protégée of the woman Matt Clarke had taken to calling Mrs Miller. Previously, Cole had known her by other names. She seemed to pick a new one for every op. This time, as what he assumed was her own little joke, she'd decided to go with Mrs Miller; she'd seen it being used in the surveillance files on Matt Clarke, Brad Bradley and Charlie Fenton. Cole had worked with Miller three times previously – at least that he knew of. With the kinds of people they answered to, discretion was mandatory. It paid not to ask any questions outside of your area of the op. Nobody liked questions. They'd been in close proximity three times: once had been a three-day thing in West Africa, standard extraction; the second had been that thing in Miami, which had been brief if rather bloody; and the other had been two years ago in Mexico. The target had been a difficult one and it had been a long-term gig. They'd been holed up on a ranch outside Puebla with nothing to do in the damned suffocating heat except watch and wait. The target was a drug lord who had gone to ground for very good reasons; they were there to put him in the ground once he finally resurfaced. They always resurfaced. Miller was in charge, but she flew in and out without explanation. Cole was left in operational control in her absence, with Lola and a couple of ex-jarheads for muscle.

Lola was not an easy person to live with, not least because, while she could speak, she chose not to. It wasn't that Cole didn't realise she was hot – he was a man, after all – but he also prided himself on thinking with things other than what was in his pants. It paid not to mix work with pleasure, especially when it was clear that Lola took such pleasure in the work. Sure, Cole had killed, but he'd never done it with the gleeful and childlike delight that Lola seemed to take in it. So, they'd lived side by side for six weeks in that compound outside Puebla, like two ghosts inhabiting the same space. Officially, when Lola went out at night it had been to check in with sources for any updates on the target. Then Cole started to notice reports in the papers about men going missing and being found in ways that made an open casket a non-starter. Cole had a sneaky suspicion that Miller knew what her pet got up to and she didn't seem to care. That shit wasn't professional, as far as Cole was concerned. He'd known all kinds of people during his time in this line of work, but Lola... He was looking forward to never seeing her again.

They pulled into the warehouse and Cole got out and closed the doors behind them. Then he and Lola got the two men out of the back seat and plopped them down in the chairs provided. Clarke sat wordlessly while Bradley, the moron, tried to run with the bag still on his head. Cole delivered a chop to the throat that sent him reeling backwards onto the oil-stained concrete. He'd not even hit the pussy that hard. He dragged him up onto the seat and placed him back down, slapping him once around the head to discourage further excursions.

Cole looked at Miller, who was sitting opposite. She nodded and then he pulled off the hoods.

Clarke and Bradley squinted into the lights. The SUV and three chairs aside, the large warehouse was empty, save for a few garbage bags in the corner. A two-story office with rusted metal stairs lay at the far end, behind Miller. The place smelled of oil, antiseptic and rotted meat. Cole didn't want to know where exactly that smell was coming from. He was very good at avoiding the wrong questions.

After giving them a moment to adjust, Miller calmly nodded at Lola, who ripped the tape off both of their mouths.

"What the fuck do you think you're doing? This is grade-A bullshit. You think you're the only ones who know people? I know people. I—"

Brad Bradley stopped talking when Cole punched him in the kidneys. In a way, it was admirable. This Wall Street guy, so utterly high on his own supply, was one of the few human beings who had the sheer stupidity to come out swinging in this situation. Even when Cole had seen cartel guys caught like this, they'd not had the cojones to start rattling out threats.

Lola leaned down and placed the tape back over Bradley's mouth, then gave the tape a big wet kiss.

Miller looked at Matt Clarke, who hadn't said a word. "Mr Clarke, do you have anything to say?"

He nodded. "I'm the one who screwed up. There's no need to take it out on Brad or Charlie."

Miller raised an eyebrow. "How noble."

"Also," continued Matt, "you need us – so let's not forget that. You want to scare us? Fine. Punish me? OK. But let's not kid ourselves."

Miller looked at him for a long moment. There was no sound, save for Bradley's whimpering. From the smell, Cole would guess that Bradley had just made his own bandages considerably more uncomfortable.

Miller rubbed the palms of her hands together and then placed them against her pursed lips, as if praying. "You're right, of course, Matt. We do need you. You have correctly evaluated the situation, but then that's what you do, isn't it? I would expect nothing less."

Clarke said nothing.

"We need you," continued Miller. "In fact, you currently have control of all of our funds, some of which are technically what you could call 'on loan' – although the people in question are not banks." Miller smiled. "If you think the banks that foreclosed on your family farm were heartless, you should meet the people behind our loans."

"OK," said Clarke. "Perhaps we could get back to business then?"

Miller stood and began to walk back and forth. "Yes, of course, Matt. Sorry for any... I was upset, after your screw-up with blurting out our plans to your... let's call her 'lady friend', shall we? I perhaps let my anger get the better of me."

Clarke said nothing. Cole had to credit him for that. The kid might have been a smug little shit, but he could sense when there was a train coming down the tracks.

Miller kept talking. "On the Amy front, by the way, we have some good news."

Clarke pulled in a breath before he spoke, the little hitch in it betraying more emotion than his face was giving away. "What did you do?"

Miller smiled. "Why do people keep asking me that? We didn't 'do' anything. Miss Daniels – oh, that's her real name by the way; you'll see it on the news soon enough. But yes, I'm afraid she has been a bad girl. There's no easy way to say this. Late last night, the NYPD were called to her apartment. It appears that during some sort of sordid sex game gone wrong, Miss Daniels overstepped the mark and killed a client."

Miller placed her hands on the back of her chair and leaned lightly on it. She let a long moment drag out as she locked eyes with Clarke. She wanted him to walk it there. Put it all together for himself.

Cole could tell Clarke didn't want to say the words, though deep down, he already knew. Miller remained silent, confident that he would blink first.

When his voice came out, it was a hoarse whisper. "You killed Charlie." It wasn't a question.

Miller shook her head. "No. Miss Daniels did that. Now she's going to be far too busy being on the run to be an inconvenience to us. If she does show up, then she can be dealt with. I wouldn't be worried about a long trial if I were you. The problem you have created has been fixed."

Cole noticed Miller glance back in his direction – an uncomfortable reminder that she didn't hold just Clarke responsible for that problem.

"Why the hell would I do anything you want me to do now?" asked Clarke. "You just killed my best friend."

Miller looked across at Brad Bradley. "Oh Matt, we all know it's the truth, but you didn't need to say it right in front of him. Insensitive."

Clarke looked down at the ground. "Go ahead; do what you want to me. I'm past caring."

Miller dragged her chair over to sit in front of him, leaning her head forward to look up into his face. "Come on now, Matt. Think it through. This is what you do, after all. You see the angles. Don't you think that I'd anticipate this? That you'd pull the martyrdom card, especially now Charlie is dead? We all know that saving Mr Bradley isn't worth anyone's time."

This was greeted by a few muffled words from Bradley that everyone ignored.

Clarke raised his head as if to say something, and then spat in Miller's face. He sneered at her. "Fuck you."

Miller held her hand up to stop Cole or Lola from advancing forward. "That's OK. Let it out, Matthew." She pulled a handkerchief from the inside pocket of her suit jacket and dabbed at her face. "It won't bring you the swift end you're craving, but that's OK. It's a Catholic thing, isn't it? The desire to be punished for your sins. Y'know, you and I are alike, Matthew. You see, we both have an eye for weakness. You see it in organisations, but I see it in people."

From side-on, Cole could see the bravado smile on Clarke's face crumble.

"Come on now," continued Miller, in a voice like that of a cajoling parent, "think it through. Work the problem. I need you to do everything I tell you to. To execute a precise and incredibly delicate plan in exactly the right order. What would be the pressure point that would achieve that?"

Clarke said nothing, his chin sinking to his chest, tears welling in his eyes. Cole could see the precise moment that his spirit broke.

"C'mon, Matt. Don't let me down. Tell me, what is behind door number one?"

"Please. Please, please, please. Don't."

Miller raised her voice. "If you please, Mr Baxter."

Every pair of eyes went to the top of the rusted iron stairs at the far end of the room as Baxter, a big red-headed dude who Cole had worked with a couple of times before, appeared from the upstairs office, dragging by the arm a woman with a black mask over her head.

Miller raised her voice again. "Say hello to your brother, Ms Clarke."

"Matt? Matt?! Are you here? Matt?" a woman sobbed.

Clarke pulled in a breath that looked like it burned his lungs. "It's OK, Jennie. Everything will be fine."

"MATT! Are you OK?"

Hearing her asking if he was OK, his head went down like he'd been punched in the gut. "I'm... I'm fine, Jennie. Everything will be OK. I promise."

Miller nodded, and the girl was dragged back into the office. Her wails could be heard briefly and then stopped suddenly.

"Don't hurt her. I'll do whatever you want."

Miller leaned forward. "I'm sorry, I didn't catch that?"

"I'll do whatever you want. I swear."

Miller moved forward and leaned in close to Clarke's head again. She spoke in a soft voice. "Oh, I know, Matthew. I know. Would you like to spit in my face once more? See if it makes you feel like a man again?"

"Please don't hurt her."

Miller stood up and walked across to Bradley, who looked up at her with eyes filled with terror.

"As for you, Mr Bradley, we also have the person you love most in the world."

Bradley's eyes darted towards the stairs.

"Don't bother," said Miller. "It does not speak well of your character, but that person is you."

Miller nodded towards Cole. "When Mr Cole here took you to get medical attention yesterday, you were put under general anaesthetic. Although you were too dim to realise, there's no reason to do that to treat burns. We have, however, installed a small explosive device in your body that we can activate at any time. It is tiny, but being where it is, trust me – it will kill you. It will be a slow, certain and excruciatingly painful death."

Bradley was crying now, too – hard. He tried to speak around the tape but Miller ignored him. "Just do as you're told and it will be fine." Miller turned to walk away but glanced back over her shoulder after a few steps. "Oh, and a word of advice, Mr Bradley. I would definitely not have sex in the next few days. That would be a very bad idea. Also, avoid microwaves."

The last thing Bradley and Clarke saw before the bags were placed back over their heads was Mrs Miller calmly walking away.

CHAPTER SEVENTEEN

"OK, look – you need to calm down."

"Calm down? Calm down!" Amy gave serious consideration to hurling the TV remote at Bunny's head, but thought better of it. "It's not your life that's in ruins here."

Evil the cat was nowhere to be seen, possibly sensing the tension in the room and rightly guessing that now was not a time when her sadistic charms would be appreciated.

Amy used the remote to flick up through another couple of channels. "Christ. CNN has got it too – that's the whole set!"

Bunny stood beside the couch and held his hand out. "Alright, give me that."

"No," said Amy, "I'm watching this. It's not every day you see your life, your future, go up in flames on national TV. Let's look on the bright side – at least New York isn't a death penalty state. Although, seeing as I'm such a depraved murderer, I'm sure there will be calls to bring it back."

"Alright, but let's not forget, you didn't actually kill anyone."

"Yes, I did – it's on the goddamned news."

Bunny stepped in front of the screen to block Amy's view and continued to hold his hand out. Reluctantly, she handed him the remote and he turned off the TV. She had welcomed the anger, embraced her fury at the injustice of it all. That was because the other option was dealing with the reality and what it meant, and that felt like too big a thing to process.

Bunny took a seat beside her on the couch. "The way I see it, we need to think this through calmly and rationally."

"That's what we've been doing. I don't know if you've noticed, but it's not going super well."

Amy was aware she was behaving like a brat. None of this was Bunny's fault. He was just the only one there.

"We need to figure out exactly what this means."

"I'll tell you what it means – it means months, if not years, proving I didn't do this thing, and even if I do, this case is the only one I'll ever be involved in, as I'll never be allowed to practice law. Even if I could, who wants the 'Dominatrix of Death' as their lawyer? That's what they're already calling me on a couple of the websites, by the way. Lord knows that nickname isn't going to impinge on my constitutional right to have a fair trial before a jury of my peers, is it? When this is all over, I'll not even be able to get my old job back, shovelling horse shit at my dad's..."

Amy stopped talking as her hand was pulled reflexively towards her mouth. "Oh God, Dad. I've got to call Dad." She sprang to her feet. "Where's the phone?"

Bunny followed her, speaking in a soft voice. "You can't do that, Amy."

She ignored him and started walking around, checking the counters and table for the cradle for the cordless phone. "I've got to... Oh God, I'm going to have to explain that... Oh God. Where do I even start? And then there'll be the neighbours and Aunt Carol and... Fuck!" She stopped in the middle of the floor. "The press will camp out on his lawn. I've seen that before. That's the kind of crap they do. I've got to tell him to get out of there."

Amy redoubled her efforts, frantically turning this way and that, her socked feet slipping on the wooden floor. "Where is it? Where is it?"

"Amy."

"He could stay with Aunt Carol or... Oh God, there's work. He'll need to close the school or at least ..." She stomped her foot on the floor in frustration. "WHERE IS THE FUCKING PHONE!"

Bunny had stopped following her around and was now standing by the faux fireplace, the cordless phone in his hand.

Amy took a couple of deep breaths and ran her hands through her hair before extending one out. "Thank you."

Bunny put the phone down on the mantelpiece. He spoke in a quiet voice. "You can't ring your father."

"What the hell? Give me the damn phone."

She moved towards the mantelpiece and he stepped forward, his outstretched arms blocking her path. "You can't do that."

"I've got to." She pushed against him, but she wasn't strong enough to get around him. "I've got to, I've got to..."

She pushed her hands against his bulk, but he didn't take a backward step. Tears filled her eyes as she pushed. "Get out of my way, you big... Irish... bastard!"

He moved his arms gently around her. She tried to push them away before eventually giving in to the hug, tears streaming down her face. They stood in an awkward embrace for a couple of minutes. Eventually, Amy broke and gently pushed away, rubbing the heels of her hands into her eyes. "Well, that was pretty pathetic," she said, with a weak smile.

"Ah," said Bunny, "'tis just nice to hold a crying woman and for once not be the reason for it."

"Yeah, I bet you've broken a few hearts in your day."

"I've had my moments."

Amy sat back down on the couch, hugging one of the oversized cushions to herself.

Bunny sat himself down in the armchair opposite.

"You can't phone your father."

She nodded. "I know. Whoever these people are, they really know what they're doing. Now, instead of having to look for me themselves, they have got the whole NYPD and the public doing it."

"And," said Bunny, "not to pile it on, but... well, looking at it logically, they have a plan here. They must know that if you hand yourself into the police or get caught, they can deal with you before you can make trouble for them, otherwise they wouldn't have gone this route with it."

Amy nodded again. "Yeah. I might not even get that day in court. If I run, I look guilty, and if I hand myself in... what are the odds I have a nasty accident in my cell or..." She trailed off, looking out the large windows at the billboard opposite, which advertised sun-kissed beaches where couples walked hand in hand.

"I know we already discussed this, but are you sure nobody knows you're here?"

Amy shook her head. "I told you, me and Jonathan met at a stupid cooking thing. We don't have a circle of friends in common. It's not like that."

Bunny nodded. "Still though, he'll be in your phone, so we need to—"

Amy shook her head, more emphatically this time. "Jonathan is... eccentric. He doesn't have a cell phone. He has a landline, but he never uses it. We'd arrange to meet most Fridays for coffee, but if I wanted to get hold of him, I had to come knock on his door or actually send him a letter."

"You're kidding?"

"Honest. He is totally paranoid about technology and the government. It's a little nuts but, well, he had an ex who worked for the IRS, and let's just say it was a very messy break-up."

"So, you think you're safe here?"

She shrugged. "As much as anywhere, I guess. Even if Jonathan realises what's happening and guesses I might be crashing here, he's the last person on Earth who would call the cops."

Bunny considered this. "Alright then, I suppose."

"None of which helps us with the bigger problem, though, does it? I'm wanted for murder and some crazy lady on the end of a phone wants me dead."

"Yeah, I've a suggestion on that front."

"Fire away. It's not like I've got many options."

Bunny absentmindedly scratched his fingers at his beard. "Well, y'know how I said I was here to find a woman."

"A particular woman," said Amy, with a weak smile.

"Yeah. Well, I sorta have a contact in the – well, I'm not sure… some part of the American security services."

"OK."

"Her name is Agent Dove. She represents a group who want to help me find that particular woman. Look, it's a long story. All you need to know is that she's something in the security services, and if we contact her, she can maybe sort this – or at least help."

"Can we trust her?"

"I've no idea but, well, she's nothing to do with this at least and she does sorta owe me a favour. That'll hopefully be enough."

Bunny looked wary as he watched hope spread across Amy's face. "This is great. Why didn't you—"

"Hang on, hang on. It's not that straightforward. Look, I'm here with no passport or anything. I basically don't exist, and if I get myself in trouble, they've made it clear they'll walk away. They got me into the New York port and they gave me an ATM card that'd get me two hundred bucks a day. And a phone – a special phone. This fancy-looking thing. It's my only way of contacting Dove."

"Oh," said Amy, realisation dawning. "This would be the stuff that…"

"Yeah, that I lost when I got robbed or…"

"But can't you just call, like, the FBI or whatever and ask to speak to this Agent Dove woman?"

Bunny shook his head. "That's not really her name. Like I said, they only want to know if I find Simone. That's her name, the woman, the particular woman."

Amy nodded. "So…"

"So," said Bunny, "I need to go and do what I was heading to do when you stopped and picked me up. Go find whoever robbed me and get my stuff back."

"Do you know how to find them?"

"Well…" Bunny looked down awkwardly at his feet, embarrassed. "I don't exactly have what you'd call perfect recall of what happened on Saturday. 'Tis a bit blurry, because of getting spiked and all."

"Right," said Amy. "Well, what do you remember?"

"I remember leaving my hotel."

"Hang on, you've got a hotel?"

"Not exactly. I had to leave pretty quickly."

"Why?"

"Don't worry about it. It'll sound bad if I tell you."

"Well now you have to tell me."

"I, kinda… well, I threw a man down the garbage chute."

"Woah!"

"See, I told you it'd sound bad."

"And what exactly did this guy do to inspire such wrath?"

"He threw a couple of punches."

"I pity the fool who throws a punch at you, slugger."

Bunny shifted in the seat. "He didn't throw them at me."

"Oh?" said Amy, before her mind caught up with the conversation. "Oh," she said again.

Bunny nodded.

"Anyway, I was hotel-less at 2am. What stuff I had was in my bag on my back, and, it being Saint Patrick's Day, the chances of getting a hotel in the city were not great. Plus, I needed somewhere that wouldn't ask for ID, and that sorta limits your options. Anyway, I slept in the Central Park for a bit and then, well… I'm not exactly sure."

"Wait. Are you telling me you don't remember a whole day? Like, you blacked out?"

Bunny pulled a face. "For a woman who is wanted for murder, you're fierce judgey."

Amy leaned back and looked up at the ceiling. Then she started laughing.

"What's so funny?"

She looked down at Bunny, which only caused the laughter to increase.

He gave her a quizzical look. "Seriously, what's the fecking story here?"

She waved her hand at him. "Sorry, sorry, sorry. Oh my God – I am so royally screwed."

"What?"

She held her head in her hands as her body shook from the laughter.

"Are you alright?"

"No," she said, tears now streaming down her cheeks, "I'm really not. People are trying to kill me, I'm wanted for murder and my one shot at survival is a drunk Irishman being able to piece back together what he did on Saint Patrick's Day."

"For the last time, I was fecking spiked."

Amy looked at Bunny and then laughed so hard she fell off the sofa.

CHAPTER EIGHTEEN

Sherlock Holmes he was not.

Embarrassed though he was to admit it to himself, seeing as he'd been a proud member of the Garda Síochána for thirty years and a detective for twenty-four of those, Bunny was not much for detecting. His skills lay in other areas. He was good with people – particularly in the area of putting the fear of God into them until they told him what he wanted to know. To be fair, the majority of police work wasn't trying to figure out who did something, but rather proving that the bastard you knew did it actually did it. For that, you needed to find evidence. Bunny was fine with evidence. But this was different. This was what you'd call "a mystery", and mysteries had clues. Bunny fecking hated clues.

It was a deeply unpleasant sensation, having a stretch of time that he couldn't recall. It had never happened before, and that was why he was sure that he must've been spiked. He remembered starting the day waking up on a bench in Central Park. Or rather, being woken by a pissed-off looking beat cop. Bunny guessed the morning rousting of the homeless was nobody's favourite duty. He was cold, homesick and hungry, all of which was, he had to admit to himself, understandable.

He'd sacrificed everything to come to America and find Simone –

literally everything. He was dead as far as all but a very small and select group of people knew. He didn't mind it; he'd do it again. But that didn't mean it was easy. He'd been in New York nearly a week, and in that time he had achieved precisely nothing in his search. He had one lead, the Sisters of the Saint – a rogue bunch of slightly out-there nuns who had first helped Simone escape New York, and then, he was pretty sure, assisted her again to flee Dublin, when her past and Bunny's present had conspired against them. That had been eighteen years ago. If the Sisters of the Saint were even still in New York, they made it a matter of principle to stay out of public view. The realisation had hit Bunny that he wasn't so much looking for a needle in a haystack as a needle in a stack of needles – and one that didn't want to be found to boot.

So yes, it would be fair to say that, even prior to Friday night, his trip to New York hadn't been going swimmingly. Then he'd had to flee the fleabag hotel he'd been staying in after he'd thrown that gobshite down the garbage chute. The place had very thin walls. He'd heard the asshole deliver the backhand slap and he'd felt the vibration as the woman had hit the floor. If Bunny had one guiding principle, it was that a man who raises his hand to a woman is no longer a man. As far as he was concerned, the fella was garbage and he got disposed of appropriately. The prick had an unpleasant landing and learned a valuable lesson. Bunny had no regrets. Still, the manager had been hollering about calling the cops and Bunny didn't need that kind of attention. He had no ID of any kind and that was a problem. It was also why he'd been staying in that shitty hotel in the first place, as it turned out all the decent hotels wanted to see some ID on check-in. Agent Dove hadn't given him any. He was pretty sure that was deliberate. He'd said he would find Simone and make sure she was safe, but he'd no intention of trusting her fate to Dove and her friends, whoever they might be. The lack of ID was their way of keeping him under control. The ATM card with a two-hundred-dollar daily withdrawal limit and the special mobile phone, he realised, were easy ways of keeping tabs on him. If he ever started getting anywhere in his search for Simone, he'd have to do something about that. Of course, ironically, he had. Getting robbed had got rid of both of them, and now he needed them back. Contacting Agent Dove was the only thing Bunny could think of to help Amy, which meant that regaining his stuff was right back at priority number one. To do that, he needed to find the day he'd lost, along with whoever had robbed him. That meant doing some serious detecting.

So, there he'd been, waking up on a park bench, cold, hungry and homesick.

Yes, homesick. It being Paddy's Day had really brought it home. Not that he'd ever been a big fan of parades: he couldn't see the point of all that marching-band nonsense with the stick twirling and all of that. No, his Paddy's Days for the last thirty years straight had been spent at the All-Ireland Club Championship in Croke Park. For most of those years, he'd got tickets and brought along any of the St Jude's under 12s team, which he'd coached, who wanted to come. That had always been his day. Getting them all into the club's knackered minibus, bringing them all to the game and then back home via a stop-off for burger and chips. That had been his life.

Now, he was a dead man wandering the streets of New York, trying to find a bunch of crazy nuns who didn't want to be found. He'd ended up spending the night sleeping on a bench in Central Park, shivering in his sheepskin coat. Clue number one, your honour, the "victim" had been cold, friendless and fecking miserable, with only a bottle of Jim Beam for company. In the morning he'd woken to find that he'd finished the whiskey and some little scrote had nicked his rucksack with all his clothes in it. He remembered thinking at the time that it was lucky his wallet and phone were zipped into the inside pocket of his coat. Being moved on by the cop was the last thing he remembered clearly until waking up at 6am the next morning. As well as a pounding headache, he had a sore jaw, indicating he may've taken a punch at some point in the evening. The lost time felt like the gap where a tooth had once been; he kept feeling around it, trying to come to terms with it. He was also worried about what exactly he'd find – the lack of details left an unsettling sense of guilt floating about, waiting for a memory to attach itself to.

Now, he sat at the bar and looked at the array of objects in front of him. Except for some loose change and a solitary twenty-dollar bill, these four items were all he'd had in his possession when he'd woken up the previous morning.

One: a gold medal – actually made of plastic that proclaimed the wearer was a tap legend. Bunny had never danced, tap or otherwise.

Two: a lady's lace bra, pink in colour.

Three: what looked like the fortune from a fortune cookie, only it read "Death comes to us all," which left a little to be desired in the motivational quote stakes.

And four: a picture.

Beside these items sat a pint of Guinness – that hadn't been in his pockets when he'd woken up, although Bunny would have to admit that it clearly played a large role in the case. The fourth item was the only one that had been in his possession long before Saturday. It was the picture of Simone and him that had been taken almost twenty years ago. His younger self beamed back joy at him, so real that it was painful to see. His arm was around her; she was giving that smile that broke his heart every time. The picture had lived in the back of his wallet, the one he no longer had. That in itself was a clue.

Cold, homesick and hungry.

Speaking of which, he was starving now. He'd not eaten anything all day. What he'd give for a full Irish breakfast.

And there it was – know thyself.

He drained the remains of his pint and shoved the clues back into his coat pockets. He picked up his change. All he had was the remains of the two hundred dollars Amy had fronted him, and he felt uncomfortable spending money that, as far as he was concerned, he hadn't earned yet.

Hopefully he'd soon start earning it properly.

He was off to Central Park – and then to go find the nearest full Irish breakfast.

CHAPTER NINETEEN

In the back of Bunny's mind, faint bells were ringing. Also, there were actual bells ringing. Somewhere in the distance, the peal of church bells could be heard. It was now just after lunchtime on Monday: somebody was either getting married or getting buried.

Still, the reasons for the bells ringing in Bunny's mind was that the bar with the sign proclaiming it "Paulie's" looked familiar. What really looked familiar was the fact that that wasn't what the sign actually said. The u was missing, leaving a faint outline where the gold letter should be, so the sign actually proclaimed "Pa lie's." Bunny had gone to Central Park, found the bench that he'd used when he'd hopped the fence a couple of nights previously and then started to walk around its outskirts, hoping that something would jump out at him. It had taken nearly two hours, but something finally had – Paulie's minus the u.

Bunny stepped in the door.

"Oh no." The exclamation came from a middle-aged woman behind the counter with a blonde perm held with enough hairspray to ensure it would survive the apocalypse. She was looking right at Bunny and didn't seem happy to see him.

He slowly approached the bar. "Hey, how are ye?"

She pouted her lips for a moment and then gave him a tight smile that didn't reach her eyes. "Hello, sir, I didn't expect to see you back here again."

"I was here on Saturday?"

He said it as a question, but she'd not taken it as such. "Yeah, I remember it well. You and the owner had quite the stand-up row."

"Yeah," said Bunny, trying to play along. "I just wanted to say sorry about that."

When in doubt, an apology seemed like a sensible way forward. It appeared to work. She leaned across the counter, and after glancing around to make sure they were still the only two people in the bar, she lowered her voice to a conspiratorial whisper. "Hey, don't worry about it. Paulie was being an asshole."

Bunny lowered his voice to match hers. "To be honest with you, I can't even remember how it got started."

"You'd just finished your breakfast and I'd asked you how it was, y'know, doing the good customer service and all. You said it was good but, y'know, sorta mentioned how it wasn't actually a full Irish breakfast, like we had on the sign."

"Right, yeah."

"To be real with you, hon', Paulie got a deal on that haggis stuff and so he just told Svetlana to cook it up and put it in there."

"Haggis is Scottish."

Bunny could see her resisting the urge to roll her eyes. "Yeah, that's what you said. Paulie overheard though and y'know, he's a little thin-skinned. Always has been. He starts in on how it was all the same. Ireland. Scotland."

Bunny saw his own knuckles whiten slightly as he gripped the bar. "Right."

"Yeah, it got pretty heated after that. Paulie said something about potatoes and, well... it was lucky your friend was here."

Bunny looked up in surprise. "Excuse me?"

"Y'know, the African American gentleman?" Bunny could see the waitress registering his confusion. "Sorta skinny kid, big ears – cute though. I don't go for the baby-faced guys myself. My friend Tina, though, she laps that stuff up. Woman sees a pair of dimples and she's on her back faster than..." She blushed as she stopped herself talking, straightening up and going back to polishing the counter. "There I go running my damn mouth again. Ignore me."

"And this black fella, he broke up the argument?"

The bartender gave Bunny a look. "Is this some kind of joke?"

It was Bunny's turn to look embarrassed. "Look, I can't exactly remember what happened to me on Saturday."

"Really, like that amnesia and shit?"

"Sort of, yeah. You could say that." Bunny preferred that phrasing. Made it sound more medical.

She didn't look fully convinced, but she cautiously continued. "Well, I s'pose. Anyway, the guy agrees with you but still calmed the whole thing down. Said he'd take you someplace else, to a proper Irish bar. He got you out of here before Paulie goes and gets his bat."

"His bat?"

"Shush, keep your voice down. Paulie is all bark. He thinks he's some kinda tough guy. Don't worry about it."

Bunny noticed that she was starting to look a little edgy. Like going over this ground might've been a bad idea.

"Look, let's forget about it, alright? Your friend got you outta here so, y'know, it was all's well that ends well."

Bunny nodded. "Fair enough. I don't suppose you happen to know the name of the bar he might've taken me to?"

"Sure." She turned around and started going through a stack of till receipts that were on a spike behind the bar. Eventually she found the one she was looking for, ripped it off and placed it down on the counter.

"Is this the name of the bar?"

"No, honey. This is the bill for your friend's breakfast that he forgot to pay before he pushed you out the door."

"Ohhh."

"Yeah. Honest mistake, I'm sure."

Bunny nodded, took the wad of twenties out of his trouser pocket and laid one down.

"He struck me as being a big tipper too."

Bunny placed another twenty on the bar, looked at the bartender's face and then placed down a third.

She gave him a wide smile. "The Porterhouse Lodge over on Eleventh Avenue in Hell's Kitchen," she said, scooping up the money, "down near the Lincoln Tunnel."

"Grand." Bunny looked at the money he had left. "I don't suppose my friend struck you as the sort who might be expecting change?"

She shook her head firmly.

"Yeah, I'd a feeling."

CHAPTER TWENTY

The Porterhouse Lodge was an actual pub. It wasn't trying to look like a pub. They hadn't brought in a team of consultants in order to achieve a pub-like quality and it hadn't engaged in customer consultations to determine what they most looked for in a pub. No, they'd just put a bar in a building and let nature take its course. In Bunny's opinion, good pubs weren't built, they were carefully grown over time. No two were the same, and if they were, then they weren't proper pubs to begin with. Bunny had strong opinions on this and had been known to explain his views at some length. Pubs, the full Irish breakfast and why soccer was rotting the brains of the younger generations were his Holy Trinity of hot-button topics.

He couldn't tell if he'd been in the Porterhouse Lodge before or if it just echoed the kind of pubs he regularly frequented. The bar was of the same dark wood as O'Hagan's in Dublin and he was taken aback by an unexpected pang of nostalgia.

It'd taken him thirty minutes to walk there. The sun was out and though it wasn't doing much to warm the place, it was still a pleasant experience. By the time he got there though, his foot was throbbing. It was painful every now and then in normal usage, but the boot he'd received to it the day before had rather knocked it up a few notches.

He'd not wanted to splurge on another taxi, as he felt bad burning through Amy's money, especially if bar staff were going to expect to be quite so well reimbursed for their helpfulness.

Another sign of the Porterhouse's proper pub status was the fact that at either end of the bar sat an old fella, each one slowly making his way through a newspaper in absolute silence. They were straight out of a Ken Bruen novel, the sentinels keeping taciturn watch over proceedings. In the background, Bruce Springsteen was singing about getting his end away in a dying industrial landscape.

Behind the bar was a portly man with a head God had taken most of the hair from, forcing him to admit defeat and shave the rest. "Hey, what can I get ye?"

Galway accent.

"Pint of Arthur's, please."

The man nodded, and Bunny climbed up onto a stool and watched with approval as the man held the pint glass at the correct angle and commenced pouring the Guinness.

"Have you been over long?" asked the bartender.

"Ah, only about a week."

"Jesus, fresh off the boat! Not that anyone comes on a boat anymore."

"Oh, you'd be surprised."

The man filled the pint glass to about the harp point and stopped, correctly leaving it to settle.

"I, ehm, I don't suppose you were working here Saturday?"

The man shook his head. "'Fraid not. Myself and the wife took the kids in to see the parade."

"Oh right. Any good?"

He shrugged. "Ah, y'know. Big crowds and all that. Lots of batons being chucked about the place. Kids liked it."

Bunny nodded. "Oh right. Only, I think I was in here and I might have lost something."

The man raised an eyebrow. "Is that so? I can go and have a dig about in the lost property. What was it? Hat? Umbrella? Coat? We'd a penguin there last month. Not a real one, of course – a stone one.

Fella came back three weeks later. He'd got pissed and forgotten it." He laughed and shook his head. "Some people."

Bunny laughed too. "I know, I know."

"So, what did you lose?"

Bunny scratched at his beard, aware he'd rather talked himself into a corner. In the absence of any better ideas, he went with the truth. "To be honest with ye, I sorta lost the day. Ended up in a bit of a session."

"I see."

"I'm trying to, I suppose you could say, retrace my steps."

The barman topped off Bunny's pint as he spoke. "I get it. Jackie is upstairs. I'll get him for ye."

"Thanks." Bunny nodded with approval and gratitude as the pint was placed in front of him. No sign of a bubble and none of that shamrock nonsense on the head. He was starting to really like it here.

He took a sip and savoured the taste, placing it back down. He glanced up the bar at one of the sentinels, who shook his head and tutted, turning a page of his newspaper.

A couple of minutes later, the barman returned, followed by a tall, white-haired man. A smile spread across his face as he saw Bunny.

"Ah, Bunny, how you doing, buddy?" he said in a strong New York accent. "I thought it might be you."

Bunny gave him a nervous smile, disconcerted to be known by someone he had absolutely no recollection of. "How's it going, Jackie?"

It was in the way he said the name – a question and not a statement.

"You don't remember me, do you?"

Bunny could feel his face redden. "Sorry."

Jackie waved his apology away. "Hey, forget about it. I've been there. Well, sorta."

Bunny took a drag on his pint. "I, ehm, I don't suppose you could help me piece together exactly where I've been?"

Jackie laughed. "Sure, no problem. You got here about ten in the morning. We open early for breakfast on the weekend. I distinctly remember you ordering the full Irish."

"Oh God."

"Yeah, you were quite, erm, what's the word... emphatic on the topic."

"What's in your version of the full Irish?"

Jackie's grin widened as he reeled off the list. "Bacon, sausages, black and white pudding, eggs, vegetables and potato all fried in creamery butter, served with a generous helping of homemade soda bread for soakage and washed down with a strong cup of breakfast tea. My wife does it on the weekends and that's the only way it gets done."

Bunny felt a wave of emotion build up inside him. "She's a good woman."

"The best."

Bunny took a long draw on his pint to regain full control of himself. As he put it down, he smacked his lips together appreciatively. "That's a cracking pint too."

Jackie laughed and then stopped himself. "Sorry, just... so far, we're mostly having the exact same conversation we had two days ago. It's déjà vu. I mean, you spent a lot of time eulogising to your buddy about the breakfast, the pint, my missus."

"My buddy?"

"Yeah, Diller? You don't remember Diller was with you?"

"Ehm..." In for a penny. "I actually don't remember ever meeting this Diller fella."

Bunny tried not to notice the look that passed between the two barmen. He was fast resigning himself to the idea that his self-respect was going to take a kicking today.

"Nice lad, has a good way with a story." Jackie turned to the barman. "He has them... What's that phrase you use, Phil?" Jackie grabbed his own ears and pulled them out.

"What?"

"C'mon, dude, y'know. It's something about soccer or something."

"FA Cup ears?"

Jackie slapped the counter. "That's it. Y'know, sticky-outie ears. Makes him look like a trophy. I mean, he's a good-looking kid – well, I say kid, like in his twenties – but y'know, the ears are a bit of a feature. I ID'd him, even though the kid doesn't drink."

"He's a non-drinker?"

Jackie nodded. "Yeah. He told us the Smithy story. You must remember that?"

Bunny shook his head.

Jackie turned to Phil. "I've not told you this yet – you're gonna friggin love this. So, this Diller kid tells us he's got this friend, Smithy. A dwarf." Jackie looked suddenly uncertain. "Is that the right word?"

"Midget," interjected one of the sentinels at the end of the bar.

Jackie rolled his eyes. "Shut up, Donal, that's definitely not right. Anyway, with apologies, if required, he's a dwarf or whatever. Diller tells us that right at that very minute, this Smithy guy is off in a leprechaun hunt."

"What the hell is that supposed to be?" asked Phil.

"I'm telling you. Says this big property developer jerk-off does it every year. Pays all these, y'know, little people to dress up in the outfits and then he and his a-hole buddies hunt them."

"This sounds like bollocks," said Phil. "Can't be legal."

"Just listen, would you. They hunt them with paintball guns, out on the estate this dipshit owns. They get five Gs just for turning up in the outfits, and the last one standing gets fifty!"

Phil shook his head. "No way. Doesn't happen."

"That's what I said." Jackie pointed across at Bunny. "That's what he said too. We all called bullshit on this story. Diller shrugs it off with a smile and we move on. I'm working serving people; Bunny here and his new buddy Diller are getting on like a house on fire – and drinking enough to put it out, might I add. Well, Diller is on the H$_2$O, but Bunny is making up for him."

Bunny gave an embarrassed shrug of his shoulders.

Jackie gave him a smile to show he meant nothing by it. "Then who comes in? Only Smithy."

"The dwarf?" asked Phil.

"Midget," repeated the sentinel.

"Shut up, Donal, or I'm barring you again."

This was followed by some incoherent mumbling and the turning of a page.

"So," continued Jackie, "with God as my witness, Smithy is sitting on that stool right there" – he indicated the one Bunny was currently sitting on – "dressed as a leprechaun, with a big red paintball mark right in the middle of his chest."

"So he lost?" asked Phil.

"Wait," said Jackie, "I've not got to the best bit. Smithy, he tells us that he fucking hates this thing. He's an actor." Jackie pointed at Bunny. "So is Diller – that's how they know each other. Anyways, he hates this hunt thing, you can really tell by how he says it. Pure hate. Says it is a dehumanising atrocity."

"Fair play," said Bunny, and the barmen both nodded their agreement.

"Thing is," Jackie continued, "he's in the hole to some guy in Chinatown. Had himself some bad cards. He's in the shit and he needs money fast."

"So, he agrees to do the thing?" asked Phil.

"He agrees to do the thing," nodded Jackie. "Only, y'know, he's in it to win it. The five Gs will clear his debt, but if he has to go through this degrading bullshit, he wants the fifty."

"Fuckin' A."

"So, he's there, they're all there – ten of 'em, I think, all in their outfits. They're told they have gotta stay on the estate, gotta stay in costume, all these rules. They get a twenty-minute head start and then these rich butt-munchers are after them – get this – on quad bikes."

"Jesus," said Bunny.

"I know, un-be-fuckin-lievable. So, Smithy, he's playing it cool. Laying low. Sees a few of the other, y'know, little people..." Both Jackie and Phil looked down the bar at Donal, who was busy pretending not to be listening. "He sees them heading back to the house, covered in paint. He thinks, I'm pretty close to winning this."

"Fifty grand," said Phil.

"Exactly. Smithy is ducking and diving, bobbing and weaving. He ends up in this clearing, there's him and this other contestant. They've heard the shouting; they know it's just them left."

"Let me guess," said Phil, "the other little guy calls the hunters or something."

Jackie slowly shook his head. "Nope."

He let it hang there, letting the tension build.

"Jesus, Jackie," said Bunny. "C'mon then."

Jackie grinned at them, displaying a full set of white teeth. "The other fella pulls out a paintball gun and shoots Smithy – BAM! Right in the chest!"

"No!" said Bunny and Phil in unison.

"With God as my witness."

"And this Smithy fella just takes that?" asked Phil.

"Fuck no. When the hunters find them, the other guy is running for his damn life. Smithy is losing his shit, demanding justice, mad as all hell. They say no deal, throw him in a van and drive him back into the city. They don't even let him pick up his clothes."

"What a shower of pricks," said Bunny.

Phil shook his head. "Nah, I mean, it's a great story, right enough – but I'm not buying it."

"Straight up, buddy," said Jackie, "I was the same. Then he takes off the damn leprechaun hat and shows us five Gs in cash!"

"Damn!"

Jackie turned to Bunny. "And you don't remember none of that?"

Bunny shrugged. "Not really. I mean..."

"Jeez, Bunny, that's scary, man."

"I think somebody spiked my drink." Bunny noticed the facial expressions and quickly clarified, "I mean, not here, obviously. Somewhere else."

All three men turned their heads as the other sentinel cleared his throat to speak. "How did he get up on the stool?" he asked.

"What?" said Jackie.

"The little fella. You said he got up on the stool there. How'd he do that? It's a tall stool."

"Really, Paidi?" said Phil. "He sets down that story and your only question is how did the little fella get up on the stool?"

The old man shrugged.

"In answer to your question," said Jackie, "pretty easily. He's a nimble little so and so."

"Midget."

"Final warning, Donal."

A page was turned; mumbles were mumbled.

"So, any idea where I went after I left here?"

Jackie rubbed his hand around his neck. "All three of you guys were here for another couple of hours maybe, then Smithy said he had to go pay the loan shark in Chinatown, and you and Diller went with him for, y'know, support."

Bunny nodded. "Right." With a slow reverence, Bunny finished his pint and placed the empty glass on the bar. "I'd better get back on the trail then. What's the damage?"

Phil nodded. "That's six bucks for the beer."

"Oh," said Jackie with an embarrassed smile, as he picked up a pad from beside the register, "and if you wouldn't mind, Diller never paid for his breakfast."

"Yeah," said Bunny, pulling out the wad of cash from his pocket, "he does that."

CHAPTER TWENTY-ONE

What were they again, the five stages of grief? Denial, anger, bargaining, depression and acceptance? As far as Amy was aware, you were supposed to go through them in some kind of order. The reality was much more chaotic than that. She jumped back and forth through all five stages at random pretty much every time she flipped the channel.

She'd been watching TV rolling news continuously since Bunny left. It was impossible not to. The salacious story of the dominatrix who murdered her client was too good for the media to not milk for all it was worth. She watched as news anchors and reporters tried to look dignified and appalled, even as the light danced in their eyes. This was so much juicier for them than the annual bit about UN officials not paying their parking tickets, which came up every year at this time. That got a couple of minutes and then it was back to the fun stuff. It was laughable how they threw in "allegedly" every now and then, like that was covering the broadcaster's ass when their caption screamed "Dominatrix of Death". The coverage in itself was interesting: violence against women wasn't exactly front-page news, but when a woman supposedly kills a man – woah, we're going to need a snazzy graphics package and some new music.

They'd started with the facts, as they'd known them. A man had been found "brutally murdered" in a dominatrix's apartment in Astoria. Law enforcement sources said that there had been signs of what they termed "severe violent activity" and the tenant of the property was wanted for questioning. The press had got hold of some neighbours. Mrs Beasland from upstairs said she was shocked, that Amy seemed so quiet. How the hell would she know? The woman did Zumba so much and at such a high volume, starting at 6am, that Amy doubted she could hear much of anything. Mister Rainer said he'd never liked her. Amy had once helped that a-hole carry a couch up three flights of stairs.

Then the police had started naming names. Amy had seen her picture up on the screen. They'd initially used a driver's licence photo, but then they'd got a picture of her from her college course's end-of-year bash. It made her look like some kind of party animal. It didn't matter that the drink in her hands was a virgin cocktail or that she'd been home in bed by eleven o'clock that night. The public were actually warned not to approach her.

Then they'd named the victim. That was surprising. She recognised the guy. Charlie Fenton, the guy who worked with Matt. The one that had tried to strong-arm her two nights ago and quite possibly shoot her yesterday morning. She'd never met the guy before that and she sincerely wished she never had. She kept trying to think everything through like a lawyer would. It came down to evidence. When the hysteria calmed down, what was the actual evidence?

Then they'd shown the CCTV footage: Amy leaving her apartment building, taken from the camera on the front door. In the pictures she was rushing out, looking panicked. She remembered it well. The footage they were showing was from Saturday night, just after that Charlie a-hole had tried to rough her up. The police had stated that it was footage taken on Sunday night and showed her fleeing the scene of the murder. Not only was she being set up, but somebody was going to great lengths to make sure it stuck.

If that was bad, the worst had been yet to come. The news had only broken about 9am, but by 2pm they were doorstepping her father. Her dad's stunned and hunted look was lifted straight from Amy's worst nightmares. It reminded her of the horrible footage of a calf in an abattoir that'd convinced her to go vegan. Dazed and terrified all at the same time. His voice was low and it was hard to hear him over the questions being shouted as he tried to make his way from his car to the house. It took a moment for Amy to make it out. He was repeating over and over again, "There's been some mistake, there's been some mistake, there's been some mistake." Amy had gone to the bathroom and retched up what little she had inside her. Then she'd cried until she'd run out of tears.

After that she'd gone back to the TV and watched some more because, well, what else was she going to do? Once they'd gone over the scant facts they had and harassed her poor father, they'd started in on the talking heads. On one channel, they wondered whether "militant feminism" had gone too far. On another, a woman Amy didn't recognise but who was described as her friend defended her by saying the guy probably had it coming. Another station discussed what other kind of jobs students were doing to help pay their way in New York.

The truth behind how Amy had wound up doing what she did for a living was that it had happened almost entirely by accident. When she'd first come to New York, she had started going out with a guy who she'd thought might be "the one". Once, late at night, while drunk, he confessed that his fantasies ran to the slightly kinkier side of things. Amy, being Amy, had decided to do some research. She read up on it and started frequenting a forum where she got talking to a dom who had been full of helpful advice. The woman, Michelle, had been very frank and open, eventually meeting Amy for a drink to talk her through it. Amy's boyfriend had been blown away. There'd been a couple of months of exploration and that side of things had gone from strength to strength. Unfortunately, in other areas, once they'd got past the initial "best behaviour" phase of the relationship, he gradually settled into being his true self, and he'd turned out to be an inconsiderate waste of space. So that had been that on the relationship front. Besides, between starting her studies and having to waitress forty hours a week to try and meet her living expenses, Amy didn't have time for anything like a private life. Still, she had found a side of her own sexuality that shocked her, and she wanted to explore it further. So she'd gone to a couple of parties with Michelle, mainly as an observer, and found it all to be surprisingly, well, odd as it sounded, nice. The scene was mostly full of people expressing themselves and there were sensible rules in place to ensure that, behind all the roleplay, everyone was safe and having a good time. Amy had ended up helping Michelle out with a couple of clients and then, when Michelle had unexpectedly gone back to Miami to manage the family business, Amy had pretty much been handed an ongoing business on a plate. The stars had aligned. Or at least, they had until now – when it felt like the sky was falling. One of the many things that annoyed her about all this was that she was renowned for taking safety seriously and being a stickler for rules. It seemed silly, given the severity of the accusations made against her, but a part of her was offended by the implication of a lack of professionalism on her behalf.

Then she'd looked at the door, and from beneath the waves of emotion that had battered her remorselessly all morning, a feeling of doubt finally bobbed back to the surface. She was putting all of her hopes on a man she had known for twenty-four hours. She'd given him a couple of hundred dollars and he'd disappeared to chase down what he said was her one way out of this situation, leaving her alone. She looked at the clock on the mantelpiece. He'd been gone four hours now. He could be out of the state by now. He might sell her out. How did she know she could trust him? OK, he'd helped her out yesterday – twice, in fact – but still. Amy had always had some trust issues, and that was before someone she'd considered a friend, in a way, had told her something he shouldn't have and then tried to have her killed.

There was one further wrinkle. Amidst the ambulance chasers and talking heads on TV, there was one man she recognised. Amy was definitely having a worse day than him, but she was guessing his

Monday wasn't all sunshine and lollipops either. His name was Douglas Randall and he was the afternoon anchor on Channel 8 News. He was the ultimate professional – reading the teleprompter, asking guests the expected questions, his expression the appropriate mix of dignity and journalistic endeavour.

The reason Amy was so impressed with Douglas's quiet dignity was that normally when she saw him, bent over with a ball gag in his mouth, he was quite the screamer. She wondered if he felt like screaming now? He must be thinking it: *I was a client of the Dominatrix of Death. What are the odds of that not coming out?*

Amy had had just about enough of sitting around doing nothing. She was going to do what she did best – take control.

CHAPTER TWENTY-TWO

"Hello again, fathead," the woman said with a dazzling smile.

Bunny had been walking around Chinatown for a couple of hours now without much luck. He was starting to think that this might be the point where the trail ran cold. He knew this Smithy character owed some guy money from a card game, but Bunny wasn't sure what to do with that information. You couldn't just ask about for a loan shark. The closest thing he had to a plan was to find out where the card games were. How many dwarfs could be frequenting them, after all? Someone would know this Smithy fella. But that still left the problem of how he was supposed to find an illegal card game he wasn't invited to. Bar anything else, it was only lunchtime – Bunny assumed most such games happened after dark. If this were Dublin, he'd know what to do. Of course, if this were Dublin, he'd have a hundred trees he could shake for information. As it was, he found himself wandering the streets of Chinatown, treeless and fast becoming hopeless.

Then, in its way, inspiration hit.

As he'd walked around, people in suits on their lunch break, plus the normal mix of tourists, thronged the pavements. Shops had fruit and vegetables on display outside, or arrays of suspiciously cheap branded merchandise. The place also smelled gorgeous, with aromas flying at you from every direction. Bunny had been tempted to eat, but he was on a budget, and filling his face was not an option. He'd passed a restaurant as the hostess opened the door to let out a family of four, all in matching "I Heart New York" T-shirts. The hostess gave a cheery wave and shouted, "Don't come back with your ugly kids!" This was met with a gale of laughter and cheery waves back. The hostess went back inside and Bunny stopped to look in the window. The sign on the door proclaimed it was "Madam Wong's – home of the world's rudest staff. Guaranteed offence or your money back." That wasn't what caught Bunny's attention though. It was what was written below it: "Home of the unhappy fortune cookie." He remembered the piece of paper in his pocket: "Death comes to us all."

The hostess followed up "Hello again, fathead" with an equally cheery "It pains me to see your stupid face again so soon." She was a pretty girl of diminutive stature in a blue patterned kimono, and she delivered each insult with a beaming smile.

"Yes – ehm, yes," said Bunny. "I was here at the weekend."

"I remember it well. We have still not removed the stink."

"Right. Sorry about that. Ehm, I was wondering if it, if I..." Bunny looked at the woman, at a loss for what to say next. "Ehm..."

She lowered her voice and leaned in, her accent suddenly becoming a lot less Peking and a lot more Pittsburgh. "Is this about your card, sir?"

Bunny's face lit up. "Yes. Yes, it is. Did I leave it here?"

The woman gave him a confused look. "No, definitely not. And I double-checked this morning – the payment was definitely cancelled correctly."

"Right. Ehm, could you... Would you mind explaining what happened, exactly?"

She nodded to another woman in a similar dress and touched Bunny's arm to guide him to the side. She raised her voice – "Come with me, poison-breath" – then lowered it once more to a conspiratorial whisper. "Sorry, we get into trouble if we don't, y'know... Owner wants us to always stay in character. Now, as I said, I really do think everything should be fine with the payment, but if you'd like me to check again..."

"No," said Bunny. "I'm sure it's fine. Could you... My memory is a little fuzzy on exactly what happened. Could you just remind me?"

She nodded as if this was a natural request. If there were an illegal poker game nearby, they'd better hope this lady and her poker face didn't ante up, as she would clean the place out. "You were here having dinner."

"With my two friends?"

She nodded. "The black dude and the..." She looked momentarily unsure.

"The little fella?"

She smiled. "Yes. He was dressed as, like, a leprechaun or something? Anyway, all of you had the early bird special and, well... your waiter, Jimmy, is new and he's not familiar with the card machine. So, when you went to pay, he mistakenly put through nine thousand dollars instead of ninety."

"Fecking hell!"

"Yes, but he noticed it and then came to me. We rang the company and the payment was stopped, I assure you."

"But, like – it could've gone through?"

"Yes." She gave him a nervous smile. "It was a lucky escape, I guess."

Bunny nodded, no doubt doing a much worse job with his poker face than the hostess had. He had been told the card had a $200 withdrawal limit per day. Apparently, that didn't hold for direct card payments. He could imagine that this news had been pretty exciting at the time.

"So it all got sorted out?"

She nodded again. "Absolutely, and your whole party left looking very happy, may I say."

"Yeah, I'd imagine we did alright. Did we happen to say where we were going?"

"Actually, you asked me to recommend a bar. I suggested the Rhinestone Lounge Karaoke Bar over on Grand Street."

"Oh God, really?"

"Is everything OK, sir?"

"Sorry, yes, thank you. You've been very helpful. I've just not got a great singing voice."

"Oh, on the contrary, sir."

"What?"

"You and your two friends treated us all to a very rousing rendition of 'Danny Boy' before you left. It was pretty epic."

"Oh God, did we? I'm so sorry."

"It's OK. You got a round of applause."

"We did?"

Bunny looked around, suddenly self-conscious, as if the diners would still be the same people two days later.

"Is that everything?" she asked.

"Yes, ehm – thanks for your time."

Her accent and volume returned to its default setting. "Do not mention it, donkey-face."

CHAPTER TWENTY-THREE

Bunny was unsure how long his first visit to the Rhinestone Lounge Karaoke Bar had lasted, but the second one lasted about twenty-six seconds.

The neon signage was off and the place was clearly not open for business, but Bunny spotted some movement inside. He knocked on the doors but got no response. He walked around the corner and down the alley at the side of the building, where he found a fire exit that had been propped open. A delivery van stood there with its doors open, and two men were arguing over the best way to get a table through a door that it definitely wasn't going to fit through. To the side of the van lay the smashed remnants of the old furniture. Bunny gave the delivery men an "I'm supposed to be here" nod as he walked past.

The inside of the Rhinestone Lounge Karaoke Bar was like every other nightclub Bunny had been in outside of work hours. It looked smaller than it no doubt appeared when full of high-spirited punters, and in the dim daylight that fought its way through the frosted glass, the furnishings looked cheap and worn, the silver looked tarnished and the whole thing felt a bit tawdry. It was like seeing somebody you knew making the walk of shame dressed in glittery spandex on a Sunday morning as you were heading to mass.

Not that Bunny had much time to take in the ambience. Behind the bar stood a short Asian man wielding a clipboard with menace. The collar of his shirt could compete with a commercial airliner for wingspan. He also looked like he was in a bad mood.

Bunny cleared his throat politely. "Excuse me, I'm sorry to bother you..."

He stopped talking as recognition closely followed by rage spread across the other man's face.

"You! Stay there! Where's my motherfucking gun?!"

Throughout his life, Bunny had picked up many rules for survival. While it had never come up before, staying where you were while someone tried to find their gun rocketed to number one on the list of stupid mistakes you don't get to make twice.

"Alright," Bunny said, raising his hands in contrition. "Look..."

"MANNY!" screeched the man.

Bunny heard a rumbling from the back of the building. He turned and headed out the door, unfortunately just in time to meet the two men who delivered tables for a living and yet, inexplicably, couldn't see when a table wasn't going to fit through a door. Their efforts to figure this out were further hampered by some lunatic with a beard jumping onto and sliding across the table, making a surprisingly nimble landing on the other side. Five seconds later, they found a solution to their problem when the table met Manny and suddenly it was in several considerably easier to carry pieces.

Bunny turned at the sound of shattering furniture to see an enormous slab of humanity standing in the middle of the remains of an awkwardly sized table.

Without being boastful, Bunny McGarry could describe himself as a big man. He'd boxed as a heavyweight in his younger days. He had a bit of heft to him. But behind him in the alleyway appeared to be half of the entirety of human existence rolled into one Hispanic man and placed in a suit that Bunny guessed was not off the peg. The last time New York had seen something this big, it was climbing up the Empire State Building with a girl over its shoulder while being shot at by biplanes.

For the second time in two days, Bunny found himself running from a fight. While that may hurt his pride, he could live with it, on the proviso that he actually got to live. Unfortunately, as well as his pride, it was hurting his foot. The old injury was now sending stabbing pains up his left leg which meant he was able to engage only in a shambling run that was about half his normal speed, and it wasn't like he was much of a runner to begin with. Manny wasn't built for velocity, but he didn't have to be. Bunny was the wounded animal at the side of the herd and the predator could smell blood.

Bunny tried to bob and weave his way down the street, half on and half off the sidewalk. If he'd been in a film, he'd have dodged around some people and then Manny would've ploughed into them. That always annoyed Bunny, how film directors did that to give an easy reminder to the audience of who was a goodie and who was a baddie. It was also unrealistic. Bunny was the first through – he was the one having to clear obstacles. Behind him, people were diving out of Manny's way. Bunny made a decision and turned a corner at the side of a convenience store.

When Manny followed him into the alley a few seconds later, he found his foe leaning over a metal trash can, gasping for breath.

Manny stopped. The alleyway was a dead end. He advanced slowly towards Bunny, who was panting heavily, bent double and defenceless. Out of the corner of his eye, he noticed Manny glancing around nervously.

Bunny was indeed a big man, but throughout his life, he'd fought plenty bigger. It was in his nature that he didn't like a bully, which meant that since his school days, bigger had frequently come looking for him, quite often with company.

Bunny spoke through gasping breaths. "Look, fella, I don't want any trouble."

"Yeah, well, the boss does."

"Fair enough."

Manny didn't have a weapon, which was what Bunny had been counting on. Manny was the weapon.

Bunny bet that throughout his life, Manny hadn't had many fights with bigger. Bar anything else, he'd have had difficulty finding it, unless he went around accusing buildings of looking at him funny. This meant that, crucially, he'd never learned guile. A kind of feral, street-smart guile was the primary reason that, despite what a gravestone in Glasnevin Cemetery might suggest, Bunny McGarry was still alive. It was also the reason a lot of other people walked with limps and, in at least one instance, spoke with a stammer.

Without seeing it, Bunny felt the movement in the air above him that meant Manny's right fist was heading down towards his head. When it got to where Bunny's head was supposed to be, Manny's fist found the lid of a steel trash can hurtling towards it at a well-judged angle that caused him to howl in pain as it connected with his wrist. Bunny, now standing, was proving considerably more sprightly than Manny had expected. Manny's left fist came around in a haymaker that found nothing but foul-smelling air, as his opponent had ducked down again and was busy vigorously applying the steel trash can lid to Manny's left kneecap.

Manny stumbled forward, which was when his unprotected face met the trash can lid, now ascending at maximum velocity. His head flew back, blood spurting from his newly broken nose, and, slowly, an avalanche of stunned humanity, Manny started to fall backwards. It took a while – there was a lot of him for gravity to get hold of. Bunny stood there watching, holding a trash can lid that would from now on bear an indent of what Manny's face looked like when presented with a very unpleasant surprise. He dropped the lid. It hit the ground a full second before Manny did.

Of all the peculiar phrases that Bunny disagreed with in life, the one he found most inexplicable was "You shouldn't kick a man when he's down." As far as Bunny was concerned, when he was down was the perfect time to kick a man. You may've put considerable effort into getting the man down, and a well-judged kick was an excellent way of making sure he didn't get back up again. Bunny admired people who didn't think like that, generally while he was standing over them while their noble blood coloured the ground.

Bunny was therefore morally fine with delivering a well-judged boot to Manny's head. His yelp of pain was not from his conscience – he'd just forgotten not to use the left foot, which wasn't going to do much for his limp.

Manny came to a couple of seconds later when a shaft of pain bolted up his arm from his shattered right wrist.

"You broke my wrist!"

"I know," said Bunny, "that's why my foot is on it. It's up to you to decide how much more pain there'll be."

"None!"

"Good answer. Now, what's your boss's problem with me?"

Bunny looked down and was surprised to see he didn't have Manny's undivided attention. Instead, he was looking at the trash bags and discarded crates that lay on the ground beside him. His voice was surprisingly high-pitched. "Do you think there are rats around here?"

Bunny glanced around. "I'd imagine there are alright."

Manny's eyes widened with real terror. "I hate rats."

"Well, you shouldn't start fights in alleys then."

"It was nothing personal. I was just following orders."

Bunny tutted. "I don't know if you've read much history, but that isn't typically considered a great justification."

Manny's head was now swivelling back and forth so much that Bunny was forced to apply a bit more pressure with his boot.

"Manny! Focus!"

Manny nodded his head furiously. "Alright, alright, alright!"

"What's your boss's problem with me?" Bunny repeated.

"What are you talking about? You smashed up his place."

"I did?"

"Well, you and the..." Manny's eyes darted back and forth again. Bunny increased the pressure a little.

"Ahhh."

"What exactly happened?"

"OK, OK, OK, OK! Jesus! What? You want me to say it wasn't your fault? Fine. They started it."

"They who?"

"What do you mean 'they who'?"

"Let's assume I'm unaware of the incident."

"But you... Ahhh! OK, OK."

"Be quick, Manny. I can hear rustling over there."

"The fucking – the, the, the..."

"Deep breath."

"The Aussies! The rugby team. Your homie, the midget—" Bunny applied a little more pressure. "Ahhh, ahhh, ahhh."

"He prefers dwarf."

Bunny had no idea if this was true or not.

"The dwarf. They – they kept trying to touch him for luck."

"I see."

"He went crazy, man. That dude has some issues! I mean, seriously. I've never seen anything like it. And he's a biter. Please let me up."

"So what happened?"

"What do you mean? They touched him; he said stop. Your friend, the black dude, tried to calm them down. One of them says, 'Your friend has a short temper' – next thing the midg— I mean the dwarf – dwarf! He's in there like a fucking demon and you're backing him up. Five guys went to the hospital."

"Including the dwarf?"

"No, man. You three all hightailed it out of there."

"Let me get this straight. Me and two other guys put five guys in the hospital?"

"One other guy," corrected Manny. "The black dude hid under a table."

"Me and this dwarf fella took on a rugby team?"

"Yeah, I guess. I dunno. Maybe they were a soccer team."

Bunny nodded. "Yeah, that seems more likely."

"Please let me up."

Bunny thought for a second. Then he pulled the medal out of his pocket. "Any idea where I got this?"

"We used to give 'em away to people who drank a yard of ale."

"Used to?"

Manny was back to scanning the bags again. Bunny was a little hurt. The guy must really have a thing for rats. "Yeah," he said. "Clint says we ain't doing it no more – attracts the wrong crowd." Manny glanced back up at Bunny. "No offence."

"None taken. What about this?"

Bunny pulled out the pink bra.

"Seriously?"

"I think I've got some cheese here somewhere."

"I don't know. The Pink Slipper Gentlemen's Club is two blocks west of here."

Bunny nodded and then took his foot away. "Thank you for your assistance. Count to ten and then you can get up."

"Can we make it five?"

"Seven – but only because I like you, Manny."

"Feeling ain't mutual."

Bunny shoved the bra and medal back into his coat pocket as he limped out of the alley. "Jesus, Manny, there's no need to be so mean."

CHAPTER TWENTY-FOUR

Matt took a long drag on the cigarette and looked out at the view. Even on a dull March day it was impressive. You could feel like the king of the world up here.

The offices that Lanark Lane Investments had moved into only three months previously were on the seventeenth floor of an eighteen-floor building on Park Avenue. The eighteenth floor was taken up by the South African consulate. The story Matt had heard was that the whole building had been paid for using South African rands back in the days when apartheid was alive and well. It wouldn't surprise him. It's not like it'd be the only beautiful skyscraper in this skyline that had been built using blood money. Of course, these were very different times now. The South African consul general was black, as were about half of his staff. Very friendly they were too. Brad had got to know one of the top aides when he'd been kind enough to hook him up with his favourite dealer for what Brad called "fun-time Fridays". The aide had repaid the favour by getting them access to use the consulate's balcony garden when they needed to smoke in a city where doing that anywhere was now frowned upon.

Matt had tried to give up smoking during a health kick he'd gone on a few months ago. He'd been spending too much time with Brad, and Charlie had staged a one-man intervention. Jesus, Charlie. Every time someone said the name, Matt felt a knife being stuck into him. OK, he hadn't been perfect, but Charlie had been Matt's best friend, and now he was dead. Jennie was still alive though, and Matt had to focus on that. Right now, the only thing he cared about in the whole world was not having his sins passed on to his blameless baby sister.

The door opened behind Matt.

"For fuck's sake, dude."

Matt didn't need to turn around to know it was Brad. He stood beside him for a moment, struggling to light one of those ridiculous thin brown French cigarettes that he'd recently taken up smoking. The guy really was a douchebag of the highest order.

They stood there for a second, smoking.

"How did it go with the cops?" asked Brad.

"Fine," responded Matt.

They'd been interviewed separately. Cole had explained how it would happen. Their housemate and colleague was dead, and the cops would naturally want to talk to them about it. Matt had stuck to the story: Charlie was his friend, but he had no ideas about his sexual preferences. Well, the guy liked women, he knew that. That was why it wasn't a big surprise when he didn't come home last night, as he was quite the fan of the sleepover. He and Brad had been beyond stunned to find out both about his death and the particular circumstances. The police assured them that there would be an arrest soon; they had a very strong suspect.

It had been surreal. Matt had felt like he was having an out of body experience while he watched himself lie with such ease. Once Cole had dropped them outside the office that morning, he'd gone upstairs and taken a pill and a few minutes to calm himself. He had known that he needed to keep it together for whatever came next.

"Did you cry?"

"What?" asked Matt.

"Did you cry?" repeated Brad. "Y'know, when the cops talked about Charlie?"

"No."

Brad nodded. "I did. Bawled like a baby. I felt it was expected, y'know? It was easy – I rubbed my hand on these fucking burns – soon had the tears flowing, dude. Niagara Falls."

Matt stubbed his cigarette out in the free-standing ashtray provided. "So the police told you that your friend had been brutally murdered and you sat there the whole time weeping and rubbing your crotch? Nice job."

"Shut the fuck up, man!" Brad was angry now. Matt watched as his features fell into the little snarl that Matt was beginning to suspect was his true face. "This is all your fault!"

"Fuck you."

Brad shot out his right hand and pushed Matt. "What did you fucking say to me?"

Matt giggled.

"Jesus, are you high?" said Brad.

Matt shrugged one shoulder. "I wouldn't say high. I've taken the edge off a little."

"All your fault," Brad repeated.

"Yeah," said Matt, "I made you make the deal with the devil, did I? You're full of crap."

"We'd have been fine if you'd kept your damn mouth shut!"

"Define 'fine' here. I mean, I know you don't understand the whole plan, but you do get the bit where—"

"Shut up, shut up, shut up! Fuck, man! You don't know who the hell is listening."

Brad looked around. The reason they liked this garden so much was that they knew the South Africans got their entire office scanned for listening devices once a week. Brad's buddy had explained it to him one night over a few lines of blow. These days it was mostly industrial espionage stuff, but still, you had to make sure nobody was listening in on you. It had struck Matt a few months ago, when they'd started to realise the full extent of Miller and company's reach, that they were probably being watched. This space was the only one they could use and at least have a reasonable hope of privacy.

Matt stepped forward and leaned on the metal railing of the waist-high glass wall that surrounded the terrace.

"I've been thinking, dude," said Brad.

"Oh? Always a treat."

Matt could tell Brad had a lot on his mind, because he didn't automatically snap back as he usually did at any perceived slight.

"The... Miller and... I'm worried, man, that if we do what they say and fulfil our end of the bargain, they might still... y'know, kill us."

Matt burst out laughing.

"What the fuck, man?"

Matt looked over his shoulder at Brad's outraged face and that just made him laugh harder. He turned and leaned his back on the railing, his laughter now taking on a manic edge.

"Jesus! Pull yourself together, dude. This is serious." Brad lowered his voice to a whisper. "They might kill us."

"I wouldn't worry about it."

"Really?"

"Yeah. They're definitely going to kill us."

Brad flicked his foul-smelling cigarette at Matt. "Screw you, you fucking degenerate. It's OK for you – I've got a fucking bomb inside me."

His face was turning red now. Charlie had called it defcon 4 – the point where you had to calm Brad down or bad shit would happen. Matt didn't care. Bad shit was already happening.

Instead he made the sound of an explosion and wiggled his fingers in the air.

Brad went for him, charging like a bull.

They came together and wrestled like two men who had never been in a proper fight. They fell to the ground, limbs interlocked. Matt had fifty pounds and a few inches of reach on Brad, so he managed to get Brad's head locked in the crook of his elbow. After a moment, Brad stopped wiggling.

"Understand something, you entitled little fucktard: I don't care if I die, and I certainly don't care if you die, but whatever happens, I'm getting my sister out of this. So, shut the fuck up and let me get on with—"

The door opened and Piet, Brad's buddy from the consulate, popped his head out. Behind him, Matt could see a few other concerned faces peering out at them.

"Hey, fellas," he said. "Everything alright?"

Matt let Brad go. "Yeah – sorry, Piet. We're... a bit emotional."

"Yeah," said Brad, quickly getting back to his feet. "We had some really bad news."

"Yes," said Matt, lying back on the grass and looking up into the gloomy sky that threatened rain. "Brad is dead."

"Christ, yeah." said Piet. "I heard. Shocking. You mean Charlie though, obviously."

Matt looked up at Brad and their eyes locked for a long moment.

"Sure," said Matt, before adding quietly to himself, "him too."

CHAPTER TWENTY-FIVE

"We're closed."

Bunny had been having a conversation with the bouncer at the Pink Slipper Gentlemen's Club for nearly five minutes now. It was a conversation only in the sense that two people were both talking. No information was being imparted.

"I know you're closed. You've already said you're closed. What I'm trying to say is I'm not a customer. I was a customer here on Saturday, I think, and I just need to speak to someone who was working then. Were you working then?"

"That ain't none of your business."

The guy had two earrings in his left ear, one eyebrow and zero intention of being helpful. He had the kind of muscle that you got from picking heavy things up and putting them down in the exact same spot. As he stood there, Bunny could see him literally flexing his pecs through his T-shirt. Either that, or it was where he was keeping his scant supply of brain cells and he needed to wiggle them to accomplish thought. In which case, his man boobs needed considerably more jiggling.

"Could I talk to the manager then, please?"

"No. Know why?"

"I'm going to guess it involves—"

"We're closed," finished the bouncer. "Nobody is allowed in."

"You don't say. If you're closed, what're you doing here?"

"What?"

"If the place is really closed, as in closed closed, as in nobody gets in, then why have a doorman on duty? As opposed to say, just a closed door."

"We're closed."

Just then, a nervous-looking girl in her early twenties walked up to the door.

"Hi, I'm here for the..."

The doorman picked up a clipboard. "Name?"

"Clare Cleaver."

The doorman took a step to the side. "Go see Tiffany."

"Thanks." He shifted to the side to let her pass and then resumed his position as a human door.

"So," said Bunny, "when you said nobody was allowed in?"

"I meant you. You ain't allowed in. Know why? I don't like you."

"That's a real shame, because I felt we were really connecting. Look, it's been a long day. I'm not here to cause trouble, I just need to talk to the manager."

"Oh, you should have said." The doorman picked up the clipboard and pretended to read it. "Yeah, it says here, we're closed."

"I'm trying to ask nicely."

The doorman took a step forward and put what little neck he had to use by rolling his head around his shoulders. There was a cracking noise as he did so.

"You can ask un-nicely, if you like."

Bunny sighed. "Un-nicely isn't a word."

"I ain't finding you funny."

"Trust me, gobshite, you'll be rolling around on the floor in a minute."

"You can—"

"Bunny – hey! I thought that was you!"

A redheaded woman in sweats had just appeared behind Bunny. She was carrying a gym bag and smiling warmly up at him.

"Cheryl, you know this guy?"

"Yes, Bruno, that's why I just said his name." She turned to Bunny. "What are you doing here?"

"I, ehm, just dropped by for a quick chat."

"Come on in."

Cheryl moved towards the door.

"He ain't coming in."

"What did you say?" said Cheryl, in a melodious Texan drawl.

"He ain't coming in," repeated Bruno.

"The hell he isn't. He's here to see me."

"He didn't say."

"I just said."

The doorman folded his arms. "No. No way."

Cheryl furrowed her brow at him. "Excuse me?"

"I said no."

"You said no. Really? *You* said no?" She fished her phone out of her pocket. "OK."

"What're you doing?"

"I'm calling Mrs Kane – y'know, the owner of this here establishment. I think it's time we clarify if my rights as manager supersede yours as doorman. Let's see which of us she sides with."

He unfolded his arms. "Don't do that."

They locked eyes for a long moment and then Bruno stepped to the side. He muttered something under his breath as he did so.

"What was that?"

"Nothing, Cheryl."

"That's what I thought. You've been a real bitch since you gave up smoking, y'know that, Bruno?"

"Sorry, Cheryl."

Bunny took a seat in the booth in the back that Cheryl directed him to.

"Just hang on there for one sec." Then she walked over to the half-dozen girls that were milling around near the stage. "Good afternoon, ladies, I'm Cheryl. Thanks for coming down. If you would all just grab a seat. Has Tiffany given y'all your application forms?"

This was greeted with nods and held-up clipboards.

"Awesome. Well, I'll be with you in a couple of minutes and then we'll go through the rules and all that fun stuff. Then, once I've answered any questions you might have, we can move on to your audition pieces. OK?"

Heads were nodded again.

"And relax. Y'all look like you're waiting for a pregnancy test!"

This was greeted with smiles and laughs.

Cheryl executed a neat turn and headed back towards Bunny. She slid into the booth opposite him and offered him a warm smile. Now he got a proper look at her, he could see she was stunning. Make-up free, her heart-shaped face had a warm glow to it, with a dimpled grin and lively blue eyes that could really carry a smile. Gun to his head, Bunny would've guessed she was late thirties, but she could certainly pass for ten years younger.

He nodded towards the stage. "Looks like you're going to be busy."

"Yeah," said Cheryl. "Donna is going off to have her second baby and Ellen finally finished her master's, so..."

Cheryl noticed something change in Bunny's facial expression. "What? Shocked that a pole dancer can have a master's?"

"Well, I mean, no offence like, but it's not what you'd expect."

"Oh, I think you'd be surprised. Let me guess, you imagine this profession being filled with broken women from broken homes?"

"Well, I..."

"I run a good club. Do you have any idea how many applications we get for jobs here? The girls are taken good care of, strict no-drugs policy and woe betide the man who thinks this is one of those clubs where the rules are really just guidelines."

"Yeah, I've met your bouncer."

Cheryl pulled a bottle of water from her bag. "Oh, forget Bruno, he's window dressing. I'm about to be a certified Krav Maga instructor. You want a demonstration of my own policy on personal space?"

Bunny raised his hands in surrender. "Sorry, I didn't mean to be rude. I apologise."

She waved his apology away. "Don't worry about it. I guess I get a little defensive on the topic. Seriously though, we run a good club here. See those girls over there?" Cheryl took a gulp from her water as she waved in the direction of the stage. "They're here because they know they can earn six figures. Eighteen months from now, I'm out of here – and I'll own my own dojo outright. I'm a businesswoman, and I ain't the only one in the building."

"I could use a couple of classes myself."

She gave him a lopsided grin. "I dunno. From what I remember from Diller's report on the incident with the Australians on Saturday night, it sounds like you held your own."

"Oh Christ, look – I don't go about getting into fights in bars."

She gave a little laugh. "Well, you seem to have a flair for it. So, what brings you back here?"

Bunny drummed nervously on the table. "Well, I know I was here on Saturday but, to be honest with ye, I don't actually remember much about it."

"Oh," said Cheryl, her eyebrows raised. "Well, you were pretty drunk."

"Ah shite, was I?"

"Oh yeah, big time!" Cheryl gave him a stern look. "You don't remember what happened?"

Bunny clenched his eyes shut. "Oh Jesus. I didn't make a show of myself, did I?"

After three seconds of silence, Bunny opened one eye, at which point Cheryl collapsed onto the table laughing. "Relax," she said. "You were fine. In fact, you were a total sweetie pie. I mean, you were drunk, but you'd also got a fair old knock on the head. You honestly don't remember?"

"I don't remember anything."

"Damn," she said. "Well, rest easy. You were the perfect gentleman. Here, at least. From what I could gather, some Australian gentlemen may not have such fond memories of meeting y'all."

"So I believe," said Bunny. "From what I can gather, this Smithy fella really doesn't like to be touched."

Cheryl grinned. "Oh, I wouldn't say that."

Bunny reddened. "Oh right, sorry. Are you and him...?"

"Now, that is a complicated question. Short answer, I'd like to be, but Smithy wants to focus on his art."

"Really?"

"Well, you know what he's like."

Bunny shifted nervously. "Not really. To be honest with you, I've been hearing about him all day, but I don't actually recall him or this Diller fella at all."

Cheryl's expression darkened. "Really? Damn, that ain't good, honey."

"I know," said Bunny. "It's never happened before. First thing I knew, I was waking up at 6am, minus my wallet and phone."

"Ouch."

"I'm hoping the two lads might be able to help me figure out what happened."

"Well, you and Diller left here about 2am."

"Right. Was Smithy not with us?"

It was Cheryl's turn to blush. "No. He came home with me. I'm afraid I've no idea where y'all ended up."

"I see. Would you know where I could find either of the lads?"

"Right about now, I'd imagine Smithy is at his current job. Although" – she glanced at her watch – "it is 3pm, so I can't guarantee he hasn't quit by now."

"Is that likely?"

Cheryl laughed. "Man has an artistic temperament, and a bit of a hair-trigger to boot."

"He sounds like a nightmare."

"That ain't giving you the good side."

"What's that like?"

Cheryl grinned. "Now that is a personal question."

"Sorry."

"I'll write the address down for you."

She opened another pocket in her bag and started rummaging around in it. "Oh sorry, I meant to ask. Any luck finding Simone?"

Bunny froze. "What?"

"Your good lady."

"I told you about that?"

Cheryl looked up. "Yeah. You really opened up. Told us all how much she meant to you. Showed us the photo you got."

Bunny held his head in his hands. "Oh God."

"Oh God nothing. A man trying to reconnect with the love of his life, that's a beautiful thing. It's straight-up romantic, in fact, and that ain't something you hear much in this building."

"What did I say, exactly?"

"You were... a little emotional."

"Oh Jesus."

"Oh hush. Ain't nothing wrong with a man crying."

Bunny raised his head up. "Oh, for feck's... I was crying?!"

Cheryl nodded as she reached across and took Bunny's hand. "Like the sweetest little drunken Irish baby." She started writing on the back of his hand. "Sorry, no paper."

"Well, it seems I made a show of myself in a whole different way than I expected." Those words triggered his memory, and he reached his hand into his pocket, pulling out the pink bra. "Speaking of which, I had this on me."

Cheryl nodded. "Cool. Aliyah's been looking for that."

"I'm afraid to ask, but why did I have that?"

"You were using it to dry your tears."

Bunny put his head back into his hands again. "Oh, for feck's sake!"

CHAPTER TWENTY-SIX

Bunny wasn't sure what he'd been expecting, but this wasn't it. He double-checked the address that Cheryl had written on the back of his hand. This was the place alright.

The bell above the door tinkled as he pushed inside. There was a waiting room with four chairs and framed pictures of smiling customers with their dogs on the wall. At a quick glance, Bunny saw a lot of people he didn't recognise and one person who may have been a supporting actor in something that got cancelled. Celebrity is a relative term.

Behind the counter was a woman with jet-black hair and a pinched face. She favoured him with a grin so wide that Bunny was pretty sure he could see every last one of the teeth she possessed. Her smile dominated the room in a way dental work rarely did. Somewhere, a dentist was rightfully proud.

"Hi! Welcome to Doggy Do-Dos. Whether your poodle needs a perm or your terrier needs a trim, we're the ones to help bring forth the beauty from within."

"Right," said Bunny, not sure what the correct response was when greeted in verse. He was girding himself for the possibility that, before the conversation continued, he might be forced to "answer me these questions three". He didn't say anything for a moment, which only caused the woman to put even more effort into smiling, which had the opposite result to the relaxing effect she was presumably going for.

"I, ehm, I was actually looking for Smithy."

The smile went down harder than the *Hindenburg*, replaced with a scowl and a distinct lack of poetry as she raised her voice. "Smithy, I'm not your fucking secretary."

A shouted response came from the back. "What now, Bernice?"

"You got a fucking visitor."

"Could you just say that? There's no need to... " Smithy, a four-foot-five white guy in a grey beanie hat and sleeveless T-shirt, emerged from a door to the side of the counter. "Oh – hey, Bunny." He turned back to Bernice. "Could you not just tell me without all the aggression? Your negativity upsets the dogs."

"Hippy-addled fucking bullshit." Bernice opened a door that led into an office. "Just get that fucking last job done. I promised the owner it'd be ready by seven and it's a fucking big one."

"Alright, just..."

Bernice entered her office and slammed the door behind her.

Smithy shook his head. "That Swiss finishing school was worth every cent. C'mon in."

Smithy turned back towards the door he'd just come through and Bunny walked around the counter and followed him in. "You'll be shocked to know that Bernice and I met on a court-assigned anger management course. She was the 'fun' one in the group."

They entered a workshop where several dogs sat in large cages, either panting happily or dozing. Soft jazz played in the background. Smithy waved a hand around. "Welcome to my office."

"You don't seem surprised to see me?"

"Cheryl rang, said you'd be coming over. Hey, can you really not remember anything about Saturday?"

Bunny shook his head.

"Damn, that is messed up. Speaking of which, not that you can remember it, but sorry about the thing in the karaoke bar. What can I say? Like the judge said, I need to get better at controlling my rage. Pull up a seat."

Bunny sat in the proffered chair. "Ara don't worry about it. I've a few issues in that area myself."

"Well, thanks again. You don't need to be dealing with my shit. You got enough of your own to be handling."

As he spoke, Smithy was picking up various trimmers, scissors and combs and dipping them in and out of a beaker containing disinfectant.

Bunny found the change of subject they both wanted. "So, you groom dogs?"

"What gave it away?"

"The little limerick the lady did when I walked in."

Smithy gave a derisive laugh and shook his head. "Don't."

He picked up a broom and started sweeping up the black dog hair that littered the floor. Behind him, a bright-eyed schnauzer, which looked well-trimmed to Bunny's untrained eye, sat in its cage, happily lapping water from its bowl.

"You worked here long?"

"Almost a month. Getting close to a personal record." Smithy put the broom down and looked around his workspace. "I also don't get on great with authority. Besides, I'm an actor, so, y'know, lots of part-time work. We talked about all this on Saturday. You really don't remember?"

Bunny shook his head.

"Damn. That must be scary."

"'Tis. To be honest, this whole day has felt weird – chasing a version of myself I don't remember. It's felt a bit like dancing on me own grave."

"Yeah," said Smithy. "I can see that."

"No choice though. I promised a lady I'd help her out, and to do that, I really need my stuff back."

"I see," said Smithy, before turning to take a clipboard off the next cage, which contained a Siberian husky.

"Cheryl double-checked," Bunny continued. "We left before you two did on Saturday night. About 2am."

"Uh-huh."

"Me and Diller, I mean. Then, next thing I know, I wake up at 6am in Times Square, and my wallet and phone are gone, but I do have—"

"Sorry," said Smithy, walking towards the door. "One sec." He raised his voice. "Bernice! What the hell is this?"

"Fucking what?!" came back the screamed response.

Smithy read from the clipboard in his hands. "'Make dog look like Gene Simmons from Kiss.' Are you kidding me?"

"What's the problem?"

"Gene Simmons from Kiss," Smithy repeated. "I assume this means the black and white face paint and… " Smithy flipped the page over. "Oh yeah, look – they included a picture too. Helpful."

Bunny looked at the Siberian Husky. Bunny didn't think a dog could manage to pull off trepidation as a facial expression, but there it was, a Siberian Husky proving him wrong.

"Just do your fucking job," screeched Bernice.

"Do my job? What? Dye the hair? Paint it?"

Bernice's door slammed open. "Jesus fucking Christ, how hard is it to understand a simple fucking instruction."

"I understand fine. I'm just not doing it."

"What the owner fucking wants, the owner fucking gets."

"Bullshit. This is abuse. I'm not painting a poor dog for no damn reason."

"He's paying fifteen hundred fucking bucks – there's a damn good reason."

"Give him his money back, because I ain't doing it."

"The fuck I will."

"Seriously, Bernice, I have to know: how did someone who hates dogs end up owning a dog-grooming business?"

"Screw you. Look – do the thing and I'll pay you double."

Smithy folded his arms. "No way. This ain't a money thing, it's a principle thing. By the way, you didn't say fuck in that last sentence. You broke a great run you had going there."

"How would you and your fucking principles feel about getting fucking fired?"

Smithy tossed the clipboard onto the counter. "You won't find out, because I quit."

"The fuck you do."

Smithy turned to leave the room. "Y'know, Bernice, the reason you're so angry is because you think the world doesn't like you. Here's a newsflash: it doesn't. That's because the world has met you and you are utterly unlikable. You are a truly terrible person."

"Fuck you. You can't walk out on me."

Smithy took a jacket from a hanger on the wall. "Not only can I, but I'm going to do it moonwalk-style." Smithy turned to Bunny as he moonwalked towards the back door. "Fancy buying an unemployed actor a drink?"

They sat at the counter in silence and contemplated the drinks that sat in front of them. Bunny had a beer, Guinness being unavailable in this establishment. Smithy had a whiskey.

Bunny scratched at his beard. "Did you really take part in a leprechaun hunt?"

"Really?" said Smithy, sounding incredulous. "You thought now would be a good time to bring that up?"

"Fair point. Sorry."

Smithy stared at his whiskey some more. "Yes, I did. Most humiliating experience of my damn life. When I make it, with God as my witness, I'm going to find everybody that was there and shoot every last one of them."

"Oh God."

"With a paintball."

"Well, that's a relief."

"Although," said Smithy, "if I ever meet that short-arsed backstabbing midget again..."

Bunny paused for a moment, and then, "Are you—"

"I'm allowed use that word, yes. You, not so much."

"Right."

They both went back to looking at their drinks. Bunny ran his finger down the side of the glass.

"So…"

"Y'know," said Smithy, "I really liked that job."

"Really?"

"I mean, not Bernice – she'd have been a modern-day Hitler if she'd got the breaks in life, but the dogs were nice. Certainly better than people, on average."

"Yeah," said Bunny. "I'm sure you could get a job doing it somewhere else. It looked like you were good at it."

Smithy shrugged. "Maybe. I need to do some work on my one-man play idea anyway."

"Oh, right, yeah. The acting. That must be tough."

"It is."

"I mean, there must be limited roles for… "

Smithy turned to look at Bunny. "For what? A midget?"

"I thought that wasn't the good word?"

"I couldn't give a shit about the word. There are lots of words. In all honesty, 'little person' pisses me off more. Makes us sound magical or some shit. No, I don't care about the word, but I do care about the label. Do you know how many times, in his entire portfolio of plays, Shakespeare specifies the height of any of the actors?"

"No."

"Never! He never does. Where does it say Hamlet can't be a dwarf? Or, come to that, that Macbeth can't be black? That King Lear can't be an Asian dude with a cleft lip and a limp? It's acting, for God's sake. It's all about pretending, inhabiting a character. How many gay actors have played straight for decades – and not just on screen? A black man can be president, but he can't be James Bond? Bullshit. Despite their acting chops, Arnie isn't really a robot, Tom Hanks isn't really a cartoon cowboy and Andy Serkis isn't anything that Andy Serkis has ever played. It's make-believe. Step into any multiplex in America and you'll see white dudes of retirement age taking on whole cities with their bare hands, played by guys who, in reality,

166

throw a hissy fit and won't leave their trailers if someone messes up their coffee order, but I can't be anything but the midget? There ain't a word for the kind of bullshit that is."

Bunny tapped a spare beer mat on the countertop. "Fair play. I mean, I never really thought about it, but you're absolutely right."

"Yeah, well," said Smithy, picking up his drink, "it doesn't mean the next time I'm sitting outside an audition with a bunch of chisel-jawed male models with two facial expressions between them that I won't be asked if I'm in the wrong place. Diller gets something similar. Do you know why he started talking to you on Saturday morning?"

Bunny shook his head.

"He's up for an audition for a role in *The Field*, y'know, the John B. Keane play?"

"I know it well."

"So he went looking for a real Irish person. Wanted to develop an ear for the accent."

"Oh."

"Now, don't go feeling weird about it. It's not like you were being used. Hell, he probably told you and you can't remember."

Bunny picked up his pint. "That's true."

"I ran lines with him. He was really good."

"Did you two meet through the acting then?"

"Yeah," said Smithy. "Something like that. We're in the same situational acting troupe."

"A what?"

"Ask me some other time. I'm not in the mood to explain it now."

"Right," said Bunny. He took a sup of his beer and put it back down. "He sounds like a nice lad, this Diller fella."

"Yeah, he's a good guy. You'd like him. Fuck, you did like him? You do like him? You know what I mean. He's a nice kid and he hasn't exactly had it easy. His domestic situation is... well, complicated doesn't begin to cover it. He grew up in and out of the system. He's skinny as a rake and a sensitive soul and yet, somehow, he managed to not get eaten alive. He isn't like you and me. He doesn't have that nasty side he's holding in check all the time. Despite all the shit he's been through, only a little of which I know about, he actually seems to really like people. He's a damn good actor too, and I'm guessing it's because he had to develop that just to survive. Makes him more real than ten of those Stravinsky method narcissists, and odds are still that the part will go to some California pretty boy."

"Here's the thing though," said Bunny. "He's got his flaws too."

Smithy said nothing for a couple of seconds, before adding a reluctant "Yeah."

Bunny went to speak but Smithy put a finger up to stop him. "You don't remember my... " Smithy turned his finger to point at his own head.

Bunny gave him a blank look.

Smithy shook his head. "Man, not for nothing, but that shit is scary. You can't be blanking out, losing whole days."

"I was spiked."

Smithy just looked at Bunny. The McGarry stare was legendary amongst the Dublin criminal fraternity. The legend was that when Bunny, with his lazy left eye, locked in on somebody, nobody could hold his gaze. He'd used it throughout his career in law enforcement to great effect. It was therefore doubly disconcerting when he found himself wilting under Smithy's gaze. His big brown eyes gave the unnerving impression that he was looking right into Bunny's soul.

"Yeah, alright," said Bunny. "I wasn't spiked."

Smithy nodded. "The first step is admitting you have a problem."

"I'll drink to that."

Bunny held his drink out, and with a shake of his head, Smithy clinked glasses with him.

Smithy took a sip and then put his glass back down, placing his hands flat on the bar either side of it. As he spoke, he stared at the drink as if he were expecting it to do something. "So, my thing. Diller, by the way, was the first person I ever told about this. On Saturday, you became the second." Smithy glanced up to see Bunny's blank expression and gave an exasperated smile. "And now you're going to be the third too. I wasn't... I wasn't always a good guy. I was angry at the world and, well, I wasn't too bothered about right and wrong, or legal and illegal. To be honest, I'm still not overly concerned about the second part of that. Still, a few years ago, I was involved in a hit and run."

"Oh."

"I was the 'hit' in that equation. Some stoned housewife in her SUV reversed over me in the car park of a 7-Eleven and then hightailed it out of there. They caught her plate on CCTV. She said she thought she'd hit a dog. Can you believe that? A dog! So anyway, I ended up in hospital – broken collarbone, broken leg, head injuries. Quite the delightful smorgasbord of pain. I'm lying there, angry at the world, just, y'know, basting in my own rage and then – bam! Clear as crystal and live in stereophonic sound, I hear in my head, the voice of God."

Smithy stared at his whiskey once more.

Bunny wasn't sure what to say. "Jesus. That's a hell of a thing alright. Are you very religious?"

"No. Stone-cold fundamentalist atheist. Dust to dust, all that."

"Oh. That must be a bit awkward?"

"Yeah, no kidding. So, I ignore it. It's the drugs. It's PTSD. It's whatever. But it keeps happening. And happening. And happening. I try blocking it out, but it just gets worse. I try drinking myself to oblivion, but it keeps coming back. It is driving me crazy. I would've gone to see a shrink, but I couldn't afford it. Then one day I gave up fighting it. I just started listening to the voice."

"Right."

"Do you know what it kept telling me? 'Help this person, help that person.' And I did, to see if it'd shut up, and guess what? It did – at least for a little while. This nurse who took care of me, nice Puerto Rican lady, her son had got mixed up with some bad people and run off. I went and found him, got him to go back home."

"Fair play."

"Look, I know how this sounds. 'The Voice of God.' But here's the thing: after I did that, I felt better than I had in such a long time. It felt good to help somebody else. So y'know, PTSD, mental illness –

hell, it could be the actual voice of God, I don't pretend to know. All I do know is, pain in the ass that it is, that voice makes me a better person and I... I guess I kinda dig it. Don't get me wrong, I ain't no saint now or nothing like that, but I do listen to the voice when it comes to me."

Smithy picked up his drink and took another sip. Bunny did likewise. They both savoured it for a moment.

"Can I ask," said Bunny, "why did you decide to tell me this if you've only ever told Diller?"

"Because you told me how you were here looking to save your woman. On a big mission and all that and, well, I could relate. Plus, I was really, really drunk. Your bottomless ATM card is the work of the devil."

"Well," said Bunny, "I can't remember it, so I'm guessing you're right. So, hang on – not even Cheryl knows about this?"

"Christ, no!" said Smithy, giving Bunny an appalled look. "The woman comes from Southern Baptist stock, and me and her... Let me put it this way: do you think you could have sex with someone if, right at that moment, you thought God might be talking to them?"

"Oh. Right."

"Yeah. I'm trying to be a better man; I ain't trying to be a celibate one. Only you and Diller know, and to be honest, that's more than enough."

"Speaking of Diller," said Bunny.

"How I know him," Smithy interrupted, "Diller, I mean, is the voice told me to help him, so I did. One of the first. I'm glad I did too. He's a good kid."

"Yeah," said Bunny, "but like I said, he's got his flaws too."

Smithy sighed. "Yeah."

"All today," continued Bunny, "I've been chasing my own tail. I'm not much for this detecting lark, but I got there eventually. Whoever robbed me when, let's be honest, I almost certainly passed out, took my wallet and my phone, but they left me with twenty dollars and the picture of Simone."

"OK."

"The picture, no matter how pissed I am, I always put back in the pocket of my wallet, because drunk or not, I don't stop being me."

Smithy said nothing.

"So, somebody took my wallet, then took the picture out and put it back in my coat. That means they knew what it meant to me."

Smithy let out a deep sigh and put his forehead down on the countertop. "Shit."

"I wasn't ripped off by a stranger."

"No," said Smithy, lifting his head and running his fingers through his hair. "No. I'm guessing you weren't. Damn it, Diller!"

"Did you know?"

Smithy shook his head. "Not for sure, but I had a suspicion."

"I need my stuff back – and fast."

"OK, but..." Smithy turned about in his chair. "But first, I need you to understand. Yeah, he's got a propensity for larceny. It's... it's like a compulsive thing. He's not in control of it."

Bunny pulled a face.

"Need I remind you" – Smithy first pointed at himself – "inveterate gambler who starts fights in bars and then hears the voice of God" – then at Bunny – "heavy drinker who blacks out and wades into fights in bars."

"I was backing you up! Well, I assume I was."

"Exactly my point. I'm just saying, none of us is perfect. He's done wrong, but I'm not telling you where he is until we come to an understanding. No cops and nothing too heavy."

"I'm not a big fan of crime," said Bunny.

"Really? Have you been one hundred per cent inside the law today at all times when trying to track down your stuff?"

Bunny thought about this as he sipped at his beer. "Alright, but that was mostly self-defence."

"Yeah, but not all of it was, was it? Same as I consider myself a moral man, but odds are that, after another drink, I'm going back to Bernice's and stealing a Siberian husky because he deserves a better life than having an a-hole owner who thinks it's OK to turn him into a punchline. Gene frickin' Simmons!"

"Did..." Bunny hesitated.

"What?"

"Did..." Bunny lowered his voice. "Did God tell you to steal it?"

"No, this is all me."

"And nicking my stuff, that was all Diller," said Bunny.

"Yeah, OK. I get it. I'm not saying the kid isn't responsible for his actions. I'm just saying, nature versus nurture. Diller's a good kid by nature but he's a damned thief mostly by circumstance. He had to be, just to survive this long. So, just, y'know, go easy."

"What am I supposed to do? Ask nicely?"

Smithy gave him a look. "We haven't known each other long, Bunny, but I'm going to guess you're really good at knowing how to ask a question."

It was Bunny's turn to sigh. "Alright, you have my word."

"OK."

"So, you know where he is?"

"No," said Smithy. "But I know where he'll be in about an hour."

CHAPTER TWENTY-SEVEN

Douglas Randall smiled.

He was good at smiling. It was an underrated skill. When he'd first got into TV news, he'd been a "weather reporter" on a nothing channel in Montana. They'd only used the title of weather reporter because the producer said it gave the job a bit of gravitas. Plus, it meant the kid that did the weather could also be sent out to state fairs to report on the size of livestock and pies – and people after they'd eaten all those damn pies. Doug Randall, as he'd been known back then, had been the know-nothing, eager puppy yapping at the heels of the revered top dog of channel MNN, Terry McNamara, the face of Montana news. Terry had called himself a mentor. In reality, that meant Doug spent a lot of time sitting at bars with Terry before pouring him into the back of a cab and making sure he got home in as many pieces as he'd been in when he'd left that morning. Terry was a master. He could've made the phonebook sound exciting. After the broadcast, Doug would stay behind for hours and read and reread Terry's script off the teleprompter, trying to learn the skill. Doug had always been ambitious. He'd wanted to be a news anchor ever since he'd been old enough to know what one was. He owed Terry for that.

One night, when they'd been out drinking, Doug had helped a particularly smashed Terry all the way back to his "in town" apartment, which he'd got for convenience – Terry's wife no longer being able to stand the sight of him having proven particularly inconvenient. After Doug had managed to get Terry onto the sofa, he'd been instructed to sit down. Terry told him that if he wanted to succeed in the news business there were three things he needed to do.

The first thing he needed to do was drop this Doug crap and be Douglas. Doug was a guy who helped you move a wardrobe and came over to your house on Super Bowl Sunday and dominated the dip. Douglas, on the other hand, was a man of importance who could be trusted to handle the news.

The second thing Doug, now Douglas, needed to do was work on his smile. It wasn't a dental thing. Douglas's teeth were perfect – he'd spent large chunks of his first few pay cheques making sure of it. Terry explained the all-important smile. Anyone could look serious talking about the economy going down the toilet or bombs being dropped – that was easy. The tricky bit – the bit that made a career – was the "other news" smile. At the back end of the broadcast, when the stories got lighter, that was where you made hay. It was the finest of balancing acts: too jolly and you couldn't be trusted; too sombre and you lacked personality. As Terry had explained it, "You're in people's homes every night. A lot of the time, they're eating dinner with you. Alone. You give 'em that soft half-smile, it's like you're sharing something. You're a friend. A partner. You have a relationship. You're someone they can trust." Then Terry had given Doug that patented McNamara smile, the one that made him beloved throughout the state by people who didn't even know why.

The third thing that Douglas needed to do, in Terry's opinion, turned out to be Terry. In one fluid motion, he stood and dropped his pants. Douglas stood, slapped Terry fraternally on the shoulder, thanked him for the great advice and walked out. The last thing he saw as he closed the door was Terry standing there, holding his penis, his confused expression that of a guy who couldn't understand why the empty cab that'd passed him by hadn't stopped when he waved.

Terry had been right on all three counts. Doug had been Douglas from that moment forth. Douglas had spent hours with a camcorder and in front of the mirror, perfecting the "other news" smile. And, to the surprise of both of them, Terry's penis had indeed made Douglas's career – in particular, the crippling urinary infection that hospitalised him in the first week of April 1996. Douglas got to step in as emergency anchor. As luck would have it, that was the week Theodore John Kaczynski, aka the Unabomber, was arrested at his shack in the mountains, just up the road near Lincoln, Montana. Three days later, Terry was back, by which time "the kid" had been given the kind of exposure that makes a career. A year later, he was picked up by Philadelphia's number two station, and then a few years after that, Channel 8 News, New York. Then, Douglas had hit his ceiling, although he hadn't known it for quite some time. Still, it had been a good run. Tonight, he and his wife Tina were out with the station's owner, news director and three of the producers, ostensibly celebrating Douglas's fifteen-year anniversary with the station. Ostensibly, because really it was about the other person at the table – Kristy Munroe. She was Harvard smart, California pretty and Tonya Harding ambitious, and she was his new co-anchor. Douglas knew that the higher-ups were making sure that Douglas felt like he was still the alpha dog in the newsroom – mainly because he wasn't, and everybody knew that. This time yesterday, Douglas had been hunkered down with Tina, strategising his defence of the big chair. After all, there had been other Kristys. This wasn't his first Kristy and it wouldn't be his last. This time yesterday, that fight had been all-consuming. Now, Douglas couldn't give two shits about Kristy. That was because today, the news had stood right in front of him and dropped its pants.

When the first reports had come in, he'd thought that maybe it was someone else. There had to be hundreds – thousands – of dominatrixes in New York. Statistically, lots of them probably had places in Astoria. Every new titbit tossed out by the NYPD had been another hole below the waterline for the version of events Douglas had been trying to construct in his head. Then he'd sat there, on camera, reading out the news that confirmed that his world was indeed crumbling around him. The cops would be looking into the client list of Amy DeSilva, real name Amy Daniels, sooner rather than later. If she had kept a diary, any records – anything – he was done for. Up until that point, it had been easy to convince himself that he could keep his ordinary life and that other thing separate. He'd constructed a world where they could peacefully co-exist. He loved his wife. Seeing Amy had not been about that.

Nowhere in all of that carefully constructed narrative had he considered what would happen if his dominatrix became America's most wanted. He'd briefly considered coming clean, but he hadn't known where to start. Tina would divorce him, Channel 8 would drop him, and Kristy would feast on his carcass while being careful not to get any on her Armani suit. So, in the absence of any form of plan, Douglas did what he did best and smiled.

The head of news had just finished telling a story that everyone at the table had heard at least a half-dozen times. Kristy laughed so hard that the TV comedian at the next table looked over a little envious. Douglas chuckled appreciatively and then excused himself. He'd needed to pee since the first course, but he'd been holding it. He couldn't risk going to the john twice in a meal; it'd emphasise his age. Dan Rather could sit there in a nappy if he had to, but Douglas knew that he wasn't Dan Rather.

He moved through the tables, nodding smiles at faces he knew or people who looked at him like they knew him. This was La Mora – everyone in this restaurant was somebody, you had to be just to get in. He headed down the hall towards the bathrooms, passing a large African American gentleman coming the other way. Douglas was ninety per cent sure he was that rapper, the one who was supposed to be leading a revolution against the fat cats. Hey, even the voices of their generation needed a little hundred-dollar lobster every now and then. As he walked towards the gents, a blonde woman in sunglasses poked her head out of the disabled bathroom on the right. Maybe that was where the rapper had just come from. Rumour had it, that very room was where the former backup quarterback for the New York Jets had managed to get a waitress pregnant between courses. The joke had gone that it was the only pass he'd completed successfully in years.

Douglas smiled at the blonde as he walked by.

"Douglas!" She spoke in an urgent whisper. He gave her a second look but kept moving. While it was flattering, the last thing he needed was a quickie in the disabled bathroom. He had more than enough troubles already.

"Douglas, get in here."

He froze, his foot hanging in mid-air. It couldn't be. It could not be. There was no way it could be. "Douglas!"

He closed his eyes. It was. He knew well what she sounded like when she was annoyed with him. For three years, he'd been paying her to be angry with him every second Thursday.

The blonde who wasn't a blonde slipped her head back inside as the door to the ladies' opened and someone who used to be someone stepped out. Douglas smiled and, thinking fast, fished his phone out of his pocket.

He could just go to the john. Maybe she'd be gone when he got back out? Being a wanted murderer surely meant you couldn't hang around in disabled bathrooms indefinitely. How did she even get in here? It had taken him six weeks and some begging just to get a reservation for his anniversary last year.

"Douglas! Get in here."

Maybe it was the fact that he was used to doing what she said, but he found himself checking the coast was clear and then stepping into the disabled bathroom. She closed the door behind him. "We don't have much time."

"Much time?" Douglas said. "We have no time. You can't be here. We don't know each other."

"Relax, Douglas."

"Relax? My wife, my boss, my... everything is outside, and I'm in the disabled bathroom with a murderer."

In some part of his brain that didn't seem to understand the severity of the situation, Douglas registered that the blonde hair was a wig. Still, she'd look pretty good if she went that way.

"I'm being set up. A client told me something he shouldn't, and someone wants me gone really badly. Come on, Douglas, you know me."

"I... I... No, I don't. We've never met. How did you even find me?"

"I followed you from your office."

"You've been to my office?" His voice rose a half octave. "What if somebody saw you?"

"Then I'd be in handcuffs now." She held out a piece of paper. "Here, take this."

"What?"

"Lanark Lane Investments are into some dodgy shit. There's a couple of phrases the guy said that must mean something."

"The guy you killed?"

The slap stung his face and focused his attention. It also gave him a slight erection. "Focus, Douglas. I'm innocent. I'm being set up and what is on that piece of paper will prove it. You need to look into it. It's some kind of insider dealing shit."

"That's not really my area."

Amy clenched her fist and held it to her forehead. "I'm being hunted, Douglas – I'm not looking for a stock tip. Just do it."

"Go to the police then."

"I can't. They're... Just look into it. If it's nothing, then it's nothing. What've you got to lose?"

Douglas felt light-headed. "What've I got to lose? Are you kidding me?"

"Stop whining, Douglas. Just do it. My life is in your hands." She opened the door and glanced out quickly. "I'll be in touch."

"Oh God, please don't..."

She was gone; the door closed behind her.

Douglas leaned over to lock it and then he unfolded the piece of paper. In a neat hand was written "*Millennium Falcon* – Admiral Ackbar – or something like that." Gibberish. Great. Douglas scrunched up the piece of paper and made to toss it into the toilet. He couldn't do it. After a moment's hesitation, he smoothed it out and placed it in the inside pocket of his jacket.

Then he looked into the mirror, but, try as he might, he couldn't make himself smile.

CHAPTER TWENTY-EIGHT

He sat there, breathing.

All around him, people were doing vocal exercises, reading and rereading lines, closing their eyes to focus.

All he was doing was breathing. Slowly, calmly. In. Out. In. Out. He'd not gone anywhere to learn this technique; he'd picked it up as a baby. God-given talent.

He smiled, because looking confident was important – Smithy had told him that. When they shouted action, it was as much about acting the part of someone who knew what they were doing as acting the actual part. They didn't actually shout "action" much though; that was a TV thing. In an audition they just fed you a line and off you went.

Beside him, a well-meaning guy with an English accent leaned in and held out a sheet. "Have you got a copy of the lines?"

He smiled back. "I'm good, thanks."

Everyone else in the room had an agent, and probably a few auditions a week. He didn't, and so he found out about calls by scouring *Backstage* or through a couple of other techniques he'd come up with. Still, he got an audition every other week – at best – and a lot of the time he turned up without being on the list, which occasionally worked. He didn't need the pages. Since last Tuesday, when he'd heard about this, he'd learned it. Not the audition piece, not all of his character's lines – he'd learned the whole damn play. Maybe they'd need another role filled, you never knew. You gotta want it. Nobody wanted it more than him.

A woman walked in carrying a clipboard. "Jackson Diller?"

He raised his hand and smiled.

Every time he walked onto a stage, he got a thrill. It didn't matter that there wasn't an audience – at least, not a proper audience. Diller had only been in a couple of am-dram performances up until this point, but he'd treated every one like it was career defining. He put his satchel down at the side of the stage. You learn that after a few. They like you to get straight out after you're done, often through another door.

"Jackson Diller?" said someone that he assumed was the director.

He nodded. "That's correct, sir."

He could hear it in the voice – that touch of surprise that he was black.

"We don't seem to have your headshot?"

"Oh," said Diller, "that's weird. I'll send in another one."

"Great. Thanks."

The reason they didn't have his headshot was that, unbeknownst to the woman at the casting agency, Diller's résumé had been slipped into the pile of candidates for the role by her secretary. The reason there was no headshot was because that way he wouldn't receive a call beforehand to tell him the role had been filled. He was a big believer that half the battle was getting in front of people. Still, that question in the voice... Too polite to directly say anything, of course, but still, two strikes down before the first pitch. It didn't matter – he was going to swing for the fences anyway.

"I see here that you're Irish, Jackson?"

"That's right, sir, I am indeed."

He'd given the casting agent's secretary a dozen variations on his

CV by now, each giving him a different nationality, because any bump was a bump. Besides, he was good at voices and he did his research.

"Great!" said the voice. "We've heard some interesting attempts at your accent throughout the day."

Diller laughed. "I can imagine ye did alright."

"Where are you from?"

"Cork, as it happens."

"OK, well then. You're reading for the role of Tadgh. In your own time..."

Diller's eyes were adjusting to the lights. He could see the director and his producer clearly now. They were smiling up at him wearily. He wasn't sure which was which, but one looked intrigued while the other was mentally ordering his dinner. It had no doubt been a long day. This was the last casting call of the day for a play with quite a few roles in it.

Diller's eyes shifted. A few rows back, he could see another figure sitting there, smiling up at him too. For a moment, he froze. It felt like a bowling ball had just thumped into the bottom of his stomach. Instant karma's gonna get you...

Diller turned and ran off the far side of the stage.

The theatre had been taking advantage of the dark week by getting some necessary repairs done. The manager was new to the job, which was why he hadn't realised that they couldn't have workmen banging away while auditions were going on. He'd been forced to send them home when they'd come in that morning. Unbeknownst to him, the work would be even further delayed, as right now the crew's foreman was behind bars, having unexpectedly returned home to find his wife and his brother in flagrante on top of his kitchen table, which was covered in his collection of *Spiderman* comic books. This traumatic incident would inspire the manager to follow his secret ambition to become a playwright, with his debut play *What A Tangled Web* opening on that very stage eighteen months later – and closing after two badly received performances.

In the foreman's defence, before he'd left the site he had at least put up some yellow tape indicating that the far side of the stage was out of bounds, displaying a concern for health and safety not commonly found in multiple murderers. He was told nobody needed to be over there for the auditions, so it should be fine. He'd double-checked with the manager that this was definitely the case, because he was a suspicious man by nature – although, as it turned out, he was suspicious in all the wrong directions.

To be fair to the manager, he hadn't anticipated somebody needing to run for their life.

For all his preparation, Diller hadn't seen that coming either.

The other thing he hadn't seen coming was the piece of scaffolding that he ran into, knocking himself out cold.

CHAPTER TWENTY-NINE

Diller opened his eyes, saw Bunny McGarry looking down at him and promptly shut them again.

The toe of a boot nudged him gently in the side. "I saw ye. C'mon. Wakey-wakey, rise and shine."

Diller opened his eyes wide and looked around him. "Where am I?"

"We're in an alley. For some reason I seem to be spending a lot of today in them."

Diller looked at Bunny, his big eyes full of fear. "Who are you?"

"What?"

"Who are you?" Diller repeated.

"I'm Bunny, we met on Saturday and then you—"

"I've never seen you before in my life!"

Diller looked around the alley, with its unhelpfully high walls and Bunny standing between him and the exit.

"Diller, stop pissing about."

"Wait, I think... I can." He lowered his head. "Oh no, it's happened again."

Bunny tilted his head and looked at Diller. "What has?"

"I... I was in a serious car accident about eighteen months ago and it affected my short-term memory. I can't form new memories. It's a medical thing. Every morning when I wake up, it's like the morning of the accident, and the days since then have never happened."

"Bullshit."

Diller shook his head. "I'm serious. I'm sorry that I don't know you. I don't know a lot of things. It's really confusing."

"Oh," said Bunny. "Right."

"Is Barack Obama still president?"

"No."

"Oh. Who—"

"Let's not get into that."

Diller stared off into the distance for a moment and then started slowly getting to his feet. "Well, I should probably get home." He stopped, a thought hitting him. "I hope I haven't moved."

"So," said Bunny, "you don't remember anything that's happened in the last eighteen months?"

Diller shook his head.

"So how do you know it's been eighteen months since your accident?"

"Umm, what?"

"For future reference, while this is a nice idea, there are a couple of flaws in it. One, the date issue previously mentioned, and two, you're relying on the person you're talking to having not seen the 2004 film *50 First Dates* starring Drew Barrymore and Adam Sandler."

"I don't know what you..." Diller feinted left and then darted right, trying to get around Bunny, who easily stepped into his path and shoulder-blocked him into a dumpster. Diller cringed as Bunny grabbed two fistfuls of his T-shirt and moved his face to just a couple of inches from his.

"Sorry, Bunny, sorry. In my defence, I didn't expect you to be a big fan of romantic comedies." He tried to give a winning smile.

"I am, as it happens. *Four Weddings* is an all-time classic. I cry every time. Are you much of a crier, Diller?"

Diller looked up into Bunny's lazy-eyed stare and then looked away. "I think I'm about to be."

And then Bunny let him go. "You're not, actually."

"Oh?"

"Yeah."

Bunny turned his back and took a couple of steps away. Diller looked at the mouth the alley, to which he now had an unobstructed path. He was fast, too. In one of the high schools he'd attended, he'd unofficially come fourth in the 200 metres, despite not being in the race. It had just happened to coincide with a linebacker's discovery that Diller was going above and beyond in his attempts to help his girlfriend with her homework.

His instincts told him to run, but for some reason his legs didn't move.

"I'll be honest with you," said Bunny. "I'm hurt that somebody who I think I considered a friend screwed me over."

Diller opened his mouth to speak, but the lies wouldn't come. He looked at the ground instead.

"Well," continued Bunny, "I suppose that's New York for you. It's dog eat dog."

Diller let his legs go from under him as he slid down the side of the dumpster and sat on the ground, suddenly very tired. "Honestly, for what it's worth, I felt awful."

"You could've fooled me."

"Seriously, I know you aren't going to believe me, but as soon as I got home, I knew I'd made a terrible mistake. I went back to Times Square the next morning, trying to find you, but you were gone. I... I can't make my rent this month and, well, your card... I figured... I'm sorry, it was an incredibly shitty thing to do."

Bunny stood looking at the wall. "Yeah, you won't get any arguments from me on that score."

"I never even tried to use the card. I was going to go talk to Smithy – see if he had any ideas on how I could find you and give it back. I know you've no reason to believe that, but honestly..."

Diller put his hands to his satchel and stopped, suddenly aware he was wearing it. He'd not been when he'd knocked himself out. He flipped it open and felt around inside, past the now squished peanut butter and jelly sandwich he'd made for himself and the battered copy of the script to *The Godfather* that he brought everywhere with him. His fingers found the zip pocket at the back. He pulled out the wallet, the charger and the phone and held them up. "Here."

Bunny took them without a word and placed them in his pockets.

"I owe you the eighty dollars cash you had in there. With God as my witness, I'll pay you back." Diller started slapping his pockets. "I think I got twenty bucks here."

Bunny waved him away. "Keep it."

Diller stopped and then stared at his own feet. "I really am sorry."

"Yeah, you said."

"I feel like shit. If you're going to work me over—"

Bunny shook his head. "No. That's not me."

Diller should have felt better, but he didn't. He looked down at his hands. "Can I ask… why didn't you just take your stuff while I was out cold?"

"I wanted to give you the chance to give it back to me."

"I see. Well, thanks for that. I didn't deserve it."

Bunny started walking away, back up the alley. "No, you probably didn't. G'luck, Diller."

Diller sprung to his feet. "Wait, you can't just…"

"What?" said Bunny, not turning around.

"Don't just… Let me make it up to you."

Bunny turned the corner and started walking down the street. Diller realised that they'd been behind the theatre the whole time. Bunny strode purposefully towards the 215th Street subway station.

"C'mon," said Diller. "Don't be like this."

"Like what?"

"All quiet and shit."

"I've nothing else to say, Diller. Good day to you."

Diller dodged around Bunny and started walking backwards in front of him. "Come on, we can't leave it like this."

"What would you prefer, me passed out drunk and you skipping off with my stuff again?"

"Ouch. OK, I deserved that."

"D'ye think?"

Diller hopped left and then right to avoid a dog and its owner, a woman in a furry hat who looked appalled at whatever this new type of walking was.

"OK," said Diller, "how about you hit me?"

"It's a kind offer, but no, thank you."

"Please? You'll feel better, I'll feel better."

"I seriously doubt that. When I punch someone, they rarely feel better – that's assuming they can feel anything."

Bunny glanced around, noticing that they were getting noticed. "Would you stop pissing about?"

"Is it annoying you?" Diller stumbled slightly as his foot caught on a loose paving stone, but he recovered quickly.

"Yes, it is."

"Enough to hit me?"

"No."

A Hispanic-looking guy with large headphones glowered at Diller as he walked by.

"So, what'll it take?"

"I'm not some violent lunatic, y'know."

"I know a karaoke bar that says different."

Bunny grabbed Diller's T-shirt again, this time to prevent him bashing into the back of the pedestrians stopped at the crosswalk they'd just reached.

Diller glanced around and then raised his voice. "Ladies and gentlemen, my name is Jackson Diller and I have wronged this fine and decent man."

In the group of a dozen or so people, Bunny noticed the split was about fifty-fifty between those looking at them and those pointedly not looking at them.

"He is too kind-hearted to do it himself, but if anyone would be kind enough to punch me on his behalf, I will give them ten dollars."

"Oh, for feck's sake," said Bunny, blushing. "Don't mind him."

Diller pulled a twenty-dollar bill from his pocket and held it aloft. "I'm serious. One punch, ten dollars, zero repercussions."

Some of the pedestrians smirked; others just looked confused.

"Ten dollars?" said Diller, waggling his eyebrows and rubbing the note back and forth between his fingers. "It is a once-in-a-lifetime offer."

A short Latina lady in a maid's uniform stepped forward and punched Diller right in the stomach. He folded faster than a badly written play by a theatre manager who had no feel for theatre, crumpling to the ground at Bunny's feet.

Diller's voice came out in a pained croak. "Thank you."

The maid bent down and took the twenty-dollar bill from his hand.

"I'm gonna need change."

Bunny stepped forward and patted the maid on the back. "'Tis alright. Consider it a bonus."

She went to kick Diller and Bunny pulled her away. "Ah-ah, no overtime. Mind how you go."

The pedestrian light changed and the crowd moved off, a couple pulling out phones, no doubt to tweet about what they'd just seen.

"You're a fecking eejit, d'ye know that?"

"I've no idea what that is, but OK."

Bunny bent down to pick Diller up. Diller grabbed his outstretched hand and then stopped. "Wait – I have to know: at the audition, was my Cork accent any good?"

Bunny thought about it and then nodded. "'Twas spot on. Fair play to you."

"Thanks."

CHAPTER THIRTY

Bunny sat on the bench and looked up at the gathering clouds. The day had started bright and fresh, but the humidity had built steadily, and now he looked up into an evening sky filled with angry purple clouds, ready to dump on New York. He looked down again at the phone in his hand. It was unlike any other phone he'd ever seen.

The fella on the boat, the one who'd met him and then brought him into America via the back door, had made a big deal of the phone when he'd given it to him. They'd been sitting in his cabin at the time, two men perched uncomfortably on the edge of an unmade bed. "It's a RoamZone, encased in hardened rubber and Gorilla Glass – it is indestructible."

The guy was in his mid twenties and had a face that Bunny had instantly disliked. It was based on nothing bar a strong suspicion that he was the sort who owned a Bluetooth headset. He had that look about him.

"Jesus," said Bunny, "that's incredible! Indestructible, you say? That'll come in handy. Can I get the GAA results on it?"

"The what?"

"The results for the games back in Ireland."

"Erm, no. It doesn't have a browser function."

Bunny tutted. "Feck."

"I don't think you understand. This phone is untraceable and works anywhere in the world. It has a special NSA-designed software on it that offers an incredible level of encryption. The signal is bounced off seven satellites."

"Yeah, I suppose. I just, y'know... It'd be good if it could do all that *and* get the scores. Never mind. So, you say it's indestructible?"

"Yes."

Bunny had then heaved it at the wall so hard it had bounced off and hit him on the foot.

"Fuck!"

"What?" asked Bunny.

"What in the hell are you doing?"

"What do you mean what am I doing? Sure, I'm testing it!"

"Stop! You're going to break it."

"You said it was indestructible?"

"Virtually. Almost. I didn't say... Look, just don't do that."

Bunny had picked it up. "Yeah, look – there's a bit of a crack there now. Oh no, wait..." He blew on it. "It was only a bit of hair. Best of three."

Bunny had pulled his hand back to try it again and the junior spy dude had grabbed it to stop him. "Jesus, are you insane?"

He had clearly been upset. This wasn't how the Q scenes in Bond movies normally went.

"So, what kinda plan is it on?" asked Bunny.

"It's not on a plan!" he'd snapped. "This phone rings one number. It will get you through to Agent Dove—"

"Who?"

"Agent Dove."

"I don't know anyone by that name."

"She..." He'd stopped and looked at Bunny. "Are you trying to get me to tell you her real name?"

"Absolutely not."

He absolutely had been. Bunny didn't like not knowing who he was dealing with. He'd been hoping to wangle it out of the lad while he was discombobulated.

"Look," said the junior spymaster, "it's really simple. This phone rings, it'll be Agent Dove on the other end. And if you need to contact her, unlock it with your thumbprint, like we just did, and press that one icon there…" He pointed at an icon of a green phone that sat alone on the screen. "That'll get you through to Agent Dove, 24/7, 365 days a year."

"Wait, I can only ring her and nobody else?"

"Yes."

"Feck's sake, what you're essentially giving me here is the world's most expensive two tin cans and a piece of string. What's the next bit of kit? A magnifying glass and some talcum powder to take fingerprints?"

Bunny looked at the icon, took a deep breath and pressed it. This was the first time he'd tried it – or at least, he assumed so. He really hoped the drunken eejit version of himself that he'd been chasing all day hadn't made a fool of him in yet another way on Saturday.

There was a series of small electronic sounds, possibly the sound of the signal bouncing off seven satellites. Bunny glanced up again into the New York sky that at 9pm was probably about as dark as it ever got. It started ringing. On the third ring, she picked up.

"Hello, Mr McGarry." He'd only met her once, but it was the voice of the woman he knew as Agent Dove.

"Howerya, how's it going?"

"I was intending to call you."

"Were ye?" said Bunny. "Isn't that lovely? Great. Well, this'll save you a few bucks off your bill."

"Have you made some progress in your mission?"

"Ehm, yeah, yeah. 'Tis going well. Lot of irons in the fire. Strong leads, all of that."

"I see. Is there something I can help you with?"

"Well, now – I'm glad you asked. I don't know if you get the New York news in your secret base in a volcano or wherever you are, but there's been a murder in New York."

"You killed someone?" Her voice dropped a couple of degrees, and it hadn't been that warm to begin with.

"No. God no. Not at all."

"Good."

"In fact, the person accused of it didn't do it either."

"I see. Does this have a point?"

"Yes. You see, the murder in question is all over the news. It involves a woman called Amy Daniels—"

"The dominatrix?"

"That's the one, yeah."

"That has been national news, Mr McGarry."

"Has it? Fancy that. Well, the good news is she definitely didn't do it because, y'see, she was with me at the time."

There was silence for long enough at the other end of the line that Bunny wondered if one of the seven satellites had banged into one of the other six. Finally Dove spoke again. "Let me get this straight, Mr McGarry. You've been in New York around a week and you have been spending your time with a dominatrix?"

"Well, not like, y'know... None of the spanky spanky. Not like that."

"You are supposed to be keeping a low profile."

"I'm trying to."

Her voice became a near snarl. "Not hard enough, apparently. I also received an email about some expenses on your card. Would now be a good time to question a charge from a strip club?"

"Now, I can explain that."

"Really?"

"Yes, ehm... I was, well, I was in a strip club."

"I see."

"Look," said Bunny, "I'm trying to tell you – this woman, Amy

Daniels, she's being set up. There's some Wall Street lads up to something naughty and they've got some serious people working with them. Linked into law enforcement in some way. I think something very dodgy is going on."

"I'm confused. How exactly does any of this relate to finding Simone Delamere?"

"Well, it doesn't."

"That is what you are here to do, Mr McGarry. We went to great lengths to allow you to do so."

"Look, I'm trying to do that, alright? This just happened. What am I supposed to do? Walk away and leave the poor girl on her own?"

"Yes, Mr McGarry, yes. You are here to find a woman, a particular woman."

"That's exactly what I told her."

The temperature of the call dipped below freezing. "Excuse me?"

"I mean..."

"You are telling people why you are here?"

"Well, only – I mean, not the full story, only like a bit."

"I see. I'm afraid this will not work, Mr McGarry. You are not the person we thought you were and we need to pursue other solutions to the Simone Delamere problem."

"Now hang on."

"Consider yourself cut loose. Goodbye."

"Wait!"

The line went dead. Bunny jabbed at the green phone icon, but nothing happened. He tried turning the phone off and on again. When he did so, and then placed his thumb on the reader, nothing happened.

A passing jogger jumped with fright as he screamed "Feck it!" at a volume that no noise-cancelling headphones in the world would've been able to keep out.

He slammed the phone on the sidewalk and jumped up and down on it.

After about sixty seconds of this, he stopped and took a few deep breaths. The first few thick drops of rain had started to splash onto the pavement around him.

He started to walk off and then he stopped, turned around and went back to pick up the phone.

The screen was still intact. That was pretty impressive alright.

CHAPTER THIRTY-ONE

Cole took a deep breath and knocked.

"Enter."

When he opened the door into the suite, Mrs Miller was running on a treadmill. The suite was large – the kind that New York has for when sheikhs or CEOs drop by. Mrs Miller was a CEO, of sorts. Amidst the cream carpets and tasteful furnishings, the treadmill she was on faced the floor-to-ceiling windows that looked out across the city. They were currently providing an excellent view of the city being hammered by torrential rain. Brief flashes of lightning could be seen skittering across the horizon. A laptop sat on a stand beside Miller. It was playing ABBA.

"Oh," he said, "sorry if this is a bad time. I can come back."

"No, now is fine."

He crossed the room, stopping beside her. She lowered her speed a couple of notches and kept running.

"And how are your charges?"

"Messrs Bradley and Clarke are back at their apartment. Jameson and Newton are on them until morning. They know we're up on their phones and laptops, so won't try anything stupid, although Mr

Bradley has been googling 'explosives inside the body' and all variations thereof."

"I'm sure he has."

"He has also carried out an extensive self-examination. He tried to get Mr Clarke to take a look, but he refused."

"Understandably."

"They're complying. They won't do anything stupid."

Miller took a glug of water. "I wish I shared your confidence. Stupid things are apparently what they do."

Cole said nothing in response. He wasn't sure why he had been called here, but this was not an organisation that, when it met triumph and disaster, treated those two imposters just the same. In fact, those responsible for the meeting with disaster had the tendency to suffer their own personal disaster soon after. Cole knew that better than anyone, which was why he was glad the meeting was here. His death would be difficult to get out of these carpets without questions being asked, even for someone with Miller's reach. Still, he was relieved to see there was no tarpaulin on the floor.

Miller slowed her run to a brisk walk and ran a towel over her face. "How would you describe your recent performance, Mr Cole?"

"Poor, ma'am."

"Yes. Poor would certainly be one word for it. Catastrophic would be another."

"I wish to apologise again. I messed up on the Clarke thing with the dominatrix. I should have known about the second phone."

"Yes, you should have. I assume that all avenues of communication have been..."

Cole nodded. "Firmly closed. I guarantee that he has no way of communicating with anyone without us knowing about it."

"And how is the police investigation going?"

"They have yet to find the girl's client list. They are still looking for the email account. When they find it, all of the correspondence with Mr Clarke will, of course, be gone. There are a few names there that will attract press attention though."

"Yes. I will also be adding a couple more."

Cole paused. "Is that wise, ma'am?"

She glanced in his direction. "Certainly wiser than questioning me has proven in the past."

Cole berated himself internally. "I apologise. I just meant—"

"Music off."

Cole hesitated for a moment and then took a step towards the laptop.

"Music off," repeated an electronic voice.

Cole felt embarrassed as Miller raised an eyebrow at him.

"Seeing as we have incurred such considerable unforeseen expense in dealing with the unexpected issue, I've decided to turn it to our advantage."

Cole nodded, before adding, "We have people in the investigation. Rest assured. We will get an hour's head start if they get any real intel on the location of the girl—"

"Woman," interrupted Miller. "She's twenty-three. Let's not infantilise her, shall we?"

Cole nodded. "Woman. Or if somehow she ends up in custody, we have contingencies in place to ensure she won't have much time to talk."

"Yes," said Miller. "Yet more expense."

Cole went to speak and then said nothing, reasoning that he should stop digging.

"Then," continued Miller, "there is the matter of this supposedly homeless Scottish man."

"Irish," Cole corrected.

"Mr Bradley said…"

"Irish," Cole repeated. "I heard the accent when he and I fought."

"When he beat you, you mean?"

"With all due respect, ma'am, he did not beat me. I had him and then…"

"Yes, yes," she said, not even attempting to keep the frustration out of her voice. "You allowed a junior patrolman to pull a gun on you and then disarm you."

"With all due respect, ma'am, what would you have had me do?"

"At any point in our time together, did I give you the impression that I would be unduly upset about collateral damage?"

"A dead cop would bring attention."

"Nothing we can't handle. Not compared to the problem Ms Daniels presents."

"As soon as we have a lead," said Cole, "rest assured, I will deal with that."

"No," replied Miller, "you will not. I have taken that out of your hands."

Cole opened his mouth to say something, but stopped.

"I also sensed that you were" – she paused to consider the appropriate term – "uncomfortable with our recently acquired guest."

Cole shrugged. "I understand the necessity of the hostage."

"Yes," said Miller. "Necessity is a good word. Do you believe Mr Clarke will stay in line now?"

"Absolutely. He won't do anything to endanger his sister. As long as he..."

They were interrupted by a male voice – human, this time – coming from the laptop's speakers. "Thirty-minute check – no confirmation. Brief sighting but subject wearing a hooded top covering face. No confirmation."

Cole looked at the laptop, expecting a clarification from Miller that was not forthcoming. Instead, she pressed a button on the treadmill and began to slow to a stop.

"Do you enjoy your work, Mr Cole?"

Cole paused, taken aback by the question. "I don't know if 'enjoy' is the right word."

"Lola enjoys her work."

"Again, with all due respect ma'am, Lola is—"

Miller stepped off the treadmill and faced him. "What Lola is, Mr Cole, is efficient. Yes, she has her... peccadilloes, but they do not impact on her work. Quite the opposite. She maintains her edge – something you seem to have lost."

Cole stiffened. "I assure you, I am still one hundred per cent committed to the mission."

"Good. I would be so upset to lose you." She said it in such a way that he was left in no doubt the loss would be permanent, terminal and entirely his.

The voice from the laptop chimed in again: "Contact. Someone at the door. Male entering…"

"Screen on," said Miller, and the laptop screen sprung into life. The picture showed a view of a brownstone building with large windows, focused on one apartment in particular. The view was obscured by the heavy rain teeming down.

Miller picked up a headset and placed it on her ear. "Stand by for confirmation."

Miller and Cole stood side by side, looking at the screen. "Ms Daniels used a landline to call her aunt an hour ago, to reassure her father that it was all a big mistake."

"How did the police—"

"They didn't. I had other sources," said Miller, as if that explained how the tapping of a subject's relatives could be so easily achieved.

And now Cole knew why he was here. It was so he could witness others fixing the problem that his mistake had created. It was for him to be humiliated.

The camera was pointing down at a forty-five-degree angle, meaning that they could only see two sets of legs as they walked across the hardwood floors.

They watched for a couple of minutes as they shifted about, then the larger figure walked towards the window.

He stood there – framing himself perfectly.

"That's him!" said Cole. "The Irishman. One hundred per cent confirmed."

Miller pressed a button on the side and spoke into the headset. "That is confirmation on both. Sweep team, stand by. Eagle One, you are go."

"Roger that," said the voice. "Should I take the secondary now?"

"Negative. Wait for a clean shot on the primary. He will be dealt with afterwards."

"Confirmed."

Miller looked at Cole. "The woman has a list of high-profile clients who are no doubt very nervous right now. It would appear one of them may be about to go to great lengths to ensure her silence."

CHAPTER THIRTY-TWO

Amy opened the door.

"Did you check the peephole?" asked Bunny.

"Yes, Grandma," she said, "I checked the peephole. I'm not an idiot."

She turned and walked away. Bunny followed in behind her and shut the door.

Bunny held a bag up. "I picked up some doughnuts. I couldn't think of anything hot that didn't have meat in it."

"Really?"

He shrugged. "Sorry."

"So?"

"What?"

Amy rolled her eyes. "Did you get your stuff back?"

"Ehm, yes. Yes, I did."

"Fantastic! Have you called this Agent Dove woman then?"

"Yeah, I have." Amy could see it in his body language before he said it. "It's not good. She won't help us."

"Why the hell not?"

"It... Well, look, it doesn't matter, but she wants nothing to do with it. To be honest, she was horrified that I'd anything to do with this."

"Great." Amy moved away and sat back down on the couch.

"Don't worry," said Bunny, "I'll think of something else."

"Actually, I already have." Amy picked up one of the oversized cushions and hugged it to herself as she spoke. "When I came back, I was checking up on the news."

"Came back?" Bunny's tone was horrified. "You went out? Are ye fecking mental?"

"Relax," said Amy. "What was I supposed to do? Sit around waiting for you to come charging in on your big white stallion and save me? Screw that. Where would I be if you hadn't got your stuff back, or you'd not come back at all or... Well, look at what you just told me. The woman was useless to us. It's lucky I didn't sit home."

Bunny moved across the room. "But what if someone had seen ye?"

"The only person who saw me was the one who was supposed to. I took precautions."

"Alright, but..."

"Look," said Amy, "forget that and listen to me." She pointed at the muted TV. "I'm trying to tell you, I just saw a news conference. The lead detective said that they believe the time of death to have been between 5pm and 8pm yesterday."

"And?"

"And, you big dummy, I was with you then. You're my alibi!"

She smiled across at him. Bunny stood there not saying anything.

"I know what you're going to say – that whoever Matt and his asshole buddies are in league with, they've a link to the cops – but, I've been thinking. I have a law professor who is pretty cool, we could go to her first. Or, I, umm, happen to know a guy from Channel 8 News. In fact, it was him I went to see." Amy looked at Bunny expectantly. "You've stopped talking. Why have you stopped talking? This is good news! Although it's been so long since we've had any, I can see how it might throw you." She could hear the giddy energy in her own voice. Finally, after the longest two days of her life, there was a light at the end of the tunnel.

When Bunny's voice re-emerged, it did so quietly. "I can't."

"Excuse me?"

He lifted his eyes to meet hers. "I can't."

"What do you mean, you... What?!"

"I told you – I'm here to find someone. That's the whole reason I'm here. If I walk into a police station or anywhere else and start giving a statement, it's over. I'm supposed to be here under the radar. That's the only way it'll work. If they find out I'm here, that I'm still alive, the whole thing is shot to buggery."

"What? How can you..."

"I'm sorry, I really am, but I can't."

He turned and walked over to the window, watching the rain as it hammered down outside.

"Oh," said Amy, "I see. I'm not the 'particular woman' you're here to save, so I get screwed? Great. Just fucking great!"

"Amy."

"No, don't start justifying it. You've made your position very clear. You won't help. You won't do the one thing you're good for."

He turned to look at her. "Amy, you need to calm down."

She tossed the cushion at him. "Screw you! Ever since I met you, it's been nothing but shit. You were supposed to help and you haven't. You've just made it worse."

He barked her name out with such ferocity, it caused her to pause. "Amy! Would you fecking listen to me? Are you sure you weren't followed?"

"Don't change the subject."

"Amy!"

She glared at him and then spoke slowly, as if speaking to an unruly child. "No, I was not followed."

"Did you do anything else?"

"What does that matter? Who the fuck put you in charge of me?"

"Amy, for the love of Christ, would you please just answer the question?"

He stood with his back to the window.

She bunched her fists together as she spoke. "Yes, alright. They've been hassling my dad, on the..." She waved a hand at the TV. She reacted as Bunny pulled a face. "I'm not stupid. I didn't call him directly. I called my aunt Crista on the landline and left a message. They can't trace that."

"They have."

"You're being paranoid. I'm a law major, remember. No judge in the world is going to grant a wiretap on somebody's entire family tree. I've not seen the woman in six years."

Bunny took a casual sidestep to his left to move to the far side of the window, and then he stood very still as he spoke. "Listen to me now. I think I saw something."

"Where?"

"Outside. On the billboard opposite. There's a shape."

"What do you mean, a shape?"

"I don't... I can't say for sure. I didn't look directly at it – corner of my eye – but I think there's something up there."

"Right. Maybe it's Batman? Is he a friend of yours? Perhaps he can help me? After all, I am a damsel in distress in need of a hero, and you're taken."

"Just calm down."

"You're full of crap. This is typical male bullshit – you're losing control of the situation, so you make up some nonsense rather than dealing with the reality of the situation. Patriarchal crap."

"Please, just—"

Amy stood, jabbing her finger in his direction. "Don't you dare, don't you fucking dare tell me to calm down." She turned away now, addressing the ceiling. "What the hell am I doing? I've allowed my actions to be dictated by some lunatic with no name. What have I been doing, trusting my survival to some drunken fucking idiot who can't even get his shit together, when I could've had Batman?"

"Look. Stay where you are. I'll go and check—"

Amy twirled around to face him. "No, no need. I'll just open the window and invite him in."

She started walking across the loft towards him. Bunny put his hand out.

"Stop! Seriously."

Amy reached the window and started waving, her voice laced with sarcasm. "Hey, Batman, just..."

She was interrupted by Bunny tackling her to the ground.

"What the—"

Amy stopped talking, her brain registering the strange noise. It had happened a fraction of a second after she'd hit the ground. Then she noticed the pane of double-glazed glass with the hole through it, cracks spiderwebbing out from it.

Bunny rolled over into a coiled crouch. "Stay down."

CHAPTER THIRTY-THREE

"Shot missed," said the voice on the laptop.

Miller did not attempt to hide her displeasure as she spoke. "Yes, I can see that, Eagle One. Maintain position and cover the fire escape, if that isn't too difficult."

"Text me the address," said Cole. "I can be there in ten minutes."

"That will not be necessary. Sweep team, you are go."

Miller hit a button on the laptop and Lola's bright smile filled the screen. She nodded, then the camera spun around. She appeared to be wearing it on a headset. Cole had used similar kit back in his Special Forces days. Only on certain missions, as on other missions it was very important that there was no record.

The camera jerked as Lola got out of a car. Two men got out of the front seat and quickly strode up the steps ahead of her, into the building and out of the torrential rain. Cole recognised Baxter; the other guy was new to him. With a stocky build and tightly cropped brown hair, though Cole didn't know him, he could tell what he was. The way he moved as they climbed the stairs to the fourth floor told him all he needed to know. Former military.

They reached the door to apartment 406 and flanked it. They

could see Lola's hand come out and signal at the new guy and then at the door.

His whispered voice crackled on the feed. "Fuck that. They know we're coming. I ain't going in first."

Lola's other hand pointed towards him. The one holding the gun.

"Lola." Miller's tone carried a warning.

The new guy looked at Baxter, whose face was filled with fury. Cole guessed that he'd vouched for the newcomer and was now deeply regretting doing so. The new guy shrugged. "Fuck it."

He took a couple of steps back to build momentum and then delivered a forceful boot to the door. It splintered, but an additional shoulder charge was required to complete the breach. Then the new guy rolled himself through the doorway and up into a crouch. The camera spun around as Lola entered, her gun held double-handed in front of her.

Miller and Cole watched in silence as the three-person team swept through the apartment. The main room was maybe thirty feet long, with a high ceiling. The windows filled the right wall and the kitchen was on the left, stretching down to the dining and living room area, which culminated in a fireplace over which sat a large flat-screen TV. As boltholes went, it wasn't half bad.

Lola spun to check the left-hand corner behind the door.

"Jesus!" exclaimed Cole, which earned him a withering look from Miller. There was a large stuffed gorilla in the corner, captured in mid roar for all eternity.

Lola turned back and began moving through the apartment efficiently and silently. Baxter checked the open-plan kitchen area before shaking his head. They watched as Lola moved around the couch and checked the fireplace. Nothing behind it but stone – no chimney. A rack of clothes that prominently featured sequins, feathers and fake diamonds lay to one side of the room. Lola swept them before doubling back to the life-sized toy gorilla. She ran her hand across it and then, wordlessly, withdrew a knife and rammed it straight into its guts and then slicing across. Stuffing spilled out onto the floor.

Then she moved down the hallway to the left of the kitchen. The first door on the right led to the bathroom – shower, sink, toilet – a good size by New York standards, but still just enough room to fit two people and certainly nowhere to hide them. The other door opened to reveal a cupboard containing laundry.

That left the final door – the bedroom. Lola entered alone. The camera scanned the room quickly before it jerked as Lola checked behind the door. Then she moved inside the room proper. An old wooden wardrobe sat to the right-hand side; the bed was central, with just a nightstand bearing a lamp to its left. She bobbed left, checking the dead area between the bed and the window, then the screen filled with carpet as Lola silently hit the deck and spun to check under the bed. She was back on her feet a second later. That just left the wardrobe.

She approached it from the side, conscious that anyone in it could be crouched with a gun, waiting for the door to open. She got low and then, in one quick movement, darted her hand out and flung the door open before stepping back.

Nothing happened.

She moved swiftly across and threw open the other door. After a moment, the picture steadied to reveal a wardrobe full of sombre suits and simple shirts. The flamboyant out on display and the mainstream hidden away. Welcome to the Village.

Miller swore under her breath and hit a button on her headset. "Eagle One, can you confirm that there have been no further sightings of the subjects."

"Negative. I have only seen the sweep team. They're still in there."

"Fucking incompetence," said Miller, although it was unclear who the remark was aimed at. She glanced at Cole, who had the good sense to suppress the smile he felt tugging at the corner of his lips.

"Boss." It was Baxter addressing Lola.

The picture on the screen jerked as Lola hurried from the bedroom. He was standing to the left side of the room, where he had opened a small cupboard they'd passed by on the initial sweep. It sat only three inches out from the wall and had initially looked like it couldn't hold anything more interesting that a fuse box.

Once opened, it revealed a chute embedded in the wall.

"Damn it! A dumbwaiter," said Miller. "Get down to the basement, now."

The two men rushed past the shattered remains of the apartment's front door. Lola stayed and looked down the chute, nothing visible but darkness with a hint of light at the end. Then the camera jumped as she climbed in.

She was about to descend when she stopped. Cole had heard it too. In the apartment – movement.

She silently climbed back out of the shaft and into a crouch. She didn't move, just stayed completely still, listening.

After a few seconds, there it was again: the faintest of movements. On silent feet, Lola padded across to the kitchen area. She ducked low behind the counter and then slowly moved around it. Nothing. There were a couple of cupboards under the counter. Perhaps Baxter had been sloppy.

Lola moved quietly and then, as she had with the wardrobe, leaned across and quickly opened the doors – revealing nothing but pots, pans and a spice rack. She stood back up.

She spun around as she heard the noise again and looked up just in time to see a white shape descend from above.

"Jesus!" said Cole and Miller in perfect harmony.

The camera jerked wildly before Lola fell to the carpet. An animal's howl mingled with her scream.

They watched as a cat darted away and through the remains of the front door. Feathers flew up from a cushion and a vase shattered as shots from a silenced pistol followed quickly in the feline's wake.

"Lola!" said Miller into the headset. They could see her feet following towards the front door.

"Lola!" Miller repeated.

They watched the running feet halt and then turn back towards the camera. She picked it up and looked into it. Her previously flawless skin was marred by a large, bloody scratch down the right side of her face.

"Check in on the others and then get out of there."

Her beautiful face twisted into an ugly snarl but then she seemed to compose herself and gave a curt nod.

Miller slammed the laptop's lid down and then stood silently, looking out into the New York night as the rain hammered against the window.

"Have you anything to say, Mr Cole?"

"No, ma'am."

"Very wise."

CHAPTER THIRTY-FOUR

The rain helped.

It was coming down hard, and the wind swirling between the blocks caused it to cut into your face no matter which way you turned. This meant that Amy, walking hunched over with her hoodie up, looked entirely natural. They'd walked all the way down Seventh Avenue and then cut across to Spring Street, just in case their pursuers were watching the nearby subway stations. The sidewalks were empty bar the occasional hardy soul rushing to be elsewhere. As they'd walked, the gutters had flowed like rivers, carrying wayward crafts of litter. Bunny walked beside her, his coat pulled tight around him, the upturned collar offering scant protection from the elements.

The rain also meant they'd not needed to talk. She was angry at him. Somewhere in the back of her mind, a snapshot of the bigger picture fluttered in the breeze, asking to be looked at, but she was refusing. Everything was going wrong. She had lost so much. Right now, she wanted to hold on to her anger at Bunny. It felt like the only thing in her life over which she still had control.

He hadn't spoken since they'd left the parking garage under the building – at least not to her. All he'd said was that someone who owed him a favour would provide them with somewhere to stay. He'd not known anyone in New York this time yesterday. Still, she didn't question it. It wasn't like they had an excess of options. Jonathan's was gone. She couldn't go home. She couldn't go to the police. She couldn't fall asleep in the hope that the waking nightmare of the last few days would indeed turn out to be a bad dream. Near the station, Bunny had stopped at a phone booth to make a call. As he'd been in there, briefly, for one mad second, Amy considered running. She didn't know what she'd be running to, but maybe it'd just feel good to run. Perhaps she could go over to the stables and bust Mabel out and they could ride off into the sunset. It didn't feel like the worst idea.

She'd found the dumbwaiter earlier in the day while cleaning Jonathan's apartment. It was what she had decided to do to try and gain some control over her surroundings. Her life had been falling to pieces on national TV, so she'd dug the cleaning products from under Jonathan's sink and gone to work. In this regard, she was very much her father's daughter. Amy remembered when her grandfather had been sick, when she was a child. He'd undergone a six-hour bypass operation. Her dad had cleaned the entirety of his father's house in that time, lifting things that had never been lifted, finding dust in places most people didn't even know existed. When Gramps had come home, he'd left the windows open for a fortnight to try and remove the smell of bleach.

She wondered if that was what he was doing now. His diligent daughter was now a deviant murderer and public enemy number one. She bet the kitchen floor gleamed like a new Corvette.

Time had dictated that the argument they had about the dumbwaiter was brief and to the point. Amy had insisted Bunny went first, reasoning that he needed more assistance in forcing his bulk into the confined space. He'd huffed and puffed, disliking both the idea and the fact it wasn't his. He seemed keener to try and fight his way out against idiotic odds, typical male. Grudgingly, he'd agreed and gone first, followed by Amy with his coat. As she'd pulled the door closed behind her, she'd heard the front door shattering. As they turned another corner and the rain once more pelted into her face, she wondered what Jonathan would think when he returned to his shattered door, not to mention the window and floor featuring bullet holes and heaven knows what other damage that had occurred after they'd left. She added him to the list of those she had let down.

Bunny stayed between her and the road, keeping a watchful eye on passing traffic to see if anyone was taking an undue interest in them – public enemy number one and the man with no name. He could leave her at any time and, in a way, she wished he would. Then she could just file him in the "people I shouldn't have trusted" column and get on with what little life she had left. He wouldn't provide the alibi that could save her, and yet he wouldn't take the out and leave either.

They'd boarded the 6 train bound for Pelham Bay Park. She'd kept her hoodie up the whole time and tried to avoid cameras where she could. Nobody took any notice. At 10pm, the passengers on the train were lost in their own worlds, too tired to care about anything but getting where they were going. Nobody seemed in the slightest bit interested in trying to get a look at the girl behind the hood, to see if her face matched that of the monster on the front of most of that day's papers, soggy copies of which lay strewn on spare seats.

When they'd reached Hunts Point Avenue station, they'd been met by a fresh-faced, cheery guy who had introduced himself as Diller. Amy had kept quiet and Bunny had introduced her as "a friend". They'd walked. Diller had offered her his umbrella, but she was so soaked through by now, she doubted she'd even notice a difference. Amy had never been to Hunts Point, but she knew it by reputation and had read a special report on the place last year. Half of its residents lived below the poverty line. Drugs and prostitution were rampant. It mostly got talked about at election time, when politicians debated who was to blame for it. But none of this came across from Diller, who was acting as an unasked-for tour guide. He proudly pointed out that it was home to one of the world's largest food distribution centres. Even as he did so, they crossed back and forth across the street in various locations, following the unspoken rule of avoiding certain spots where figures huddled in doorways or under awnings. In other places they passed women, and a few men, getting what cover they could and then walking out into the rain when cars passed by.

The rain rat-a-tatted against plywood on several houses where windows had once been. Graffiti tagged the walls and only every third streetlight worked. Still, Diller chatted on happily, like he was showing them around a stately home. They reached a row of tenement houses where Diller excused himself and disappeared down an alleyway. Bunny and Amy stood there for a couple of minutes in silence, neither expressing what they were both thinking: *I really hope he's coming back.*

Bunny stood tense beside her, feeling eyes watching them from the shadows. At the far end of the street, there was a fire in a barrel and several figures standing around it. Amy watched as two of the figures broke off from the group and started making their way towards them. Amy could have sworn that Bunny had been looking in the other direction the whole time, and yet he said, "Them lads come near us, just let me do the talking. Alright?"

Amy nodded.

She looked away and counted the time it'd take the men she wasn't looking at to reach them. She was about to glance again when there was a thunking noise from inside one of the tenement houses. Then a section of the wood over one of the ground-floor windows slid up and Diller stuck his head out, beaming cheerfully.

"C'mon in, folks."

As they walked towards the window, Diller hopped out and pulled over a breeze block to be used as a step up. From the corner of her eye, Amy saw the figures move by, reminding her of the sharks she'd once seen in the New York Aquarium, gliding silently through the waters.

She climbed through the window and into a room stinking of damp, mould and God knows what else. A bare lightbulb hung from the ceiling, swaying backwards and forwards, causing the shadows to leap and lurch. Bunny followed her in, with Diller behind him. Diller must've caught her facial expression. "Don't worry, this ain't it. Nobody uses this room – leaks too bad."

He pointed at the sagging ceiling. Amy smiled and nodded, feeling rude and ungrateful.

Diller walked to the corner and untied a rope, which caused a sheet of metal to descend over the hole. "My little invention. I rigged it up as a security measure."

Bunny nodded. "That's very clever."

Diller led them out into the hall.

"Jackson, that you?" The voice came from upstairs.

Diller shouted back up, "It's alright, Mrs James, it's only me. I got some company."

"Ohhh," said the voice, sounding much happier now. "Finally got yourself a lady friend, huh? You get goin' now!"

Diller blushed and glanced back at them. "That's Mrs James; she lives upstairs. Nice lady."

Amy and Bunny nodded, both diplomatically ignoring that Mrs James was now belting out the Marvin Gaye classic "Sexual Healing". She was getting the words wrong but singing it with gusto nonetheless.

"The kitchen is through there," said Diller, nodding at a closed door in front of him. Then he pushed open a door to the back room of the house.

Amy walked in and then stopped. She wasn't sure what she expected, but it hadn't been this. The room was warmly lit from several mismatched lamps dotted around and every last inch of wall was covered with drawings of flowers, birds and animals of all manner and description. It was as overwhelming as it was unexpected. A cornucopia of colour surrounded them.

"Jesus," said Bunny. "This is incredible."

Diller blushed. "My mom loves nature and animals and stuff so I, y'know, tried to make it special for her."

Amy glanced at the two far corners, noticing the mattress that sat in each. "Where is she?"

"Oh, erm... She's not going to be here for a while."

Amy nodded and avoided further questions.

"Did you do all this, Diller?" asked Bunny.

He nodded enthusiastically. "Yeah. I, erm, I used to go up to the Bronx Zoo and one of the custodial staff would sneak me in. I'd sketch the animals and then come home and... y'know." He shrugged. "It's something to do."

"Ye got talent."

Diller shrugged again, clearly uncomfortable with praise.

Once Amy had taken in the four walls of smiling animals and bountiful nature, she was able to process the rest of the room. There wasn't much else. The mattresses, complete with sleeping bags, were positioned in each corner. Paperback books with cracked spines lined two of the walls, piled ten or so high all around, so as not to block the view of the Bronx Zoo collage. There was a table of sorts, coffee-table sized, although it was really a piece of wood, painted with yet more smiling animal faces, and balanced on four stacks of paperbacks for legs. On it sat a laptop. A thick cable ran in from a hole high up in the wall, the plugs that ran from it held together with a worrying amount of electrical tape.

"Can I ask," said Bunny, looking awkward. "When you said you couldn't make your rent...?"

"Well," said Diller, "not rent as such. Gotta pay to be left alone. Plus, I get to piggyback off the electricity the Roberts next door got. We got Wi-Fi too. Wi-Fi!"

Bunny nodded. "Right. That's great, yeah."

"So," Diller said, pointing at the two mattresses, "the two of you can sleep here and I'll go upstairs and sleep on the landing."

"Diller," said Bunny, "this is really good of you."

Diller shook his head emphatically. "No, it isn't. Least I could do after my... y'know. And sorry again about that."

It was Bunny's turn to shake his head. "Listen, if you're helping, you deserve to know what you're getting into." He nodded at Amy, who took down her hood. "This lady is called Amy Daniels. She's currently wanted for murder."

"For a murder," interrupted Amy, "that I very definitely did not commit."

"Yeah," agreed Bunny. "But I've got to be honest with you, Diller, there's a lot of police after us – and people who are a whole lot worse. She's the main story on the news so, y'know, you need to be aware of the risk you're taking."

Diller shrugged and smiled. "Hey, if you didn't do it, you didn't do it. And I owe Bunny a big favour, so…"

"It might be dangerous, though. Us being here," said Bunny. "We'll stay tonight and then we'll try and figure out our next move."

"Well," said Diller, "I don't know if you noticed the neighbourhood I live in. I mean, I took you here by the nice route, but still. Point is, it wasn't exactly that safe to begin with – the paper called us New York's war zone last year."

"OK," said Bunny. "I just didn't want to leave you in the dark. Didn't seem fair."

"And I appreciate it. Sorry to be the bearer of bad news though, but you ain't the big story on the news no more."

"Oh," said Amy, "that's a relief."

"Yeah," said Diller. He pointed to the laptop. "I was watching just before I came to fetch you. There's been another terrorist attack."

"On New York?" asked Bunny.

Diller nodded. "Well, on the outskirts. Some big data warehouse or something. I didn't really get it, but apparently it's a big deal. Some massive building, blown to smithereens with the poor janitors inside. They said the company's called Millennium something or other."

Bunny and Amy looked at each other.

"*Millennium Falcon*," they said together.

Diller looked back and forth between the two of them. "Is everything OK?"

Bunny puffed out his cheeks. "Yeah. That sound you just heard was the other shoe dropping – hard."

CHAPTER THIRTY-FIVE

Douglas Randall sat in the chair in his office and looked up at the ceiling. He was supposed to be on air in seventy-four minutes and he really needed to clear his head. He was wishing he'd actually paid attention in those meditation classes his wife had made him go to. Instead, he just kept running it around in his head, again and again and again. Maybe it was just a big coincidence. The piece of paper Amy Daniels had handed him had said *"Millennium Falcon"* on it, but how was he to know that had anything to do with Millennium Faction Data? After all, lots and lots of things were called Millennium. He was pretty sure some British pop star had a song called that. And there was a TV show, wasn't there? At the turn of the century, lots of things had been called that. It had been quite the buzzword. No, his mind was made up: there were a thousand very good reasons why this was just a big coincidence.

Then the phone rang. "Hi, Douglas, I've got a Miss Bates on the phone. She says you asked her to give you a call about some investments."

"I don't think— Oh, wait..." It had taken him a moment to realise. They'd only used that name a couple of times, when they'd been doing certain scenarios. "Sorry, yes, I think I know her. Put her through."

"Douglas," said the woman he'd feared it would be.

"Hi, Miss Bates. OK, I've got it from here, Sally."

He waited until he heard the click. He had long had the suspicion that Sally listened into his calls, the nosy old busybody.

Amy sounded tense on the phone. "Well, Douglas?"

"Well what?"

"Oh, come on. Millennium Faction Data – that's got to be it. The thing Lanark Lane Investments are into."

Douglas watched as Kristy walked by his office, all bright smiles and false warmth. She waved at him happily. She'd brought cakes in that morning for one of the camera guy's birthdays. What a devious bitch. Douglas gave her a cheery wave back and pulled the blinds down.

"Goddamn it, Amy, do you have any idea how many things are called Millennium something or other? I just Googled it – thirty-eight and a half million."

"Yes, and how many of them got blown to smithereens last night?"

"It's just…"

"Have you looked into it? See if Lanark Lane Investments has anything to gain from what happened. Jesus, Douglas!"

Douglas sat on the edge of his desk and looked at the pictures on the wall opposite. The one of George Foreman pretending to punch him was a real favourite. He took a deep breath and then spoke with a calmness he didn't feel. "Look, Amy, you've been through a lot. Maybe you should just go to the police and explain—"

"For Christ's sake, Douglas, people are trying to kill me and you can't be bothered to investigate it? That's all I'm asking. You're supposed to be a journalist."

Douglas worked the stress ball furiously in his left hand. "No, I'm not. I'm a newsman. I read the goddamn news – that's it! I can't be who you want me to be. Alright? I'm sorry."

"No, Douglas, it's not alright. You're all I've got, and I need you to do your fucking job!"

There was a knock on Douglas's office door.

"Hold on a sec." He put his hand over the receiver. "Who is it?"

"Hey, buddy, it's Tony. You asked to see me."

"Sure, c'mon in." Douglas spoke into the receiver again as Tony Fracero entered his office. "OK, honey, I gotta go. Go with whatever colour you prefer. Bye."

"Don't you dare—"

Douglas hung up the phone and gave Tony the patented Randall smile. "Tony, my paesano, how you doing?"

"Great, I—"

Douglas pointed at the visitor's chair and moved around to sit behind his desk. "The missus is redecorating again." Eye roll. "Like I care about the colours. I couldn't tell you what they are now." He gave a hearty fake laugh; Tony followed suit. He was almost exactly the same age as Douglas, although his hairline had retreated and waistline advanced more than Douglas's. That was OK for him. As the station's security correspondent, actually knowing things made the look less crucial.

"Doug," said Tony, "you know I'd love to catch up, but this bombing at the Millennium data centre has got us all running around like headless chickens, so..." Tony looked at the door, an unsubtle manoeuvre which Douglas studiously ignored.

"Yeah, I know. Just crazy. I mean, terrorism these days, Jesus! Right?"

Tony nodded. "Insane."

"So," said Douglas, "fill me in a little. I feel like I'm not really getting this."

"I'd love to, but..."

"C'mon. For old times' sake."

A look passed between the two men. What wasn't being mentioned was Tony's blissfully happy home life with Martha and the three kids. One of the main reasons said home life was so blissful was that when Tony had got an intern pregnant, Uncle Douglas had been her shoulder to cry on. He'd got her a well-paid job in a friend's ad agency and the number of a doctor. Tony owed Douglas.

"OK, well you know the general stuff already. The company was formed back in 2002, Millennium Solutions having made a ton of money from the Y2K nonsense and then taking over Faction Data, who were a big disaster recovery firm. They really hit the big time a few years ago when they moved into comprehensive storage solutions, hence the enormous data centres, one of which went boom last night. Homeland has their suspect, but they're not officially releasing the name yet. What we officially know is that at 11:14pm last night, a bomb went off at the Millennium Faction Data building out in Queens, pretty much taking it out and killing a security guard, three technicians and two janitors in the process, plus several more injuries. It would've been a lot more, except it was at their quietest time. Homeland's suspect is believed to be one of the dead too."

"Thank God. I mean, that there weren't more people there. What is the place though?"

"Well," said Tony, "it's basically an enormous data storage facility. No company stores their own data anymore; they rent space in enormous data farms like this one. Billions of gigabytes all securely stored and then instantly backed up to two different locations – y'know, for redundancy. A large chunk of the Fortune 500 have their data there."

"Right. It's not your normal ISIS target, is it?"

Tony shook his head. "Well, no, but what we're hearing is that the suspect, a member of staff, left a detailed online journal full of anti-American hate. And you've got to remember, these guys don't have what you'd call a conventional hierarchy. The suspect had the opportunity through what he did for a living and he took advantage. Initially, what we couldn't figure out was the why – I mean, what he'd thought it would accomplish, but we just got a tip on that." Tony leaned forward and lowered his voice to a conspiratorial whisper. "So, we don't have this confirmed yet, and Millennium have flat-out denied it, but we're hearing that the redundancy may've been messed with. We're hearing that they might have lost data."

"Oh," said Douglas, frankly unimpressed. "That'll be a big hassle, I guess."

"Hassle?" said Tony, sounding incredulous. "Dougie, you ain't getting this. Today's economy doesn't run on oil or steel or even money. It runs on data. This is Wall Street. This is online retailers. This is credit card companies. All of them might have lost a couple of days of data. If this is real, this is a fucking digital Pearl Harbor. Companies will fold; confidence will take a serious hit. Right now, the authorities are talking about loss of life and saying the data situation is fine. But if the whispers are even a little bit true, you're going to have companies having to come out tonight and tell the world that they've just taken enormous hits to their businesses. It's going to be chaos. Wall Street will be running red with blood in the morning. Your 401(k) is going to take a pounding, I'm afraid."

"Right," said Douglas. "I see. So, if you knew about this beforehand, before it was public knowledge, you could make a killing?"

Tony turned white. "Shit, Doug. Don't go calling your broker. That's insider dealing, we'll both be—"

"No, no, nothing like that." Douglas leaned back in his chair and looked up at the ceiling again. He stayed that way for nearly a full minute.

"Erm, Dougie?"

Douglas leaned forward again and looked Tony in the eye. "Tony, I need you to trust me. What I'm about to say goes no further than this room. OK?"

"Sure."

"I had a... let's call it a source, come to me yesterday and give me a garbled tip. It made no sense at the time but..."

"OK," said Tony, looking really unsure as to where this was heading.

"It was, like, a snippet of overheard conversation. She – I mean, they, the source – wrote it down. I think it's just a coincidence, but..." Douglas took a folded piece of paper from his inside jacket pocket and held it up between two fingers. "This is probably bullshit and we'll be laughing about it tomorrow, but... what is the name of the suspected bomber?"

Tony stared at the folded piece of paper in Douglas's hand for a long moment.

"Tony?"

"Well," said Tony, "we only just got this from our guy at the NSA, and it is on deep background right now, but he was commonly known as Addy Wilson."

Douglas felt his whole body relax, like the electric current that had been going through it since last night's newsflash had finally been turned off.

"Although," continued Tony, "that wasn't his legal name. It's funny – kinda sounds like a character from *Star Wars*. His name was Adaal Ackbar."

Douglas closed his eyes and reached his hand across the desk. Tony took the piece of paper and opened it. "You have got to be fucking kidding me!"

"I really wish I was."

CHAPTER THIRTY-SIX

You had to know what to look for.

Bunny was in the queue at a taco truck with a lot of people in suits. It wasn't lunchtime yet, and he guessed that they were trying to beat the rush so they could get back to their desks faster. He himself was in a windbreaker with an NYPD baseball cap and cheap sunglasses, all of which he'd picked up in the kind of tourist shop that never saw the same customer twice. Everyone around him was talking, either on their phone or to the person next to them. Half a block west was the building on Park Avenue that housed the offices of Lanark Lane Investments.

Bunny and Amy had been staying at Diller's place since Monday night, although Bunny hadn't been there much. He'd spent most of the previous day and all of that morning doing surveillance on Matt Clarke. Once the news of the bombing had broken, he'd tried to ring Agent Dove, reasoning that whomever she represented might be considerably more interested in a major terrorism incident than a murder with a rather lurid set of headlines attached. Regardless, the phone had been dead. He really had been cut adrift. He'd spent most of Monday night trying to come up with a plan while staring at

Diller's ceiling, which was also covered, rather alarmingly, with the smiling faces of members of the animal kingdom. He'd had his fill of running and hiding. Somehow, they needed to take the initiative back. He had no idea how to do that, but he figured he needed to start at the source – namely one Matt Clarke, he of the big mouth and the bottom in need of a spanking. He had indeed been a very naughty boy and Bunny was inclined to give him the kind of spanking that'd fulfil his needs in that area for the rest of this life and possibly the next one.

So, on Tuesday morning, Bunny had been up with the lark, staking out the building that Matt Clarke and his amigos lived in. Not that Bunny had been dumb enough to approach it directly. From a distance, he'd scoped out the two guys in the SUV and the other fella in the BMW. Between them, they had all exits and entrances to the building completely covered. He'd watched as Bradley and Clarke had been hurried into a minivan by the big black fella who'd handed Bunny his arse a few days beforehand. They'd driven away in convoy. Bunny reckoned that the only people under closer personal protection had either won an election or just taken over a small Third World country.

He'd not attempted to follow them, instead guessing that they were heading for their offices. He'd been right. Once Bunny reached the building on Park Avenue, he spent the next few hours scoping around it, seeing the same level of protection. The two guys in the SUV were parked in front of a fire hydrant on the far side of the street; they'd flashed some form of ID when a traffic cop had shown an interest. The guy in the BMW was down one of the side streets.

He'd then seen Clarke and Bradley being accompanied back home to West 88th Street. He'd hung around long enough to see the shifts change. The security around their apartment was even tighter. The logic was sound: the office was safer due to its own security and the sheer volume of people. Bunny's plan, as much as he'd had one, had been to try and reach Clarke at home. He could go in, smash the gobshite over the head and then, well, he didn't have much after that.

Even if he could get hold of the lad and get him out of there, what would that get him? Bunny wasn't exactly Snow White, but he drew the line at torture. The options were limited. Very limited.

He'd reached the front of the queue for the taco truck.

"What can I get you?"

"What's good?" asked Bunny, never making eye contact with the guy in the truck above him. A second SUV had just pulled up and the bearded black guy had stepped out.

"Everything is good, *ese*. We don't sell it if it ain't." The guy leaned forward and pointed at the menu on the side of the truck. "Now, what you want, bro?"

"Right. Grand. I'll have that." Bunny jabbed a finger at the menu without looking at it.

"Cool, one *lengua* taco platter coming up. Five bucks."

"Lovely." Bunny reached his hand into his pocket and pulled out a note. The black guy had entered the building.

Bunny held the note out and felt it slip from his fingers.

"Dude."

He glanced up to see the Styrofoam tray being held out, and the pissed-off expression behind it.

"Sorry. Miles away. Thanks very much."

Bunny took the tray and stepped to the side. A woman had just got up from the bench behind him, so he slid in and took her place. Just a tourist, eating his lunch. As he picked up his taco, the black guy re-emerged, flanked by Matt Clarke. As they walked to the vehicle, Bunny noticed the guy's hand was on Clarke's elbow, guiding him forward. Clarke jerked his arm, but the man maintained his grip. With his free hand, the black guy opened the rear door of the black SUV and firmly guided Clarke inside before slamming the door. Then he put his hand on the rear door handle, double-checking it was locked.

There it was. To see it, you had to know what to look for. Clarke wasn't being protected. He was being held prisoner.

As the SUV pulled out and joined the flow of traffic, the other

SUV and the BMW following behind, Bunny bit into his taco. It was nice, if a bit chewy.

He glanced over at the menu. It was cow tongue, apparently.

He took another bite.

Not bad.

It'd go well with a nice cup of tea.

CHAPTER THIRTY-SEVEN

Water. Whiskey. Pint of stout.

Bunny put the three drinks down on the table and sat back.

They were back in the Porterhouse Lodge because they had to meet somewhere and they all knew where it was. Jackie the barman had greeted Bunny warmly, and then when the other two had walked in, he'd roared a genial laugh and said, "Holy shit, they're putting the band back together."

Now they were sitting in the back room. The place was at the tail end of a steady lunch business of sandwiches and such, but on a bright and sunny March day, the dark back room was theirs alone.

Amy was back at Diller's, it being way too risky for her to be out in public. She had Mrs James, Diller's upstairs neighbour, for company. Mrs James was convinced that Amy was Diller's girlfriend. Initially, Bunny had been wary of anyone seeing Amy, but he'd quickly understood why Diller had been unconcerned. The sweet old lady was "off with the fairies", so to speak. She didn't know the year, much less who was or wasn't America's most wanted.

Bunny glanced at the muted TV up in the corner. Whether it could be considered a positive development or not, Amy wasn't the main story on the news anymore. The attack on Millennium Faction

Data was unsurprisingly dominating. It had been weird, watching as Adaal Ackbar went from innocent victim to lunatic jihadi to evil genius as the "truth" of the attack had come more into focus over the last two days. Shares in several affected companies had been suspended for the day yesterday, but the stock exchange had been back to business as usual that morning, and apparently it had been bloody. Billions were being wiped off the valuations of companies. Fortunes would be lost and, Bunny guessed, at least one made. He didn't pretend to understand what was happening, but he knew enough. Matt Clarke and his boys at Lanark Lane Investments had known about the attack beforehand and some very bad people were clearly in cahoots with them. The whole thing just came down to good old-fashioned greed.

Amy's newsman contact was useful to a point, but it didn't get them anywhere near a solution. The note she had given him – "*Millennium Falcon* – Admiral Ackbar – or something like that" – wasn't exactly a smoking gun. No news organisation was going to go on air with what amounted to an eavesdropped coincidence. Randall had said he had people looking into Lanark Lane, but Bunny guessed it'd be way too little, way too late. Whoever was behind this, they weren't afraid of dropping bodies, and they'd undoubtedly clean up their loose ends on the way out the door. All of that was why Matt Clarke was somewhere between protectee and prisoner. Getting to him and finding some way of showing the truth to the world was the closest thing Bunny had to a plan, but right then, it didn't feel like very much of one.

Smithy raised his whiskey glass in toast and then tossed it back in one fluid motion. Diller sipped on the straw in his water.

"So," said Smithy, "what can we do for you, Bunny?"

"Well. 'Tis a bit of an ask, but basically, I need to get into a building up on Park Avenue."

"OK," said Diller.

"Woah, hang on a sec," said Smithy. "When you say 'get in' – I'm not a burglar and, larcenous tendencies aside, neither is Diller. I'd like to help, but I'm not doing B & E at an uptown address."

"No, no," said Bunny, "nothing like that. I just need a distraction. Some way of getting me in to talk to someone without being spotted. I thought maybe you could do one of your situation things."

"Situational acting event," said Smithy.

"That's the one."

"OK," said Smithy, "well, that we can probably do. If there's one thing we're good at, it's distracting people. What's the address?"

Bunny slid across a piece of paper. "Here, I wrote it down."

Smithy took out his smartphone and started tapping away.

"We'll figure out something," said Diller. "Our recreation of the *Ghostbusters* scene in the New York Public Library is still talked about today. We're the reason it is now their official policy to turn away people dressed as ghosts."

"Is that right?" said Bunny. "Just explain this to me again. Yous recreate scenes from famous films?"

Diller nodded enthusiastically. "Yeah. It's acting with a punk aesthetic. That's what Smithy calls it."

Smithy nodded. "That's the idea."

"Right," said Bunny, sounding a tad sceptical.

"Our 'I'll have what she's having' from *When Harry Met Sally* is really popular," said Diller. "Y'know, the one where Meg Ryan does the—"

"Everyone remembers that scene," said Bunny. "'Tis an all-time classic."

"Oh yeah," agreed Diller. "People love it. We got paid to do it at six different restaurants on Valentine's Day."

"So this is a business?"

"Yes," said Diller.

"No," said Smithy. Then he looked at Diller. "Well, it didn't used to be, but, well, the thing about actors is that we're all broke, so a few bucks does come in handy. It also paid a couple of fines."

"Yeah," said Smithy. "Recreating scenes from *Dog Day Afternoon* wasn't our finest idea. Some cops showed up who hadn't seen the movie. We all spent a night in the cells."

Diller nodded. "The thing about recreating an armed siege is that it can quickly become an actual armed siege."

"Yeah," said Smithy. "We really…"

Smithy stared transfixed at his smartphone for a moment and then shut his eyes.

"Smithy?" said Bunny. "Ye just stopped talking there."

Diller shushed him. "He's thinking. This is his process."

Bunny stayed quiet but looked back and forth between the two of them: Smithy, head down, eyes closed, with an almost pained expression; Diller, wide-eyed with his tongue hanging out, giving him the air of an excited puppy. In the back of Bunny's mind, he was starting to worry this was a terrible idea. Unfortunately, it was also his only idea.

"I've got it," said Smithy.

"He's got it," said Diller.

Smithy opened his eyes and looked at them both. "*Lethal Weapon 2*."

"Oh my God," said Diller. "The exploding toilet scene?"

"No, not the… Why would we do the exploding toilet scene?"

Diller slapped the table. "Guy getting decapitated with the surfboard."

"No."

"Mel Gibson shooting the aquarium."

"No," said an increasingly exasperated Smithy. "And I would never hurt fish."

"Guy jumping off the building and Mel goes, 'Do you really wanna jump? OK then—"

"No," interrupted Smithy, sounding exasperated. "Stop guessing!" He then saw Diller's hurt expression and felt instantly bad. "I mean… no, Dill, none of them. And the jumping off the building scene is in the first film anyway." Smithy turned to Bunny. "You want a distraction, I can do you one hell of a distraction. When do you need this?"

"As soon as possible."

Smithy nodded. "OK. First thing tomorrow good enough?"

"I guess it'll have to be."

"OK," said Smithy. "I need to go take a look at this place. Diller, you need to call the crew and get hold of some cardboard and markers."

Bunny pulled out his wallet and handed Diller a couple of bills. He now had twenty bucks left.

With that, Smithy hopped off his stool and started pacing. "Do these people know what you look like?"

Bunny nodded. "Well, at least one of them. The big black lad who I had a bit of a tussle with."

"OK," said Smithy. "We're going to have to figure out how we can get you in there without getting seen." Smithy nodded to himself and kept pacing back and forth. "OK. This is going to be challenging but doable."

Bunny picked up his untouched pint of Guinness. "I'm getting too old for this shit."

CHAPTER THIRTY-EIGHT

Darryl Habana smiled to hide the wince that had reflexively appeared on his face when the elevator doors opened. In his defence, he had no doubt that Jessica Wallsop almost certainly did the same when she saw him. Darryl worked on the top floor, for the South African consulate; Jessica worked three floors down for an insurance company. They'd met at the previous December's building Christmas party. That was one of the big things Darryl had noticed when he'd moved to New York from South Africa: the sheer amount of Christmas parties. The consulate had theirs, and the other consulates had theirs, each trying to outdo each other, which meant that December was one long, cheaply acquired hangover. Then the building had one too. Darryl had gone as one of the consulate's representatives, as it paid to be friendly. Besides, it clashed with the night of the Swiss consulate's bash, and ever since a regrettable tackle against the Swiss trade attaché during the inter-consulate five-a-side soccer tournament, he had been persona non grata at their bashes. Darryl regretted it, not least because their wine list was the stuff of legend.

Speaking of regrettable incidents, Jessica Wallsop gave Darryl a tight smile and then turned to face the doors, punching the button for the ground floor with more force than necessary, as if trying to convey to the elevator her keenness for the trip down to be over as quickly as possible.

It would be hard to put their "coming together" at the Christmas party in overly romantic terms. Their eyes had not met across a crowded room. He had been hitting on her friend and Jessica had still been there when the friend had left with some gym-toned tool from the risk-management firm on the third floor. They didn't have a great deal in common other than two things – they were both drunk and horny. It was not a love story for the ages.

At the party, Jessica had seemed, if anything, a bit shy and mousy. Once they had sneaked upstairs to the consulate, on the pretence of slipping out to their much-prized balcony garden for a sneaky joint, things had changed. A beast had been unleashed. They had never made it to the balcony. Darryl had brought her into the boss's office because, well, who doesn't want to screw on their boss's desk? She had been eager virtually ripping his clothes off. It had also become apparent that Jessica was quite the talker when she got going, lying across the vast expanse of mahogany desk. Initially, Darryl had been in to it; a bit of filthy talk just added to the experience. Then it had taken a turn. As Jessica had become more and more excited, her dirty talk had taken on a racial element. At first, it had been frankly hot – this petite all-American white woman talking to the big black man. But her choice of language had gone south fast. Soon Darryl found himself appalled by the woman he was still having sex with. It was like his body and mind had split in two. Then, he'd glanced up to see the framed picture of Nelson Mandela on the wall. The eyes of the great man had looked down on him as if to say, "Darryl, is this how far we have come?" He had realised there and then that he couldn't keep quiet. Unfortunately, his body was not entirely on board with the plan. This was how the stern talking-to about unacceptable language that he was delivering to a suddenly mortified woman from Vermont was interrupted by his orgasm. It sent extremely mixed messages. He still shuddered at the memory, and he still couldn't look at sweet Papa Madiba without feeling shame.

When the doors pinged open on the reception floor, Jessica bolted out as if shot from a cannon. Her left shoulder bounced off the opening door and then she all but leaped the security barriers as she beeped herself out. Her heels skittered across the marble floor of the reception area at as close to a run as someone could manage without actually running. It was "building on fire but not near me" speed.

Darryl watched her go and then calmly put his pass down and beeped himself through the barriers. He'd seen Jessica meeting an Asian guy outside the office a couple of weeks ago; he did not want to think about what was going on there.

He turned the corner to the reception desk. Marcia was on her throne, queen of all she surveyed, as ever. She was a grandma from Brooklyn, and took what she considered to be a "healthy interest" in the building's to-ings and fro-ings. Most people considered this being a busybody. Darryl liked her though, possibly just because she reminded him of his auntie JuJu.

"Hey, Marcia, my love, I hear you had to see me?"

She pursed her lips at him and sucked at her teeth. "Don't you be trying none of that silver-tongued charm on me, Darryl. I'm on to you, mister."

He grasped his chest in mock offence. "Why've you got to treat me so mean, Marcia!"

"Because you love it, you incorrigible flirt."

Darryl smiled and glanced across at the reception's waiting area. It was standing room only.

"Wow, busy down here today."

"Yeah. Apparently there's a bunch of people waiting for a meeting with that recruitment company on the fourth floor. Trish doesn't know anything about it and that Andy guy is out of the office."

Marcia said the words "Andy guy" with the tone normally kept for international war criminals. He had committed the sin of dumping half a cup of coffee into one of the potted plants near the door that, while technically belonging to the building, Marcia considered to be very much hers.

"So, you got someone for me?" asked Darryl.

"I do. He insisted on speaking to someone from the consulate. I told him, you gotta make an appointment like everybody else, but he refused to leave. Said it's life and death or some such nonsense."

Darryl lowered his voice so he couldn't be overheard. "Probably just someone who's lost their passport. They always think it should be treated like a national emergency." Darryl glanced over at the waiting area again. "Which one is it?"

"It's the... it's the..."

In the nearly three years he'd worked here, he'd never seen Marcia short of a word.

"Black guy?"

"No, don't be stupid. He's..." She leaned across and whispered it. "The really, really short guy. I don't know what's the right word these days."

"Ah, OK. No problem."

Marcia ripped off a note from her pad and handed it to him. "Here's his details."

Darryl took it and turned towards the waiting area. Floor-to-ceiling windows showed the bright and beautiful going about their days on Park Avenue.

The reception area consisted of a square of couches, with individual chairs at the corners, arranged around a massive wooden coffee table where various magazines that nobody ever read were splayed out in fans. Every available space on the couches was taken. One of the seats was occupied by a very attractive redhead with a pair of legs that Darryl did well not to make direct eye contact with. There was also a large guy with a handlebar moustache, sunglasses and a seafarer's cap.

Darryl glanced over to the corner and nodded at Tito, the security guard. These walk-ins could be a little cuckoo.

Sitting on one of the chairs was a dwarf, who watched Darryl walk towards him with a look of expectation. Darryl glanced down at the piece of paper.

"Mr Leo Getz?"

The man smiled. "That's me, attorney-at-law. Anything you want, Leo – gets! Get it?"

Darryl smiled. He had a peculiar feeling of déjà vu that he couldn't quite put his finger on. He extended his hand. "I'm Darryl Habana, from the South African consulate." The man shook it firmly. "I believe there is some kind of emergency?"

"Yes. Very important. Really important!"

"OK." Darryl looked around at the lack of available seating. As a rule, he didn't like to bring anyone upstairs until he'd determined what the purpose of their visit was. It was a lot easier to end a meeting if it had never got past reception.

Darryl pushed a couple of the magazines out of the way and perched himself lightly on the edge of the thick oak coffee table. It also put him down at his visitor's eye level, which seemed polite.

"So, what can I help you with?"

"OK, OK, OK. A friend of mine wants to emigrate to South Africa."

"I see. Well, there is plenty of information on our website. There are restrictions as we only accept skilled workers in areas of need, or entrepreneurs with assets—"

"Sorry, sorry, sorry," said Getz. "You're misunderstanding me. I need you to talk him out of it."

"OK. And why is that?"

"Well, it's just a really bad time for him to go over there, with all the trouble."

"Mr Getz, I assure you that, despite what you've heard about our crime rates, South Africa is actually a very safe—"

"No, no, no. Not that." Getz gave him a wide smile. "The guy's from Jersey – Syria would be a holiday. It's just... Well, you can meet him and then it'll be clear."

Darryl glanced around at the other people in reception.

"Oh, he's here?"

"Yeah, yeah, yeah." He raised his voice. "Alphonse!"

A young black guy with a warm smile and rather large ears

stepped out from behind a column and strode forward, hand extended.

"Hello, I'm Alphonse, erm... Glover."

Darryl stood to shake his hand. "Nice to meet you, Mr Glover."

"Alphonse, please."

"Alphonse. So, you want to emigrate to South Africa?"

"But... but you're black!"

Shocked, Darryl turned towards the source of this last statement. It was from the white guy with the handlebar moustache and sunglasses who had just stood up from one of the other sofas. He spoke in an Afrikaans accent. Actually, as Darryl would realise when thinking back on it later, he didn't. He spoke in what people who'd never properly heard one thought an Afrikaans accent sounded like.

"Excuse me, sir," said Darryl. "Who are you?"

Before he could get an answer, Alphonse raised his voice. "That's right! I want to go to South Africa and join my black brothers and sisters in the struggle against the white oppressor."

"What?!" Darryl gawped as Alphonse held his fist aloft and proudly proclaimed, "Apartheid never. Freedom forever."

It was then that all hell broke loose. Suddenly most of the waiting area was on its feet and joining in the chant.

"APARTHEID NEVER! FREEDOM FOREVER!"

Darryl noticed that the half-dozen or so people, now including the not-really-Afrikaans man, had taken out signs, all with various poor attempts at spelling the word apartheid.

"Is this some kind of a joke?"

"No," said Alphonse. "The freedom of the black South African majority is no joke, sir."

"What the hell are you talking about? Apartheid hasn't existed for twenty-five years. I am a black South African."

Darryl turned at a tap on his shoulder to find Tito the security guard standing there. "Erm, Darryl, I think they're doing a scene from *Lethal Weapon 2.*"

"What?"

The man with the handlebar moustache had now started up a chant of "Free Nelson Mandela", and other people were joining in.

"Shut up," said Darryl, his patience now a distant spot in the rear-view mirror. "What are you people talking about? The great Nelson Mandela is dead."

The crowd fell suddenly silent – a brief moment of respite – like they had reached the calm eye of the storm of madness. Then the dwarf – who Darryl was beginning to realise probably wasn't called Leo Getz, and whose law qualifications were looking increasingly doubtful – stood on the oak table and pointed an accusing finger. "They killed Nelson Mandela!"

The next ten minutes were pure chaos, as Tito the security guard, Darryl, and even Marcia, out from behind her desk, struggled to get the "protesters" out of reception. A crowd had started to form out on the street, watching as the protesters chanted their resistance to a long-gone political system. Eventually they got everybody out onto the street, which is when the cops finally showed up. The consulate's donation to the NYPD's Christmas fund would not be quite so generous this year.

Alphonse then raised his hand and pulled it down, clenching it into a fist. "And – scene!"

The protesters immediately stopped protesting and instead burst into applause.

"Well done, everybody," said 'Leo Getz'. "That was absolutely fantastic work. Really committed. Beautiful."

Darryl looked around at the half-dozen people who were now smiling warmly at him. "Who are you people?"

The black guy who called himself Alphonse produced a business card and extended it to Darryl with a bow. "We are the Situational Actors' Collective, bringing great scenes from the cinema to life."

Darryl took a few seconds to process this, and then said, "But... why?"

Tito was standing at Darryl's shoulder again. "Erm, Darryl, the cops want to know if you want to press charges?"

The question was met with a murmur among the actors and a few worried glances.

"Yeah," said Darryl, "like 'South African consulate charges people for protesting against apartheid' is a headline the boss wants." He turned to Alphonse. "Can I assume this is over now?"

He nodded. "Well, unless you'd like an encore?"

"Thanks, but I'll pass." He turned to Tito. "Tell them it's fine." Then he turned back to the actors. "Who put you up to this?"

"I'm afraid I'm not at liberty to say," said Alphonse.

"It was Frederick from the Swiss consulate, wasn't it?"

This was met with just a smile.

Darryl tapped the business card against his chin. "I bet it was. That son of a... Hey, can you guys do scenes from *The Sound of Music*?"

Three minutes later, Darryl walked back inside, one of the misspelled signs under his arm so he could show the rest of the office. As he beeped himself through the security barrier, Marcia was behind her desk, complaining loudly. "Goddamn it, one of the fire exits has been opened now. Tito, can you go to the back and check it. It must be a full moon or something. Crazy is out to play."

As he walked down the hall, Darryl noticed the attractive redhead with the killer legs walking towards him. She gave him a wide smile. "Hey, sweetie. Hope y'all are having a good day."

Darryl smiled back and tried to think of something to say, but nothing came to mind. Instead he watched as she caught the security gate just before it closed behind Tito. Then she was out and walking away.

Darryl sighed and pressed the elevator button and one of the sets of doors reopened. He entered, stepping into an elevator containing a large man in a black coat with a thick beard.

"Thanks."

"Not a bother."

CHAPTER THIRTY-NINE

Matt Clarke walked into the bathroom stall, locked the door behind him, closed the toilet lid and sat down. He didn't need to use it. Apart from a burger yesterday – or was it the day before? – he'd hardly eaten in the last four days. What little had been in his system on Monday had been spewed up as soon as they'd got back from their meeting with Mrs Miller. He'd barely slept since then either. Every time he closed his eyes, all he could see was his baby sister, terrified and alone, in the situation he had put her in. He'd needed to be sharp over these last two days in order to do what Miller expected of him, so his stomach fizzed with a cocktail of coke, Adderall and something Brad had begrudgingly given him for the anxiety. It wasn't working. Matt could feel his heart thumping, like it was building up momentum to lift off, rip through his chest and make a break for it. A half sob, half giggle slipped from his lips at the image of his internal organ scampering off down the hall. He was aware his mind was only hanging in there by a thread.

What was torturing Matt wasn't the fear of getting caught, it was the certainty that he wouldn't be. He had spent the last three hours in his office, willing the phone to ring. Someone from the SEC – "We'd like to discuss your recent trade patterns, Mr Clarke." Elizabeth the receptionist – "Matt, Detectives Gregaro and Mason from the NYPD are back; they want to talk to you again about Charlie's murder." Hell, he'd take the FBI barging in, seizing computers, slapping on cuffs. He was carrying off the most audacious insider trade in Wall Street history and nobody seemed to care.

He knew the SEC was not going to come looking. David King, one of their lead dogs, had come to see him last month. The man had a fearsome reputation. Amongst a largely toothless organisation, he was one of the few who was happy to go hard if he smelled something was off. King had asked for a private meeting, and Matt had been concerned but not fearful. He had gone in with all of his stories well prepared. Over the last couple of years, he'd got very good at covering Lanark Lane's and the fund's tracks. All of the big moves they'd made were backed up by compelling research and analysis. It was a much easier gig when you started from the point of knowing the result and worked backwards. Still, when he'd gone into the meeting with King, he'd been better prepared than he'd been for any exam he'd ever taken, although it turned out he hadn't needed to be. King had made awkward small talk for twenty minutes before they'd come around to the purpose of the meeting. "I just want you to know," King had said, "that I've looked at Lanark Lane's deals from over the last couple of years, and as far as I'm concerned, they're all absolutely fine and above board."

Matt had been bemused, as this was a very odd statement for someone in King's position to make unbidden, and he'd suspected some kind of trap. King must've interpreted his reaction differently, as he reached across the table and touched Matt's hand, his voice suddenly low and shaky. "Please, tell them I said you were OK. I've got a family. Everything is fine. Tell them I said that."

Matt had been freaked out. "I... I don't know what you're talking about."

King had pulled his hand back, like a guy who'd made a misjudged pass. "Right. Of course. I just meant... I wanted you to know that after a careful investigation, we at the SEC are happy the Lanark Lane are a top-notch firm. You're just the man with the golden touch." Then he'd pushed out an overly forced laugh and the meeting had ended soon after.

King had thought he'd been sent to send a message to Matt's employers, but he hadn't. He'd been sent by those employers to send it to Matt. We are untouchable. In hindsight, it was preparation for getting Matt committed to what came next, in all of its terrible, horrifying glory.

As expected, shares in Millennium Faction Data had been suspended; they'd file for bankruptcy by the end of the week. The initial wave of sympathy for the company was turning to anger, now that the flaw in their system had been exposed and the true impact of the lost data had been realised. Matt felt for them. How could you anticipate that an employee would rig your mirroring software to send phoney data to the backups for three days and then blow up the primary site with him still inside it? Not even Matt had thought of that, and he'd gone looking for disaster scenarios.

People on the TV were calling the attack a knife to the economic heart of America, and everybody seemed to accept that Adaal Ackbar, a thirty-six-year-old data engineer, born and raised in Delaware, had, out of nowhere, become a jihadi radical. The guy had coached his kid's baseball team and sung in a barbershop quartet, and yet nobody questioned it. Nobody smelled a patsy. Adaal Ackbar and five other people were dead, and it was Matt's fault.

A few months ago, Miller had asked him for the biggest target imaginable, and after weeks of painstaking research, he'd come up with this. Thinking back, he couldn't remember what he'd thought they would do with the information – or if he'd even thought about it at all. Had he really been dumb enough to believe that there might just be a fire and the building would be evacuated? Or that they'd use hackers, or the wrong cable might get cut? Had he really been that naive? Then, twelve days ago, Miller had sat him down and explained in great detail exactly what would happen. She'd said that she had to, as the investment would be far too great to risk any misunderstanding. They were going all in, and there could be no mistakes. The only time there'd previously been an issue had been last year, when Matt had been informed that a certain airplane manufacturer would have a serious issue with the engine on one of its aircraft. They'd not given Matt enough details, and so, when an older model, no longer sold by the company, had indeed experienced an issue, resulting in a cargo plane going down in the Philippines, it had not had the effect Matt had expected. The plane had been out of all warranty and, due to cost-cutting measures, the recommended service schedule had not been maintained by the airline, so the manufacturer could easily wash their hands of it. Hell, seeing as it'd pushed two other airlines to order up-to-date planes from the same manufacturer, it had actually nudged their stocks up slightly, rather than causing the expected dip. Matt had shorted their stock heavily and the fund took a hit. Not a big one in the overall scheme of things, but enough to require an explanation. So, this time, Mrs Miller had told Matt everything. She had even told him the name – Adaal Ackbar. More than anything, he wished she'd never done that. The name had made it real. He was aware that other people had died previously – the pilot of the cargo plane, for one – but this had felt different. As much as he'd been able to coherently assess what had gone so wrong in his life since that meeting with Mrs Miller twelve days ago, that was one conclusion he'd reached: she should never have told him the poor patsy's name.

Matt pulled some sheets of toilet paper from the dispenser and wiped the sweat off his brow. It had been a "big day" on the markets. Lanark Lane had cashed in their chips the day before so that the money would be clear by tomorrow, as instructed by Miller. The traders on the desk were giddy with excitement, although even there, Matt could see that the smarter ones were highly suspicious. How could they not be? This had been The Fund's last big score, so even the pretence of subtlety had been abandoned. They were smashing the piggy bank and pulling off one of the biggest heists in Wall Street history. Matt's greatest creation. Disaster Inc's crowning glory.

The worst part was that he'd got it right. He'd sat there all week, watching as the three screens on his desk, full of reds and greens and flashing numbers, played out a symphony of his composing. No, no –

that wasn't it. It was like one of those massive domino displays, where someone painstakingly lays out the pieces and then from one teeny, tiny nudge they all fall in a perfectly choreographed sequence. The money had flown out of the companies affected by the data loss, causing the whole market to tumble as the tide was sucked out. Then, once the initial wave of panic had passed, much of it had flown back in again, the incoming tide lifting the unaffected competitors. It wasn't a crash as such, because while some shares were tanking, others thrived. It was a thing of beauty – terrible beauty – and it was all Matt's work. What had Miller said? That he had an eye for weakness. She'd been right. He'd made hundreds of millions for the people who were holding a gun to his sister's head, and he had the irrational craving for someone, anyone, to notice. But there was nobody he could call. Miller and her people were all over his phone lines, his PC – everything. His office and home were surely bugged. He was a prisoner in his own life and there was no escape. They were everywhere and there was nothing he could do other than exactly what they wanted. Or Jennie would be killed. What tortured him more than anything was the idea that, after these deals were closed, they wouldn't need him or Lanark Lane Investments again. It hadn't been openly stated, but this was clearly going to be the last massive pay-off. After the dust had settled on this, someone would come looking. A small, detached part of Matt's lizard brain had run the numbers from their perspective. Once this was done, Matt and Brad were not just expendable, they were unacceptable risk. Matt was past caring about himself, and he couldn't give any less of a fuck about Brad and his whiny boiled balls, but Jennie... Dear God in heaven, he had to save Jennie.

Matt heard a noise from the cubicle beside him and sat up a bit straighter. He'd thought he was alone. Come to think of it, that cubicle had an out-of-order notice on it, didn't it? Before he had time to process that thought, Matt jumped in surprise. In the corner of his eye, he felt sure he'd seen a face – a bearded face, looking down on him from over the partition wall. But when he looked properly, it was gone. Maybe it was God, looking down on him in judgement.

Then the bearded man shouldered the stall door in and Matt realised he wasn't God at all. Whatever the large guy with the wonky eye was, he was not celestial. There was a smell of booze and Mexican spices on his breath.

Before Matt could make a noise, the man had his hand wrapped tightly around his throat and was pressing him up against the wall. As you'd expect from a high-end office building such as this one, the bathroom stalls were larger than average. Still, as the man who wasn't God slammed the stall door closed behind him, there was precious little room in there for the three of them: Matt, this man and this man's wild, demented anger. His face was two inches from Matt's as he spoke, his crazed eyes the stuff of nightmares.

"Howerya, Matt, nice to finally meet you. I'm a friend of Amy's. You remember her? The woman you framed for murder because, thanks to you, she knows that a certain terrorist attack isn't what it appears?"

"Please, I—"

"I strongly – and I mean strongly – suggest the rest of that sentence prominently features the word 'sorry'. Thanks to you, that poor girl has had a fecking shite week." The man pushed his face even closer. "In all honesty, I'm not your biggest fan myself."

Matt tried to speak but the man's hand was wrapped too tightly around his throat. He dismissed the idea of trying to fight back in any way. Nothing about this man indicated that that would go well.

"I'm going to..."

The man stopped speaking as the door to the restroom opened and a whistling presence entered. It was Jimmy – or whistling Jimmy, as everyone called him. The man spent his life whistling tunelessly to himself. It was an annoying habit he himself acknowledged and apologised for repeatedly. He just whistled away, the happiest son of a bitch you've ever met in your damn life. They'd had to give him a desk on his own at the far end of the office, because the trading team complained about the whistling. There had also been a stapler-throwing incident which had needed to be dealt with. As it happened, being the company's compliance officer, it did make sense for Jimmy to sit apart anyway. He was supposed to be separate from the traders, as it was his job to verify all they did. This had given him the other nickname he had, the one Charlie had come up with, which only he, Matt and Brad had shared. Rubber Jimmy. So called because he was happy to rubber-stamp anything they put in front of him. It had been a long and exhaustive interview process, finding someone who was bad at their job in just the right way.

A zip was unzipped and the tune meandered in a new direction, accompanied by the sound of liquid hitting porcelain.

A strangled groan escaped Matt's lips, which resulted in the bearded man looking even more annoyed, a development Matt would not have thought possible.

The whistling stopped.

After a hesitant moment, Jimmy spoke. "Hey, everything alright in there?"

The bearded man glowered at Matt, who tried to form his face into apology. The hand around his throat was released and appeared in front of Matt's face, making a talking motion.

"Hey, Jimmy."

"Oh, hi, Matt. You OK, buddy?"

"Yeah. Sure. Bad tacos."

"Ouch. Been there!" Jimmy even sounded cheerful when discussing severe dietary discomfort. A zip was re-zipped and Jimmy proceeded to wash his hands.

"You want me to hang around, give you some company?"

Matt and the bearded man shared a peculiar moment, oddly bonding over the sheer weirdness of a grown man offering to give another grown man moral support through a bowel movement.

"Erm, no," said Matt. "I'm good thanks, Jimmy."

"Okely dokely," said Jimmy, tossing some paper towels into the bin. "Hang in there, buddy boy. Later, gator."

And then the door swung open and closed, delivering whistling Jimmy back into a world he was all but utterly oblivious to.

The bearded man pointed in the direction of the door. "Who the fuck?"

Matt shook his head. "Don't ask."

The bearded man puffed his cheeks out. "This is a weird fecking country. Anyway, where were we? Oh yeah." He slammed Matt back up against the cubicle wall. "I was going to beat the truth out of you."

"Alright. Look, I'm really sorry. I never meant for Amy to get hurt. I fucked up. This whole thing, all of it, is my fault, and I'm so unbelievably fucking sorry."

"You're not yet, but you're going to be..." The man stopped talking and tilted his head to the side. "Ah, for... Now what are you doing?"

"What?"

"You're fecking crying. Stop with the – ara Jesus."

He stepped back, tugged some sheets of toilet paper from the dispenser and handed them to Matt.

Matt took them, wiped his eyes and sat back on the toilet. "Sorry, I'm..."

"Alright, you can quit saying sorry now."

"Sor— OK. Yes. Sorry – shit – sorry."

"You need to make this right."

Matt looked up at the man. "I know, but... how?"

"How? You need to tell the truth. Contact the authorities. Spill the beans on the bad guys."

"I can't." Matt raised his hands as he saw the big man's expression darken. "No. Listen. I would if I could. Honestly. I don't care what happens to me, but they've got my sister."

"What?"

"Jennie, my kid sister. She's only twenty. Miller took her."

"Who the feck is Miller?"

"I don't know. Mrs Miller... that's just a name I gave her, because she looks like... It doesn't matter. The point is... Look, I know I know too much. These people, they don't care about leaving bodies in their wake. Once they get their money, I'm as good as dead after all that's happened. I know it. They know it. I got too much on them. It's why they took Jennie. They know I'll do whatever they want to protect her."

The man leaned back against the door and looked up at the ceiling. "Oh, for Christ's sake."

"I've been racking my brain," continued Matt, "trying to come up with some way out of this."

"So this whole thing is about money?"

Matt nodded. "A shit-ton of it. Miller described the fund as belonging to some people who formerly worked for the US government but are now 'retiring from public service' – her words. She joked about government pensions not being all that. They said, when they came to me, that they'd give me certain useful information, so I could invest their money and…"

"Fantastic. You're running a pension fund for mass murderers. You must be really proud."

"Look, I've made mistakes – so many God damn mistakes. More than anything, I want to try to make it right. But they got Jennie and I can't do anything until she's safe."

Silence filled the cubicle. Outside, the auto-wash system of the urinals whooshed.

The two men looked at each other for the longest time until, finally, the big man spoke. "So, if we were to get your sister to safety, you'd—"

"I'd do anything you asked," interrupted Matt. "Anything. Please." He reached forward and grabbed the hem of the big man's overcoat. "I'll do anything you want."

He reached down and gently pushed Matt's hands away. "That's a dangerous thing to be telling a strange man in a toilet cubicle. Alright, so you're their devious little prick. Let's see if we can't use that mind of yours against them. We'd best be quick, before anyone notices how long your shit is taking."

CHAPTER FORTY

"And that," said Bunny, "is what we agreed to."

He looked around nervously at the other three people assembled in Diller's front room: Amy, Diller and Smithy, whom Bunny had invited due to his previously demonstrated flair for creative thinking. None of them seemed particularly happy, which was in stark contrast to the members of the animal kingdom beaming at Bunny from all four walls and the ceiling.

There was also a live member of the animal kingdom in the room: a Siberian husky that Bunny happened to know wasn't Smithy's – or at least it hadn't been the first time he'd met him. On the upside, he bore very little resemblance to any of the members of Kiss. Bunny couldn't see its face, which was buried in its nether regions, lapping away enthusiastically as it had been throughout the brief presentation Bunny had just given.

"If I may," said Smithy. "I see a slight problem with your plan."

"OK," said Bunny. "What is it?"

"It is the entire lack of a plan."

"I'll admit, it's a bit short on detail."

"Short?" said Smithy. "I'm short. This shit is Peter Pan. As in, it doesn't exist. What you have laid out is a set of circumstances, which is entirely different to a plan."

"I thought," said Diller, "the plan was, we got you in there and then you slap the guy around a bit until he agrees to help."

"That was the plan," admitted Bunny, "but then circumstances changed. I mean, in a way, this works out better for us."

"Really?" said Amy. "How?"

"Well, we'll know where he, and hopefully his sister, will be at a certain time, and if we can get his sister back, then, y'know, it's all gravy." Bunny gave a thumbs up and then quickly rethought it. Once he'd successfully exited the building on Park Avenue without being seen by the watching men, it had dawned on him that he may have been better off knocking Matt unconscious and taking him with him. It had been the sister stuff. He was aware he'd allowed that to knock him off plan, and now they were royally screwed. Again.

"I can't believe I'm going to be the one to say it," said Smithy, "but wouldn't now be a good time to go to the authorities?"

"With what?" said Amy. "We don't have anything. We can't prove a damn thing. I can claim I heard a few words that sounded a bit like the target and prime suspect in a terrorist attack. The only people who have any idea I'm not completely making that up are" – she pointed at Bunny – "the invisible man with no name and a TV newsman who doesn't want to admit knowing me, never mind that I gave him a really weak piece of evidence about a massive conspiracy."

"Did you ring him again?" asked Bunny.

"I did. It took Diller and me an hour to find a working phone booth, but we got there eventually. His guy thinks it sounds very suspicious and he's looking into Lanark Lane Investments, but like we said, we don't have anything remotely close to evidence at the moment. Randall can't report anything that wouldn't lead to his company ending up in court, facing a defamation case they'll lose."

Bunny scratched at his beard. "Fair enough. And besides," he said, turning to Smithy, "whoever the people behind this are, they're linked into the security services or law enforcement or something. I saw the guy who tried to shoot me getting handed back his fecking gun and apologised to. If we go to the authorities, we have to assume it'll get right back to them."

"He's right," said Amy. "Believe me, I've done nothing but think this through again and again. The only way anyone will believe us is with a smoking gun, and that means getting Matt. Speaking of jerk-offs, is there any way you could stop your damn dog from doing that?"

Smithy and Amy glared at each other. "He's not my dog."

"What are you, a dog-sitter?"

"No. I stole him."

Amy threw her hands in the air. "Great. We're bringing stolen goods to meetings now."

"It's either that or he starts barking at all the weird pictures on the wall again." Smithy glanced at Diller. "No offence, Dill." Then he looked back at Amy. "And besides, suspected murderers in glasshouses shouldn't throw stones."

"Alright," said Bunny, stepping forward, "enough of that. Can we focus on the problem in hand, please? We know where they'll be and when. We also know that this Mrs Miller and her lot are highly trained and heavily armed."

"And they've got a sniper," said Amy.

"What?" said Smithy and Diller in unison.

"Oh yeah," said Bunny. "They do."

The room fell into silence. Or at least what would've been silence, if not for the sound of a stolen dog enthusiastically fellating himself.

"Jesus Christ, Not Gene Simmons," said Smithy. "Could you stop doing that?"

To everyone's surprise, not least Smithy's, Not Gene Simmons immediately did as instructed.

"Oh," said Smithy, "I wasn't expecting that."

"First thing that's gone right in a while," said Bunny.

"Hey," said Smithy, "I think you'll find *Lethal Weapon* 2 worked pretty well."

Bunny nodded. "No, it did. That was a great idea – and do thank Cheryl again for me. She was great."

"Yeah, she is great," said Smithy.

"She seems to think very highly of you. What's going on there? If you don't mind me asking."

Smithy shrugged. "Look, she deserves better than a guy with no decent prospects, a stolen dog and a propensity for getting himself buried up to his neck in stupid shit. Case in point," he said, holding his arms out wide.

"Fair enough."

The room lapsed into silence as they each fell into contemplation of the problem.

Not Gene Simmons took a gander at his own nether regions again, then, noticing the four sets of eyes locked on him, decided against it.

Upstairs, they could hear Mrs James singing a song about young lovers in a warbling voice.

Diller cleared his throat. "I have an idea."

"OK."

"Great."

"Good."

"I'm..." He hesitated. "Look, it's probably really stupid."

"It's got to be better than the nothing we have so far," said Amy.

"Go on, give it a lash," said Bunny.

"There is no such thing as a bad idea," said Smithy.

Diller then explained his idea.

When he'd finished, he looked around at the others. The only one that seemed excited was Not Gene Simmons.

"Yeah," said Amy, "that definitely won't work."

"Sorry, Dill," said Smithy, "but I take it back. That is a terrible idea."

Bunny nodded. "Afraid so."

Diller shrugged. "Well, worth a shot."

They lapsed back into contemplative silence.

Over the next hour, they rehashed what they knew and took shots at pitching ideas, more often than not bailing halfway through their explanations as they realised why a plan definitely wouldn't work.

After two hours, the best idea they had was Diller's – mainly because it was the only idea.

For want of anything else to discuss, they discussed the many reasons why Diller's idea definitely wouldn't work.

An hour later, they'd worked through what they'd have to do if they were going to carry out Diller's stupid idea, which they definitely weren't doing.

An hour after that: "Look," said Bunny, "we need to stop talking about Diller's fecking stupid idea. It'll not work."

Another hour after that: "Look," said Diller, "can we stop referring to it as Diller's stupid idea."

"It is pretty stupid though, Dill," said Smithy.

"I know. That's why I'm disowning it. I don't want us to try it, fail and then have everyone blaming me afterwards."

"That won't happen," said Amy in a kind voice.

"Yeah," agreed Bunny. "Besides, the odds are very good that most of us would be dead, so you'll be fine on that score."

Bunny had meant it as a joke, but it had been too close to the truth.

The room lapsed into silence again.

Another hour later, due to the absence of any other form of plan, they were doing Diller's stupid idea.

Not Gene Simmons went back to vigorously engaging with himself. They left him to it.

CHAPTER FORTY-ONE

Matt typed in the commands to the various windows on the laptop in front of him. They were sitting at the large mahogany conference table in his office. Back on his usual desk, the three monitors filled with numbers were showing Wall Street's nervous rebound continuing at a hesitant pace.

Matt's was a big office. He remembered how happy he'd been on the first day he'd moved in. Now, it was like a prison, same as everywhere else in the waking nightmare his life had become. Speaking of nightmares... he looked across the desk, where Brad sat looking eagerly back at him while Cole observed, his face the emotionless mask it always was.

Matt spun the laptop around and placed it in front of Brad. "OK, Brad, just log in and give authorisation and I can confirm the transfer."

Brad bit his lips nervously. "Before we do this," he said, in the whine his voice seemed to have permanently become, "can I just confirm about the bomb you put inside me?"

"Relax," said Cole. "You're doing as you're told. As long as you both keep doing that, you'll be fine."

"But," said Brad, sitting forward, "can I just clarify, after we do this and, y'know, you get your money, is someone going to take it out?"

"It degrades naturally," said Cole. "Nobody needs to take it out."

"I'm sorry, I just... No, I need more clarification than that." Brad's eyes were full of watery pleading. "Please, I'm being good. I don't want to die."

"You won't."

"I will. I know I will. Once you've got your money, I'm expendable."

"Brad," said Matt in a firm voice, "pull your shit together and do what needs to be done."

"Fuck you, Matt. That's easy for you to say. You haven't got a fucking bomb inside you."

Matt's voice came out as a snarl. "They've got Jennie, you asshole. Shut up and do what you're told."

"OK," said Cole, "just relax. Like I said, the device degrades – just like, as soon as this is verified, Matt's sister will be released. We're right at the finishing line here – let's not get stupid. In fact, if it'll make you feel better." He pulled out a small white device, not much bigger than a cigarette lighter, and held it in front of Brad. "This is the detonator. Once you complete your part, I'll hand it to you. OK?"

Brad stared in wide-eyed fear at the innocuous piece of equipment that Cole placed on the mahogany desk – to his right-hand side, away from Brad.

"Give it to me first!"

Cole didn't say anything, just moved his hand a fraction towards the device.

"OK, OK, OK," said Brad. "Jesus!" He started typing furiously into the laptop while glancing at the detonator every other second, like he had a nervous twitch.

The laptop gave an unhappy beep.

"For Christ's sake, Brad," said Matt. "Concentrate. You've put your password in wrong."

"Shut the fuck up!"

Brad refocused and typed in the passwords. Then he turned the laptop back to Matt. "There. Done."

Matt pulled the laptop towards him, checked the windows and then started typing away again. After a minute, he said, "Ok, and… we're done."

"I've gotta call the boss," said Cole. "Verify."

"Sure," said Matt. "Call away."

Cole pulled out his cell phone. As it rang, he calmly slapped away Brad's hand, which had been moving across the table. "Fucking idiot. Oh no – sorry, ma'am, not you. Yes, it's done."

Cole listened for a minute in silence. His eyes bored into Matt, who was sitting on the other side of the desk, smiling at him.

Finally, Matt looked at his screen again. "Oh, I see what's happened here. Can I have a quick word with her, please?"

Cole gave Matt a suspicious look and then passed the phone across.

"Hi, it's Matt. Yeah, there's a slight problem. You see, I just executed a script on my end and all of your money got transferred into a password-protected account in the Cayman Islands. One that only I have the password for. And it has to be given in my voice."

Cole and Brad tensed on the other side of the table.

Matt held up a finger to still them. "Don't…" Then he continued, "See, here's the thing. You get what you want, and me, Brad and my sister are all as good as dead. So here's what's going to happen. It's now" – Matt looked at his watch – "2:47pm. At 4pm, I'm going to walk down the road to Madison Square Park, where I'm going to meet my sister. I'm going to say my farewells, watch her get into a cab and drive away, and then you'll hand me a phone and I'll make the call that will get you your dirty fucking money."

"I see," said Mrs Miller on the other end of the line. "And what exactly is to stop Mr Cole extracting that password from you?"

"Well," said Matt, as he dipped his hand into his desk drawer, "here's the problem with that, you sociopathic bitch. Seeing as I don't believe you'll really let my sister go, you've left me with nothing to lose." He pulled out a certain razor-sharp letter opener and held it to his own throat. "So, I've just taken a hostage of my own. Me."

CHAPTER FORTY-TWO

New York was a weird city in general and in March in particular. You could get snow storms, typhoons and vicious thunderstorms like they'd had a few nights ago, or it could be like it was now – an unseasonable heatwave, with the temperature touching seventy degrees. People who weren't insane, or making some kind of a point, were out in shorts and T-shirts. It was warm enough that an idiot could kill a dog by leaving it in the back seat of a car, although, it being Manhattan, if you could afford the parking, then you could certainly afford a dogsitter, the extra expense being justified by saving your soul from burning in hell for all eternity.

It was into this balmy day that Matt Clarke stepped at 3:50pm from his office on Park Avenue, intent on making the short walk down four blocks to meet his sister in Madison Square Park. It was the kind of thing normal people did. He was wearing an overcoat, as if he'd not checked the weather forecast before leaving the office or, indeed, just looked out a window. He appeared to be chatting on his phone, although an observant person might have noticed that, while he held his phone to his ear, he wasn't talking much. An extremely observant person might notice that under the sleeve of his inappropriate overcoat, a razor-sharp letter opener was held tightly to his right wrist by his watch strap, inches from his own neck. If anyone tried anything funny, he could slice through his carotid artery at a moment's notice, and before anyone could do anything, the only key to millions of dollars in the Cayman Islands would bleed out over his inappropriate overcoat.

Behind, keeping the agreed distance so as not to spook him, walked Mr Cole.

"Do you think he'd really do it?" asked Mrs Miller through the earpiece he was wearing.

"I am not qualified to give that assessment."

"What the fuck is that supposed to mean?"

"What it means is I'm not a psychiatrist, although if you'd like my unprofessional opinion, as a man who has seen a lot of people lose their shit over the years, yeah, I believe he would do it. That's the thing about pushing someone to breaking point: you can never be sure how they're gonna break."

"Is that a criticism, Mr Cole?"

"It's an observation."

"I notice you've stopped saying 'ma'am' when you address me. Please direct your astute observational skills to Mr Clarke. Also, where is Mr Bradley?"

"He became emotional. I knocked him out."

"Was that—"

"Yes," interrupted Cole. "The idiot still believes we actually did put a bomb inside him and he was losing his shit. I removed the variable."

"Very well, but—"

She was interrupted when another voice intruded over the line from Cole's end. "The end is nigh, madam. Gobble ye not the hot dog of Satan..."

"What the hell is that?" asked Miller.

"Some lunatic street preacher with a sandwich board."

"Fucking New York," said Miller. "We are still in control of this situation. Lola has just done a brief sweep of the park. It is busy with civilians but there is no sign of any law enforcement. I have contacted our NYPD contact and he has diverted foot patrols, citing a national security operation. Lola and Baxter have the girl. When she leaves the park, she will flag a taxi; we have two of them waiting. They'll either get her or follow the one that does and reacquire the girl when appropriate."

"Why not just let her go?"

"Excuse me?"

"I mean, lying to the guy has got us into this mess. Perhaps we should try—"

"I am not interested in your opinions, Mr Cole. Operational parameters say leave no trace and they have not changed. Why don't you—" Miller gave out a moan.

"Are you OK?"

"I'm fine. Do your job and let me do mine."

With that, Mrs Miller hung up the phone. "Christ, Jorge, go easy," she said. She didn't feel bad about shouting at Jorge, not least because he couldn't hear her. He was mostly deaf and entirely Guatemalan, with the toned physique of someone who enjoyed the company of a mirror. His grasp of the English language didn't extend much beyond what was required for his job. Having severely limited communication abilities as a masseur could be seen as a handicap in certain ways; however, for the right client, it could be very useful. He couldn't overhear the wrong thing, and even if he did, he wouldn't understand it. Mrs Miller appreciated his inbuilt ironclad discretion, as well as his willingness to go above and beyond in certain areas for tips.

She was in her hotel suite, lying face down and naked on Jorge's massage table. Initially, she had booked him as a treat for when the mission was completed. She hadn't cancelled because that would have been a concession to the idea that the situation was out of her control – which it was not.

Through the hole in the table, she could see the screen of her laptop, which she'd placed beneath it. She reached a hand down and pressed a button. "Lola, the primary is on his way. Are you in position?"

The view changed from the back of a leather car seat to Lola's face. She nodded at the camera. She had tried to conceal it with make-up, and she was wearing her hair down, but the scratch on her face was still visible.

"OK, wait for my go."

Miller pressed another button. "Eagle One, are you in position?"

"Confirmed."

"Then turn on your damn camera."

"Sorry."

After a moment, the screen sprung to life, showing an angled view down onto the busy park.

"Where are you?"

"I was able to gain access to the roof of a building on the west side."

"Do you have an angle on the whole park?"

"Negative. About eighty per cent. Best I could manage on this notice. There's also some foliage cover."

"Yes. Well..."

Miller watched the feed. It seemed like an ordinary day for the oblivious civilians below. She could see people playing frisbee. Eating picnics. Walking their dogs.

"You've a lot of tension around de glutes. Would you like de special?"

"Shut the fuck up, Jorge."

"Excuse me?"

Miller cursed under her breath. "Never mind. Eagle One, stand by for further instructions and, erm, well done."

She hit a button on the laptop to mute it and then slapped Jorge's hand. He giggled, misconstruing entirely what this meant.

Madison Square Park took up three blocks of the world's most expensive real estate, slap bang in the middle of Manhattan, flanked by Madison Avenue and Fifth Avenue on one axis and East 23rd street and East 26th on the other. In a world of perpendicular lines, Broadway delighted in doing its own thing, running at a more or less forty-five degree angle, and so where it met Madison Square Park it sliced off the corner where East 33rd met Fifth Avenue, ruining the park's otherwise perfect symmetry. Broadway then went along its merry way, its peculiar path giving rise to the iconic Flatiron Building across the road, a slim triangle in a world of boxes. Looking down from Madison Avenue, amidst the trees you could see that the paths in the park formed two bicycle-like wheels, each with six curving spokes, the rear one looking a bit squashed by Broadway's intrusion. The fountain was at the centre of that wheel. It was never not busy, but on an unexpectedly sunny day, more people than usual went there to enjoy the rarity of green amidst the skyscrapers and traffic, or to let their kid calm down after they'd become over-stimulated in the nearby Lego store.

Amy took a deep breath. Under her helmet she wore a Bluetooth headset, connected to the phone in her pocket. When Bunny had explained the need for communication if the plan was to have any hope, she'd given Diller the cash and he'd gone out and bought them a bunch of burner phones.

The plan felt absurd now. It had felt absurd yesterday, but in a "so crazy it just might work" kind of a way. Now it felt straight-up absurd. She'd only known Bunny for five days, and Diller and Smithy even less; the chances they were taking for her felt like lead weights attached to her body. She wanted to hit the speed-dial numbers, tell them all to forget it, go away – hell, run for their damn lives. They were playing Russian roulette with a fully loaded gun.

Some impatient idiot in the line of traffic on Fifth Avenue honked their horn and Mabel shifted nervously beneath her. "Easy, girl. Easy." The traffic for this time on a Friday was as advertised, moving at a crawl in almost every direction. She shot the driver with the happy horn hand a dirty look and he gave an apologetic wave.

Amy nodded, trying to stay in character.

Despite being New York's most wanted for most of the week,

today she had committed two crimes for the first time in her life, at least as far as she was concerned. The first was technically rustling – the unlawful acquisition of a horse. She'd left a thousand dollars and a note at the stables, promising Mabel would be back that evening. But still, theft was theft, and Amy was sure they'd still have called the cops. Speaking of which, that was the other crime. Smithy's girlfriend had got her the outfit. From a distance, it did more or less look the part. Only close up would people perhaps notice that the pants were spandex and the shirt didn't have proper buttons, this version having Velcro that allowed for instant easy removal. The gun on her belt was also fake. Of the many things that were feeling ridiculous now, the fact that all of the weapons in this situation were held by the other side was possibly the most ludicrous. And for a wanted murderer riding a stolen horse while dressed in a stripper's cop outfit, that was really saying something.

Douglas Randall sat back in his office chair and took the first moments of silence he'd had in the last hour to try to calm his breathing. It had not been easy. When Amy had called, he'd told her it wouldn't be easy, and he'd been right. Still, he had managed to get them to agree to it. The director of news had looked at him like he was losing his damn mind, but when he'd laid it out and threatened to resign if they didn't grant him this one unusual request, he'd agreed. He knew right now that he'd be up in his office talking to the station heads, informing them that the reliable old lapdog that presented the evening news had just gone rabid, but still, they'd at least let it play out.

There were two versions of how the rest of today went. In one, Douglas Randall would be a punchline – divorced, disgraced and derided. In the other version, he'd receive the Pulitzer Prize. He looked at the empty space on his shelf beside the picture of him with George Foreman. He was either going to get some serious hardware to go alongside it, or else this time next week, it'd be someone else's shelf.

"This is nice," said Cheryl.

"Excuse me?" said Smithy.

"This. Having a picnic in the park. It's nice. It's the kind of stuff real couples do."

"We're not really having a picnic though."

Cheryl rolled her eyes. "I know that, dummy, but you're the method actor. The easiest way for me to look like I'm having a picnic with my boyfriend in the park is to, y'know, actually have a picnic with my boyfriend in the park. Here, have a Twinkie."

"No thanks. Look, hon' – you've got to take this seriously."

"What, the picnic? I am. You're the one who isn't committing. Alright, the food is Twinkies and a six pack, but you didn't give me much time to prepare."

Smithy leaned in and put his hand on top of hers. "Seriously. This isn't a game. These are some bad people."

"I know that, Smithy. I'm not an idiot. I've got an IQ of 148 and a full understanding of the situation as it has been explained to me. However, I also have a bag full of Twinkies so, y'know, for just a hint of normalcy in our fucked-up relationship, be a doll and eat the goddamned processed sugar."

She held a Twinkie out and Smithy bit into it. "Christ, I forgot how horrible these things are."

"Well, I'm a lot of things, but Little Miss Homemaker ain't one of 'em. If I get gunned down in the forthcoming firefight, make sure your next squeeze is into home baking."

"Don't say that. Christ, I should never have asked you to do this."

"Oh, calm down. Alright, I'll stop with the jokes. It's your loss though; I'm quite the dazzling conversationalist."

"I know just... promise me you'll be careful."

Cheryl rolled her eyes but didn't say anything more when she saw the look on Smithy's face.

"Just please, I'd never forgive myself if something happened to you."

She put the remaining half of the Twinkie back into the bag. "Y'know, you're one sweet little bastard when you want to be. I promise I'll be careful. Also, y'know, I am a black belt in Krav Maga, so I'm pretty much the most dangerous person in this park."

Smithy looked over Cheryl's shoulder. "Sadly, that isn't the case." He pressed a button on the phone lying on the blanket in front of him. "Heads up. They're here."

Marilyn Jessop was trying to make the best of a bad situation. She was in New York for a week with her friend Becky and it was supposed to be the trip of a lifetime. They were freshmen at Penn State, and when this idea had first come up, it had felt like an amazing adventure. In Marilyn's defence, New York was amazing, it was just everything else that was a disaster.

She'd met Danny a couple of years ago at a debate camp. They have camps for everything: Christian camps, fat camps, baseball camps, band camps. If you looked hard enough, there was no doubt a camp to assist weight loss through baseball, percussion and Jesus. Yes, debate camp may have been a bit nerdy, but it had been a chance for her to get out of Laguna Falls for a couple of weeks, and back when she was in high school, she'd have done anything for that.

Danny was a year older than her, and she'd thought he was possibly the most interesting guy in the world. He was into bands she'd never heard of, authors she'd never read and philosophies from countries whose takeout wasn't even available in boring old Laguna Falls. At the time, most boys Marilyn's age had been monosyllabic and only interested in trying to get their hand on a boob. What was it with men and boobs? Jesus, they're just devices to deliver milk to babies, get over it! Danny had been different: he'd been deep, he'd been artistic, and he'd been so engaged with the larger world around him, while, admittedly, having his hand on her boob. Still, it had been special.

It had been almost two years and they'd stayed in contact. They hadn't been pen pals, because it wasn't the 1980s, but they'd texted,

WhatsApped and twice FaceTimed. It had been a very casual thing. Marilyn had given herself panic attacks while playing it cool. She'd obsessed over each message received and studiously waited the required time before replying. Danny was her high school crush, unobtainable and miles away – and even further once he'd gone to NYU. Of course he had; he was so damn cool. He was studying architecture but considering dropping out to focus on his poetry, and besides, conventional education was so restrictive. He'd invited Marilyn out for a few days, while his roommate was away. She'd brought Becky because, well, she wasn't some kinda easy girl. Besides, Becky had an aunt upstate and they'd agreed she could go visit her if sparks flew.

Sparks did not fly. Danny was going through a "natural" phase, so he didn't wash his hair and only bathed in the rain. In the thunderstorm a couple of nights ago, he'd stepped out on the fire escape naked, to become one with nature. A neighbour had hit him with a beautifully tossed pineapple. In the eighty-nine hours that she'd been back in his company, Marilyn had realised what that neighbour already knew: Danny was a pretentious ass-hat and quite possibly the dullest man on Earth. Reality had come crashing down brutally fast – so much so that Marilyn viewed the version of herself who'd got off the plane ninety-one hours ago as a naive idiot. That had been bad. Then they'd all got drunk and Becky had made out with Danny.

Why they were in Madison Square Park at that moment sitting on a bench beside the fountain was because she'd spotted a shout-out on social media and leaped on it like a life raft. She had wanted to have a unique New York experience and this was her chance. She'd seen a tweet about a special event happening here after one of the girls from her sorority had retweeted it from a girl who was a presenter on one of the channels that was like MTV but not MTV – cooler than MTV – although it had turned out to be owned by MTV. The point was, it was a chance to be part of something other than the embarrassing love triangle that'd become her trip. Danny could not ruin this.

Danny was trying to ruin this.

"Yah, I mean these things started as kind of a social experiment but then, y'know, popular culture got hold of it and ruined it like so much else. The first one actually happened right here in Manhattan. It was organised by an editor at Harper's y'know as, like, an ironic thing. But then..."

"Shut up," said Marilyn. She ignored Danny's smug little look of outrage, which she now hated more than anything else in the entire fucking universe, and instead went back to looking at happy couples walking by, wondering which one it was going to be.

Matt took a look over his shoulder and saw Cole exactly where he'd been for the previous few blocks: ten feet behind him. Cole stopped and raised his hands in an "everything is cool" gesture.

Matt's mind was racing. Running over everything that he'd said to the big man. It turned out that the most important meeting of his life had happened in a toilet stall. All they'd agreed was that Matt would find a way to hijack the money transfer and then refuse to do anything until they'd let him see and talk to Jennie in the flesh. He'd thought of Madison Square Park just because it was nearby, but it was also where he had met Jennie the one time he'd convinced her to come to New York. They'd been off to see a Broadway show. Matt had skipped out in the intermission, saying he had stomach cramps, and then he'd gone and got high. She hadn't visited again. Christ, he had been such an asshole.

The big man had told him to get her to the park and he'd take care of the rest. Matt was putting his and his sister's fates in the hands of some wild-eyed lunatic he'd never met before, whose name he didn't even know. All he knew was that he matched the description of the guy who'd flash-fried Brad's balls. As references went, it was a pretty good one. Brad, like Matt, deserved everything that he had coming, as far as Matt was concerned. Matt knew that he had been numbing his conscience with drugs and whatever else for months now, but the last few days had acted like a *shakubuku* – a swift spiritual kick to the head that alters a person's reality. He wasn't sure it was a real thing; he may have just seen it in a movie. Right now, his only concern was Jennie and getting her away safely. She was an innocent in all of this. He and Brad, on the other hand – they'd made their deals with the devil.

Finally, Matt ran through the words that the black kid outside his office with the "The End is Nigh" sign had shouted at him on his way by. The big guy must have needed to get a message to him, even if the message itself made no sense.

Matt stepped into the park.

Here goes nothing.

CHAPTER FORTY-THREE

Cheryl nodded across to the other side of the park. "That's her."

"How do you know that?" said Smithy.

"Because I googled her. Damn, did you people not even do that? I need to be in on the planning meeting next time."

"I don't think we'll be making this a regular thing."

Smithy turned his body as if opening a beer, which allowed him to glance in the direction of Cheryl's nod without looking obvious. It was true that he didn't know what Matt Clarke's sister looked like, but he didn't need to. He could have just looked for the girl who looked utterly terrified. She wore a yellow fleece and jeans, her hair tied back in a ponytail. She had just entered from the Broadway side of the park and now stood in the middle of the path, flanked on either side by an admittedly smoking hot Latina woman and a large white guy with tightly cropped red hair, who was cute enough but not really Smithy's type, although he did have a thing for redheads.

Smithy looked in the other direction and saw Matt Clarke walking towards the fountain. The expression on his sister's face when she saw him was hard to miss, and her legs nearly went from under her. It reminded Smithy of some footage he'd seen on the news of a woman who'd been freed after two days buried in the rubble of a building that had collapsed in an earthquake. Jennie tried to move towards her brother but was held back by her guards.

Matt marched forward and stopped beside the fountain, looking carefully at the sunbathers, benchwarmers and picnic-ers, fearful of some kind of trap. About fifteen feet behind him was a black guy. Smithy assumed this was the man Bunny had tussled with previously.

The trio took a step towards Matt Clarke, but he held out his hand to stop them. Then he pointed at his sister. The redhead glanced at the Latina, who gave the briefest of nods, and they both released their grip. Jennie rushed towards her brother, tears in her eyes.

Smithy and Cheryl carefully got to their feet, like a real couple who'd just finished the real picnic they had been having.

"Here we go," said Cheryl. "D'you think Diller got him the message OK?"

"We're about to find out."

"Remember," said Smithy, "you promised me that, no matter what, you'd get the hell out of here."

"But—"

"You promised."

"Alright. But this is a bit like bringing a gun to a gun fight and still using a knife."

"I love you."

Cheryl did a double take. "Really? You pick now to say that for the first time?"

"I'm unconventional."

"I love you too, you irritating son of a bitch."

Matt hugged his baby sister tight. "I'm so sorry, I'm so sorry."

"Matt, I... I don't... They wouldn't explain to me. I don't understand."

Matt gently pulled away and held her at arm's length. "We don't have much time." He glanced around, noticing that there were more people than just Cole, Lola and the redheaded guy now looking at them. "Listen, Jennie, this is really important. Whatever happens, know that I'm so sorry that I got you involved in this. I got in over my head with some really bad people. Whatever you hear about me, know that I tried to make it right."

She gaped at him in confusion. He got an unwanted flashback of when he'd told her about their father's passing and a little bit of his heart broke all over again. "I'm getting you out of this. Some people are going to help."

"But..." Jennie looked back at the people who had held her captive. "How are you going to—"

"There's no time. Just... just trust me and play along."

She nodded her head furiously. Even now, even after all he had put her through, she still trusted her big brother to make it all OK.

As Matt had left the office, the black kid with the sandwich board had been hollering the typical nonsense. Initially he'd ignored him, but the dude had stepped directly into his path and pointed at him. "You, sir, repent your sins. Get down on your knees and propose to the girl. It's the only way to save her. So sayeth the big man with the beard and the weird eye."

Matt had paused for a second and then walked on. The kid had turned and harangued a woman walking by in the other direction. "The end is nigh, madam. Gobble ye not the hot dog of Satan..."

He took one last look around at the park full of people enjoying the sunshine and then fell to his knees. He looked up at his sister, the only person left in the world he cared about. "Will you marry me?"

Jennie looked down at him in confusion. "What?"

Before she could say anything else, a voice roared from somewhere behind him. "SHE SAID YES!"

Then a world that had seemingly lost all reason really went totally fucking crazy.

Once the shout went up, Marilyn was up and on her feet and running towards the happy couple. She was doing it. Ever since she'd first seen the videos on YouTube, she'd wanted to be part of a flash mob – and now she was finally doing it! Much to her relief, other people all around her were on their feet too. The thought of how mortifyingly embarrassing it would be if she were the only person to join in had occurred to her, but she pushed herself through it. It was really happening. Forget Danny. Forget Becky. She was doing it. The tweet had been really clear in its instructions.

Flashmob!! I'm proposing to my girlfriend just after 4pm tomorrow by the fountain in Madison Square Park. Please be part of a massive group hug & make the best moment of my life even more special. Join in when you hear SHE SAID YES!! #GroupHug #SpecialMoment #FlashMob

"What the fuck is happening?!"

Miller screamed it at the picture on the laptop. Suddenly, the world had gone insane. Most of the people in the park had simultaneously stood up and begun running towards the Clarke siblings. She watched as the pair were engulfed in a sea of humanity. "Fuck, fuck, fuck, fuck!"

Jorge, with his 10% hearing, entirely misunderstood this too.

Marilyn had run track in high school so she'd been the second one to reach the happy couple. "Congratulations!" she'd hollered in a near scream. The first person there was a redheaded woman with a Texas drawl. She was weird. Even as people were charging in from all sides to join the congratulatory group hug, she grabbed the bride-to-be and then spoke to the groom. "I've got her. That way – go now!"

"But—"

"Go!"

Marilyn found herself in the middle of a mass of humanity. It was like a mosh pit, only not at all, seeing as it was so friendly. People were cheering and shouting their congratulations. Somebody attempted to start a sing-song. "All you need is…"

And then there were three loud bangs and people started screaming.

Cole looked across at Lola, who had her gun pointed in the air. Goddamn her, she'd never been a fan of the subtle approach. Miller was screaming in his earpiece: "Lola, secure the primary. Cole, get the sister." People were running every which way, in any direction that took them as far away from Lola as possible in the shortest amount of time. A fat guy in a "Where's Maggie?" T-shirt nearly bowled Cole over. New Yorkers four days after a terrorist attack were always going to be a powder keg of tension, and Lola had just casually tossed the match.

Cole looked around, trying to locate Jennie Clarke's yellow fleece amidst the chaos. There, running into the park. A woman was guiding her away, but Jennie had stumbled and fallen in her panicked state. As the other woman picked her up, she looked back to see Cole running towards them, the look in her eyes one of terror. People were scrambling for cover around him, forcing Cole to bob and weave. The two women took off running again, heading towards the centre of the other wheel. Cole was gaining fast, Jennie Clarke's yellow fleece almost within touching distance. He had just begun drawing his Glock from the holster under his right armpit when something crashed into him, sending him hurtling into the bushes and the gun flying from his grasp.

Cole regained his footing fast, because everything in his training had always taught him that only dead men, or those destined to soon join them, stayed on the ground. The bearded Irishman was similarly getting himself upright just a few feet away.

"How's it going?"

"I'm getting really sick of you."

"To be honest with ye, I hear that a lot."

Cole hurled himself towards the man, sending them both pinwheeling over a park bench and sprawling to the ground once again.

Lola scanned the crowd. Behind her, Baxter was on the ground, while a stocky child seemed to be kicking him in the head. Lola did not have the time nor the inclination to care.

She spotted Matt Clarke rushing out the exit at the corner of East 23rd and Broadway, one amongst many in the fleeing crowd. She stopped and trained her sights on him. Miller screamed in her ear. "Alive, Lola! We need him alive."

With a snarl of frustration, she pulled her gun up and started running towards the exit. Clarke reached the sidewalk and stood there like a rabbit in the headlights. Lola was closing fast. She could see the delicious terror in his eyes. Forty feet away... thirty... twenty...

A cop on horseback moved in front of Clarke and blocked him from Lola's view. She slowed her pace. This was a problem. Shooting a policeman was certainly doable, but it would be inconvenient. Then she looked again and corrected herself. Policewoman. Lola redoubled her pace as she saw Matt Clarke climb up behind the policewoman and into the saddle. Lola lunged at the horse, narrowly missing it as the cop kicked and the animal took off down the pavement at a canter, sending pedestrians hurtling out of its way.

"Goddamn it!" screamed Miller in Lola's ear. Lola trained her gun on Clarke's rapidly disappearing back. "Alive!" screamed the voice again.

Lola pulled up her gun and looked for something to kick. Then she noticed something that gave her a much better idea.

Miller pressed a button to flip through her feeds.

"Ms? Excuse me, Ms..."

Miller was far too busy to notice, but at some point she had clamped her legs together, trapping the masseur at the wrist. She had very strong thighs for a woman her age.

The bird's-eye view of Madison Square Park filled the screen. "Eagle One, shoot the horse."

"Say that again?"

"Shoot the horse!"

She watched as the angle of the video feed jerked and then zoomed in on the horse and its two riders, currently galloping along the East 23rd Street side of the park.

All Amy knew was that she couldn't stop, so while people screamed all around her, she had to keep moving forward. She dug her heels into Mabel's flanks and spurred her on. "C'mon. Good girl. Good girl."

"Oh God, oh God, oh God." Matt had his arms wrapped around her waist so tightly, there was a real chance he could break one of her ribs.

On the sidewalk in front of her, she was confronted by three mothers with strollers rushing straight at her, away from where they seemed to assume the danger was. Amy cursed under her breath and tugged the reins to turn Mabel out onto the road and into the bus lane, causing an oncoming X12 Staten Island Express bus to judder to a halt in a squeal of outraged brakes and hydraulics. Mabel reared up on her back legs and neighed in terror. Amy's years of experience allowed her to ride it and Matt's sheer desperation kept him clinging on. The world seemed to slow as Amy saw the outrage on the bus driver's face. His mouth formed a large O, ready to shout some abuse that never came – his outrage turning to disbelief as his front windscreen exploded.

Lots of people screamed, Matt amongst them. Amy didn't have that luxury. She didn't know where the shot had come from, but she wasn't going to wait around to find out. Instead, she urged Mabel on, and the horse, more terrified of what was behind it, bolted forward into the next lane, causing the westbound cars to similarly judder to a halt.

Amy tugged Mabel left, allowing them to move between the two flows of traffic. A taxi driver on the west side jumped out of his vehicle to remonstrate with her and then gawped at the bonnet of his car, where a smoking hole had inexplicably appeared. Amy guided Mabel around the open car door in her path before spurring her on again to pick up some speed.

Through a cacophony of car horns, they zoomed across the intersection with Madison and then back onto the sidewalk, sending pedestrians scurrying to get out of their way. As she did so, a bullet fizzed by her ear and an advert that implied the secret to a long and happy life was well-conditioned hair shattered.

"Damn it," said the voice. "Target has escaped."

"Eagle One, you are a disgrace!"

"Fuck you, lady."

"Excuse me, miss," said Jorge.

The screen went dead.

"Excuse me, you have my hand. Between your legs... Ahhh, ahhh, ahhh – it hurts!"

"Lola?" screeched Miller. "Where are you? And where the fuck is Cole?"

If anything, Bunny was losing worse than the first time. He concentrated his efforts on just trying to tie the big black guy up as he rolled about on the floor. Bunny had gone for a headbutt but the guy had dropped his chin, causing Bunny to ram his own nose into his opponent's forehead. He'd broken his nose a few times before, but this felt like a messy one. There was a lot of blood on his opponent; unfortunately, none of it was his. Still, at least Bunny had ruined an expensive-looking suit.

Bunny went for an eye gouge and yelped in agony as the middle finger on his right hand was snapped back and broken. The black guy used this distraction to twist himself and get his weight on top of Bunny, pinning him to the ground.

In a fight, if both participants are on the ground, then the most important thing is who ends up on top. On top, you can drive your fist down into your opponent and you can use your weight to pin him. It is an accepted truth amongst self-defence specialists that there is nothing but advantage to being on top in a grapple on the floor. Those experts, however, have not taken into account that being on top of a portly Irishman, your knees pinning his arms to the floor and your fist cocked back, puts your head at the perfect height for a dwarf who has built up a fair bit of momentum to jump and slam his forehead straight into your exposed face. Admittedly, that is not a situation that comes up in most fight scenarios.

Cole fell away as Smithy tumbled over the prone figure of Bunny.

Never one to look a gift horse in the mouth, Bunny rolled himself over and slammed his left fist into his opponent's jaw. The blow didn't have much behind it, but it at least allowed Bunny to turn his body around and get himself on his knees. The first one back to his feet wins.

As Cole, dazed, tried to regain his footing, a roundhouse right with some real feeling behind it caught him on the jaw and sent him sprawling backwards. Bunny screamed as lightning bolts of pain from his shattered finger ripped up his arm. He planted his right foot in preparation for aiming a left-footed kick somewhere memorable.

"Bunny!"

He turned to see Smithy, with Cole's Glock in his hand.

Bunny took a step away. Cole turned and sat on the ground, looking up at them: a professional dispassionately reading the situation.

"Right," said Bunny, looking down at him, "Well, I think we can call it one-all now."

Cole spat out a bloodied tooth. "Bullshit. I had you until..." He pointed towards Smithy.

Smithy shrugged. "He does have a point."

Bunny looked outraged. "Who's fecking side are you on?"

"I did headbutt him. Neither of you won the fight."

"Yeah," agreed Cole.

"I did," finished Smithy.

"I wasn't fighting to win, anyway," said Bunny. "I was fighting to slow him down, so your lady and the hostage could get away." Bunny turned back to Cole. "By the way, count yourself lucky that this chauvinistic gobshite insisted his girlfriend got the feck out of here. She's like a black belt in crack major. She'd have had you on toast. Now, finger and thumb only – slowly – take your wallet out and toss it here."

Cole did as instructed and the wallet landed on the grass in front of their feet.

Bunny put his left hand out and Smithy handed him the gun.

"So, what's the move here?" asked Cole.

"Excuse me?" replied Bunny.

"Holy shit," said Smithy, who had picked up Cole's wallet and was flipping through it. "This guy is NSA – no, wait... FBI... CIA... Homeland Security!" Smithy looked up. "Who the fuck are you people?"

"I'll tell you who they are," said Bunny. "They're the people who slaughtered a load of innocent civilians for the sake of some dirty fecking money."

"You say that like we're the first to think of it. It's just business."

"It's just business," repeated Bunny. "That's the 'I was just following orders' of the twenty-first century." Bunny waved the gun between himself and Cole, never taking his eyes off the other man. "Just so we're clear – if the positions were reversed, I'd have two in the chest and one in the head by now."

Cole spat out some more blood. "Ain't too late for that to happen."

"Bunny?" said Smithy, trepidation in his voice.

Bunny took a step forward.

Cole closed his eyes.

"Bunny!" said Smithy.

For a moment, the world held its breath.

"Well," said Bunny. "Guess this is just another way I'm better than you." Cole opened his eyes. "But not that much better." And Cole screamed as Bunny shot him in the left shin.

"Jesus, Bunny."

Bunny turned and headed towards the Madison Avenue exit. "C'mon – cops will be here soon."

As if on cue, sirens began to wail in the distance.

Bunny quickly cleared the bullet from the chamber, unclipped the ammo magazine, wiped the handle clean and then tossed the gun in one direction and the clip in the other. "Let's see how well that prick does with a bullet hole in him and no ID to help avoid awkward questions." He grabbed Cole's wallet from Smithy's hand and shoved it into his coat pocket. They rushed out onto the sidewalk. Some people were taking cover while other commuters just walked by, headphones in, oblivious.

Bunny noticed people looking at them – specifically at the blood that was running from his shattered nose in a steady stream. "Jesus," he said, pointing over his shoulder towards the park, "there's some nutter in there with a gun. Everybody stay back!"

And then they were across the street, the grey granite mass of the Sony building towering over them to the right.

"So, what does God have to say about that?"

"It's not a… it's not a running commentary. It's just an occasional thing."

"Oh right," said Bunny. "Did Amy make it?"

"I didn't see. I was a little busy."

"Well, fingers crossed. She's a resourceful girl."

"What're we going to do now?" asked Smithy.

"Pint?"

CHAPTER FORTY-FOUR

The plan had been straightforward. Actually, the plan had been a chaotic mess, but this part of it had been relatively simple. Amy was to pick up Matt at Madison Square Park and bolt up East 23rd Street. Before the opposition knew what was what, they'd be out of there, heading for their salvation up by the NYU Medical Center. Once they reached Channel 8, there were going to be a whole lot of questions, but when you were a wanted murderer who was trying to expose a massive criminal conspiracy, the least you could expect was questions. Matt had attempted to make conversation, but Amy had been too busy concentrating on getting them to safety for much of it.

"Where are we going?"

"To fix this mess."

"I'm really sorry."

"Save it."

They'd made it up to the intersection with Second Avenue without much incident. Well, at least without confrontation. Amy hadn't noticed in the panic, but when Mabel had reared up, Matt's tight grip around her had caused the not-really-a-policewoman's blouse to rip open – which was, after all, what it was designed to do. Amy had tried a couple of times to reattach it, but it didn't seem to be working so, yes, she was now galloping up the 23rd Street bus lane on horseback with a terrified man riding pillion and her underwear on show. She felt like a rather prudish Lady Godiva. If she got through this, she'd look back on this moment and cringe for the rest of her life, but it was a price she was willing to pay. Still, New Yorkers were a lot of things, but short of an opinion or three wasn't one of them, so there'd been more than a few things shouted in her direction.

Mabel wasn't used to keeping up this sustained pace anymore, so Amy had been easing off slightly. They could take a left onto First and then it was a straight line to where they were heading. The good thing about the Friday Manhattan gridlock was that no car could move through it with anything approaching speed, so what a horse lacked with its horsepower of, well, one, was compensated for by the fact that not much else was moving anywhere in a hurry.

Then Amy had heard it: the insistent whine, coupled with a few shouts of outrage. She looked back to see a motorbike ripping its way along the bus lane behind them. The rider had no helmet on, so Amy could see the wide grin on her face as her long hair streamed behind her in the wind.

"Shit!" screamed Matt. "It's the crazy bitch!"

With an apology uttered only in her head, Amy dug her heels into Mabel's flanks once again.

Their luck held, as the lights at the intersection had just been changing against them, so traffic going both directions screeched to a halt amidst honking and swearing as Mabel raced through. The motorbike had been maybe half a block behind when she'd seen it. Amy didn't look back, but she hoped that the renewed chorus of honking and the sound of at least one collision meant the motorbike had hit trouble and bought them more time. Mabel, even at her best, wasn't going to be able to outrun a motorbike for long.

Just before the junction with First Avenue – "Oh fuck!" screamed Matt. "She's gaining on us."

In a split-second decision, Amy didn't make the left turn to salvation; there was no way they could make it. Instead, she galloped through the intersection and, at the sound of the motorbike getting closer, tugged the reins to the right and brought Mabel over the raised tree-lined partition that divided East 23rd Street and the access road for the Peter Cooper Village apartment complex. Amy glanced left and saw the motorbike running parallel with them in the 23rd Street bus lane. The brunette wore a wide smile as she dipped her right hand under her left armpit, going for a gun.

Amy heaved the reins right again when she saw the split-second break in the fencing, sending Mabel shooting onto the pedestrian pathway to the apartment complex. A loving couple walking arm in arm, enjoying the sunny spring day, disentangled themselves and dived in separate directions to remove themselves from the path of the horse that was thundering towards them.

"What are we going to do?" hollered Matt.

"You're going to shut up."

It was a nice complex, well maintained and containing plots of greenery amidst the high-rise apartment blocks; a little village unto itself. Amy had looked into living there once. Randomly, a line from their brochure popped into her head: "The tree-lined paths provide a sense of tranquillity and calm amidst the surrounding city." Not so much now. One of the flowerbeds took a hit when a pizza delivery guy drove his bike into it in an evasive manoeuvre.

Amy sent Mabel across a lawn, where a two-foot-high hedge blocked their way. It had been a while. She felt the horse surge towards it, enjoying reliving a former life. Once a jumper... Mabel executed the jump with ease. Matt yelped like a little girl, but otherwise remained stoically silent.

Behind them, Amy heard the damned whine of the motorcycle again. The psycho brunette having to go around the hedges would buy them some time, but nowhere near enough.

They reached a road that snaked its way through the complex. A security barrier at the exit was up as a UPS truck dawdled through. Mabel accelerated, beating its descent.

As Amy turned them right, down Avenue C, she risked a glance over her shoulder and saw the bike negotiating its way around the truck.

Avenue C was a big straight road, with the FDR Expressway running parallel on the far side of the street, sixty feet in the air. Behind it, the vast expanse of the East River rolled slowly by.

Amy could feel Mabel breathing harder and harder beneath her, her recent life of slow-walking tourists around Central Park catching up on her. The motorbike would be out now and closing fast; they couldn't rely on luck for much longer.

Ahead of them, she saw the on-ramp for the FDR and inspiration struck. She urged Mabel on. "C'mon, girl, one more push!"

"Don't go on the FDR," yelped Matt. "What are you... that's a..."

"Shut. Up!"

Long lines of traffic clogged each of the arteries of the intersection, drivers waiting impatiently to get on the expressway, keen to make it home so that their weekend could start. The horse galloping straight across forced the driver of a Dodge coming from the right to slam on her brakes, which was quickly followed by a succession of crunching noises as the cars behind her domino-ed into one another. They reached the on-ramp, leaving another cacophony of honking in their wake. Amy could feel Mabel panting harder beneath her. She gave her a quick pat of encouragement. Above them, a sign showed that Exit 6, the next one, was closed.

"Don't go on the expressway," yelled Matt. "We'll be trapped!"

"That's the idea."

As a teenager, Amy's dad had taken her out to dinner every other Tuesday, to a diner called Roberto's. He'd really liked the place. He was a man of simple tastes, and the restaurant did what he liked. Amy had been less keen, but even in the worst throes of teenaged ingratitude, had never said so. She never wanted her dad to feel like he wasn't doing the best for her. They'd had this ancient video game called Frogger, which you sat down to play on a screen in a table. Her dad had loved the damn thing. For such a disciplined man, it was the one time she saw him get giddy. The concept was simple: you were the aforementioned Frogger the frog and, for reasons never fully explained, you had decided to risk life and limb to repeatedly attempt to cross first a road filled with progressively faster traffic and then a river, where you had to hop on logs and the backs of turtles – frogs, of course, being famously afraid of water.

As they reached the top and merged onto the FDR, the memory of trying to play that stupid game came back to her. The traffic wasn't moving fast by expressway standards, maybe thirty miles per hour, but when you were on a horse, that was plenty fast enough. The traffic in the right lane slowed, as much to stare as anything else, and Amy guided Mabel in.

"She's coming," shouted Matt.

"Tell me when she's close."

Amy watched the two lanes of traffic beside them, with cars moving past. *Nearly. No. Now? No. C'mon! C'mon! C'mon!*

"I can see her!" hollered Matt in Amy's ear, accompanied by the unmistakable whine of the motorbike. "She's coming fast... Shit, she's—"

"Yee-haw!" roared Amy, and dug in her heels to urge Mabel forward.

Four feet is not much of a jump for a true jumper. Hell, Amy remembered jumping that back in one of her first competitions as a teenager. There was an increased degree of difficulty, though – an exponentially increased degree of difficulty – if to make that jump you had to first veer wildly across two lanes of traffic.

Amy got a flash of the car in the middle lane swerving sharply into the outer lane to avoid them, then she heard the thudding crunch of bodywork doing its job as whatever was in the outer lane collided with it and the partition.

The partition was four feet of concrete; Amy could feel Mabel pull back. She geed her on, her body tensing. If the horse refused, this was going to be all kinds of ugly.

Mabel faced a four-foot jump with two people on her back after traversing two lanes of traffic, with three lanes of oncoming traffic waiting on the other side. Amy couldn't even hope to time the landing. It was a leap into the unknown, and God bless Mabel as she raised her front legs and went for it.

Of the many unknowns, Amy hadn't realised that the FDR on the other side of the partition was considerably lower – so a four-foot jump had an eight-foot landing.

Mabel landed with a juddering stumble but managed to regain her footing. Amy saw a brief flash of whatever vehicle had thankfully been far enough back in the fast lane, and then heard the sound of a car in the middle lane piling into the back of Buick in the slow lane.

Amy wrenched the reins left and Mabel slammed into the side of the Buick with a shattering of glass and crunching of bodywork. Both Amy and Matt howled in pain as their legs were trapped between the horse's momentum and the Buick's resistance. Amy felt something shatter around her knee. Mabel screamed but stayed upright and limped away.

Amy, biting back her own tears, patted the horse on the neck as they trotted awkwardly down the off-ramp. "Good girl. I'm so sorry. Good girl."

It was the one thing a horse could do that a motorbike couldn't. Somewhere on the far side of the FDR, the smiling brunette probably wasn't smiling anymore. It'd take her at least fifteen minutes to get off and circle back, by which time they'd be long gone.

Compared to the rest of the journey, the last five blocks to the studios of Channel 8 News were relatively uneventful.

CHAPTER FORTY-FIVE

The Porterhouse Lodge was reasonably busy with the after-work crowd, but the bar area remained surprisingly empty.

"No offence," said Jackie, "but you two guys are bad for business."

Smithy glanced at him before returning his focus to the matter in hand. He had his fingers on either side of Bunny's head and his thumbs on his nose. "Are you sure you won't go to an emergency room and get this thing done properly?"

"No, no," said Bunny. "Just do it."

Smithy sighed. "Alright, but before I do – two things. Firstly…"

"Ahhh!" Bunny screamed as Smithy jammed his fingers in and shoved his nose back into position as best he could.

"Fecking – shitting – buggering – tiny bastard!"

Jackie tried to smile at the work crowd, who were regretting their choice of establishment. "Sorry about that, folks. Just a bit of first aid. Everything is fine."

Bunny wiped the tears from his eyes. "Drinks for everybody!"

This was met with a cautious cheer. People liked free things, but they disliked scary things, and "don't take alcohol from a bleeding man" was very much the adult version of "don't take candy from strangers".

Jackie leaned in. "Can you afford that?"

Bunny nodded, pulling a wallet from his pocket. "I can indeed. Or at least the fella who busted my nose can. Speaking of which..." Bunny glanced at the clock on the wall. "Shite. Turn on Channel 8 there, would you, please."

With a suspicious look that implied the welcome mat was wearing thin beneath their feet, Jackie changed the channel. The screen was filled with the face of Douglas Randall, trying very hard not to grin like a lunatic.

"Ah," said Jackie, "I hate that smug prick. Always smiling away to himself."

"Shut up!" said Bunny, and then caught Jackie's look. "Erm, sorry. I mean, could you turn it up, please?"

Jackie gave it a second's consideration and then grudgingly did so. Douglas Randall's broadcast-quality tones rose up, the hubbub of the bar dying down to see what this new interruption to their Friday evening was.

"... will shock you. This is not an ordinary broadcast. I am joined tonight by two guests. Matt Clarke is a fund manager at Lanark Lane Investments, a hedge fund on Wall Street, and with him is a lady you may recognise – Amy Daniels, who was implicated earlier this week in the brutal murder of Charlie Fenton, who worked with Mr Clarke at Lanark Lane Investments. As we went on air, our producers made the NYPD aware of Miss Daniel's presence here, and she has agreed to fully cooperate with their investigation as soon as this broadcast ends, as has Mr Clarke. Before that, though, they have a truly extraordinary story to tell. Mr Clarke."

Matt cleared his throat and looked nervously into the camera. "Yes, hello. My name is Matt Clarke, and for the last few years I have been a fund manager. My... my main client in that time has been a group of people who identified themselves to me as current or former US government employees in the Intelligence Community. I have, under their instructions, undertaken a series of... highly unusual investments, using what could be called insider information."

"Big fecking deal," said one of the old fellas who propped up the bar.

"Shush," said Smithy.

"Feck off, ye midget."

"Donal!" said Jackie sounding outraged.

"Another word, old man, and you'll be remembered as the octogenarian who got his arse handed to him by a midget."

The old man looked at Smithy for a long moment, then nodded and went back to his paper. "Fair play."

"And what," prompted Douglas Randall, "was the exact nature of this information?"

"Well," said Matt, "most recently it was being told two weeks before it happened of the attack on the Millennium Faction Data building."

It was hard to tell if the gasps they heard were all from the bar or if there'd been some in the TV studio too.

"To be clear," continued Douglas Randall, "you are saying that current or former members of the US Intelligence Community knew of Adaal Ackbar's intentions before the attack happened and attempted to profit from it?"

Matt shook his head. "No, sir. I mean, they did intend to profit from it, but it wasn't him. I believe he was a patsy and the attack was carried out by members of this group."

This time the gasps were mixed with shushes, evening out the amount of air in the bar.

Douglas Randall looked into the camera. "We'll get into the exact details of that right after this short break."

All around Smithy and Bunny, the crowd erupted into excited conversation.

Smithy picked up his whiskey and held it out to Bunny.

Bunny picked up his Guinness and clinked it against it.

"Not a bad day's work," said Smithy.

"Nope."

"So, what now?"

"I'm going to get back to why I came here in the first place. I need to find a particular woman, and to do that, I need to find a particular bunch of nuns."

Smithy lifted his chin and nodded. "Sounds about right."

"And yourself?"

"Well," said Smithy, "I've got to find a good home for a Siberian husky that looks nothing like Gene Simmons, then I'm going to have to calm Diller down, because I bet this little adventure has given him all kinds of wild ideas, and oh yeah, I'm pretty sure I got a tad overexcited myself and told a woman that I loved her, so there's that."

"Don't you love her?"

"That's hardly the point."

"Take it from me, that's exactly the point."

Bunny felt a vibration in his coat. He pulled out a phone that had suddenly started working again.

"What's the deal with that?" asked Smithy. "You never did say."

"'Tis indestructible, apparently. Gorilla Glass and rubber something or other."

"Cool. Does it get the baseball scores?"

"No," said Bunny, shoving it back into his pocket. "But that's exactly what I asked. Well, sorta."

"Aren't you going to answer it?"

"Not yet." Bunny nodded at Jackie. "Same again, please, Jackie – and is your missus doing the breakfast tomorrow?"

EPILOGUE 1

Someone to Watch Over Me

Amy watched as the first fingers of dawn spread across the Manhattan skyline. The lights were still twinkling on the Queensboro Bridge. As views went, it wasn't half bad. She pulled her coat a little tighter around her and took a sip of her coffee, resisting the urge to check her watch. He'd be here. She could count on him. Her crutches lay on the ground beside her.

For a man his size, he did move with a deceptive grace. She only noticed him when he appeared seemingly out of nowhere to sit beside her.

"This isn't the original bench, you know," she said.

"Isn't it?"

"No. I looked it up. Apparently, the bench that Woody Allen and Diane Keaton are sitting on at the end of the movie was never here. They brought it in especially."

"Oh," said Bunny, "is that right? I'm not sure I wanted to know that."

"Hey," said Amy, "it's still a great view."

"'Tis that alright. How's your knee?"

"Fine. I mean, it will be, soon enough. The doctors said I was pretty lucky. A horse is a big animal."

"That it is."

It had been a couple of weeks since everything had happened. After their revelations, life had been intense and hectic. Not quite as bad as it had been for the five days previous, when she'd been wanted for murder, but still a long way from normal.

"Oh, sorry, by the way" said Amy. "You must've been coming here for the last few mornings looking for me. I only got your note yesterday."

"Not a problem."

"I was back home seeing my dad."

"Right." A moment's pause and then, "How did that go?"

Amy absent-mindedly turned her coffee cup around in her hand. "OK, I guess. I mean, there were some conversations that were mortifyingly embarrassing but, ultimately, I suppose it wasn't too bad. Not to be too 'movie of the week' about it, but facing death and everything else we've been through... it does help put things into perspective."

He nodded. "That it does. That it does. I see the Mayor of New York has personally promised you'll be allowed to finish law school?"

"Yeah. I'm taking some time off, but I guess I'll do it next year. I have been talking to a couple of groups. Suddenly, I'm thinking that campaigning to ensure that everyone gets a fair trial is an issue that I can really get behind. I might as well use my new-found 'celebrity' for something positive."

"Fair play. Any news on the investigation?"

Amy shrugged. "If there is, they aren't telling me a whole lot about it. Matt and that Brad guy aren't going to see any jail time as they're cooperating and they can make the case they were coerced. They've got that guy Cole in custody but he's not talking. They've got a couple of others, but the main woman, Miller or whatever, they seem to have no clue how to find her. I believe there'll be a congressional inquiry as soon as the criminal investigation is done. She's long gone, I bet. Everything else will be just talk."

"Yeah," said Bunny. "Doesn't really seem right, does it? Although, on the upside, there's that two hundred and forty million dollars that we made for the US government."

"True. I'm hoping for a really good tax rebate next year. Oh, speaking of which." Amy reached down into the carrier bag that was sitting beside her. "I got you a present, but I didn't have time to wrap it."

She had thought he might laugh, but when she held it out, real emotion filled his eyes. "How did you..."

"This is New York. Everything is here if you just know where to look."

He took it and held it up in front of him. "That's... that's a beautiful thing."

She nudged him gently with her elbow. "Steady there, big guy. Don't go ruining your hard man persona by bawling your eyes out over a box of teabags."

"Barry's teabags, though. How did you know?"

"I googled Irish teabags," responded Amy, feeling slightly embarrassed at how much credit she was getting for what was actually a pretty simple acquisition. "Oh, there's something inside too."

He opened the box to see the white envelope stuffed with cash.

"Ten thousand dollars, as agreed."

He shifted beside her. "Ah, you didn't have to do that."

"A deal is a deal, and you could use the cash."

"Actually," he said, "I've got my ATM card back and my pocket money has been upped."

"Oh really?"

He nodded. "Let's just say that Agent Dove has had to do a fair bit of grovelling and apologising for not helping us out when she had the chance."

"Damn right."

"So, honestly, you can have the money back."

He tried to hand her the envelope.

"Oh no, cowboy, that's yours. Do with it as you see fit. I'm doing OK, thanks. I'm getting a book deal. Let's just say I'll have a nice retirement nest egg. I'm also moving out of the city. I've got my eye on a little cottage in the country. Nothing fancy, but it's got a couple of acres. A certain horse's days of ferrying tourists around Central Park are over."

"Ok," said Bunny, "if you're sure." He took the envelope and shoved it into the inside pocket of his sheepskin coat. "I know a promising young actor who I think is well deserving of a scholarship."

Amy smiled. "That's a great idea." Then she caught herself. "Oh sorry, I meant to ask – how's your thing going? Y'know, the hunt for that particular woman?"

Bunny shrugged. "Slowly. I've just got back to my search for a bunch of lunatic nuns. They've got to be here somewhere."

She looked out across the river as the light of a new day crept up on the city. "Yeah. This is New York. Everything is here if you just know where to look."

EPILOGUE 2

Should Auld Acquaintance Be Forgot?

In the corner booth of a bar in a mid-range hotel in Bolivia, a statuesque older lady, her dyed mousy hair showing its roots, sat nursing a drink. A man sitting at the bar had been eyeing her for a couple of minutes, and he decided to make his move. He swayed as he walked, looking a little worse for the drink but nothing too severe.

She was a little older than he was, but then, this wasn't a normal situation.

"Hey there, I was wondering if you'd like to buy me a drink?" He gave her a winning smile.

"No, I would not."

"OK," he said, sliding into the booth opposite her, "I'll buy the drinks, but you'd better be damn good company."

"No, thank you. I'm waiting for someone."

The man raised his hands. "Me too! What are the odds?"

She gave an exasperated sigh. "What's your name?"

"Steve."

"Steve," she repeated. "Here's the thing, Steve. You've misjudged body language, verbal cues and now you've ignored a straight no. You've also crucially misjudged your own limited charm. So now I'd like you to leave."

"Hey," said Steve, "I was just trying to be friendly."

"No, you weren't. I think we both know your motives."

He grinned. "I bet you don't."

"I'm sure I do, Steve. You see, I know you. I've known a thousand yous. You are nothing special. In fact, you remind me of a Venezuelan man I once knew."

"Is that so?"

"Yes. He was also guilty of grossly overestimating his charms. I knew his motives too."

Something changed when she looked across at the man. Suddenly, it wasn't the same man. Physically, yes – but now he looked much more alert. The fake glassiness in the eyes had fallen away. There was something else there too.

"I'm not trying to seduce you."

"No?"

"No, Evelyn."

An icicle of terror slid down the back of her dress.

She looked down at her drink. "You know my name." It wasn't a question.

"Oh, I know everything about you. In particular, I know that you took a lot of money from people nobody takes money from – and you didn't give it back." Steve clucked his tongue.

She wanted to say something, but suddenly her mouth was dry, so very dry. If she were lucky, maybe they'd make it quick.

A figure pushed into the booth beside her.

The woman who had been known by many names looked up to see a smile she knew all too well beaming back at her.

"I believe you are familiar with my associate?"

"Yes," said the woman, who now knew it was definitely not going to be quick. "Hello, Lola."

EPILOGUE 3

If You Go Out in the Woods Today

"And then," said Andy, his eyes wide, "they looked behind them, and there, sitting in the back seat, was a fisherman's hat... and a *hook*!"

Andy gave the word hook extra emphasis, just like his uncle Toby had done when he told him the story. It was greeted by a gratifying series of gasps from the girls and gleeful guffaws from the other boys. Everyone looked impressed except...

"That's bullshit," said Lorraine Parks.

"Lorraine!" said Mrs Wilkes. "Mind your language, young lady!"

"Sorry. It's BS."

Mrs Wilkes looked even more annoyed by this, as if Lorraine was getting off on a technicality. "Well, why don't you tell us a story then?"

"Fine, I will. Mine is way scarier because it's actually true!"

Andy stuck his tongue out at her. Lorraine glared back. She couldn't believe that for a week last year she'd thought she was totally in love with him. "It was told to me by my aunt Mona and she's in the police."

"Answering phones," sneered Andy.

"Andy Canworth," said Mrs Wilkes, "women can be in the police force just like men!"

Andy wilted under her gaze.

"Anyway," said Lorraine, "my story is about a guy who got kidnapped by terrorists or drug dealers or something."

"She's making it up!"

"Shut up, Kyle, that bit isn't important."

Lorraine caught Mrs Wilkes's warning look and moved quickly on. She didn't want to clean pots again tomorrow while the rest of the camp went canoeing. "What is important is that this guy, to get him to do what they wanted, they put a bomb inside him! A bomb – right there in his belly!" She pointed at her belly as she looked around the fire. "The police shot the bad guy in the head – blam! – but they never found the detonator that set off the bomb. They looked everywhere. Everywhere. Doctors say they can't take it out, so this guy, he had to live with a bomb wrapped up in his guts."

"What'd he do?" asked Tina, with perfect timing.

Lorraine turned to her. "What could he do? He was scared, in case someday someone found the detonator and, y'know, didn't know what it was and pressed the button. Then he'd go – BOOM!" Lorraine was smart; she knew the noises were how you sold it. "Besides, the detonator would've had like a frequency for the signal..." Lorraine tried not to look at Mrs Wilkes, but she was hoping putting in some science might get her back into her good books. "So if anything else had a remote with the same frequency – BOOM! He walks by the wrong garage door opener – BOOM! Someone tunes their radio to the wrong channel – BOOM! Phone rings – BOOM!"

"He'd be dead by now, then – easy," said Andy.

Lorraine nodded. "Yeah, he would be – only he moved to the only place he could find where there was no technology. He moved right here, to Massapatchu Falls, Oregon, and got himself a cabin high in the woods. Away from everybody, right up that hill there."

Lorraine was gratified that even the boys looked when she pointed – and they weren't grinning now. "Up there, all alone – he's gone crazy! Scary crazy! If he sees any technology, he has to kill whoever has it before he blows up!"

Right then, because being a kid is hard, and being a chubby one is harder still, God threw Lorraine a bone. Cathy Edam's phone rang. Even the boys screamed.

"Cathy Edam!" hollered Mrs Wilkes. "Give me that phone instantly." She then looked embarrassed. "Not because of Lorraine's silly story. You're not supposed to have it. Rules are rules. You'll be cleaning pots tomorrow."

Cathy looked even more horrified now. Lorraine tried not to look too pleased, but Cathy had put chewing gum in her hair that time and no way was it an accident.

"Is he still there?" asked Tina.

Lorraine slowly nodded her head. "Uh-huh. And if you listen late at night, you can hear him – roaring crazy stuff at the moon!"

Three seconds later, even Mrs Wilkes screamed – and would subsequently be unable to justify her actions when subject to an internal review carried out by the school board. She would be put on probation and all school trips would be cancelled for five years, with nobody ever going back to the camp up on Maple Ridge.

What were the words they heard? The words hollered in the distance that so terrified a class of eight graders that they scattered in the woods in all directions, after which the services of the mountain rescue team were required in order to ensure they all eventually made it home safe and sound?

"THEY BURNED MY BALLS!!!"

FREE NOVELLA!

Hi there reader-person,

I hope you enjoyed the book, thanks for taking the time to read it. If you've not already had the pleasure, then the Dublin Trilogy books are packed full of Bunny McGarry mayhem - details are on the next page. If you're one of the hardcore who have already read them then fear not, Bunny will be back in 2019.

In the meantime, I have written what started as a short story and ended up as a novella, featuring Smithy and Diller. It's entitled *Smithy's Revenge* and in case you can't guess, it involves a certain someone wanting to get his own back on the man who dressed him like a leprechaun and hunted him like an animal.

You can get the e-book FOR FREE by signing up to my monthly newsletter. Just go to my website WhiteHairedIrishman.com/revenge/ to sign up.

Cheers muchly,

Caimh

ALSO BY CAIMH MCDONNELL

THE DUBLIN TRILOGY (FEATURING BUNNY MCGARRY)

A Man With One of Those Faces (Book 1)

The Day That Never Comes (Book 2)

Angels in the Moonlight (A prequel to the trilogy that we're calling Book 3 as it needs to be read before...)

Last Orders (Book 4)

Lightning Source UK Ltd.
Milton Keynes UK
UKHW010558130519
342540UK00001B/183/P